PLATANIDES

THROUGH THE EYE OF THE STORM

BY

WILLIAM PLANES

ISBN 979-8-9859596-0-4 (Digital)

ISBN 979-8-9859596-1-1 (Paperback)

ISBN 979-8-9859596-2-8 (Hardcover)

Prime Investment Holdings, Inc., Publisher

36181 East Lake Road, Suite 315

Palm Harbor, FL 34685

Panayiotis F. and Katherine Platanides (Πλατανιδης),

MAY THEIR MEMORIES BE ETERNAL!!!

Πλατανιδης Through the Eye of the Storm

A family's origins preserved

Contents

Dedication

I dedicate this book to my father and mother, Παναγιώτης Φωτίζουν Πλατανιδης and Αικατερίνη βεηις Πλατανιδης (Peter Frank Planes (Platanides) and Katherine Venis Planes); the loving and caring parents who brought me into this world, natured me in the tradition of the Greek Orthodox Faith and made sure that I, unlike them, through their efforts and dedication, had the benefit of a college education. They and my brother Frank have long passed away leaving me with my estranged sister, Maria, to whom I was close as a child and young adult. In our older years, our lives have taken us down different paths and convictions, most of which have left us to drift apart and become estranged from one another. Notwithstanding, to this day, I remember her in all my Prayers.

Preface

Some of what appears here may not be true, but it is as I was told and as I remember.

As I approach my eightieth birthday, experiencing an increase in the decline of my health, I find myself reflecting on my children, stepchildren, grandchildren, nephews, nieces, and cousins here in America as well as those in Greece and other parts of the world. While I am listening to television commentators, color and slant the news to favor one person's or other's political beliefs, I realize that most of us do not really know much about our heritage, origins, and family history, this being distinguished from the World and American History, which we hear the politicians recite and rewrite to their partisan preference, time and time again.

Over the past couple of years, I have looked for DNA relatives through 23andMe, expecting not to find much but I was shocked at the number of 2nd, 3rd, 4th and 5th cousins (all descendants of my Grand Parents and their Parents and Grandparents before them) that are living in America and Greece. When I talk to my children, nieces, nephew, and cousins and ask about their linage, they can name as far back as their Grand Parents, but few know much about their Great Grandparents, and none know who their Great-Great-Grandparents and their Great-Great-Great Grandparents were; where these Great Grandparents came from and what they did for a living. Most cannot remember the names of their Great Grandparents much less those that came before them.

One must wonder if "We the People" even know what our respective families looked like, their beliefs and experiences up until we became conscious of our personal surroundings and experiences? How many of us know the history of what our parents or grandparents experienced before arriving in America? Much less the life experiences of those that remained in Greece and other countries or never survived the 1922-23 Genocides of Christian of Greek and Armenian descent in Asia Minor or the Nazi occupation of Greece during World War II (1939-1945). Very few of us know, much less understand, that the 1922-23 Genocides of Christians of Greek and Armenian descent in Asia Minor was the end of the genocide of Christians of Greek and Armenian descent in Asia Minor that began thirty years before.

With the foregoing in mind, and notwithstanding that I may not remember all, much less, all that I remember may not be the entire story, I decided that I would write this book to preserve for my children, their children, and the generations that will follow them, as well as the other children of the Platanides, Tsalikidou, Donjogolou, and Venis families, some portion of the history of these families, otherwise, this history will surely be lost.

Acknowledgements

———◆———

In undertaking this book, I want to acknowledge the encouragement I received from my Cousin Fotis M. Platanidis (son of my Uncle Minas Platanidis); Andreas Spyridakis (son of my Aunt Panayiota Platanidis Spyridakis); and my cousin Georgeann Venis (daughter to my mother's brother, Uncle George Venis); and my good friends Harry and Ana Patsalides. I also want to thank Georgeann Venis, Fotis M. Platanidis, and my cousin Dr. Dean Furkioti, DDS (whose Grand Father was Pantelis Tsalikidou, brother to my Grandmother Kyriaki Tsalikidou Platanidis, and whose Grandmother was Despina Donjogolou Tsalikidou (whose Grandmother was Despina Platanidis Donjogolou, the sister of my Grandfather Fotis Platanidis) for assisting in research for this book; and Harry and Ana Patsalides for assisting me in the translating and checking the translation of some of the documents that I depended on during the writing of this book. Lastly, but not at all the least, I want to acknowledge and thank my very dear wife, Regina M Planes, who I deeply love, for her tolerance as I spent endless hours, days, weeks, and months pursuing the completion of this book and for her abundant loving care of me in these my declining years.

About the Author

The author is the first generation born of a survivor of Genocide in Asia Minor by the radical Muslim troops of Kemal Ataturk in September 1922. His father and mother, following their Greek Orthodox Faith, raised him in the teachings and traditions of the Greek Orthodox Church.

Born in New York and raised in Folly Beach, South Carolina and Coral Gables, Florida, he graduated from Coral Gables High School and Florida State University and then served in the US Navy. He engaged in the business of acquiring troubled companies, restructuring, and reselling these companies. By way of his upbringing and using the profits he earned from these business activities, he invested these funds in good works, including the good works of his Faith and Christian beliefs.

In the time that he has been home because of the COVID-19 pandemic, he questioned if his children and the children of his siblings and cousins really understood the greatness of the freedoms we enjoy in the United States. If they understood how fragile the existence of these freedoms is; the sacrifices of life and blood made by many to preserve these freedoms and this county; and if they even knew what his father and many others went through to give him and all of them the opportunity to have religious freedom so we could openly live our Orthodox Christian Faith.

To preserve the history of this heritage he undertook writing this book.

Psalm 23 King James Version

²³ The LORD *is* my shepherd; I shall not want.

² He maketh me to lie down in green pastures: he leadeth me beside the still waters.

³ He restoreth my soul: he leadeth me in the paths of righteousness for his name's sake.

⁴ Yea, though I walk through the valley of the shadow of death, I will fear no evil: for thou art with me; thy rod and thy staff they comfort me.

⁵ Thou preparest a table before me in the presence of mine enemies: thou anointest my head with oil; my cup runneth over.

⁶ Surely goodness and mercy shall follow me all the days of my life: and I will dwell in the house of the LORD forever.

CHAPTER ONE

Driven from the Land of their Birth

I n 1908 a young Greek Orthodox Christian couple, Fotis and Kyriaki, living in the city of Alasehir Asia Minor (Turkey), gave birth to their second child, a boy, they named him Panayiotis. Their firstborn was a girl, she was to be their only daughter, her name was Panayiota. Fotis was the son of Emanuel and Maria Platanidis, in her older age Maria would live out her years in Alasehir Asia Minor with Fotis and Kyriaki. The couple had four more sons, Athanasios, Pantelis, Stavros, and Minas, all born in Alasehir Asia Minor.[1]

---

[1] Alaşehir (Turkish pronunciation: [aˈɫaʃehir]), in Antiquity and the Middle Ages known as Philadelphia (Greek: Φιλαδέλφεια, i.e., "the city of him who loves his brother"), is a town and district of Manisa Province in the Aegean region of Turkey. It is situated in the valley of the Kuzuçay (Cogamus in antiquity), at the foot of the Bozdağ Mountain (Mount Tmolus in antiquity). The town is connected to İzmir by a 105 km (65 mi) railway

Alasehir stands on elevated ground commanding the extensive and fertile plain of the Gediz River (Hermus in antiquity), presenting an imposing appearance when seen from a distance. Today Alasehir has about 45 mosques. There are small industries and a fair trade. From one of the mineral springs comes a heavily charged water popular around Turkey.

Within Turkey, the city's name is synonymous with the dried Sultana raisins, although cultivation for the fresh fruit market, less labor-intensive than the dried fruit, has gained prominence in recent decades. As Philadelphia, Alaşehir was a highly important center in the Early Christian and Byzantine periods. It remained a strong center of Orthodox Christianity until the early 20th century, and remains a titular see of the Roman Catholic Church.

 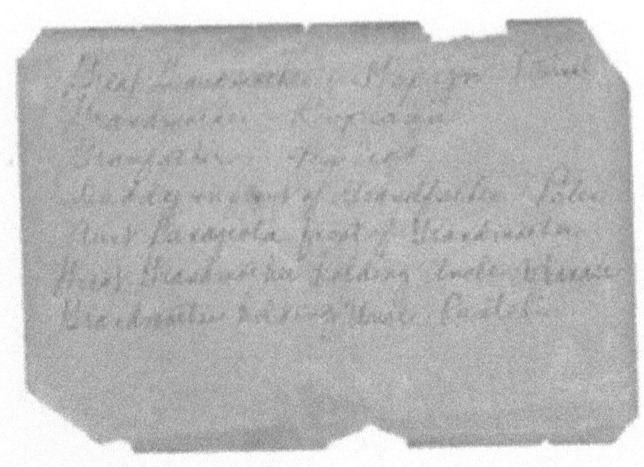

Photograph thought to be taken in 1913 or 1914. Writing on the back was at the hand of my mother, Katherine, so that my brother, sister, and myself would know our father's family. Sitting from left to right Katherine writes "Great Grandmother Mariyo Paternal, Grandmother Kyriaki, Grandfather Fotis; Daddy in front of Grandfather – Peter, Aunt Panayiota in front of Grandmother, Great Grandmother holding Uncle Athanasios, Grandfather holding Uncle Pantelis". My cousin Fotis M. Platanidis explained to me that the younger boys as shown here are dressed in girl's clothing. This was done to protect infant and young boys from being abducted by the Muslims who would abduct young and infant Christian boy and take them to the interior of the country to be raised as slave labor.

Although several ancient cities bore the name of Philadelphia, this is generally agreed to be the one listed among the seven churches written to by John in the Book of Revelation. Philadelphia is listed as the sixth church of the seven. A letter specifically addressed to the Philadelphian church is recorded in Revelation 3:7–13 (Revelation 3:9). The city's history of earthquakes may lie behind the reference to making her church "a pillar in the temple" (Revelation 3:12).

Aside from the peculiar fact that Smyrna was warned of temptation lasting "ten days" while Philadelphia was promised a total exemption, or preservation, from temptation, Philadelphia shares with Smyrna the distinction of receiving nothing but praise from Christ. This explains why modern Protestant churches sometimes use "Philadelphia" as a component in the local church's name as a way of emphasizing its faithfulness.

The Greek army occupied the city during the Greco-Turkish War (1919–1922). There is dissent about who burned Philadelphia in 1922. American consul George Horton wrote in his memoirs about the Turkish army tactics of burning every Greek city they entered culminating with the great fire of Smyrna. Other accounts put the blame on the other side. The retreating Greek army carried out a scorched-earth policy while it was retreating from Anatolia during the final phase of the war, which included the Fire of Alaşehir. According to Park, 70% of the buildings of Alaşehir were destroyed by fire, and Kinross wrote, "Alaşehir was no more than a dark scorched cavity, defacing the hillside. Village after village had been reduced to an ash-heap." It is estimated some 3,000 lives had been lost in the burning of Alaşehir.

Photograph, taken in 1920 on the occasion of the Baptism of Minas. It shows the entire family of Fotis and Kyriaki in Alasehir, Asia Minor. Seated are my paternal grandparents, Kyriaki and Fotis Platanidis; standing in the back row, from left to right are Athanasios, Panayiota, Panayiotis, and Pantelis; seated on the laps of my grandparents, from left to right are Stavros and Minas. Again, notice that Athanasios, Pantelis, Stavros, and Minas are wearing girls closing, to keep them from being abducted by radical Muslims.

Fotis was a wealthy and respected merchant who imported and exported tobacco, figs, raisins, and olive oil to and from various destinations by camel going and coming from the East and by boat going and coming from the West through the port in Smyrna[2]. He and his family

---

[2] Smyrna (/ˈsmɜːrnə/ SMUR-nə; Ancient Greek: Σμύρνη, romanized: Smýrnē, or Ancient Greek: Σμύρνα, romanized: Smýrna) was a Greek city located at a strategic point on the Aegean coast of Anatolia. Due to its advantageous port conditions, its ease of defense and its good inland connections, Smyrna rose to prominence. Today the modern name of the city is Izmir.

Two sites of the ancient city are today within Izmir's boundaries. The first site, probably founded by indigenous peoples, rose to prominence during the Archaic Period as one of the principal ancient Greek settlements in western Anatolia. The second, whose foundation is associated with Alexander the Great, reached metropolitan proportions during the period of the Roman Empire. Most of the present-day remains of the ancient city date from the Roman era, the majority from after a 2nd-century AD earthquake. In practical terms, a distinction is often made between these. Old Smyrna was the initial settlement founded around the 11th century BC, first as an Aeolian settlement, and later taken over and developed during the Archaic Period by the Ionians. Smyrna proper was the new city which residents moved to as of the 4th century BC and whose foundation was inspired by Alexander the Great.

Old Smyrna was located on a small peninsula connected to the mainland by a narrow isthmus at the northeastern corner of the inner Gulf of İzmir, at the edge of a fertile plain and at the foot of Mount Yamanlar. This Anatolian settlement commanded the gulf. Today, the archeological site, named Bayraklı Höyüğü, is approximately 700 meters (770 yd) inland, in the Tepekule neighborhood of Bayraklı.

lived in Alasehir. Their home was situated on a large piece of land which included their home along with a separate large building that supported Fotis' import and export business[3]. This large building had large doors that were high enough to allow camels to pass in and out of the building.

Fotis' father and mother, Emanuel and Maria, had other children, among them was a son named Apostolos [4] and a daughter Despina. Apostolos and Despina each had families of their own; all lived in Asia Minor, in cities North of Smyrna and Alasehir[5].

Fotis was a big man, he was strong, had big hands and long arms, and stood six feet four inches in height. On the other hand, Kyriaki was a petite woman, barely five feet tall. Panayiotis was a responsible and smart son and brother; he was very close to his sister Panayiota and his brother Athanasios.

The Platanidis, Tsalikidou, Donjogolou [6] , and many other families for centuries had lived in Asia Minor prior to and during what was then Byzantium and subsequently the Ottoman Empire, going back as two millenniums (2,000 years) before Christ when Asia Minor was the ancestral home of people of Greek Heritage. The presence of Orthodox Christians in Asia Minor goes back to the Byzantine Empire; going back beyond before to the first century and the Seven

---

New Smyrna developed simultaneously on the slopes of the Mount Pagos (Kadifekale today) and alongside the coastal strait, immediately below where a small bay existed until the 18th century.

The core of the late Hellenistic and early Roman Smyrna is preserved in the large area of İzmir Agora Open Air Museum at this site. Research is being pursued at the sites of both the old and the new cities. This has been conducted since 1997 for Old Smyrna and since 2002 for the Classical Period city, in collaboration between the İzmir Archaeology Museum and the Metropolitan Municipality of İzmir.

[3] My first cousin, Fotis M. Platanidis (son of my father's brother, Minas Platanidis) advises that our cousin, Fotis P. Platanidis, with his father (our uncle), Pantelis, have visited this area and reported that they were able to visit were our parents were born and, from a distance, were able to see, the house where they lived.

[4] My cousin Fotis M. Platanidis and I have communicated with Fotis Platanitis in Thessaloniki to reconnect our families. However, the family in Boston and Thessaloniki indicate that the suffix on the last name is different ("tis" vs "dis") and thus there is no connection. They have not taken into consideration the change in the suffix when immigrating from Greece to the USA (e.g. on Panayiotis' immigration the suffix was changed from "dis" to "des" based on phonetics. Likewise going from Greek to English, phonetically it is not unreasonable to change "dis" to "tis". Notwithstanding, we continue to work on connecting the families. See footnote 5 below.

[5] It is thought that at the time of the 1922 genocide and exodus from Smyrna, Apostolos Lost touch with his brother, Fotis, as he had earlier (before the 1922 genocide) went to Thessaloniki as a refugee, immigrating from Thessaloniki to America he settle in Boston., His son and his grandson were both Boston Massachusetts policemen, and his great, great grandson, who is also named Fotis Platanitis in Thessaloniki. In discussion, on Facebook, with Fotis Platanitis in Thessaloniki, indicated to me that it was rumored that part of the family, after leaving Smyrna in 1922 settled in Chania, Crete.

[6] Fotis had several siblings, most of which we do not know their names. However, know that one brother was named Apostolos and one sister was named Despina. Despina Platanidou marred Yoryos (George) Dajogulou. They had a son named Anastas. When Yorgos and Despina passed away, Anastas was going to live with his uncle, Fotis, in Alasehir. While young, Anastas decided not to go live with his uncle, instead he marry a lady whose name was Kyriaki (Grace) Athanasiu. Anastas and Grace, married and immigrated to the USA. They had several sons and daughters all born in Asia Minor, one of daughter was named Despina Donjogolou (a granddaughter Despina Platanidis Donjogolou). Despina Donjogolou married Pantelis Tsalikidou, the brother of Kyriaki Tsalikidou Platanidis.

Churches to whom the Apostle John, at the instruction of Jesus, wrote[7] to the seven Churches as referenced in the Book of Revelations; a time when Orthodox Christianity was prevalent in Asia Minor, a time that the Great Cathedral of Ayia Sofia was built in Constantinople[8] and the many Holy sites in Cappadocia [9] were established. Asia Minor was the ancestral home of people of Greek descent going back to the year 2,000 BC.

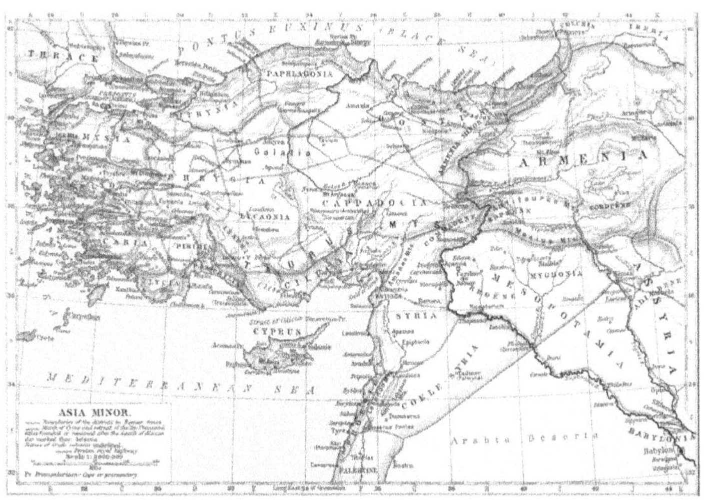

Old World Map of Asia Minor

The Ottoman Empire encompassed parts of Asia, Asia Minor, North Africa. The coastal area of what is now Turkey had access to the sea, it prospered and was predominantly Muslim with Greeks, Armenians, and Kurds being in the minority, the Greeks being the largest of the minorities.[10] While the Muslims had dominated this region since the overthrow of the Byzantine

---

[7] Read Appendix B for more information on the Seven Churches, the Seven Cities and what the Apostle John wrote to the Seven Churches at the direction of Jesus Christ.

[8] Constantinople, named by and for the Emperor Constantine.

[9] Cappadocia appears in the biblical account given in the book of Acts 2:9. The Cappadocians were named as one group hearing the Gospel account from Galileans in their own language on the day of Pentecost shortly after the resurrection of Jesus Christ. The Byzantine Empire lost Cappadocia permanently when it came under the control of the Seljuq Turks about the time that they defeated the Byzantine army at the Battle of Manzikert in 1071. Ancient rock-cut church and cave dwellings in Cappadocia, Anatolia, in present-day Turkey are among it's most distinctive features.

[10] As a result of the oppression of minority populations in Asia Minor by the Muslims, many families adopted names that they used so that they would not be singled out and suppressed as part of the minority population in Asia Minor. These names generally ended with the suffix "oglou" as is evident in the name Donjobolou. The Tsalikidou family used the name Tsalikoglou. The name Platanides comes from the Platanos, which is the name of the Platanos tree. Thus, with the suffix, Platanidis means "son of the Platanos tree". With this in mine my grandfather adopted and used the name "Tsinaroglou" which also means son of the Platanos tree. Families fleeing Asia Minor, for the most port, used their Greek names. Those immigrating to the USA further modified their names as they went through immigration at Ellis Island or latter by wanting to simplify or Americanize their names (e.g. Platanides to Planes, Tsalikidou to Chalekson, and Donjogolou to Donlou).

Empire and the Ottoman occupation of Constantinople [11], the Muslims with the Greeks, Armenians, and Kurds managed to survive their earlier conflicts and continued to live among one another. The Platanidis family had survived living in the Ottoman Empire, under the rule of the Muslims, and survived World War I. Later they would be adversely affected by the victory of the army of Moustapha Kemal, (Kemal Ataturk or Ataturk as he preferred to be called) over the retreating Greek army in what is known as the Greco-Turkish War.

Kyriaki was born Kyriaki Tsalikidou in Alasehir Asia Minor. She was one of eight children born to Yoryos (George) and Panayiota (Bessie) Tsalikidou. Kyriaki' siblings included four brothers whose names were Pantiles Tsalikidou (Charlie Chalekson), Konstantinos Tsalikidou, Yoryos Tsalikidou, and Damitri Tsalikidou, and three sisters named Stella, Stavroula, and Despina Tsalikidou. All were born and raised in Asia Minor. Some had immigrated earlier to the Greek Mainland. Pantelis had immigrated and lived in America where he had a retail neighborhood grocery store in Detroit Michigan. He would meet and marry Despina Donjogolou (the granddaughter of Despina Platanidis Donjogolou) in Detroit Michigan. Pantelis and Despina had three children, a daughter Pauline (Baptized Panayiota) and two sons, George, and Ernest, Pauline and George being named after their Grand Parents, Pantelis' mother and father, Yoryos and Panayiota Tslaikidou.

Photograph, taken in the late 1800's thought to be of Yoryos (George) and Panayiota (Bessie) Tsalikidou, parents of Kyriaki Tsalikidou Platanidis, with two of their daughters, possibly Stavroula and Kyriaki

---

[11] Constantinople was renamed Istanbul after being overtaken by the Muslim army of Kemal Atatürk.

Fotis and Kyriaki wanted to educate Panayiotis. They made an arrangement with Pantiles for Panayiotis to receive a visa to travel to his uncle's home in America to pursue his education with the understanding that he would go to school, including college, and graduate school to become a doctor and return to his family to practice medicine in Alasehir. While these arrangements had been made, no one expected what happened in September of 1922. That is when the Greek army was driven from the interior of Asia Minor West to the sea and the port of Smyrna.

Through the summer of 1922 the Greek families in and around Smyrna, which included those in Alasehir, were on high alert as news from the battle lines in the East indicated that the Greek Army was failing in holding off Ataturk's army. Ataturk's troops were driven by a theme of Nationalism, "Turkey for the Turks only"; that meant no one else, especially Christians and Jews. Ataturk sought to cleanse what is now Turkey of all persons that were not Muslim. That meant that all Greeks, Armenians, and Kurds were not welcome. Ataturk sought to establish a Muslim Caliphate.

Panayiotis was conversant in several languages, Turkish, Greek, Italian, French, and some English. He would go to the business districts in Alasehir and Smyrna, barefooted and dressed in shabby clothing, he would walk freely among the adults and listen to what they were saying. No one would pay attention to him as he looked like a poor boy living on the streets of the City. This way he would gather news of what was happening and return home to tell his father, Fotis, what he had heard. Fotis was working with other Greeks and Metropolitan Chrysostomos; Fotis needed to keep his family safe.

Metropolitan Chrysostomos (Kalafatis) of Smyrna

In September of 1922, the situation in and around Alasehir and Smyrna became tense and urgent. Through the summer of 1922, the Greek army had retreated from the East and as they retreated, they moved through Alasehir to the port in Smyrna and from there they were transported back to Greece. As this process unfolded, the tensions grew, and the Greeks and Armenians had growing concerns. Many Greeks along with the Christian Churches and Christian Organizations in the region looked to Metropolitan Chrysostomos[12] for guidance.

Fotis was more than just friends with Metropolitan Chrysostomos, they were confidants and family. Metropolitan Chrysostomos had baptized three of Fotis' sons. Metropolitan Chrysostomos was working with all the Christian Churches to unite and resist the approaching army of Ataturk. Fotis was working with Chrysostomos to unite the Churches to resist the annihilation of the Christian minorities (both Greek and Arminian).

On September 9, 1922, the armies of Ataturk, approaching from the East, passed through Alasehir and entered the City of Smyrna. With Ataturk on horseback, they marched into the cities and established control. Many Armenians and Greeks were to fight back. Ataturk sought out the Metropolitan, he did not need to look far as the Metropolitan did not hide, he was at The Cathedral Church of Saint Photini in Smyrna.[13]

Upon arrival at the Church, Ataturk and his troops sought to gain access to the Church, they sought to desecrate the Church. Metropolitan Chrysostomos stood in and block the door to the Church. Ataturk ordered his troops to disrobe the Metropolitan. He was disrobed, then his eyes were gouged out and he was stabbed many times. Then the Metropolitan, with his beard tied to the tail of a horse, was dragged through the streets of Smyrna till he was dead. Panayiotis, barefooted and wearing the shabby clothing of a street boy, witness these events[14]. Over the years he repeatedly told this story to his wife and children.

On September 10, 1922, Panayiotis witnessed the death of Metropolitan Chrysostomos of Smyrna. Not knowing that on November 4, 1992, the Metropolitan would be Canonized and Venerated by the Greek Orthodox Church, Panayiotis went home and reported the death of then Metropolitan Chrysostomos of Smyrna to his father, Fotis. Upon hearing of the death of the

---

[12] Metropolitan Chrysostomos was a Metropolitan of the Greek Orthodox Church. He was born on January 8, 1867 in Triglia, Ottoman Empire.

[13] The Metropolitan Church, or Cathedral Church, of Saint Photini in Smyrna of Asia Minor was destroyed in 1922 by Muslim Soldiers under the command of Kemal Ataturk. Ataturk desecrated the Church on September 10, 1922, and what remained burned as Ataturk and his soldiers burned Smyrna to the ground on September 13, 1922. Whatever did not burn was destroyed by dynamite. For more on the Cathedral Church of Saint Photini, go online to https://www.johnsanidopoulos.com/2021/02/the-cathedral-church-of-saint-photini.html

[14] On November 4, 1992, the Church of Greece Canonized Chrysostomos. He is Venerated in the Eastern Orthodox Church as Saint Chrysostomos of Smyrna. The Orthodox Church celebrates the Feast Day of St. Chrysostomos of Smyrna each year on the Sunday before the Exaltation of the Holy Cross which falls on a Sunday between September 7th to the 13th each year.

Metropolitan, Fotis knew that Ataturk would be coming to kill him as well, as Fotis and the Metropolitan had been working closely to resist the Muslim takeover, now that Ataturk had tortured and killed the Metropolitan and desecrated the Church, Fotis knew that Ataturk would seek to capture and kill him and his family; Fotis feared for the safety of his wife and children.

The Miter of Metropolitan Chrysostomos of Smyrna. (National Historical Museum, Athens, Greece)

In the early morning of September 12, 1922, while roaming the streets of the business district of Alasehir, Panayiotis learned that Ataturk had reached an agreement with representatives of the United States, France, United Kingdom, and Italy to allow them to take those who were citizens of their countries out of Smyrna using ships that had arrived and were anchored around the quay in Smyrna. He also learned that Ataturk's troops would allow the fires that had already been started in the Arminian sections of Alasehir and Smyrna to run out of control, thus the fires would spread and burn the balance of the cities. Only those that were citizens of the United States, France, United Kingdom, and Italy would be granted safe passage. Those that did not get removed by the ships of the United States, France, United Kingdom, and Italy would face whatever fate that would befall the Greek, Armenian, and other Christian occupants of Smyrna and the surrounding areas, this included Alasehir.

Panayiotis rushed home to report this news to his father, Fotis. On arrival his father was not home, he reported to his mother what he had learned. Shortly after arriving home, Ataturk's Muslim Soldiers barged into the home and seized Kyriaki and her children. They demanded that

Kyriaki tell them where they could find Fotis, she would not say anything to them, she refused to talk, she remained silent. Before they could take her away, Panayiotis took his visa for his passage to the United States and flashed it at Ataturk's troops, he kept yelling "US citizens, US citizens….". The troops did not know how to read English, but they saw the visa which was in a booklet that had the Seal of the United States of America on its cover. They then thought they had made a mistake and broken into the wrong house and had ceased American citizens; they retreated and left the home releasing Kyriaki and leaving her and her children behind.

St. Chrysostomos' The Cross that Metropolitan Chrysostomos used for Blessing, given to Kyriaki by the Metropolitan on the date of the Metropolitan's Baptism of her Kyriaki' son Minas in 1920 [15].

Upon the troops leaving her home, Kyriaki did not wait for Fotis to come home. Kyriaki knew that if Ataturk was able to find Fotis, they would kill him just as they killed Metropolitan Chrysostomos; and they would rape and torture her and Panayiota and take her sons to work as slave labor in the interior of Asia Minor. She, with the help of Panayiota and Panayiotis, gathered up the other children (Athanasios, Pantelis, Stavros, and Minas). With her children and some personal items of religious significance [16], Kyriaki left her home not knowing that she would never

---

[15] On November 4, 1992, the Church of Greece Canonized Chrysostomos. He is Venerated in the Eastern Orthodox Church as Saint Chrysostomos of Smyrna. The Orthodox Church celebrates the Feast Day of St. Chrysostomos of Smyrna each year on the Sunday before the Exaltation of the Holy Cross which falls on a Sunday between September 7th to the 13th each year.

[16] Upon the occasion of the Baptism of Fotis and Kyriaki' youngest child, Minas, in 1920, then Metropolitan Chrysostomos gave Kyriaki the Cross that he used to Bless. The Cross is made of stainless steel, gold and silver and has an inside chamber in which a "relic" may

see their home again. At that moment, their lives had changed, a change that would affect the family for more than just one lifetime, it has affected our family for multiple lifetimes.

Upon leaving her home Kyriaki went to meet Fotis and tell him what Panayiotis had learned about the fires and the ships at the quay as well as what had happened when Ataturk's troops broke into their home. Fotis' main concern was to save his family from the suffering and the sure death that they would experience if they were to be captured by Ataturk's troops. He was pleased with Panayiotis' quick thinking and bold conduct claiming to the Muslim troops that they were US citizens and showing the visa booklet which, the troops mistakenly thought that it was a US Passport. Panayiotis' quick thinking and the bold stance of a young boy bravely stepping in and facing down the Muslim Soldiers of Ataturk with nothing more than a visa book were nothing less than amazing. His brave stance had certainly saved his sister and mother from mistreatment and violation at the hands of Ataturk's Muslim soldiers and his brothers and himself being taken into the interior of Turkey to be used as slave labor.

Fotis decided that if the visa was mistaken one time as an American Passport, perhaps it would work again. Fotis and Kyriaki proceeded to the quay in Smyrna. Upon arrival, they could see ships at the quay, ships from different countries. These included ships from the US Navy. Access to the ships was guarded by Ataturk's troops, anyone seeking access had to pass a Muslim checkpoint and show proof of identity. Once approved at the checkpoint, they could proceed to the ships that were at the quay.

The ships of the US Navy that were in the harbor included the USS Edsall, USS Simpson, USS Litchfield, and USS Lawrence. The USS Edsall was the flagship of the American fleet.[17]

Upon arrival at the quay, Fotis lined up the family in a single file with Panayiotis in front, followed by Panayiota, Athanasios, Pantelis, with Kyriaki carrying Minas and then Fotis holding Stavros. Fearing discovery as Greek Orthodox Christians and their close relationship to their much-loved Metropolitan Chrysostomos, Kyriaki hid the items of religious significance, which included the Cross of Metropolitan Chrysostomos, upon the person of the children that were held in the arms of Fotis and herself. They proceeded to the checkpoint. Arriving at the check point Panayiotis presented the visa book as though it was a passport and smiling proudly announced in English that they were US Citizens. The Muslim soldier at the checkpoint looked at the cover of the visa book, saw the Seal of the United States, handing it back to Panayiotis, he

---

be placed. This and some small ikons were put among the few things that the family took from their home as they hastily left to escape the Muslim Soldiers.

[17] See Ships of Mercy by Christos Papoutsy for general information and the events leading up the burning of Smyrna, the genocide of the Christian Greek and Armenians and that role that the US Navy played in evacuating refugees.

then pointed in the direction of a big gray ship telling him in Turkish to enter and proceed to the ship.

Still in a single line with Panayiotis leading the way, Fotis and his family proceeded towards the gray ship. Upon arrival a sailor addressed them, and Panayiotis showed him the visa and said that he had a visa and wanted to go to America to study, that he had an uncle in America that was waiting for them and had booked passage from Greece to America. The sailor, knowing that they were not US Citizens, directed them to board a launch of the World War I Destroyer, the USS Litchfield. They boarded the launch that took them to the USS Lichfield; upon boarding, they found a space close to the rail of the ship, where they could sit and see Smyrna.

At 1:00 AM on September 13, 1922, Fotis and his family could hear the cries for help as they helplessly watched the rapes, murders, and genocide of Greeks and Armenians on the quay as the fires of Smyrna raged and burned out of control. Panayiotis would someday tell this story to his children, saying that the heat from the city burning was so hot that the gray paint on the side of the ship that faced the city had bubbled and peeled. By 3 AM on that morning all of Smyrna was engulfed in fire, Ataturk had destroyed the city.

Photograph, taken on September 13, 1922, showing the USS Linchfield at the Great Fire of Smyrna. The USS Linchfield was decommissioned on November 5, 1945; and was scrapped at the Philadelphia Naval Shipyard on March 29, 1946.

Picture, taken from a launch boat of a US Navy Destroyer (see the American flag on launch, shown in the left forefront of the picture). The picture is of the overcrowded boats of refugees as they desperately are attempting to escape the fire and genocide by the Muslim Troops of Kemal Ataturk at the quay of Smyrna.

The Clock Tower of the Metropolitan Church of St. Photini in Smyrna before it was desecrated, burned, and dynamited by the troops of Kemal Ataturk in September 1922.

Photographs of the Metropolitan Church of St. Photini in Smyrna, before and after. The upper photograph was taken before the attack by the Muslim troops of Kemal Ataturk; and The lower photograph was taken on September 20, 1922, after the fire and before it was blown up with dynamite by the troops of Kemal Ataturk.

Photograph of the desecrated graves at the Greek cemetery of Saint John's

The fire of Smyrna, a panoramic view from the opposite side of the Limani while still burning.

Photographs, before and after the destruction of the city of Smyrna after the fire.

The upper photograph shows the Bell Tower of the Metropolitan Church St. Photini; the Limani at Smyrna; and a general view of the City of Smyrna. The Bell Tower acted as a point of navigation for ships coming into the limani at Smyrna.

The lower photograph provides a view of the city of Smyrna after the fire. This photograph was taken on September 15, 1922

Having witnessed these acts of Genocide by radical Ataturk Muslim soldiers and the burning of Smyrna, on the morning of September 14, 1922, Fotis and his family were transferred from the USS Litchfield to a Greek passenger ship that took them to the port at Pieria Greece. Thus, the compassion of one US Navy sailor allowed them to board the USS Litchfield saved their lives[18]. Now they were on their way to Greece, the homeland that they knew, the homeland of their ancestors going back more than two millenniums was astern of the ship that carried them from a land that they would never see again to lands that they have never seen and events that they knew nothing about. They were alone and without a country.

USS Edsall, a US Navy Destroyer, was at Smyrna on September 13, 1922, when Smyrna was burned by the soldiers of Kemal Ataturk. On September 14, 1922, the USS Linchfield would begin to transfer the refugees that it had taken on board during the day of September 12, 1922, to the USS Edsall and Greek passenger ships that had arrived from Greece. USS Edsall received 607 refugees from the USS Linchfield and transported them from Smyrna to Salonika.

---

[18] One can only imagine what Panayiotis' innermost thought were when I (his son William), forty-four years later told him that I had accepted a transfer from the US Marine Corp to a special unit in the U S Navy; At that moment was Panayiotis reflecting on those moments when he, as a young boy, was met by a US Navy sailor who gave him and his family safe passage by allowing them to board the USS Litchfield to escape certain genocide at the hands of the Muslim troops of Kemal Ataturk?

USS Simpson, from June 29, 1922, to February 26, 1924, was involved in protecting United States citizens, and aiding the work of the American Relief Association in the Black Sea rescued mainly hundreds of Americans after the great fire of Smyrna September 13, 1922

Fotis and his family had left their homeland with nothing more than the clothing on their back, some items of religious significance, which included the Cross of Metropolitan Chrysostomos, and their very deep religious faith in Christ and the Theotokos. They knew nothing regarding the fate of other family members (Fotis and Kyriaki's siblings, parents, aunts, uncles, cousins). Fotis, Kyriaki, and their six children were survivors of genocide at the hands of radical Muslims led by Kemal Ataturk.

CHAPTER TWO

The Family is Divided

Upon arrival at the port of Pieria Greece, Fotis had nothing more than their clothing, a few personal items, and some items that were of religious significance to them, all which Kyriaki had pulled together in their hast to leave their home and escape the troops of Ataturk. There was little to no money. The port of Pieria, like many other ports in Greece and the Greek Island, were frantic as Greece was overwhelmed with refugees from Asia Minor. Many of these refugees were of Greek and Arminian heritage, but they were not Greek citizens. The population of Greece over the summer and into September of 1922 had tripled but the infrastructure and economy of Greece were not prepared, nor could it provide for the needs of so many refugees.

There was no work for Fotis, as he was a refugee, not a citizen of Greece and thus was not allowed to work. In the days after their arrival, they immediately knew that they had arrived at a critical juncture in this journey; without contemplating or planning, this all had been thrust upon them.

Panayiotis still had his visa book and along with it, he had his passenger ticket on the SS Acropolis, an Italian passenger ship. Fotis took the ticket to the office of the passenger liner in Pieria expecting to cash the ticket in and use the money for food and shelter for the family. He was not the only one to have this idea. At the office of the passenger ship SS Acropolis, Fotis found Kyriaki's sisters, Stella and Stavroula. Stella had a ticket for the same steamship that Panayiotis was scheduled to travel on as she too had intended to travel to America to visit her brother, Pantelis Tsalikidou in Detroit Michigan. Unfortunately, the steamship line advised that they were bankrupt and could not refund anything on the tickets. They either had to use the passage or lose the passage; those were the choices. In the meantime, they were reunited with Stella and Stavroula.

Stella and Stavroula told Fotis and Kyriaki how they had, in the early morning hours of September 13, ran for their lives through the streets of Smyrna attempting to reach the quay with their brothers Demetriou and Yoryos while being chased by the Muslim Troops of Ataturk. As they ran for their lives, Stella was holding hands with her brother Yoryos, they could hear gunfire, Yoryos hand went limp in Stella' hand, he fell to the ground, he had been hit by gunfire, he was dead. Stella, Stavroula, and Demetriou could not do anything for him and had to keep running, leaving his lifeless body alone in the street. They all grieved over the killing of Yoryos.

The steamship that Pantelis Tsalikidou had booked passage to New York City for his sister Stella and nephew Panayiotis would leave Pieria Greece on November 2, 1922, that was six weeks away. In the weeks leading up to the departure of the ship, Fotis and Kyriaki realized that the Greek government did not look at them as Greek Citizens, but as refugees from Asia Minor, with no citizenship rights in Greece. To settle in Greece the family would have to make and process an application to receive permission to move from the refugee camps to a permanent home in Greece. They also realized that Panayiotis was in a different situation as he had a visa to go to America, to live and study with his Uncle in Detroit. For Panayiotis there was a path out of uncertainly, he could go to America. This was also true for Kyriaki's sister, Stella. So, it was decided that Panayiotis would go with his aunt Stella to America on the passenger ship, SS Acropolis, which would leave Pieria on November 2, 1922.

On November 2, 1922, Panayiotis, at the age of 14, hugged and kissed his mother and father goodbye, expecting to see them in a couple of years when he finished his education and returned to them in Greece. Likewise, he hugged his sister Panayiota and brothers Athanasios, Pantelis, Stavros, and Minas, with the promise to return to be with them as well. Little did he know that he would never see his mother, father, and his brother Stavros again. The number of times that Panayiotis' wife and children would hear him say "Αχ, Μάνα μου *γλυκιά* " (Oh, my sweet mother) are simply too numerous to count. Not ever seeing his mother or father again was a burden he carried. He loved them and missed them the rest of his life, as I am sure they too loved and missed him.

On January 15, 1923, at 7:37 PM the SS Acropolis was towed into New York Harbor, with no coal on board to fire its boilers. This was true when SS Acropolis made port in Italy, France, and England. The steamship line was bankrupt and could not pay for all its fuel, so they obtain enough fuel to get close enough to the next port, just close enough to be towed into port.

Having left Pieria on November 2, 1922, and arriving in New York's Ellis Island on January 15, 1923, it had taken seventy-four days for the SS Acropolis to make the journey from Pieria to New York. Panayiotis and his aunt Stella, while in Alien Steerage Class, had spent Christmas, New Years, the Feast Days of St. Nicholas, St. Basil and St. Fotis, and Epiphany on board the SS Acropolis as this steamship made its way across the Atlantic Ocean. Panayiotis described this passage in Alien Steerage class as lacking many of the necessities that would keep someone comfortable, warm, and dry. The food left much to be desired and the accommodations he described as being poor. His aunt Stella would not leave him out of her sight, always holding his hand tightly and keeping him close to her. He indicated that his aunt Stella became ill on the journey and remained ill most of the time they were crossing the Atlantic.

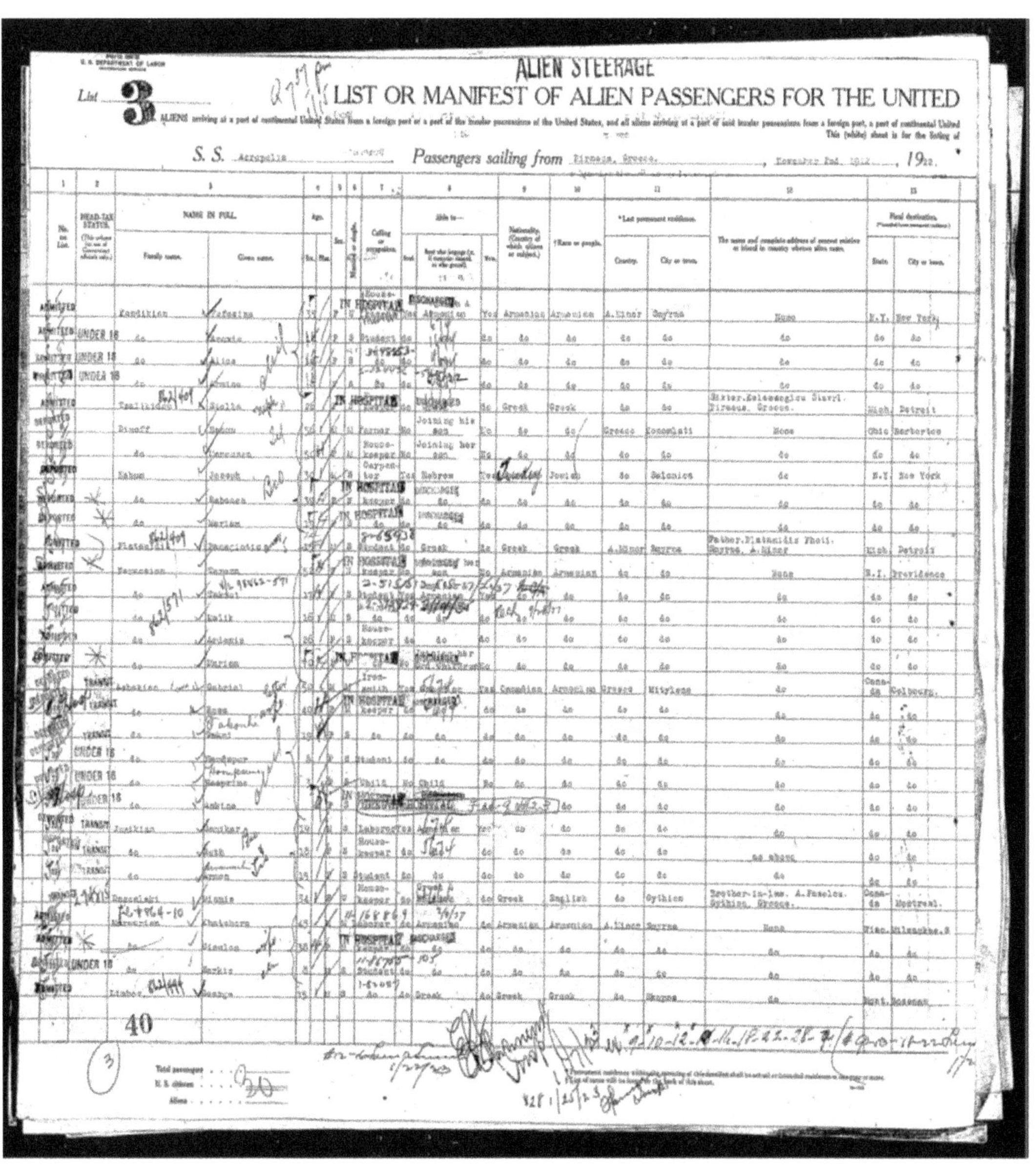

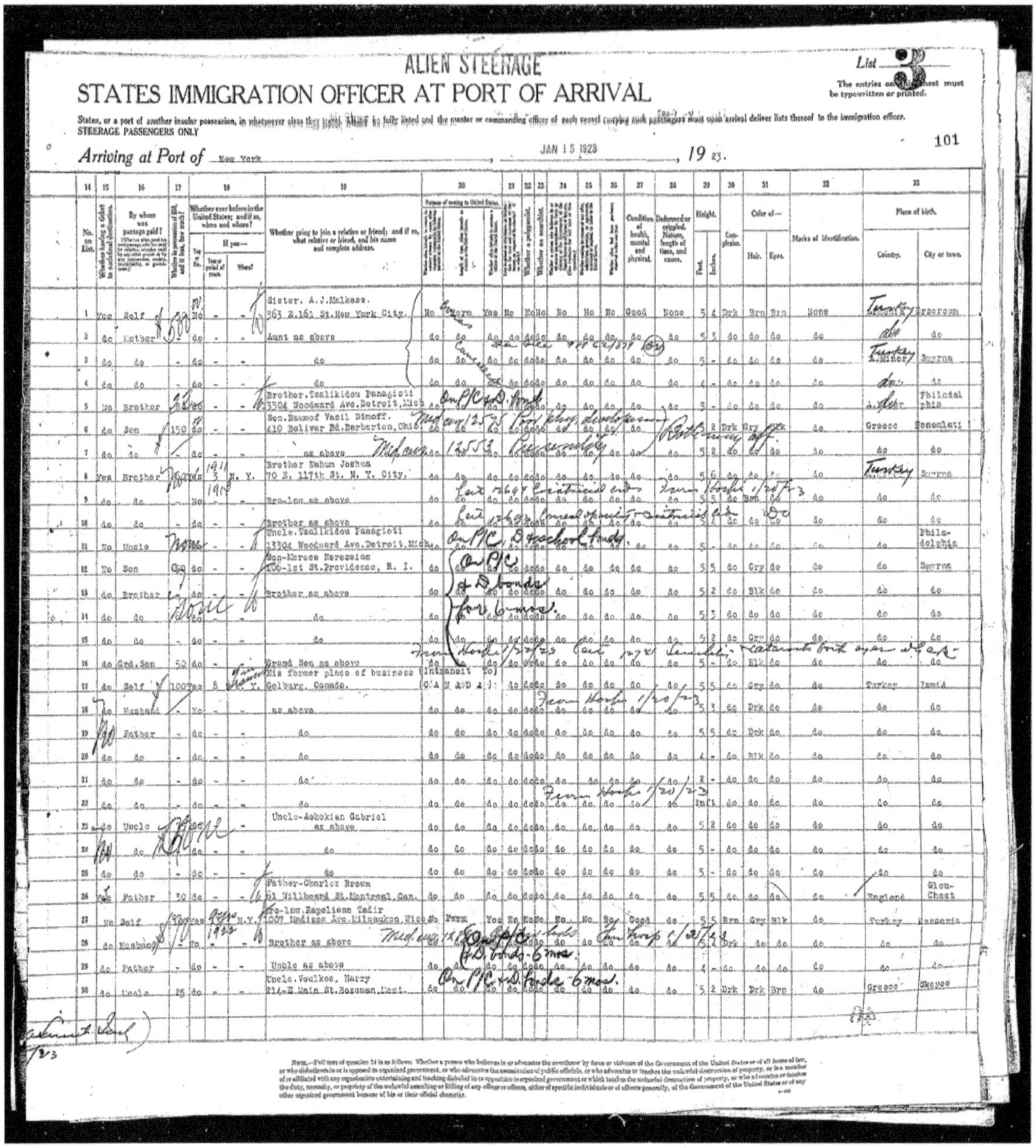

ALIEN STEERAGE

STATES IMMIGRATION OFFICER AT PORT OF ARRIVAL

List 3

The entries on this sheet must be typewritten or printed.

States, or a port of another insular possession, in whatsoever class they travel, MUST be fully listed and the master or commanding officer of each vessel carrying such passengers must upon arrival deliver lists thereof to the immigration officer.
STEERAGE PASSENGERS ONLY

101

Arriving at Port of New York, JAN 15 1923, 1923.

No. on List	Whether having a ticket to final destination	By whom was passage paid?	Whether in possession of $50	Whether ever before in the United States	Whether going to join a relative or friend; and if so, what relative or friend, and his name and complete address	Height (ft.)	Height (in.)	Complexion	Hair	Eyes	Marks of identification	Country	City or town
1	Yes	Self	500	No	Sister. A. J. Malkass. 563 E.161 St. New York City.	5	4	Drk	Brn	Brn	None	Turkey	Erzerum
2	do	Mother	500	do	Aunt as above	5	3	do	do	do	do	do	do
3	do	do	-	do	do	5	-	do	do	do	do	Turkey A. Minor	Smyrna
4	do	do	-	do	do	4	-	do	do	do	do	do	do
5	No	Brother	[illegible]	do	Brother. Tsalikidou Panagioti 3304 Woodward Ave. Detroit, Mich	5	-	do	do	do	do	do	Philadelphia
6	do	Son	150	do	Son. Naumof Vasil Dimoff. 410 Boliver Rd. Barberton, Ohio	5	2	Drk	Gry	[illegible]	do	Greece	[illegible]
7	do	do	-	do	as above	5	2	do	do	do	do	do	do
8	Yes	Brother	[illegible]	1911 3 N. Y.	Brother Nahum Joshua 70 E. 117th St. N. Y. City.	5	6	do	do	do	do	Turkey	Smyrna
9	do	do	-	No	Bro-law as above	5	5	do	Brn	do	do	do	do
10	do	do	-	do	Brother as above	5	4	do	do	do	do	do	do
11	No	Uncle	None	-	Uncle. Tsalikidou Panagioti 13304 Woodward Ave. Detroit, Mich	5	-	do	do	do	do	do	Philadelphia
12	No	Son	50	do	Son-Abraca Neressian 106-1st St. Providence, R. I.	5	5	do	Gry	do	do	do	Smyrna
13	do	Brother	[illegible]	do	Brother as above	5	2	do	Blk	do	do	do	do
14	do	do	None	do	do	5	3	do	do	do	do	do	do
15	do	do	-	do	do	5	2	do	Gry	do	do	do	do
16	do	Grd. Son	50	do	Grand Son as above	5	-	do	Blk	do	do	do	do
17	do	Self	100	Yes 5 N. Y.	His former place of business (Intransit to) Golburg, Canada.	5	5	do	Gry	do	do	Turkey	Ismid
18	do	Husband	-	No	as above	5	3	do	Drk	do	do	do	do
19	do	Father	-	do	do	5	5	do	Drk	do	do	do	do
20	do	do	-	do	do	4	-	do	Blk	do	do	do	do
21	do	do	-	do	do	2	-	do	do	do	do	do	do
22	do	do	-	do	do	Infant		do	do	do	do	do	do
23	do	Uncle	None	do	Uncle-Ashokian Gabriel as above	5	2	do	do	do	do	do	do
24	do	do		do	do	5	-	do	do	do	do	do	do
25	do	do	-	do	do	5	-	do	do	do	do	do	do
26	Yes	Father	30	do	Father-Charles Brown 51 Willibeard St. Montreal, Can.	5	5	do	do	do	do	England	Glou-Chest
27	No	Self	100	Yes 1922 N. Y.	Bro-law Kapeliene Tadir 1007 Madison Ave. Milwaukee, Wisc	5	5	Brn	Gry	Blk	do	Turkey	[illegible]
28	do	Husband	-	No	Brother as above	5	[illegible]	Drk	do	do	do	do	do
29	do	Father	-	do	Uncle as above	4	-	do	do	do	do	do	do
30	do	Uncle	25	do	Uncle. Voulkos, Harry 214-E Main St. Bozeman, Mont.	5	2	Drk	Drk	Brn	do	Greece	Skopos

List 3 of the Alien Steerage List of Manifest of Alien Passengers for the United States Immigration Officer at Port of Arrival, for the S.S. Acropolis, Passengers sailing from Piraeus Greece, November 2nd, 1922, Arriving at Port of New York, January 15, 1923. List 3 is shown on a two-page ledger, the two pages make up one document. The image on the prior page is of the left-hand side of the Ledger and the bottom image is of the right-hand side of the Ledger.

List 3 of the "List or Manifest of Alien Passengers for the United States Immigration Office at Port of Arrival-Alien Steerage" shows the ship arriving in New York City. Looking at the left-hand side of the Ledger for List 3 of this manifest as it appears on the prior page, lines 5 and 11 show the arrival of Stella and Panayiotis, each showing their destination as Pantelis Tsalikidou at 3304 Woodward Avenue, Detroit, Michigan, Pantelis being the brother and uncle to them, respectively. The manifest shows that Panayiotis had no money with him, that Stella had $33.00 and that Stella, upon her arrival, was ill and was admitted to the hospital on Ellis Island.

Taking a close look at the Manifest of Alien Passengers, one notices that a stamp was applied to the left-hand column next to each name. The stamp indicates "Admitted" or "Deported"; most arriving passengers were "Deported", Panayiotis and Stella were "Admitted". Also, on the right-hand side of the Ledger for List 3, as it appears on page 29, those passengers from Asia Minor indicated that Asia Minor was their country of origin. However, for each immigrant who indicated that they were from Asia Minor, the words Asia Minor had been crossed out, and the word "Turkey" appeared in handwriting. Asia Minor was no more, it had been taken over by Kemal Ataturk's Muslim Army. Constantinople ceased to exist, it was renamed Istanbul; Smyrna was renamed Izmir, and Asia Minor became Turkey.

When Stella recovered from her illness, she was allowed to stay, but Stella and Panayiotis remained in New York on Ellis Island for three months. Stella sent word to Pantelis that they had arrived, but it took time for her message to reach him, and then it took time for him to travel to New York to receive them.

Once Pantelis came to Ellis Island to receive them they all returned to Detroit to live with Pantelis and his family. But Panayiotis would not go to school. He insisted on finding jobs. He wanted to work and send money to Greece for his parents and sibling to have food and shelter. Panayiotis struggled between being required to go to school as he was in America on a student visa and his deep-felt need to work and help his family in Greece. At age sixteen the time had come to renew his student visa. Rather than renew it, he and his aunt Stella crossed over from Michigan to Canada and reentered the United States with a temporary residence visa. This made it easier for Panayiotis to work. On April 8, 1926, at the age of eighteen, Panayiotis filed a Declaration of Intention with the District Court of the United States, Eastern District of Michigan, Southern Division, seeking to become a permanent resident and a citizen of the United States and renouncing forever all allegiance and fidelity to any foreign prince, potentate, state or sovereignty, and in particular to Mohammed VI, Sultan of Turkey.

U. S. DEPARTMENT OF LABOR
NATURALIZATION SERVICE

ORIGINAL

No. 56055

UNITED STATES OF AMERICA

DECLARATION OF INTENTION

☞ Invalid for all purposes seven years after the date hereof

Eastern District of Michigan
Southern Division

In the _______ District _______ Court
of _the United States_

I, Peter Platanides, aged 18 years, occupation Clerk, do declare on oath that my personal description is: Color white, Complexion dark, height 5 feet 5½ inches, weight 135 pounds, color of hair darkbrown, color of eyes brown, other visible distinctive marks _______ I was born in Turkey on the 14 day of March, anno Domini 1 908 ; I now reside at 13917 Brush St., Highland Park, Michigan, I emigrated to the United States of America from Piraeus, Greece, on the vessel Acropolis ; my last foreign residence was Canada ; I am not married; the name of my {wife / husband} is _______ {she / he} was born at _______ and now resides at _______ It is my bona fide intention to renounce forever all allegiance and fidelity to any foreign prince, potentate, state, or sovereignty, and particularly to _______ Mohammed VI, Sultan of Turkey, of whom I am now a subject; I arrived at the port of New York, in the State of New York, on or about the 16th day of January, anno Domini 1 923 ; I am not an anarchist; I am not a polygamist nor a believer in the practice of polygamy; and it is my intention in good faith to become a citizen of the United States of America and to permanently reside therein: SO HELP ME GOD.

Peter Platanides
(Original Signature of Declarant)

Subscribed and sworn to before me in the office of the Clerk of said Court this 8th day of April, anno Domini 19 28

[SEAL]

Albert L. Abel

Deputy   Clerk of the U.S. District _______ Court.

Document recovered by a search of public records using Ancestory.com; Peter Platanides Declaration of Intention to become a Citizen of the United States of America

In Greece, Fotis had made an application to move the family to Chania Crete and was waiting for the Greek Government to issue a travel and settlement order that would allow them to travel and settle in Chania.

On the back of a photograph of the family in Greece, using it as a postcard, Fotis wrote a short message to his brother-in-law, Pantelis. Some of the writing is blocked out by red tape (and is so indicated below) that was used to secure the picture on the opposite side to a photo album and other writings have faded out (and is so indicated below by the insertion of periods (……)) because of their age or the possibility of water damage. Fotis writes:

"Korinthos(?) 5/5/1923…(red sticker)…America

Dear brother Pantelis Tsalikidou, greetings! When you receive this photograph of ours, I ask you please, because it is good, to communicate with Stella and Panayiotis, so we can feel relieved here in the…other places. Your sister Kyriaki and me became unrecognizable…Thanks to God that keep us still strong and we wish *for His Will to return us home. The little children Athanasios, Pantelis, Stavros, Minas as well as Panayiota, they all kiss with respect your right hand…(two lines follow that the writing comes out very dull and not readable)…(red sticker)…We wish you all the best…"*

This is signed Platanidis Fotis

On the left is the photograph upon which my grandfather on May 5, 1923, wrote a message to his brother-in-law, Pantelis Tsalikidou in Detroit Michigan. From left to right in the back row is Panayiota, with my grandparents, Fotis and Kyriaki; in front of them are Athanasios, Pantelis, and Stavros; and in front is Minas.

On the right is the May 5th, 1923, writing of my grandfather.

I had sent an image of the postcard and the writing of my Grandfather to my cousin Fotis M. Platanidis in Athens to assist me with the translation. These writings of our Grandfather on May 5, 1923 came shortly after escaping the genocide in Smyrna and their suffering the loss of Metropolitan Chrysostomos and Kyriaki's brother, Yoryos. We both felt strongly that this writing by our grandfather would give us some indication of his thoughts and state of mind. Remember, the family's escape from Genocide at the hands of the Muslim soldiers on the evening of September 12, 1922, just two days after my father, Panayiotis, witnessed the murder of Metropolitan Chrysostomos on September 10, 1022, and a day before Kyriaki's brother Yoryos was killed in the streets of Smyrna while trying to escape this genocide of Christians. The postcard with its writings is dated May 5, 1923, approximately seven months following these traumatic experiences where they lost the lives of Metropolitan Chrysostomos and Kyriaki's brother Yoryos and, only by the grace of God, was I able to escape the genocide of the entire family. Because my cousin's (Fotis) eyes are failing him and given the importance of these writings, my cousin enlisted the help of a graphologist to try to resurrect these writings which are now a little more than ninety-eight years old.

The graphologist advised my cousin that the writings expressed deep nostalgia for the Holy Grounds of Mikra Asia (perhaps referring to the Church at Smyrna and the Church at Philadelphia as referenced by John the Apostle in the Book of Revelations at 2:8-11 and 3:7-13, respectively, and the homeland of people of Greek heritage dating back to 2000 BC). He refers to their transformation from their lives in Asia Minor prior to the genocide and them, having been transformed from their life, home, and business they knew, to the hard times of a refugee without a county living in a refugee camp. The graphologist observed that our Grandfather's hand was trembling as he wrote and that some of his grammar is garbled or incohesive. The graphologist points out that the writer is probably exhausted and burned out from a constant and continued trauma that he and his family had suffered, now finding himself without a home, without a country, without a source of income to care and provide for his family and having to part with his oldest son, Panayiotis.

Having the advantage of looking back over the events that my grandfather suffered (the loss of Metropolitan Chrysostomos, his death being so violent, barbaric, and full of hate for Christ and the Christian Faith followed by an escape from certain death and genocide of his wife, children and himself at the hands of Ataturk) and the killing of his brother-in-law, Yoryos, I can see that, at this point, my grandfather was suffering from mental fatigue caused by catastrophic events and destruction that were way beyond his control; events and destruction that left him out of control of his and his family's ability to exercise control and self-determination. Today we would call this Post Traumatic Stress Disorder, PTSD, which is a disorder that people suffer from (especially soldiers returning from combat) after they have suffered a life-changing trauma. My grandfather had suffered several life-changing traumas in quick succession of each other. Trauma such as the death of the Metropolitan, Ataturk searching for him to kill him and his family, and the killing of Yoryos`; from which our Grandfather, but for the Grace of God that manifested itself in the quick thinking of a 14-year-old boy, would find a way to bring himself and his family to safety and escape what would have been his death. At this point, I have no doubt that my grandfather and grandmother were suffering from PTSD, a mental condition that was not recognized at that time and as such would go untreated and be further exacerbated during the balance of his life.

For me, reading this for the first time as I approach my 80th birthday, never having heard my grandfather's voice or read anything that expressed his thoughts in his own word, this, was moving. My heart and mind were overcome with a mixture of tears, hurt and compassion as for the first time in my life I connected with my grandfather and experienced some of the emotions and pain my grandfather was experiencing; all expressed in his own words written by his hand some ninety-eight years ago; for the first time in my life I experienced his innermost thoughts and prayers, all in his words written by his hand; those words being sent by him to his brother-in-law, Pantelis, to be shared with his son, Panayiotis, and his sister-in-law, Stella. This picture and writing were maintained by my father among his personal effects for the rest of his life. One cannot begin to imagine the emotions my father had about these writings and the picture that was on the other side of this Post Card.

In his writing to Pantelis Tsalikidou, Fotis gives thanks to God that God has kept them strong as they experience this ordeal. He also prays to God and wishes that "His Will" is to "return us home". This shows me that my Grandfather was deeply steeped in his faith. A novice would pray to God to return them home, but my grandfather prayed that "God's Will" would be to return them to home, knowing that whatever is "God's Will" is what would be done and confirming that he was ready and willing to accept "God's Will", whatever that was. This expression of faith by my grandfather I find deeply comforting as I know by these words that he was deeply committed to God and God's Will. At a time in his life that he was experiencing the most egregious events a person may imagine, my grandfather did not dictate to God to accept his will as God's Will, but he humbly prayed that God's Will would be to return them home, and in so doing he also was proclaimed that he had and would continue to accept God's Will over his own desires. He was committed to God and accepted God's Will. He engaged in "undoubting prayer".

On July 15, 1925, after living in refugee camps under primitive conditions from the time of their arrival, September 16, 1922 (one day short of two years and ten months), Fotis and his wife with his daughter and four sons obtained approval to settle in Chania Crete. At that time Fotis was 48 years old, Kyriaki was 45 years old and Panayiota, Athanasios, Pantelis, Stavros, and Minas were 18, 14, 12, 9, and 6 years old, respectively.

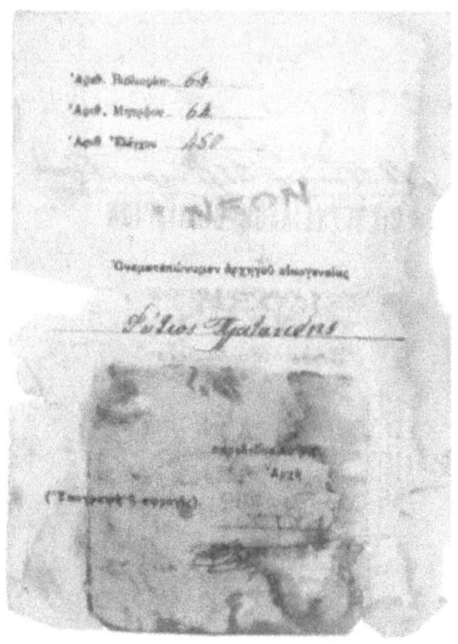

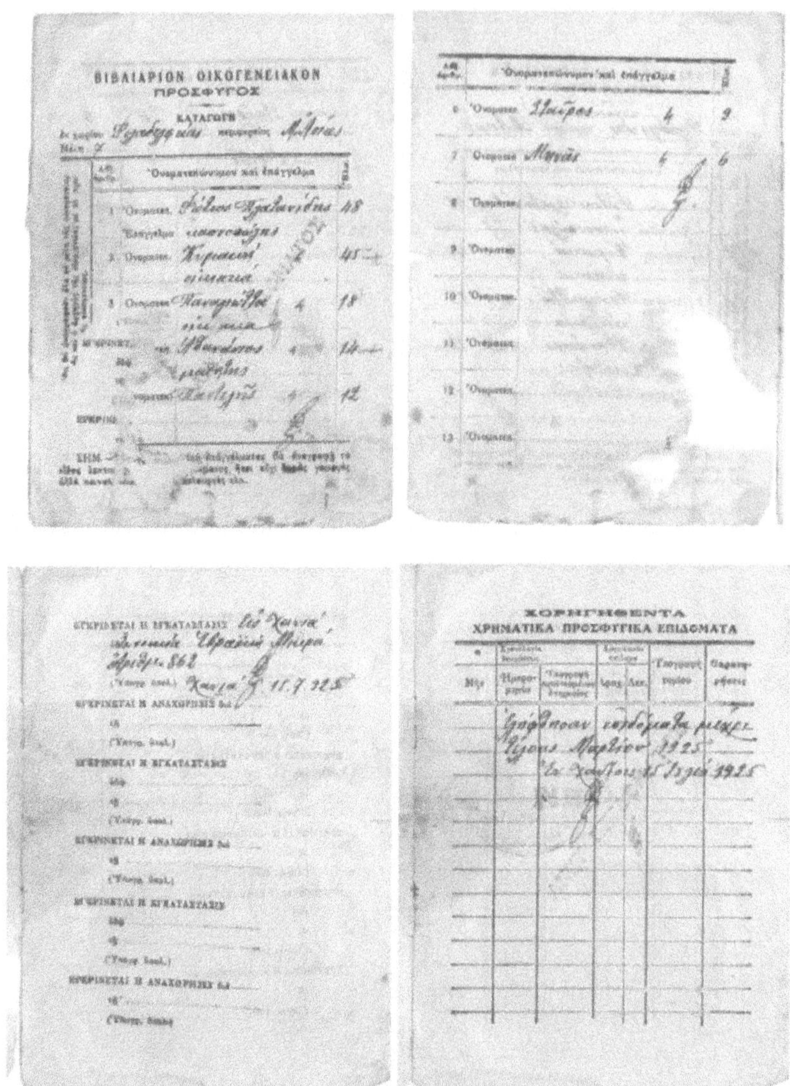

This Permit to settle in Crete for Fotis Platanidis and family was issued by the Greek government on July 15, 1925. It was found among various old papers that had been saved by Minas F. Platanidis. The document is 16 pages, but only six pages are presented here. In the photograph, my grandfather is sitting. Behind him, from left to right is my grandmother, and son Athanasios and daughter Panayiota; the second row, from left to right is his son Pantelis, my grandfather, and his son Stavros; and in front of him is his son Minas. In the picture, the three youngest boys continue to wear dresses which indicates to me that they continue to fear the abduction of their sons by the Muslim terrorist.

Panayiotis continued to live and work in Detroit, sending money to his father and mother a couple of times a month. It was this money that provided the support for his family during their time in the refugee camps and afterwards, gave his father the ability to buy a small house and store, down by the limani in Chania. Fotis would open a tobacco shop and from there work to support his family.

Throughout the balance of their lives, while keeping in touch by letters and pictures, Fotis and Kyriaki lamented not seeing their son. On his death bed, Fotis prayed to God that a sign would be given to Panayiotis that would mark the time and date that Fotis passed away, a sign to Panayiotis that his father was thinking of him at the time he passed away. At that time, living in Miami Florida, while Panayiotis was sitting at the kitchen table with his wife, a water glass sitting on the table by itself, shattered. Panayiotis told his wife, the glass had shattered as a sign so that when the time came, he would remember where he was and what he was doing at this, an important movement. Later, Panayiotis received a letter that told him that his father passed away and that when he passed, he prayed that his son would receive a sign to know when he passed.

Panayiotis would know that his father had passed away thinking of him. While time and distance had separated them, their love and connection to one another were never diminished. So, it was for Panayiotis and his father, likewise Panayiotis and his mother as well as his sibling. Torn apart and divided by acts of terror and genocide delivered by Kemal Ataturk and his army; spiritually they were never separated.

CHAPTER THREE

Panayiotis meets Katherine

Having obtained a Temporary Residence Card in 1925, Panayiotis did not stay in school, he worked to send money home to his parents in an effort that his father would establish himself in Crete. In the meantime, he continued to live with his uncle. At eighteen years of age, he made his declaration to become a permanent resident and a citizen of the United States.

Panayiotis, no longer dependent on a student visa or a temporary residence card, traveled around the county fighting as a lightweight boxer under the ring name "Peter Oaks". Yes, he was small, but he had a long reach, a reach that one would expect on a man that was over six feet tall. His hands were also those of a larger man. He was quick with his hands and had a strong punch. He earned a featherweight title, but then stopped when he took a punch that broke his jaw. After months of having his jaw sowed shut and having a liquid diet, he decided to earn money without having to fight. His new endeavors included driving trucks, working in restaurants, working construction, and other trades.

When he was about twenty years old, he noticed a lump on the left side of his neck just under the jawline. He thought that this had something to do with his having broken his jaw. When he went to the doctor, the doctor advised him that he had a tumor and that it needed to be treated with radiation. These treatments were expensive, some were still experimental. He was referred to a trial program. When he went to sign up, he was concerned that since he was not born in the USA, he may not be allowed to enter the program. Noting that he was born in Philadelphia, Asia Minor, which had been renamed by the Muslims to Alasehir, Turkey; when he was asked where he was born, he said Philadelphia (specifically eliminating the reference to Asia Minor). He was accepted into the trial and underwent radiation for the tumor. The tumor dried up, turned black, and then was removed. He had a scar there to remind him of this experience. It must have been a frighting experience as after this Panayiotis decided it was time to settle down with someone that would be part of his life and have a family with him.

Panayiotis' wandering around the county had brought him to New York. In New York, he eventually went to work as a shoe salesman in the Manhattan store of Indian Walk Shoe Company. Here he would embark on a career and a trade that would teach him to work with children and adults that needed orthopedic shoes. He was now twenty-five years old.

One day, in New York City, he was shopping at a Woolworth 5 and 10 Cent Store. Here Panayiotis noticed a petite dark-haired girl working behind the counter. She was short, only four feet eleven inches high. He approached her and asked her name, she said "Katherine Venis ". He asked if she was Greek, and she said yes. He asked if he could take her out and she said we will see. When he asked what that meant, she told him that she knew nothing about him and until she does, she is not going to go out with him. She also said that once she knew more about him, then she would have to ask permission from her parents. His being from Asia-Minor, she questioned him if he was a Greek or a Turk.

Katherine's picture from the time she met Panayiotis

Panayiotis did not give up on Katherine, as she told her children Panayiotis came back to talk to her every workday for weeks. Finally, she told him that he could take her to a dance at the Greek Orthodox Church, but her father said that he would have to take her sister, Connie, to the dance as well, as they were not to be left alone.

Katherine had a large family. She was the oldest of six children born to Theodore Venis and Mariyo Harolambopouls Venis: four daughters (Katherine, Konstantina, Eleni, and Louiza) and two sons (Thanasis and Yoryos).

Theodore had immigrated from Greece to America to join his first cousin who was also named Theodore. His cousin and his cousin's sister, Corrina Venis, had immigrated earlier to America from Greece.

At the time that Panayiotis met Katherine, her family was living in New York City, New York, and her Uncle Theodore was living with his wife and children in Summerville, New Jersey. It was not too long before the young couple would go, with other families, to Summerville to visit Katherine's uncle's family. Katherine and her sisters were close to her "Jersey" cousins. As a result of the weekend and holiday trips to Summerville, Panayiotis developed close ties to the Jersey cousins as well. For Panayiotis dealing with two families each having five and six children (a total of eleven children) was not difficult, in fact, it was heartwarming and reminded him of his big family that he had left behind in Greece. In short, he liked and was comfortable dealing with all the family and relatives. Furthermore, Katherine's mother, Mariyo, took him under her wings as though he was her son. She nicknamed him, endearingly, "Turkco" (Mariyo spoke only Greek, thus "Turkco" which meant "Turk".

There was also the contrast between life in the big city, New York, and life out on the farm, Summerville. The blend of the two environments (city vs farm) the large family with the large extended family (Katherine's family of six children in New York and her uncle's family of five children in Summerville) provided the warmth and balance that he had missed since he had left his homeland in Asia Minor.

On November 25, 1934. Panayiotis and Katherine were married. While the Panayiotis family in Greece could not come to America, the couple had a Church wedding in New York City. Of course, all the New York and New Jersey Venis relatives attended the wedding and the reception. Panayiotis' uncle, Pantelis Tsalikidou, with his family as well as his aunt, Stella Tsalikidou Pelekonos with her husband Andreas Pelekonos, came from Detroit Michigan, to celebrate this wedding. While this was a happy and great occasion for Panayiotis and Katherine, Katherine had never met Panayiotis' immediate family. Her only communications with them would be by mail and photographs.

Wedding photograph of Panayiotis and Katherine November 25, 1934

Photograph of the wedding party of Panayiotis' marriage to Katherine on November 25, 1934. Siting from left to right is the brides' maid and wife of New Jersey Cousin Ollie Venis, Katherine's sister and brides' maid Helen, Katherine's sister and bride's maid Louiza, and the wife of Michael Starycki and brides' maid Helen Venis Starycki. Standing from left to right is my mother's cousins Ollie Venis, Henry Johanson, and his wife and the maid of honor Konstantina Venis Johanson, New Jersey cousin Konstantine Venis and Michael Starycki, husband of Helen Venis Starycki.

Panayiotis and Katherine were in love, devoted, and happy with each other and the combined Venis families. Over time these relationships would prove to be life long, genuine, and unbreakable. It was a time that family was important and meant something; they all stood together.

Panayiotis and Katherine after their wedding

CHAPTER FOUR

Katherine's Family

Αικατερίνη βεηις (Katherine Venis) was the oldest of six children born to Theodore Venis and Mariyo Harolambopouls Venis. Katherine's siblings were Konstantina (Connie), Eleni (Helen), Thanasis (Tommy), Yoryos (George), and Louiza (Λουίζα in Greek or Louise in English).

Mariyo Harolambopouls [19], the daughter of George (Yoryos) Harolambopouls and Katherine (Αικατερίνη) Spiliopoulos Harolambopouls, at the age of twenty, arrived from Padagora Greece aboard the steamship Martha Washington on August 13, 1912. With her was her niece, Αικατερίνη Harolambopouls, they are shown on the passenger manifest as traveling to meet Mariyo' brother, Halalambos Harolambopouls who is also designated as being Αικατερίνη Harolambopouls' father. He is shown to have an address in Massachusetts[20].

Theodoros (Theodore) Venis, was born in Strezova, Greece, the son of Thanasis Venis and Katherine Bouta Venis. He traveled to America, immigrating on April 20, 1912, to join his first

---

[19] Harolambopouls, translating from Greek to English, phonetically, Harolambopouls may also be spelled Charombopouls.

[20] The address on the ships manifest, 490 Market Street, Lowell Massachusetts, is the address for the Greek Orthodox Church in Lowell, Massachusetts. Little is known about Mariyo' family, but DNA shows that I have a cousin living in Athens Greece (Dias Haralambopoulos) that is in his seventies that is four times removed from common grandparents.

cousins, Theodoros Venis and Corina Venis. Theodoros and Corina[21] were brother and sister, their parents raised their cousin Theodore as his parents, Thanasis and Katherine (Αικατερίνη) Venis, passed away at an early age.

Upon Theodoros' arrival, he and his cousin Theodoros, joined together and settled in New Bedford, Massachusetts. There they both met and married young ladies, one married a Romanian lady named Catherine, and the other met and married Mariyo Harolambopouls[22] . The two couples lived together sharing an apartment in New Bedford. Both couples gave birth to their first two children while living in New Bedford Massachusetts. After the births of their first two children Theodore and Mariyo, moved to New York City with their two children, Αικατερίνη (Katherine) and Konstantina (Connie)[23]   and the other couple, Theodore and Catherine, moved to rural New Jersey with their first two children, Ollie and Konstantina, where they established a farm.   Eventually, Corina settled in Charleston South Carolina where she married Kosmas Davoulos, she had one daughter, Helen. All three couples remained close and in touch with each other, they were raised as family and did not want to be separated.

Theodore and Catherine would have five children, Ollie, Konstantina (Tini), Eleni (Helen), Konstantine (Gus), and Philip (collectively the "Jersey Cousins"); all were raised and lived in New Jersey, all having children; and their children married and had children. The number of descendants from Theodore and Catherine are large and they spread out throughout the United States.

It is interesting to note that the Jersey Venis families, the Jersey Cousins, have a long history of service to the country, starting with Theodore Venis' military service during WW-II; most all his son's and many of the grandsons of Theodore and Catherine Venis served in the US Marine Corp during WW-II, Korean War, Vietnam War, and the Cuban Missel Crisis.

Theodore and Mariyo also had large families. (as noted above four daughters and two sons). Later in life, they moved from New York to South Florida. Their children had children, and

---

[21] There is an indication that Theodoros and Corina Venis may have also had other sisters that immigrated to America.

[22] Theodoros and Mariyo were marred in New Bedford Massachusetts on April 23, 1914, in the Greek Orthodox Church by Fr. D Spyropoulos.

[23] It is tradition in Greek Families that the first female child be named after the grandmother on the mother's side, thus it is possible that Mariyo' mother was named Katherine (Αικατερίνη). This thought is further supported by the fact that Mariyo' nice, daughter of her brother, was named Αικατερίνη, this showing that her father, Halalambos Harolambopouls, may have chosen to name his daughter after their mother. However, it is noted that Theodore's mother was named Katherine, thus Katherine may have had two grandmothers for whom she was named. On Katherine's birth certificate her name is spelled with a "K", not a "C", none the less from entering grade school though most of her life she spelled her name with a "C", Catherine. Subsequently we were able to isolate the marriage record of Theodoros and Mariyo in New Bedford Massachusetts on April 23, 1914 which confirmed the name of both their parents and that Mariyo' mother was named Αικατερίνη (Katherine).

likewise, they had children. Today all grandchildren, except for two that have passed away[24] , and their great-grandchildren live in South Florida, Central Florida, Tarpon Springs Florida, Atlanta Georgia, Denver Colorado, Fort Collins Colorado, North Carolina, South Carolina, and Missouri.

Patriotism did not limit itself to the Jersey Cousins. Theodore and Mariyo's sons and son-in-law served during WW II in the Army Air Corps, the US Army, and the Merchant Marines[25]. Panayiotis' son William served in the US Marine Corps and the US Navy at the time of the Vietnam War and Panayiotis' son-in-law, Dr. William Maistrellis MD (while married to my sister, Maria Platanides Maistrellis), served in the US Navy as a Navy Surgeon onboard an aircraft carrier, the USS Coral Sea, operating in the Pacific Ocean during the Vietnam War.

Of significant note is the military service of Johnny (Yannis) Georgopulos, son of my Godfather, William Georgopulos. Johnny, at eighteen years old volunteered and served in the Army Air Corp. His service was on one of the famous B-17 Flying Fortress[26]. Johnny was the belly gunner in a Flying Fortress initially based in England and flying missions over Europe. While manning the belly terret of the Flying Fortress to which his unit was assigned, the plane came under attack by German fighter planes. While under attack by Germans, this Flying Fortress was hit at its belly turret, the belly torrent housed one gunner, Johnny Georgopulos. The Belly Turret of the Fortress was annihilated and Johnny, then nineteen years old, was seriously wounded. By the time Johnny was able to receive medical care, he was in bad shape. Medics worked on him, but he lost his leg. He was sent stateside where he received medical care at various military hospitals. Gas Gangrene set in, and they amputated more of the leg. This process followed several other similar events until the Gangrene was cut out. Eventually, Johnny lost all his leg up to his hip. This all took place over a number of years and by the time that the Gangrene was brought under control, other complications set in; on March 27, 1950, approximately five years after he was wounded in WW-II, at twenty-four (24) years old, Johnny passed away; his passing away was the result of the wounds he received at age nineteen (19) in service to our country, the

---

[24] Two of my first cousins on my mother's side of the family (Venis) have passed away. Both were sons of my Uncle Tommy (Athanasius) and Aunt Sophia Venis. One was John Venis who was born with Cerebral Palsy and lived to the age of 70 and the other was Harry Venis who die from COVID-19 in April 2020.

[25] Lazarus Nicholaou, son-in-law of Theodore and Mariyo and husband to my aunt Connie, served in the Army of the United States from March 2, 1942 till his Honorable Discharge on November 8, 1945. After basis training he shipped out to England on September 18, 1942. His service took him to England, France, Belgium, and Germany. From the day of the Normandy Invasion to the end of the war, the Battle of the Bulge, he remained and served in Europe, returning to the United States and his beloved wife, Konstantina, after the end of the war.

[26] The B-17 Flying Fortress was developed in the 1930's by Boeing and saw service in both the Pacific and European Theaters of WW-II. The B-17 dropped more bombs than any other U. S. aircraft during WW-II. The plane originally designed by Boeing, was taken over by Douglas and produced for the Army Air Corp. During its production the aircraft went through several different design configurations, adding gun turrets housed in glass on the top of the fuselage as well as on the nose and belly of the aircraft, thus the name Flying Fortress. While principally deployed in the European Theater, they were deployed early in the Pacific Theater.

United States of America; a war that ended November 1945 ended the life of a fine young man in 1950.

Panayiotis had registered for the draft in the 1930s. When the war broke out in Europe and after D-Day, Panayiotis attempted to enlist in any branch of the US Military that would have him, but his job with the Hospital for Special Surgery and his work with crimpled adults and children made him necessary to remain at home to treat those who were injured and would b be returning from the war.

The offspring that followed the two Theodore Venis cousins also married and had children. They are numerous and are spread across the United States. While numerous, some live close to each other and do not even know that they are related. Some are confused over the last name, Venis. They mistake the Greek letter "Beta" in the Greek spelling of the name, βεηις, for the letter "B" in the English alphabet so they go by the last name Benis, pronouncing the letter B as you would in the name Ben, rather than Venis. This confusion stems from old documents related to the New Jersey Theodore Venis that showed his name in Greek, βεηις, thus they thought Venis was a mistake and that it was spelled with a B, thus Benis. Most of these descendants have little or no knowledge of the history of the two Theodore Venis couples and Corina Venis Davoulas, how they came here, who they were, how they and their children served this county to assure the preservation of the Constitution of the United States with all the rights and freedoms we receive under the protection of the Constitution and the depth of their Greek Orthodox religious Faith.

CHAPTER FIVE

Panayiotis, Katherine, and their Children

Both Panayiotis and Katherine had grown up in large families. Panayiotis' family had four brothers and a sister, a total of six; Katherine's family had four sisters and two brothers a total of six; and Katherine's uncle's family in New Jersey, with two daughters and three sons, a total of five. When discussing having a family, Panayiotis and Katherine always viewed the family as being large. Panayiotis knew that as the father of a large family he had to establish himself in a business that would bring him sufficient income to support a large family. For Panayiotis, supporting a family included Church, Education, housing, food, discipline, all served with an abundance of love.

At the time of his marriage to Katherine, November 1934, Panayiotis worked for Indian Walk Shoe Company in Manhattan. There he had learned the shoe business and focused on children's shoes with a special emphasis on shoes for crippled children. After his marriage, Panayiotis left his employment at the Indian Walk Shoe Company and went to work for New York's "Hospital for Ruptured and Chipped Children", subsequently known as "Hospital for Special Surgery[27]."

---

[27] Founded in 1863 as "Hospital for Ruptured and Crippled Children" in Manhattan, New York City, New York . Entering its seventh year of existence, in May 1870, the Hospital for the Ruptured and Crippled Children moved from its first site on lower Second Avenue

While at the Hospital for Ruptured and Crippled Children Panayiotis would expand his knowledge of orthopedic shoes and would learn to modify the shoes so that they would fit braces or to be worn by crippled children with features built into the shoes that would accommodate their special needs. These skills eventually extended to providing these same skills to crippled adults. This led to his opening "The Time Square Shoe Repair", a shoe repair and hat blocking shop in Time Square. Here he would apply these skills and modify shoes to meet the needs of crippled children and adults. Most of this work would flow to him by way of prescriptions issued by the doctors at the Hospital for Special Surgery on 42nd Street and Lexington Avenue in Manhattan. During WW II, much of this work involved soldiers who were injured in the war.

During Panayiotis' time at the Hospital for Special Surgery, Panayiotis met a young doctor of German descent, Dr. Karl Ackerman, M.D. Dr. Acherman was a Medical Doctor practicing as a family physician in Manhattan with privileges at St. Frances Hospital and the Hospital for Special Surgery, both in Manhattan. The friendship between Dr. Ackerman, Panayiotis, and Katherine would become lifelong. He would become their family physician, oversee Katherine's pregnancies, the health of her children, and the health of both Panayiotis and Katherine, and become the family physician for Katherine's parents and siblings.

Dr. Carl Ackerman, MD, taken at our home in the Bronx on White Plains Road

to its new home on 42nd Street and Lexington Avenue in New York City, the current site of the Hyatt Hotel. It was considered the country, as the heart of the city was south in lower Manhattan. Although there was a continuous exodus of people north from Wall Street, the lower Eastside and Canal Street, much of the city north of the 50s was open country. There were areas near 42nd Street occupied by shanties, and goats could be seen roaming. The hospital was renamed in 1940 when it became the "Hospital for Special Surgery"

Panayiotis took his father-in-law, Theodore Venis, who had worked as a "shoeblack" and had experience repairing shoes, into the business to work with him. When WW II ended, he brought his brother-in-law, Lazarus Nicholaou, who was returning from the war in Europe, into the business as well. For Theodore Venis and Lazarus Nicholaou, this would be their trade for the rest of their lives.

Panayiotis and Katherine purchased a two-family home in the Bronx, not far from the L train, this allowed Panayiotis to commute to work at the Hospital in Manhattan and eventually his shoe repair and hat blocking store in Times Square. The house was at 1256 White Plains Road in the Bronx. It was a two-family three-story home, with the first floor being a basement walkout to a back yard. The third story had its own entrance and was a separate two-bedroom one bath home, home for a second family.

Picture of the front door of the two-family home and 1256 White Plains Road, New York City, Bronx, New York. The door on the right was the door to our home. It opened to a foyer that had two doors, one to the home that we lived on and one that went upstairs to the home that eventually Uncle Lazarus and Aunt Konstantina live in with my cousins Theodore and Nicholas.

The above collage of photographs (but for the one with Aunt Helen next to a palm tree) are of photographs taken on the day of my Baptism (in 1942). The Upper left photograph shows Grandfather Theodore Venis, Godmother Evthokia Georgopulos, Grandmother Mariyo Venis, and God Father Vasilios (William) Georgopulos. Upper right is a photograph of Johnny Georgopoulos, US Airforce Belly Gunner in the famous B-17 Flying Fortress, at the time of this picture he was about 18 years old and had volunteered for the US Army Air Corps. The middle photograph is of Aunt Sophia, Godmother Evthokia, and Uncle Thanasis. The bottom left photo is of Johnny Georgopulos.

On September 17, 1942, the home would host the wedding reception of Katherine's sister, Connie, when she married Lazarus Nicholaou[28] in a Church Wedding[29] ; and later, after Lazarus return from his US Army service during WW-II[30] , the third-floor second residence would become home for Connie and Lazarus and eventually their two children, Theodore L, and Nickolas L Nicholaou.

Photograph, taken on September 17, 1942, the Church wedding of Lazarus Nicholaou to Konstantina (Connie) Venis the day before he shipped out for the UK to join the Allied Forces to free Europe.

[28] Panayiotis and Lazarus would become lifelong friends. Panayiotis would be the best man at the wedding of Lazarus to his sister-in-law Konstantina, would be the Godfather to their two children and they would be business partners in the Time Square (Manhattan) Shoe Repair. Both had common ground as they were refugees from Muslim terrorism, one from Asia Minor and the other from Cypress.

[29] Panayiotis was the best man for Lazarus when he married Katherine's sister Connie in a Church Wedding (the couple had been married in a civil ceremony on February 2, 1942, just prior to Lazarus leaving for basic training with the US Army. After basic training they wanted to marry in the Church, before Lazarus was to ship out to the war in Europe; and later Panayiotis and Katherine would be Godparents to their first son, Theodore L Nicholaou, when they Baptized him into the Greek Orthodox Faith.

[30] Lazarus Nicholaou had a three day leave between the end of his basic training and his shipping out from New York to England to be part of the Allied Forces in what was eventually know as the invasion at Normandy. He was born in Cypress and left Cypress to immigrate to the USA with his mother Chrisante, who was thirty-eight years old, and his brother Panos, who was ten years old, all of whom are shown on the Manifest of Alien Class on the steamship President Wilson arriving in New York on November 7, 1928, to join his father (Charalambos Nicholaou) who had previously immigrated and was living in St. Louis Missouri at 4251 Norfolk Avenue. On September 17, 1942, while on leave prior to shipping our, Lazarus married Katherine's sister, Konstantina (Connie) and the wedding reception was hosted at the home of Panayiotis and Katherine on White Plains Road.

Photograph of the Theodore G. Venis family on the day of the marriage of their daughter Konstantina to Lazarus Nicholaou, September 17, 1942. Standing in front of the bridegroom and bride is my brother Frank. Seated from left to right is Grandmother Mariyo, Lazarus Nicholaou, Konstantina Venis Nicholaou, Grandfather Theodore G. Venis. Standing behind the seated from left to right are my mother Katherine, my father Panayiotis, Maid of Honor Aunt Helen, and Aunt Louisa. And in the back row standing are Uncle Thanasis with his wife Sophia and Uncle George

Panayiotis and Katherine set out to have a big family, though they tried to have a large family, they had a good size family, two sons and one daughter.

The couple, Panayiotis and Katherine, would have six pregnancies in all. In 1936, 1939, and 1940 Katherine was pregnant, but while going full term she gave birth to three boys that were either stillborn or died as infants shortly after birth. Little is known about these three births as Katherine and Panayiotis did not fully share this with their children. In her older age, Katherine disclosed these pregnancies but did not provide many details.

On November 11, 1938 (a year after the first pregnancy and birth) Katherine gave birth to Fotis Panayiotis Platanides (Frank Peter Platanides). Frank would become the oldest of all the surviving children. January 14, 1942, after two more births in 1939 and 1940, Katherine gave birth to me, Vasilios Panayiotis Platanides (William Peter Platanides). I ("Billy" as they called me) became the middle child as on November 12, 1944, Katherine gave birth to a daughter, Maria Platanides, she became the baby and only girl of the family.

Photograph on the left taken in the fall of 1945 of Panayiotis and Katherine with their three children, from left to right, Billy, Frank, and baby Maria. Photo on the right of Katherine with baby Maria was taken in 1944.

Photographs, taken in 1943. Above left is Grandmother Mariyo doing her kit with me on the left and my brother Frank on the right side of the photograph. Above right is of grandmother Mariyo doing her kitting. Lower photograph, taken with my Uncle George's picture and birthday cake. At that time is was reported MIA (Missing in Action) as the US Army Bomber that he served upon as a Navigator was shot down over Burma. He was MIA FOR 90 DAY. In the picture from left to right are Uncle Thanasis, Aunt Sophia, Aunt Konstantina, Katherine, Aunt Helen and Aunt Louiza.

*Both photographs, taken in December 1944, the month after the birth of baby Maria;
here shown with Panayiotis and again with Katherine*

*Katherine, December 1944. Panayiotis in the back yard of the home on White Plains Road in the
Bronx New York, see the "L Train" in the background. This is the train that Panayiotis took to go to
work in Manhattan.*

Photograph, taken in 1944 of the Theodore G. Venis family. Siting is Grandmother Mariyo holding Granddaughter, baby Maria, and Grandfather Theodore with my brother Frank sitting on his lap. Standing from left to right are my mother Katherine, Aunt Konstantina, Aunt Louiza, Uncle George in his military uniform, Uncle Thanasis in his military uniform, Thanasis' wife Aunt Sophia, Aunt Helen, and Panayiotis holding me, Billy. Not is the picture is Uncle Lazarus who at that time was in the US Army deployed to Europe as part of the USA armed forces in WW-II.

Panayiotis' work at and with the Hospital for Special Surgery made him essential to the home country's support for the troops and efforts overseas during WW-II. He wanted to serve especially with his family in Chania falling under the control of Nazi Germany, but they would not accept him into the service, he was to stay home and work with the doctors and the hospital, caring for the returning troops that had been injured and crippled.

CHAPTER SIX

Panayiotis and Katherine Leave New York

In March of 1946, Panayiotis would leave the management of the Time Square Shoe Repair and Hat Blocking store in the hand of his brother-in-law, Lazarus, and his father-in-law, Theodore, and he and Katherine would move to a small barrier island, Folly Beach, in South Carolina. Folly Beach, for many, was a summer destination, especially sailors on leave from their ships that would come into the Port of Charleston South Carolina. In Folly Beach Panayiotis would take a five-year lease on a refreshment stand on the Folly Beach Pavilion. The Folly Beach Pavilion was one of several properties owned by the Larry Operating Company owned by John Larry. Folly Beach was just outside of Charleston South Carolina where Corina (Korina) Venis had settled with her husband, Cosmas Davoulas. She was our mother's second cousin, but we always thought that she was our aunt, we called her Aunt Corina.

In September of 1946, while only four years old, I would enter school as a first-grader. My brother and I would take a school bus from the barrier island to the James Island Elementary School. The school was also on a barrier island. It was a one-room schoolhouse on James Island. During the time that the family lived on Folly Beach, my brother Frank and I would attend school at James Island Elementary. Eventually, our sister, Maria, would also attend school at the one-room schoolhouse.

The school was organized with its desk in rows going from the front to back. The teacher's desk and blackboard were in the front of the room. All first graders set in the first row, going from front to back. Likewise, second graders set in the second row of seats; the third, fourth, fifth, and sixth rows were for the third, fourth, fifth, and sixth graders set in similar order. Here I found myself in the 1st grade and thus in the first row and my brother in the 3rd grade, thus two rows over. My brother and I were always together. At the outset Maria was too young to go to school, so she did not attend. When she was old enough, she started in the first row, I had progressed to the third row and was close enough to watch over her, as my mother had instructed. My brother Frank had progressed to the fifth row, he was to watch over me and our sister, Maria.

Panayiotis' business in Folly Beach was a seasonal business, it was only open from Memorial Day weekend to just after Labor Day each year. On Folly Beach there was the Atlantic Pier which extended out into the Atlantic Ocean. At the shore side of the pier, was a small amusement park that included a Ferris wheel and a carousel. Across the street from the amusement part, just one block off the ocean was a small white two-bedroom wood-frame house that became home to Panayiotis' family for the five years that they lived in Folly Beach.

Pictures, taken on July 9, 1992, of the house on Folly Beach South Carolina that was the home of Panayiotis and his family's from about March 1946 till September 1950. The top photo is the front view of the home and the bottom photo is the back view of the home

Photo, taken the summer of 1946 on Folly Beach of my brother Frank, my mother Katherine, and myself. Frank was eight years old, and I was four years old. Sister Maria was an infant and did not go to the beach, she stayed home with grandmother Mariyo and thus not in the picture.

Below are Scenic Photographs of Folly Beach South Carolina, the Atlantic Pavilion, Folly Pier, Folly Beach Amusement Center, and the Beach, all in the mid-1940's

Photograph of the Folly Pier and the beach in front of Pete's Hot Dogs in the Atlantic Pavilion at Folly Beach South Carolina

Arial View of Folly Beach South Carolina. From left to right side of the picture, the long building with a red roof is the Atlantic Pavilion which (starting on the left end of the Pavilion) included a gift shop and bath house (at the left end of the Pavilion) and Pete's Hot Dog Stand with the dance floor and jute box (at the right end of the Pavilion); then (continuing to the right) there is the ramp from the main street down to the beach; the amusement park (with the white house we lived in just behind it); and jutting from the shoreline into the Atlantic Ocean the Folly Pier.

Folly Beach South Carolina, Main Steet, car ramp to the beach, with Atlantic Pavilion, Amusement Park and Folly Pier.

Photograph of the North end of the Atlantic Pavilion where Pete's Hot Dogs was located. This photograph shows the ramp from Main Steet for cars to drive down on the beach.

Aerial Photograph of the View of Folly Beach, showing the Folly Pier and the Atlantic Pavilion.

On the occasions that our grandparents, aunts, uncles, and/or cousins from New York and New Jersey came to visit, everyone stayed in our small home, thus it was not unusual that we would have extra sleeping accommodations in the form of cots in the bedrooms or on the enclosed in front porch.

Just another day at the beach for these three kids (left to right are Billy, Maria, and Frank) while Dad is selling hotdogs, chili, French fries, ice cream sandwiches, and soda pop (everything a kid would like to eat) we could play on the beach. The photograph is taken in front of the Atlantic Pavilion at the bottom of the walk-up ramp from the beach by our mother, Katherine, in the summer of 1950.

Panayiotis' business was located at the North side entrance of the Atlantic Pavilion and Bath House, which was just South of the pier, intersected by "Main Street". Main Street had a ramp that led down from the street to the beach so that cars could drive on the beach. Coming into the pavilion from Main Street there was a long counter (about 100 feet long) that was a refreshment stand that served hot dogs, chili dogs, hamburgers, French fries, ice cream, ice cream sandwiches, soda pop, and beer. This was called "Pete's Hot Dogs". It faced out onto the pavilion where there was a huge dance floor with a jute box. It was here most of the tourists and military on leave came to recreate.

Everyone raved about "Pete's Hot Dogs", no one could figure out why his hot dogs were better than others and of course, there was Panayiotis' "secret recipe" for "chili sauce". The chili sauce was put on the hot dogs and French fries. The secret for the hot dogs was simple. Panayiotis did not buy his meats from the Charleston purveyors; he used his pick-up truck to make three to four trips a season to the Swifts meatpacking plant in New York City where he bought his hot dogs. He would pack them in dry ice in the back of his truck and drive them back to Folly Beach. They were Swift's "all-beef Kosher hot dogs". He would bring them to Folly Beach having removed the labels and other identifying packaging, that way no one knew that the difference was that Panayiotis' hot dogs were all kosher beef hot dogs.

The chili sauce was a little more complicated. He never shared this recipe, but he did tell Katherine where he kept it and told her that when the time came to pass it on that she should take it, without opening the envelope, and give it to me, his son Billy. Katherine gave me the envelope with the recipe after my father passed away, I retain the only copy and have not shared it with anyone. One day I will pass it to my two children, Rhea and Billy II.

While living on Folly Beach, Panayiotis had an abundance of time each year that began just after Labor Day to just before Memorial Day each year. With this time Panayiotis and Katherine obtained Frank and Billy's school work from James Island Elementary School and each year set out to see America. These trips generally occurred between the Feast Day of St. Basel (New Year's Day) and the Orthodox Christian Easter. Each year Panayiotis would buy a new four-door Pontiac sedan, usually the Pontiac Silver Chief, the one with the amber Indian head on the hood of the car; the Indian head lit up when the car's lights were on. Each year they would put their three children and the family's collie dog "Duke" in the back seat and set off for two to three months to see America.

With their children and Duke, they traveled the United States and saw the Petrified Forest, the Grand Canyon, the Redwood Forest, Yellowstone, Grauman's Chinese Theater, Niagara Falls, the Mississippi, the Great Lakes, and (several times) traveled route 66 West across the Mojave Desert and through the Rocky Mountains to California. In California, we would visit Uncle Pantelis Tsalikidou and his family. On one of these trips to California my grandmother and grandfather, Theodore and Mariyo Venis, also made the trip. While the car was crowded (four adults, three children, and Duke, the Collie dog), this was good family time. In all, our parents traveled with us four consecutive years; we, as a family, over a total of the seven-year period, while we were still children, visited 46 of the then 48 states. While traveling, Katherine kept a schedule on our schoolwork and assignments; mailing our homework and test back to the teacher at James Island Elementary School.

Photograph of Billy, Maria, and Frank at the Petrified Forest; and of Billy and Maria sitting on the back bumper of Panayiotis Pontiac Silver Chief four-door sedan in 1947 as we traveled West on a family trip.

1947 wedding photograph of Paul and Helen (Venis) Karp. Our family traveled by train from Folly Beach to New York City to take part in the wedding.

Photographs, taken on the rooftop of the apartment building that my grandmother lived at 1288 Sheridan Avenue in New York City, Bronx, NY. In the photograph on the left, standing in front is my brother Frank, sister Maria and myself, Billy; and standing behind us are Uncle George and Grandmother Mariyo. The photograph on the right is of my brother Frank, sister Maria and myself, Billy, all three of us were at Aunt Helen's wedding as an usher, flower girl, and ring bearer, respectively.

Photograph on the left, taken in Redondo Beach California, with my grandparents, Theodore and Mariyo, we visited the family of my father's uncle, Pantelis Tsalikidou. In the picture from left to right starting in the back is Panayiotis, his first cousin Panayiota (Pauline, daughter of Pantelis and Despina Tsalikidou), Katherine, Grandfather Theodore Venis, Grandmother Mariyo Venis, Despina Tsalikidou (granddaughter of Despina Platanidis Donjogolou); in front of the adults is my sister Maria and brother Frank; and in the foreground is Ernest Tsalikidou, son of Pantelis and Despina Tsalikidou.

The photograph on the right was taken at the rim of the Grand Canyon as we traveled to Californian. My Grandfather Theodore is standing behind; and sitting on the wall from left to right is Grandmother Mariyo, Frank, Maria, Billy, and Katherine. Panayiotis took the picture.

While living in Folly Beach, Panayiotis decided to build a shrimp boat with his brother-in-law, George T. Venis. Uncle George had returned home from the war in the Pacific and was looking to get started in a business. The boat was built in Folly Beach, on the back side of the island. Panayiotis named the boat "The Lady Maria" and assigned George to be her captain. The Lady Maria operated as a commercial shrimp boat out of Charleston South Carolina for some time, but later moved to St. Augustine Florida and eventually to Key West Florida. Subsequently, they would expand and add more boats as they began to build a fleet of Shrimp Trawlers to operate in the Atlantic.

*Uncle George and a worker looking inspecting the paint on **The Lady Maria**, built on the backside of Folly Beach Island by Panayiotis and his brother-in-law, George.*

My Grandfather Theodore and Grandmother Mariyo with my father, Panayiotis, outside the pilothouse onboard, the shrimp trawler Cayo Hueso.

In 1950, after Labor Day, Panayiotis' lease on the refreshment stand ended, it had been a five-year lease. Panayiotis and Katherine moved back to their home on White Plains Road in New York City. In their absence, Lazarus and Connie lived in the third-floor apartment, so Katherine and Connie again had a combined family. Once there, Panayiotis traveled between New York and Key West to take care of the shrimping business that he had developed with his brother-in-law George. This was somewhat short-lived as Panayiotis' son, Frank became ill, and was restricted to complete bed rest, he had been stricken with Rheumatic Fever.

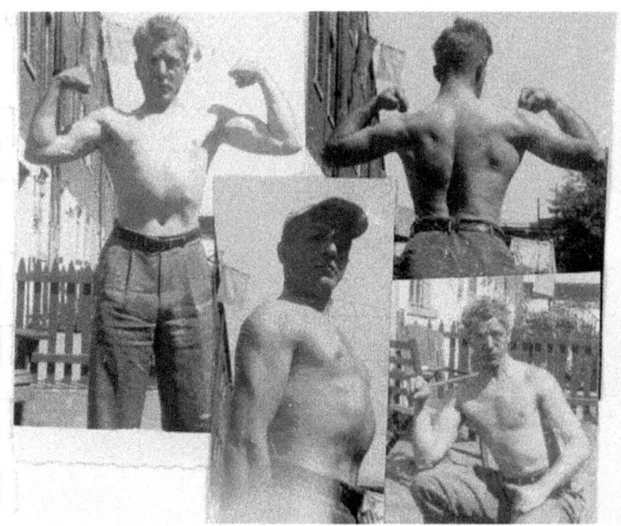

Photographs of Panayiotis in the back yard of our home on White Plains Road in the Bronx New York taken in the fall of 1950

Frank's illness was difficult on the family, especially my mother. He was on total bed rest, could not get out of bed at all, for nine months[31]. Eventually, Panayiotis gave up his interest in the shrimp business and sold it to his brother-in-law, George, as he needed to stay in New York and help care for his son. Now knowing that my parents had three other sons who died as infants, I realize that my father and mother's emotional concerns over Frank's illness were much heavier than my sister and I could have understood at that time. I also wonder how much my brother Frank knew or what he was told about the two sons born after his birth and before my birth.

Frank and I were separated in age by four years. As an infant and a small child, he was exposed to the events of the two births that intervened after his birth and before my birth. In an interview for 1940, United States Federal Census Panayiotis provided information stating that he, aged 32, lived at the house on White Plains Road with his wife, Katherine Planes, and his son, Francis and that he had another son, but that son no longer lives.

---

[31] I shared a bedroom with my brother Frank. I remember waking to my mother's crying with my aunt Connie while attending to Frank's needs during the long nights. This was endless, he was confined fully to that bed for nine months; but eventually Frank recovered but was marked for life with an enlarged heart and other illnesses that he had to struggle with. With Frank's recovery, Dr. Ackerman recommended the family move out of the Northeast to a less sever climate. He recommended Coral Gables Florida. With that recommendation, in 1951, Panayiotis and Katherine packed up their family, sold their home and moved to Coral Gables Florida.

CHAPTER SEVEN

Panayiotis, Katherine, and an unexpected new start

In the summer of 1951, Frank's illness required Panayiotis and Katherine to leave New York and move to Florida. Leaving New York, selling their home, and setting out to drive to Coral Gables Florida, with three children and a Collie dog, Duke, in the back seat of a 1949 Pontic Silver Chief four-door sedan was an adventure.

Photograph, taken in the summer of 1951 at our home at 1256 White Plains Road in the Bronx, New York. From left to right in the back is me (Billy), Grandmother Mariyo, and sister Maria. My brother Frank is sitting on the step and is supported by our mother, Katherine. He had not been out of bed or walked for a period of nine months.

It was an exciting day for the children when the Mayflower Moving Van came to the house at 1256 White Plains Road in the Bronx to pack and load up the family's household goods to take them to Coral Gables Florida. For me, I was happy to leave New York and the New York Public School System (PS 119 in the Bronx). I was used to a one-room schoolhouse; being able to see my brother and sister in the schoolroom; liked cooling off under the ice house with my friends during the hot Folly Beach summers; going crabbing with my brother for blue claw crabs at low tide under the Atlantic Pier; fishing for Whiting from the Atlantic Pier; running barefoot up and down the beach; eating chili dogs, French fries, milkshakes and ice cream sandwiches at Pete's Hot Dogs; and the smell of clean saltwater ocean air. I simply did not like it in the city.

At low tide, under the Folly Beach Pier was a great place to catch Blue Claw Crabs, what kid would not prefer this, over New York City and PS 119 in the Bronx.

My brother, sister, myself, and our Collie Duke were used to traveling, and the trip, while for other reasons was a challenge for Panayiotis and Katherine, it was almost routine to us. For Panayiotis and Katherine, there was no family living in South Florida, they had no home there, had never been there (other than Panayiotis driving back and forth from New York to St. Augustine and Key West to tend to the shrimp business with his brother-in-law, George, they had no business operating there to support the family); for them, this was a trip into uncertainty. They had the funds that Panayiotis had strapped under his clothing in a money belt. That was to be the seed money to start in a new place with new people and who knows what kind of business.

In leaving New York, Panayiotis sold all that he owned, his store in Time Square to Theodore and Lazarus, his two-family home in the Bronx to someone else, and the shrimp boats to his brother-in-law George. To that, he added approximately $36,000 that he received from his good friend Dr. Carl Ackerman as extra seed money if it were needed. The home furniture and household goods had been picked up by Mayflower Van Lines[32] to be moved to Florida and kept in storage until they were able to locate a home. But Panayiotis did not want to buy a home, he would first find and buy a business; after the business, he would decide about buying a home.

Heading South we would stop for one week in Summerville New Jersey to visit with Aunt Tini and Uncle Henny Johanson (Kostontina Venis, daughter of the New Jersey Theodore Venis and married to Henry Johanson) and their four children (Maryann, Richard, Tommy, and Corrin). For me, this was a good time to be with my cousin Richard[33]. From New Jersey, we would stop and visit for several days with Aunt Corina (Corina Venis, sister to the New Jersey Theodore Venis) and her husband, Uncle Cosmas Davoulas, their daughter Helen and their dog "Dolly", an all-white spit terrier. After Charleston, we stopped in St. Augustine Florida to visit Aunt Helen (Eleni Venis, daughter of the New Jersey Theodore Venis) and Uncle Mike Starycki at their "Blue Skies Café" located just off the St. John's river in St. Augustine Florida. Aunt Helen was our second cousin on our mother's side of the family, but as children, we knew her as our aunt and called her as such, Aunt Helen. St. Augustine was the last contact with any family or friends. Arriving in Coral Gables, the family was truly among strangers.

Upon arrival in Coral Gables, Panayiotis and Katherine sought out the location of the Greek Orthodox Church. It was the St. Sophia Greek Orthodox Church on Coral Way in Miami Florida. There they met Very Rev. Father Demosthenes Mekras, his wife, Presbytera Cynthia (Tula), and their two children, Evangelia (Evan) and George[34] . They sought advice from Fr. and his

---

[32] As we traveled South from New York to Coral Gables, my brother, sister, and I would watch for Mayflower moving vans traveling South. At each siting of a Mayflower Van, we would wonder if it was carrying our belongings.

[33] Richard Johanson was born two months before me, our mothers were more like sisters than cousins, so from an early age we share a play pen and generally played together when our parents visited each other. My mom and dad Baptized Richard into the Greek Orthodox Faith before he was a year old, thus they were his Godparents. As a high school graduate, Richard came to Coral Gables and enrolled at the University of Miami where we both started as freshmen in September 1960. In our older age, Richard, with his wife Linda, traveled with Regina and I on our yacht, The Lady Regina; one time we went as far North as Halifax. Regina and I enjoyed being with Richard and Linda on those trips, Richard, and Linda were special. On April 15, 2020 Richard passed away in the critical care unit of a New Jersey Hospital from COVID-19, May His Memory Be Eternal!!!

[34] At the time we arrived in Coral Gables Evan was just turning five years old and George was about to turn three years old. Father and Tula Mekras would have a third child, John in December of 1954. I would become good friends with both Evan and George. George passed away on May 18, 2014 at the young age of sixty-six, and Evan and I have remain friends.

Presbytera. They wanted to know about the area and how to get in touch with businesspeople that were Greek Orthodox. Father and Tula were very accommodating, they would become close lifelong friends.

Panayiotis and Katherine took a short-term lease on a furnished house on Anastasia Avenue in Coral Gables and began looking at businesses. Their seeking business opportunities settled around two businesses that they liked and eventually bought both.

The Photograph upper left is of our Collie Dog, Duke. The photograph upper right is me (Billy), Duke, and my sister Maria.

The photograph lower left is of my brother Frank, sister Maria and I. Photograph lower right is of us going fishing (Frank, Maria, and myself), I remember that she did not like fishing because she did not want to touch the worms. All these photographs were taken at the house on Anastasia Avenue, Coral Gables Florida in August 1951.

One of the two businesses was a seasonal business at 4316 SW 9th Court Miami Florida. The property was named "Tropical Court". It was a winter seasonal business and included fourteen one-bedroom bungalows in a garden setting. For the most part, the bungalows were seasonal rentals with long-standing repeat reservations for the winter months to "snow-birds" coming from the Northeast. The season would begin about Thanksgiving of each year and end in the Spring, prior to Memorial Day. While the guests came South to escape the cold winter weather and the snow, they liked to go to the horse races, dog track, and the Jai Alai Fronton. Betting was their big thing, especially when they were winning. This property consisted of three lots; one lot had fourteen bungalows; the middle lot was for parking, and the third lot had a single-family 3-bedroom two-bath residence. This was ideal as with this property they would have a good income and have a home for their family.

Above photographs are Panayiotis, Katherine, and Duke in front of one of the bungalows at Tropical Court; Our family from left to right Maria, Panayiotis, Katherine, Billy, and Frank; and Maria, Duke, and Billy in the front yard of our home at 4318 SW 9th Court, Miami Florida (adjacent to Tropical Court).

The other business was a restaurant called the AirChief Diner. It was truly a diner located in Miami Florida on Northwest 36th Street across the street from the Eastern Airlines maintenance facility at Miami International Airport. This was a seven day a week 365 days a year business, 24 hours a day, it never closed. It catered to the airline industry employees most of whom provided the maintenance of the airplanes for Eastern Airlines, National Airlines, Pan American Airlines, and others. After the first several months of operations, Panayiotis realized he could not cover the full operations of the diner as, when he was not there the shrinkage of food and cash, could not be controlled.

To solve the managerial/operations problem Panayiotis took on two partners, men he met through Fr. Mekras at St. Sophia Greek Orthodox Church, Mr. Chokanis and Mr. Roussos. Prior to finalizing a partnership, Panayiotis and the two other gentlemen did a week appease on each of the three shifts, this was to allow them to see the volume of the business and to show them that with a foot on the farm the shrinkage of the cash and food ceased. With this new partnership, one partner was on duty for eight hours a day, thus they had 24-hour coverage; weekends and holidays were shared, thus each of the partners had time for their families, and the operations and oversite of the business were secured.

All went well for a couple of years, and all three partners did well. During this time Panayiotis sought out contacts in the medical community so that he could open a children's shoe store that would provide orthopedic shoes for crippled children. During this period, his father-in-law and brother-in-law sold the store in Times Square and moved to Florida as well. They established a shoe repair shop in a strip center at Bird Road and SW 67 Avenue in Miami, one block outside of Coral Gables[35].

---

[35] It did not take long for Katherine's parents and sibling to leave New York and move to Florida. Within a couple years they all left New York and joined Panayiotis and Katherine in Florida.

Photograph marked with a date of November 1954 of grandmother Mariyo and Aunt Konstantina (Nicholaou) at grandmothers' new home in Florida; and a photograph was taken on November 1954 of Grandmother Mariyo, Katherine, and Panayiotis sitting by the Christmas Tree at our home at 4318 SW 9th Court, Miami Florida. This would be Mariyo's last Christmas with us as she passed away in June 1955.

Panayiotis eventually sold his interest in Air Chief Diner to his two partners and established a children's shoe store, "Peter Planes Shoes", at 48 Miracle Mile, Coral Gables, FL... He and Katherine established a relationship with the Florida Cripple Children's Commission at Variety Children's Hospital in Miami Florida. Katherine would give of her time without compensation[36], working with the doctors and the children, identifying the children's needs and scheduling appointments for them to be fitted and have their orthopedic prescriptions filled by "Peter Planes Shoes".

At the store, Panayiotis took as much time as necessary to work with each child and their family, personally fitting the shoes, then modifying the shoes to fill the doctor's prescription. He personally did all the work to modify each pair of shoes. The business struggled the first two years, they thought that they would have to close the store, but both Panayiotis and Katherine were persistent. Over time the doctors saw the value of Panayiotis' work and talent and Katherine's dedication to the children; the orthopedic doctors found respect for Panayiotis and

---

[36] Over the decades of work that followed Katherine would be recognized by Variety Children's Hospital of her over 20,000 hours of volunteer work with crippled children

his knowledge of orthopedics and his personal attention to the fitting and filling the prescription for each child, their business was a success.

They sold Tropical Court and built a home in Coral Gables at 625 Villanella Avenue on the Coral Gables Deep Waterway. Arriving in Coral Gables in the summer of 1952, by 1957 Panayiotis had transitioned his family from New York to Coral Gables; had re-established himself as a respected resource in the children's orthopedic shoe industry, and had repaid Dr. Karl Ackerman the seed money that Dr. Ackerman had made available to him at the time that Panayiotis and Katherine left New York City.

Panayiotis and Katherine were good friends with John and Katherine Pisaris. Once they had opened the shoe store, Mrs. Pisaris insisted that Panayiotis start the new year off with his meeting her at Peter Planes Shoes in the morning on New Year's Day. Upon arrival at the store, Panayiotis would find Mrs. Pisaris waiting at the front door to come into the store and be their first customer of the new year. It was done each year so that the new year would start with good wishes.

On November 25, 1961, Panayiotis and Katherine celebrated their Twenty-fifth Wedding Anniversary. Mrs. Pisaris wrote them an Anniversary Poem in Greek and hand-delivered it to them (note she called them Renee and Pete).

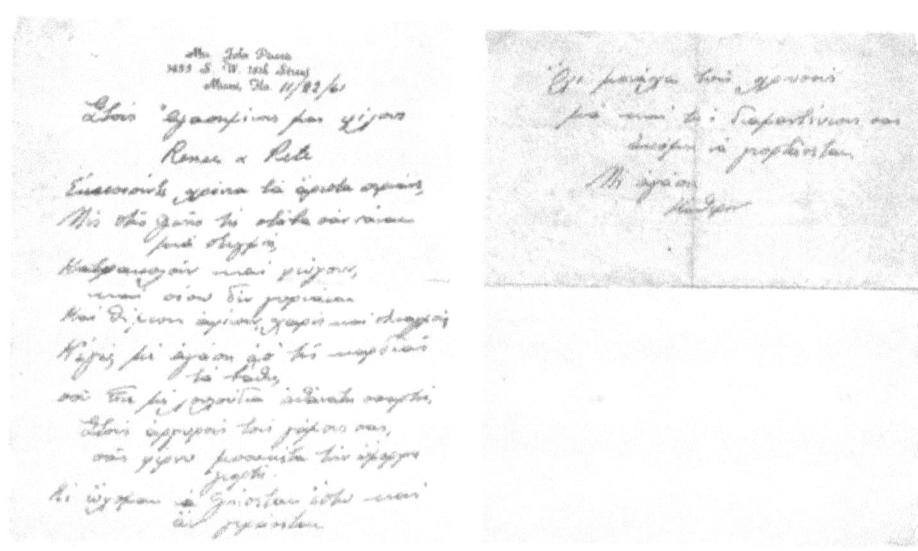

Above is the poem written in Greek by Katherine Pisaris on November 22, 1961,
which was among some of the personal items that Katherine (Renee as Mrs.
Pisaris called her) had chosen to keep, I found this after she had passed away.

Panayiotis and Katherine were well-liked. This poem written for them by Katherine Pisaris says:

To our dearest friends

Renee and Pete

Twenty-Five perfect years have gone by

In life's raindrop as if it were one moment,

They tumble and depart,

and do not come back

And the years buried the joys and worries

And I, with love, from the bottom of my heart

which is forever full of bouquets of flowers.

Bring to your silver wedding's beautiful celebration.

And I wish that you live, even though you may be old,

To celebrate not only the Golden

but the Diamond too.

With love

Katherine

While Panayiotis worked hard and had many activities at Church and with his family, he also enjoyed sports. His favorite sport was bowling. He and Katherine, with Chris and Bee Gorges, joined a bowling league. As time progressed Panayiotis' game excelled. Keeping score for him one evening while he was practicing, I marked him making sixty-four strikes in succession. Twenty strikes is a perfect game, so this was equivalent to three perfect games in succession. In his later years, he became a semi-professional. Because his use of the bowling ball was so fast and precise, they nicknamed him "Jet Planes".

Panayiotis bowling, while his bowling partner, Chris Georges in the background keeping score.

1967 American Bowling Congress Championships in Miami Beach, Florida, Panayiotis was a semi-professional bowler.

Panayiotis and Katherine always looked to set a good example for their children, be it in their home, business, or church life. They freely showed warmth and affection to their children; always stressing the importance of Church, Faith, Prayer, and the Orthodox traditions; they were active in community philanthropy such as the Coral Gables Soroptimist Club; were members of the Mason's and the Eastern Star; and were active in the various Church organizations, both locally and nationally, such as Philoptochos, AHEPA, Daughters of Penelope, and various committees that supported Church functions at St. Sophia. Attendance to Church was a way of life, it was connected to you just like a limb of your body. For the children these activities included Sunday School, Greek School, GOYA, the Sons of Pericles, and the Maids of Athena.

Photograph on left is Panayiotis and Katherine attending Church at St. Sophia Greek Orthodox Cathedral in Miami Florida with their children, Frank, Billy, and Maria; and photograph on the right is Panayiotis and Katherine on a family outing on Key Biscayne at Crandon Park with their three children; Katherine, Maria, and Billy sitting on the palm tree with Panayiotis and Frank standing in front of the palm tree.

Panayiotis started each day with prayer standing in front of his Icon of the Theotokos holding the Christ Child to say his prayers; and likewise, each evening he repeated this practice to end each day with prayer. While he started and ended each day with prayer, throughout the day he would not hesitate to stop what he was doing and take a moment in prayer. Faith and prayer were as much of his life as breathing. He did not speak of this, but he demonstrated it by his daily acts of kindness and compassion coupled with his practice of prayer every day of his life in full view of his wife and children. Katherine was as much devoted to Christ and the Theotokos as was Panayiotis. They both believed in Christ and they both believed in education; they made no secret of this to their children. While the strength of body and mind were important, the strength of character and Faith in Christ was paramount. They lead by example.

Left is a photograph from January 6, 1966, with Archbishop Iakovos blessing Emmanuel Tsavaras, who retrieved the Cross that year. Also in the picture is Katherine Planes (Platanides) Grand (National) Governor of the Daughters of Penelope. Photo on the Right is of Mrs. Peter Planes (Katherine) Grand (National) Governor of the Daughters of Penelope from Coral Gables and Miss Elizabeth Athanasakos, Grand President of the Daughters of Penelope from Ft. Lauderdale, both attending the 1966 Epiphany Celebration in Tarpon Springs, Florida

Panayiotis knew the Patriarch Athenagoras, from the time he was Archbishop of America; he also was friends with Archbishop Iakovos, the Archbishop of America that succeeded Athenagoras when Athenagoras was elevated as the 268th successor of the Apostle Andrew and Ecumenical Patriarch of Constantinople on November 1, 1948. When Archbishop Iakovos would visit St. Sophia in Miami[37] , he would often come to dinner at our home with Fr. and Tula Mekras and close family friends, Chris and Bee Georges. Panayiotis looked forward to these visits as it was one of the few times he could sit and converse with someone using the Turkish language.

[37] On one of Archbishop Iakovos' visits to St. Sophia, Fr. Mekras had the Archbishop tonsured me to enter and serve in the Holy Alter of the Greek Orthodox Church.

Fr. Mekras and His Eminence, as did everyone else, looked forward to Katherine's baking Καλαμαρι Υεμιστα (stuffed squid), a dish she had perfected with her own receipt.

Upon arrival in Coral Gables, Panayiotis and Katherine enrolled their children in public school. To their surprise, the Florida Public School would not accept me into the fifth grade. This was because of my age, I had started school a year earlier than most children, thus they wanted me to repeat the fourth grade so that I would be with children similar in age. It is at Coral Gables Elementary School, while in the fourth grade, I met my friend Alan Clark with whom I attended school from the fourth grade till the eleventh grade; after which he and his mother moved away to Kentucky. Alan and I would stay connected with each other for several years, but in 1967 he simply disappeared from my life. I have spent much time searching for him over the fifty-plus years that followed.

PORTABLE NO. 6—first row l to r: Biff Kerr, Jo Ann Rubel, Linda Kassel, Sally Wassenberg, Leslie Armstrong, Maria de la Roza, Roberta Truppman, Esther Kopelman, Alan Clark. Second row: Robert Jordan, William Carpel, Laurence Niven, James Powell, William Platanides, John Porter, Scott Singleton, George Charukas, Randy Cox, Peter Hazelwood. Third row: Elaine Kranzler, Marcia Kodish, Miriam Rissman, Diane Plasman, Michele De Hart, Judy Klien, Shannon Shields, Judy Kapner, Nina Deutsch, Barbara Townsend. Fourth row: Charles Kimbrell, Nickolas Condon, Stuart Cockerill, Billy Nettles, Michael Costello.

Group photo, taken on June 1954 of my homeroom class graduating from Elementary School. In the first row on the right end is my friend Alan Clark" I, William Platanides, am in the second row, fifth from the left

Maria and I attended Coral Gables Elementary, Ponce de Leon Jr. High, and graduated from Coral Gables High School. Frank attended Ponce de Leon Jr. High and graduated from Coral Gables High School. Coral Gables High School was very special, it was ranked among the very highest of high schools in the United States. There, I would enjoy taking advanced (college level) chemistry and physics from Mr. Bulbee, as well as classes in wood and metal shop, mechanical drawing, and classes in mathematics. After graduating from high school, I had already completed advanced courses in quantitative and qualitative chemistry and advanced physics. My brother Frank, when he went to Coral Gables High School, likewise enjoyed, and accelerated in these same advanced courses.

The graduation of all three children from high school was something that Panayiotis reflected upon with delight as he never graduated any school, much less high school[38]. But this was not the end of the education that Panayiotis and Katherine desired for their children; they encourage and made the opportunity available to each of their children to attend college and obtain a college degree.

My sister Maria with Panagiotis and Katherine oh her graduation from high school in June 1961

---

[38] Panayiotis attended school to the 9th grade. He chose not to go to school but to work so he can send money home to his parents for food and to purchase a home and start a business.

My brother Frank graduated from high school in June 1957. In the photograph from left to right, Maria, Katherine, Frank, Panayiotis, and Billy

Highschool Graduation Photograph of William P. Planes (Platanides), June 1960

Junior Tycoon Gets Double Bonus
...kiss from mom and dad for Bill Planes, 17.

Teenage Tycoons Report Profits

By JOHN MORTON
Herald Staff Writer

South Florida's youngest business tycoons got together Friday night and decided things are pretty good.

Some 350 members of Junior Achievement, teenage students who form their own corporations, assembled for the program's second annual banquet and award session.

While the big businessmen — their sponsors — sat back and listened, some of the top "executives" reported on what they have done in printing, plastics and a dozen other industries during the past year.

How does it add up? "It has enabled me to gain an understanding of American business — and my own abilities," explained 17-year-old Bill Planes, 625 Villabella, Coral Gables.

Bill, a junior student at Coral Gables High School, is president of Futures Unlimited Co. He and a group of other teenagers made more than $1,600 for their stockholders last year in developing, manufacturing and selling chalk boards.

Bill's firm was named "Company of the Year" for J.A. and its youthful president also figured in a number of other awards.

Principal speaker at the banquet was Edgar J. Forio of Atlanta.

Forio, senior vice president of Coca-Cola Co., told the achievers, "This training will give you the ability to just feel in your dreams and make 'em walk around the street."

The executive was a last-minute stand-in for Sen. George A. Smathers, who wired the group that "developments in the legislative program" made it impossible for him to attend.

Other major awards presented to the achievers included:

NATIONAL INDUSTRY AWARDS — Mike Hocker, 17, Miami Edison.

COMPANY OF THE MONTH — Dennis Bahr, 18, Miami Edison.

BEST SALESMAN — Iris Atwell, 18, Jackson High School.

$100 SCHOLARSHIPS — Les Gillespie, 17, Miami High; Barbara Denison, 18, Miami High; Michaeleen Hard, 18, Coral Gables High; Burton Maxx, 17, Miami High.

Having set up and operated a successful business ("Futures Unlimited") in his senior year of high school, William P. Planes (Platanides) is named Achiever of the Year by Jr. Achievement.

All three of Panayiotis and Katherine's children went to college. There were no student loans, grants, or scholarships. Panayiotis and Katherine paid for their children's education by working and saving their earnings. Each child was afforded the opportunity to attend college and pursue upper education as far as they would like.

Frank never finished college. He came home after the first year and went to work at Peter Planes Shoes[39] assisting our father in opening two more stores; growing the business so that it

---

[39] Peter Planes Shoes was very successful. Panayiotis became aware that others were seeking to play off the name. When he went to his attorney, Irving Kaulback, Esq. to copyright the name, attorney Kaulback had another solution, simply claim the name "Peter Planes" by filing with the Dade County Courts to change his name to Peter Planes and the last name of his wife and his three children from

served all of Dade County Florida, not just Coral Gables. When Panayiotis retired, Frank took over 100% of Peter Planes Shoes. Frank and his wife, Claudette, had three children. The oldest, Peter F. Planes was named after his grandfather, Panayiotis F Platanides/Planes. Frank's second child, Catherine, was named after her grandmother, Katherine; and his third child was named Khristina. Catherine attended college but did not finish. Catherine married and divorced then remarried. She had one child, Coltan, with her first husband. She was devoted to raising Coltan. Khristina was the only one of Frank's three children to pursue a college education. Khristina earned a Batchelor's degree and subsequently pursued graduate-level studies. Peter and Khristina have never married. Coltan's grandfather, Frank, encouraged him to go to college as did his Uncle Peter, Aunt Khristina, and his mother; he attended college and graduated.

On November 26, 2012, just fifteen days following his seventy-fourth birthday, Frank died from the cumulative effects of an enlarged heart, diabetes, bladder cancer, leukemia, and a host of other ailments. The stress from the Rheumatic fever he had as a young boy, followed and affected him his entire life.

I, Billy, began my higher education at the University of Miami. Initially my Cousin Richard Johanson attended with me. We both started as Freshmen together, but he was homesick for his girlfriend and left school during the first semester to go back to New Jersey. Later he attended and graduated college at the Citadel in South Carolina. Richard and I attended the University while living at home with my parents, his God Parents. After Richard withdrew from school, I pledged a national social fraternity, Sigma Chi. Making my grades the first semester, I was initiated into Sigma Chi. In my second year of college, I took up residency in the fraternity house, visiting home frequently to see my mom and dad.

After my second year at the University of Miami, I transferred to Florida State University, principally because my mother was concerned that my sister, who had attended Florida State University the prior year, had done so with no family there to look after her. Knowing this was important to my mother, I offered and transfer to Florida State University. I graduated from Florida State University with a Bachelor of Science Degree in Accounting. At that time, I was in the US Marine Corps Reserves and wanted to continue to work on a Master's Degree in Accounting; but with the war in Vietnam, it was obvious that I would not have that opportunity, so I committed to going on active duty. Once committed, I was offered an opportunity to transfer from the Marine Corp to the US Navy, I accepted the transfer and reported to active duty with the Navy, otherwise, I would have pursued a Master's Degree in Accounting.

Platanides to Planes. Thus, he became Peter Planes and others could not use that name in the name of their business as it was his name. And so that is how the Platanides name came to be changed to Planes.

The Sigma Chi Chapter at Florida State University in my Senior year of College. I left
school at the end of the first trimester of the 1965-1966 school year (December 1965),
having completed all but one course for my Bachelor of Science Degree in Accounting,
completing one course by correspondence over successive months, this allowed me to
begin the fulfilment of my military duty. While not there for my graduation, I graduated
in April 1966.

1967 photographs of me in my Navy Dress Uniform

Returning from active duty in the Navy I sat and passed my CPA examination and established my own CPA firm; merged my CPA firm into a national firm, and subsequently retired at an early age to work in private industry[40]. In 1987 I began to work for an agricultural enterprise owned by James W. Keen and Regina Margulies. On August 24, 1992, this business, Florida Lime Growers, Inc., which included 580 acres of producing lime, avocado, and mango groves with a packing house to process and ship the produce of these properties was totally destroyed by Hurricane Andrew. The eye of Hurricane Andrew passed directly over the home that I maintained with Regina, the packing house, and the groves that we operated in South Dade County Florida. Once the storm had passed it was obvious that 100% of the groves had been destroyed. With the destruction of the groves, there was no basis to revive the business.

With the agricultural business destroyed, in 1994 I moved to Tarpon Springs Florida and established a consulting firm that provided services to small and distressed businesses. Often loaning them money to reverse their fate, or sometimes buying the business and operating it while

---

[40] In 1983, after retirement from practice as a CPA, I became engaged in a court appointed position to manage a bankrupt mortgage business. Here I made a mistake which resulted in my having to serve time in Federal Prison. Upon return to Coral Gables, I began to engage in various business which ultimately led me to relocate to Tarpon Springs Florida where, with Regina, we established a private consulting firm that grew into a multi-state privately owned conglomerate that embraced multiple industries and business disciplines. In subsequent years, James W. Keen would also become a shareholder, director and officer of this privately owned conglomerate.

it was revamped to be sold five to seven years later as a successful enterprise. While I was the senior consultant for this firm, Steve E. Pallos was the President and Regina was, at that time, the sole owner of the firm. Later, James W. Keen would also become a shareholder.

The consulting company grew into a privately held conglomerate that eventually operated in eight locations in multiple states; these operations included the largest HVAC sheet metal company in the Southeast United States; two Long Term Acute Care Hospitals; mortgage lending; accounts receivable factoring and other types of secured lending companies; a healthcare management company; and an assortment of other businesses. In addition to the conglomerate, there was a privately held real estate company that owned and operated an assortment of commercial real estate in multiple states which included more than 100 acres of vacant land in Tampa Florida. All together, these companies employed more than 650 employees.

Regina, 1983

My second wife, Regina, is a Registered and Advanced Nurse Practitioner; she is now retired, as am I. She was active in the medical side of the conglomerate and in the administration of the private Orthodox Christian school that we established to provide education to children that had special needs. While successful in business, my primary success remains with my Church, my accomplishments, and my philanthropy to and through the church (these types of activities were instilled in me at an early age by my grandmother, Mariyo, and my parents, Panayiotis and Katherine.[41]

In 2005 I was to receive the Ellis Island Medal of Honor; its being bestowed on those who have made substantial contributions to others as they immigrated to America. As I explained in my letter to Archbishop Demetrios, the then Archbishop of the Greek Orthodox Archdiocese of America and Exarch of the Ecumenical Patriarch Bartholomew I, I would be happy to accept such an award posthumously for my father, Panayiotis, as he is the one that immigrated to America, escaping genocide at the hands of Ataturk's Muslim Soldiers; arriving here and building a life and a family in this country that was exemplary for anyone that seeks to come to America and become a part of this country's heritage, while never forgetting his parents, sister, and brothers in the old county. It is Panayiotis that deserved the Ellis Island Medal of Honor, not me, as I was simply the beneficiary of his works, commitments, and Faith.

In the spring of 1965, Maria graduated from Florida State University with a bachelor's degree in Mathematics. My parents continued to encourage her to pursue more education. With their support, from 1965 to 1967 she continued post-graduate education at Boston College in Boston Massachusetts and obtained a Master's Degree in Math Education. While she was pursuing her post-graduate degree, in 1966 she met Dr. William Maistrellis, MD. She married Dr. Maistrellis on November 25, 1967. After Dr. Maistrellis returned from active duty in the Navy they settle in Clearwater Florida where he joined a medical practice specializing in vascular surgery. While living in Clearwater they had three children, all girls, Stephanie, Christina, and Alexandra. From 1981 to 1983, while married with three young daughters, with my mother assisting in the care of her children, Maria entered Stetson College School of Law and earned a Juris Doctorate Degree in Law. After law school, Maria entered the practice of law. In later years she and her husband divorced. Today Maria is remarried and lives in Atlanta Georgia where her three daughters settled, two of her daughters are married, and had children.

Maria's oldest daughter, Stephanie, married and then divorced, she has no children. Stephanie graduated college and then went to graduate school where she earned two master's degrees, both in the field of healthcare. Maria's middle daughter, Christina, graduated from Dartmouth College and continued her studies at Emery University where she obtained a Juris Doctorate in Law. She married Michael Broxterman, has four children, and while raising her children she is practicing law. Her two oldest children are now in their first years of college, the

---

[41] William Planes, son of Panayiotis and Katherine Platanides, in recognition for his devotion and work for the Greek Orthodox Church has been awarded the God Metal of St. Paul; elevated to the status of an Akron Notarios of the Mother Church, the Patriarchate and the Order of St. Andrew by His All Holiness Bartholomew I, Ecumenical Patriarch of Constantinople; has been, with his wife Regina, the recipient of the 2006 Very Reverend Father Typhon Theophilopoulos Philanthropist of the Year award; and the Gold Seal of the State of Florida by the Board of Regents of the St. Petersburg College for their Philanthropic service to the Community in Pinellas County Florida.

other two children intend to go to college after they graduate high school. Maria's youngest daughter graduated from college from the University of Florida, is married and has two children. Maria has six grandchildren.

Photograph of Katherine with all her grandchildren and one great-grandchild, taken at the wedding reception of my nice, Christina Maistrellis Broxterman. Katherine is seated in the middle of the photograph. The young boy next to Katherine is her great-grandson, Colton (son of Frank's daughter, Catherine). Starting at the left of the photograph and going to the right behind Colton and Katherine are Frank's daughter Catherine Planes, Alexandra Maistrellis, Christina Maistrellis Broxterman, Stephanie Maistrellis, my son William (Billy) P. Planes II, Frank's daughter Khristina Planes, my daughter Rhea Planes Martinez, and Frank's son Peter F. Planes II. At that time there were three more great-grandchildren of Katherine that are not in this picture, these being the three children of Rhea Planes Martinez (Mathew, Andrea, and Andrew Martinez)

While Maria and I were close as children, in college, and as young adults, our views on Christ, Faith, and marriage were different. We drifted apart and today are estranged from one another.

Panayiotis and Katherine set out to raise their children in the Orthodox Christian Faith and to see that they were educated to the highest degree that each of them could individually attain. While I and my brother Frank remained Orthodox Christians, my sister, after her divorce, left the Orthodox Church.   After the divorce and moving to Atlanta Georgia, she met a man and remarried. Today she is a member of a Christian Church and has, while not in communion with the Orthodox Church, accepted Christ in her heart and in her life.

Panayiotis and Katherine were devoted to each other and their children. They committed themselves to support the educational desires of each of their children, always encouraging them to pursue higher education. They always involved Christ and the Church in their daily lives and instilled the need for Christ and undoubting Faith with each of their three children. To these ends, Panayiotis and Katherine accomplished making all these opportunities available to their children. While it was up to my brother, sister, and myself to make use of the opportunities and teachings that our parents pursued with us, for sure, our parents accomplished all that they attempted in life, especially when it came to the teachings for their children.

Picture of Panayiotis and Katherine Planes (Platanides)

Panayiotis passed away on December 3, 1970, from blood poisoning (gram-negative septicemia) resulting from a surgical procedure that he had a couple of weeks before his death. He was 63 years old and had retired a couple of years before his death. Katherine passed away on May 12, 2016, just fifteen days after her 99th birthday. On her 99th birthday, she had been enjoying good health and had no illnesses. On the day of her 99th birthday, I told her in Greek "Θα του εκατοστίσεις!" ("you are going to make it to 100!")   She looked at me and smiled then, responding in Greek, saying, "Γιο μου, κουράζομαι, σε λίγο ώρα θα πάω στο Χρήστος!" ("my son, I am growing tired, in a short time I will be going to be with Christ!"). At the time she passed away she had all her faculties about her and could challenge anyone to a good debate, especially if it was regarding the Orthodox Christian Faith.

Both my parents, Panayiotis and Katherine, had full and eventful lives. During their lifetime they received an abundance of blessings from God. Receiving these Blessings, they were not greedy; they did not retain the Blessings selfishly for themselves; they used these God-given Blessings to provide Blessings to others as what they received was not theirs, it belonged to the

God, they were stewards of Gods' gifts. Quietly, but decisively, they lived a life of philanthropy, giving freely and unselfishly to others and to their Church without restraint. God always provided them with what they needed, and they gave the abundance of what was provided to others so that they too could be Blessed.

Photographs, taken on the occasion of Katherine's 80th Birthday

Katherine with her first cousin, Konstantina (Tini) Venis Johanson.

Katherine seated with her sisters Louise and Konstantina standing behind her

Seated next to Katherine is Tula Mekras. Standing behind them is Fr. Mekras and Bee Georges

CHAPTER EIGHT

Platanidis Family in Chania during WW II

Once my Grandparents received immigration papers from the Greek government, they were allowed to settle in Chania Crete. Using money sent by my father, Panayiotis, my grandfather was able to purchase a small home[42] and establish a shop that sold tobacco and other items in Chania [43]. This is where Panayiota met her husband, Ioannis Spyridakis, and also where my uncles grew up and established their families. At the beginning of WW II, Panayiota, Athanasius and Pantelis had married, Stavros and Minas had yet to marry. This was where Panayiotis' family were living when WW-II broke out.

---

[42] The house was small, it was two stories built on a plot of land that was 55m square at Skoufon 43, Chania, Crete. It was built coved the entire plot and was not in good condition, but it could be repaired and would provide basic shelter for the family. Ironically this house belonged to a Muslim Creatin who abandon the house after the genocide in Smyrna, leaving Chania to join the new califate in Turkey.

[43] From this shop, located down by the limani, Fotis would sell tobacco, newspapers, candy, and other small items that he may acquire so that he could sell at a profit to make money to feed and clothe his family.

Fotis Platanidis in front of his shop in Chania, Crete, before WW-II

Photo of Σαντριβαγι (Sadrivani) Square at the Limani of Chania, taken in April 1940. Six months before the attack of Italy on Greece and the Greek participation in World War II. In the center of the photograph, you can see a huge Greek flag, posted on a little corner shop. This is the shop of my Grandfather, Fotis Platanidis

Wanting to present my father's family in Chania and what they experience during the German occupation of Crete, I asked my cousin Fotis M. Platanidis to write an account of what transpired with the family during this period. Fotis has provided an account of these events. When he provided me with these materials, I decided that I would not attempt to summarize or paraphrase his thoughts and expressions. His emotions regarding this period in the family's history are starkly clear and apparent. As such his presentation of the family during WW-II is presented, unabridged, in Appendix A of this book. In that regard, understanding the family and the environment that they were facing requires some knowledge and understanding regarding Greece, Crete, and WW-II.

May 1941, the day it rained "umbrellas" in Chania

The *ΠΛΑΤΑΝΙΔΗΣ (Platanidis) shop in Σαντριβαγι (Sadrivani) square at the Port of Chania. It was destroyed due to the air raids of Luftwaffe (German Airforce) on the Port of Chania, at the beginning of the Battle of Crete in May 1941. You can clearly see the family name written on the shop, ΠΛΑΤΑΝΙΔΗΣ (look at the upper left-hand side of the photograph). The motorcycle with a sidecar that is parked in front of it, is a Zundapp of the German Military Police. Photograph supplied by my cousin Andreas Spyridakis.*

The three photographs above and the following description were supplied by my cousin, Fotis M. Platanidis on September 9, 2021. These represent the devastation suffered from the bombing of undefended civilian homes and shops in Chania by the Nazis as WW-II began to effected Chania Crete. Fotis says:

"Fotis Platanidis family house is placed at Skoufon 43 street, within the old city which is surrounded by the medieval castle walls. In simple words, their house found itself in the middle of the bombing zone of the German air-bombers!! Three out of hundreds of photos follow to show how Chania looked like after these criminal air raids that targeted the civilian population.

Our family house had a German bomb falling next to it, destroying the neighbor building and causing severe damages to ours. One floor was fallen but the ground floor stood. This new disaster Fotios Platanidis with his wife Kyriaki had to face alone....."

In Appendix A, Fotis, son of Minas, addresses some of the histories regarding Greece, Crete, and Chania as it relates to the Italian attempt to enter Greece on "Oxi" Day (the day that Greece stood up to an invading army from Italy and simply said "No" and held them off); the invasion of Greece by the Nazis; the invasion of Crete; the Battle of Crete, and the liberation of Greece. Thus, his writings follow the lives of his father and his three uncles as he walks us through this period of history, a period which is the backdrop of what the family experienced during WW II. He also deals with the activities of our grandfather and our grandfather's sons in an organized urban guerilla resistance that our grandfather fostered and pursued on the island of Create during WW II.

Fotis M Platanidis goes into detail to present the activity of his father, Minas, and our uncles, Athanasios, Pantelis, and Stavros Platanidis. In so doing he received help from Andrew (Andreas) Spyridakis, son of my father's sister, Panayiota Platanidis Spyridakis; Joanna Platanidis, daughter of George A. Platanidis and granddaughter of my father's brother, Athanasios F. Platanidis; Koula Platanidis, daughter of my father's brother Pantelis F. Platanidis; Chrisoula Spyridakis, daughter of my father's sister, Panayiota Platanidis Spyridakis; and his mother, Eleni (Nitsa) Platanidis.

Fotis M. Platanidis also depends on his own recall of conversations he had with our uncle Athanasios Platanidis and his wife Maritsa; our Uncle Pantelis Platanidis and his wife Artemisa; our Aunt Panayiota Platanidis-Spyridakis and her husband Ioannis; and his father, (my uncle) Minas Platanidis and his wife, Eleni (Nitsa) Platanidis. Thea Nitsa is still living, the youngest of the spouses of my father's generation, she is now in her nineties and lives with my cousin Vasilios M. Platanidis, brother to Fotis M. Platanidis, she is the last of that generation.

While I do not attempt to paraphrase all that Fotis presents in the accounting of the family at the time of World War II, I do present what my father told me and what I heard my father discussed with my mother over the many years of their marriage and in 1965 when I visited Chania and met my uncles with my father. One point in fact, what Fotis presents on this subject compares favorably with what I was told by my father and what I heard my father, and his brothers discuss during my visit to Greece in 1965.

I clearly remember my father's frustration as he described to us what his parents and siblings had suffered at the hands of the Nazis; how he mourned the death of his brother Stavros who died a young man from the wound he suffered in WW-II and inflicted upon him by the Gestapo during his imprisonment for his efforts in the urban gorilla resistance; and his quiet discussions with his brothers Athanasios, Pantelis, and Minas when I visited my uncles with him in 1965. Regarding these events, my cousin and I are in unison on all these events, except one; that being when Uncle Stavros died.

We all agree with what is presented here, in that his death was attributed to the wounds, torcher, and treatment he suffered as part of the 5th Cretan Division of the Greek Army fighting the invasion from the Italian military on the Albanian front combined with the wounds, torcher, and treatment he suffered at the hands of the Gestapo after he was arrested in Crete for his part in the urban gorilla resistance. My cousin's understanding is that Uncle Stavros died because of what he suffered during WW II and after WW II when the Nazis and Gestapo continued to occupy and exercise control over Create until their subsequent withdrawal in August of 1945, the war having ended on May 9, 1945.

This has been confirmed to me by my cousin Andreas Spyridakis, who at the time that the war ended and the subsequent withdrawal of the Nazis and Gestapo in August 1945, was a child. He remembers helping and handing wood to Uncle Stavros while Uncle Stavros worked to rebuild parts of the family home that had been damaged during the war. While we cannot determine the actual date of death of Uncle Stavros, he died sometime after August 1945, perhaps in 1946 or 1947... His death is attributed to the wounds he received fighting on the mainland of Greece as well as the treatment, and torcher by the Nazis when he was part of the resistance in Chania, these having a profound effect on his physical health. MAY HIS MEMORY BE ETERNAL!!!

From what Fotis summited to me and what I was told, one must only be amazed at what my Grandparents suffered during their lifetime, being confronted from July 28, 1914, to November 11, 1918, with WW-I; having lived through and narrowly escaping the genocide in Asia Minor, and then the Nazi invasion and occupation of Crete. The sacrifices they endured during WW-II including the injuries incurred by all four of their sons (Athanasies, Pantelis, Stavros, and Minas) in the battles fought by various of their sons at the borders with Italy ("Oxi Day[44]"); with the Germans on the mainland of Greece; the Battle for Crete[45]; the urban gorilla resistance movement in Crete that resulted in Minas being arrested, tried and sentenced to two death sentences by the Nazis; Stavros being arrested for his activity in the urban gorilla resistance; Stavros standing Trail and sentenced to death by the Nazis; after the armistice and the respective release from prison of Stavros and Minas; and the eventual death of their son Stavros because of the wounds suffered in WW-II and the torture and treatment the Gestapo subjected him to while imprisoned.

As my cousin Fotis codified what had been the photographs, documents, and other items that were left behind by our grandparents and parents, it became apparent to both of us that our grandparents and our parents in Greece did not want to discuss these events with our generation as they did not want our generation (as my cousin expresses it) "to be aroused and fan the flames of rebellion and hate" that would inspire our generation to engage in more fighting. In reading Appendix A, one can feel the heat of the emotions expressed by my cousin Fotis as his frustration and anger over these events become apparent in what he expresses. Our Grandparents had come

---

[44] Oxi day commemorates the victory of Greece over the Italian Forces that sort to invade Greece at the beginning of WW-II. While out manded and against unbelievable odds, Greek patriots overcame a superior force from invading Greece, the fought and had banner with the work Oxi on them ("Oxi" meaning "No" in Greek). This national holiday is celebrated on October 28th each year.

[45] Fotis and Kyriaki were told of the death of their son Minas in the battle for Crete. Only after having a Trisiuon for him and a Memorial at 40 days after his death, five months later to the contrary of the reports that he had been killed they found out and were reunited with him. Minas had been badly wounded had survived and was in a prisoner of war hospital. He escaped the hospital and made it home to be reunited with his parents.

to the point that had concluded that the flames of resistance simply had to burn out as they wanted us, their grandchildren, to live in Peace and not experience the pain and heartaches of radical terrorist, genocide, and war that they had experienced at various times throughout their lives.

On the other hand, my father, Panayiotis, did not approach these matters from the same perspective as his siblings and parents. Panayiotis wanted his children to know the value of freedom of speech, freedom of worship, freedom of choice, all of which comes at a very steep price paid in blood by those that came before us; and to realize that every day we have to be vigilant to protect these values as there is a forever lurking line of dictators, sultans, monarchs, and politicians who oppose such freedoms and, given a chance, they would subject all that come under their rule to such tyranny, taking such freedoms away from people, in favor of their own thrust for power, domination and wealth.

My grandparents, Fotis and Kyriaki, possessed and relied upon their great amount of Faith in Christ; their Faith was at the forefront of their maintaining their composure to endure all these atrocities. Through these events they prayed and held close to their hearts the Cross that Metropolitan Chrysostomos had given them at the time of Minas' Baptism at The Metropolitan Church at Smyrna (one of the Seven Churches in the Book of Revelations) in 1920, remembering him, praying for his intercession (not knowing that the Metropolitan would be canonized and venerated by the Church of Greece as a Saint on November 4, 1992). They would keep the Cross of St. Chrysostomos close to them until the time came that they passed away. Then it would pass to my aunt, Panayiota. Panayiota would pass it to her brother, Minas, and his wife Eleni on the day of their wedding as her mother had wished Minas to carry it through his life and pass it to the next generation of the Platanidis family. Today, the Cross of St. Chrysostomos has passed to my generation and is in the hands of Minas' son, Fotis M. Platanidis.

CHAPTER NINE

The Donjogolou, Tsalikidou and other Families

Piecing together a family tree is made difficult when many records that would have originated in Asia Minor, especially marriage, baptism, and death records that would be available through the Orthodox Churches in Asia Minor, were destroyed with the Churches. Likewise, burial records were also destroyed as most cemeteries were desecrated, the grave markers destroyed and many of the graves simply uncovered.

A key document that assisted us with the family trees of the Tsalikidou and Donjogolou families was written by Gordon Donlou and provided to me by my cousin, Dean Furkioti. Gordon Donlou's graphs of the Donjogolou family tree were of great assistance in my research. Gordon Donlou was the son of George Donjugolou (aka George Donlou) and Julia Trabaoum Donjugolou; the grandson of George and Julia Donjogolou; grandson of Anastas Donjugolou and Kyriaki (Grace) Athanasiu Donjogolou, and great-grandson of George Donjobolou[46] and

---

[46] In Gordon Donlou's writings he spells the family name two ways. At the beginning he states with George and Despina Donjobolou; then moves to Anastas and Grace Donjogolou; then back to Donjobolou and finally to Donlou. We could not find an explanation for the change in the spelling. The spelling should be Donjobolou and Donlou.

Despina Platanidis Donjobolou. In his writings regarding the history of his family, he writes that this motivation of his, having gathered this information regarding the family and backgrounds of his parents, George and Julia (Trabazoum) Donlou, was to have this information available to his family that was then living and families that would subsequently follow. He indicates that this information was compiled by his parents, George Donjobolou and Julia Trabazoum Donjobolou, and aunt, Elizabeth Donjobolou Georgeadis, all with the hope that this information will be passed down through the years to the generations to come. Gordon Donlou, born on September 5, 1929, passed away on March 1, 2020, at the age of 90.

From the information provided in his Obituary and various birth, death, military service, and census record, we can determine that Gordon Donlou was a well-respected son, brother, husband, father, grandfather, and educator. He was born in Detroit Michigan on September 5, 1929, and moved to Redondo Beach California with his parents (George and Julia Donjogolou) in 1936. He earned a Bachelor's and Masters' Degrees in Education from the University of Southern California. He served in the US Army during the Korean War. He was a professional educator in the South Bay Public School system for thirty-eight years. He was an active member in various of the Greek Orthodox Churches in Los Angeles and Long Beach California and assisted in the founding of St. Katherine's Greek Orthodox Church in Redondo Beach California. His value of family is evident in his attempt to codify the history and the roots of the Donjogolou family back to Great Grandparents, George, and Despina (Platanidis) Donjogolou, who were born, lived and passed away in Asia Minor,

Through immigration, marriage, death, military, census, and other public records maintained by Federal and State governments here in the United States I was able to confirm and, in some cases, add to the information provided by Gordan Donlou. For example, Gordan Donlou's information combined with public records in Detroit Michigan gave rise to identifying the names of the father and mother of Pantelis Tsalikidou. The marriage license of Pantelis Tsalikidou and Despina Donjogolou identifies the place of their birth and includes the names of their respective parents. While we knew that Pantelis had several sisters (Kyriaki, Stavroula, Despina, and Stella) and three brothers (Constantinos, Demetri and Yoryos), with their birth records being lost in Asia Minor, we did not know the names of their parents. Through this marriage license, we were able to establish that the parents of Kyriaki, Pantelis, Constantinos, Demetri, Yoryos, Stavroula, Despina, and Stella (all brothers and sisters of one generation of the Tsalikidou family) were George and Bessie. Bessie is a nickname for either Panayiota or Vasiliki, this was verified with the Church. Pantelis chose to name and baptize his firstborn as Panayiota (calling her Pauline in English) and Pantelis' sister, Kyriaki, named and baptized her only daughter Panayiota. It would be safe to say that both, in the Greek tradition, named these daughters after their mother, thus Bessie is used here as the nickname for Panayiota. But to further confirm the name of their mother as Panayiota, we found the marriage record of Stella Tslikidou to Andrea Pelekonis, where-in Stella confirms that her mother's name was Panayiota.

Gordon Donlou also provides additional history about the times that his ancestors live in and the hardships that they encountered. He establishes that:

George Donjobolou was born in Ankara Turkey into a middle-class family; George's father had little formal education and manufactured covered wagons for farmers and for a short time was in the jewelry and silversmith trade. George Donjogolou died of pneumonia at about the age of 25. Before his death he married Despina Platanidis and had one son, Anastas ("Ernest" in English);

Despina Platanidis Donjobolou, married to George Donjogolou. She was the daughter of Emmanuel and Maria Platanidis and is thought to have been born in Philadelphia, Turkey. She had one son, Anastas, with whom she lived with, after her husband's passing. She died in 1910 or 1911 at about the age of 40;

Anastas Donjogolou, the son of George and Despina Donjogolou was born in Ankara Turkey. In Ankara, Anastas had a neighborhood grocery business. He had a wealthy uncle and aunt in Smyrna that wanted to raise him at the time of his father's death. But Anastas stayed in Ankara, married Kyriaki (Grace) Athanasiu. They had seven children in all (all born in Ankara), but many of them did not live long, dying in infancy, only four grew up to be adults (John, Elizabeth, George, and Despina). To avoid military duty in the Turkish army during WW – I, Anastas immigrated to the

United States where he joined his son, John who had immigrated a year and a half earlier. Once WW-I was over, not knowing if his family had survived the war, Anastas returned to Ankara to gather his wife, Grace, and the other three children (Elizabeth, George, and Despina) and bring them back to America. Upon Anastas' return to Ankara, he located his wife and children and arranged for passage back to America. His time in Ankara was about 15 days in total. Finding and returning to America with Grace, Elizabeth, George, and Despina, arriving in New York, they first settled in Springfield Massachusetts, then moved to Detroit Michigan. Anastas and Grace were both employed as factory workers, first in shoe factories in Massachusetts and subsequently in the automobile factories of General Motors and the Hudson Car Company. Anastas died in 1921 at age 50 from a heart attack.

Grace Athanasiu **Donjogolou** was born in Ankara, Turkey, she was the oldest of seven children that lived (a total of thirteen children were born of her parents). In Detroit Michigan, she worked at the factory store of General Motors. Grace lived to ninety years of age and was living with her eldest daughter, Elizabeth at the time of her passing.

John Donjobolou was born in Ankara, Turkey, and came to the USA at about the age of eleven with his uncle. They arrived in 1912. John lived with his uncle on his uncle's farm in New Hampshire. John was a confectioner, making and operating candy stores most of his life, most of the time in partnership with his brother, George. In 1924 John moved to Detroit and married his wife, Helen. In 1937 John moved to Redondo Beach California. He and Hellen raised their two children, Grace and Ernest in Redondo Beach. They named their children after John's parents. Ernest (Anastas) became a dentist and Grace became a teacher.

George Donjobolou was born in Ankara, Turkey. When his brother John and then his father Anastas left Ankara to immigrate to the USA, he was about eight years old and remained with his mother. After WW-I was over, Anastas returned to Ankara to gather his family and he returned with them to the USA. Passing through Springfield Massachusetts for a short time they all settled in Detroit Michigan. In 1928 George, then 23 years old, traveled to Athens Greece and married Julia. Julia was the oldest of six children. Returning from Greece they initially settled in Detroit and had two children, Gordon, and Ernest. In 1937 Gordan and Julia moved to Redondo Beach California.

Elizabeth Donjobolou was born in Ankara, Turkey. When her brother John and then her father Anastas left Ankara to immigrate to the USA, she was about ten years old and remained with his mother. After WW-I was over, Anastas returned to Ankara to gather his family and he returned with them to the USA. Passing through Springfield Massachusetts for a short time they all settled in Detroit Michigan. Elizabeth, at age fifteen, married Socrate Georgeadis. Elizabeth and Socrate lived in Royal Oaks Michigan. They had two daughters, Sophia, and Georgia. In 1938, Socrate and Elizabeth moved to California. Socrate passed away in 1965. Elizabeth lived with and was cared for by her two daughters until she passed away.

Despina Donjobolou was born in Ankara, Turkey. When her brother John and her father Anastas left Ankara to immigrate to the USA, she was about four years old and remained with his mother. After WW-I was over, Anastas returned to Ankara to gather his family and he returned with them to the USA. Passing through Springfield Massachusetts for a short time they all settled in Detroit Michigan. She left school after the eighth grade. At the age of sixteen, she married Pantelis Tsalikidou. While living in Highland Park Michigan Despina and Pantelis gave birth to two of the three children they would have, Pauline (Panayiota) and George. In 1938 they with their two children moved to Redondo Beach California. Their third child, Earnest, was born in California. It is during this period of time they shorten their name from Tsalikidou to Chalekson. Pauline would marry Arthur Furkioti and have two children (Dean and Kathy); George became a schoolteacher and school administrator, and Ernest became a dentist.

During the process of passing through immigration in New York, the spelling and/or baptismal names of those immigrating to the USA were augmented. The immigration agents tended to spell the foreign names phonetically. Such was the case with my father, while in Greek the name is Πλατανιδης which translated by converting the Greek letters of the Greek alphabet to the English letters of the English alphabet is Platanidis, as papers were processed through immigration the spelling of my father's name became Platanides. This has caused some confusion, but for the most part, after these initial generations of immigration from Asia Minor, the names were changed to accommodate ease of recognition, pronunciation, and spelling. We have Platanides to Planes, Tsalikidou to Chalekson, Donjogolou to Donlou, etc.. Additionally, in the old country, they used the suffixes to identify the gender, thus a male member of the Platanidis, Tsalikidis, and Donjogolis family would use a suffix at the end of the name showing "is" and a female member of the same family would use the suffix "ou". While this practice is still used in the old country, in North America, and within the English language as spoken in the USA and Canada, the use of suffixes to identify the gender of the person is none existent, thus with Platanides, Tsalikidou, Donjogolou, and others the name is constant and the suffix has no meaning and carries no indication as to the gender of the person. These variations in the names and finding these name changes to continue the research to find descendants of the families is a tedious job, one that may never be completed.

Gordon Donlou did his family and our project a great service as he left us a road map prepared by himself, George Donlou, Julia Donlou, and Elizabeth Georgeadis. Beyond the above-stated information, Gordon has also provided a form of the family tree which has been used to assist in constructing the family trees of Platanidis, Venis, Donjogolou, and Tsalikidou families. In his writings, he has also included information and narratives for the Kolomoratolou and Georgeadis families, all of which are interwoven and interrelated to the Platanidis, Dongogolou, and Tsalikidou families.

The book, Ships of Mercy – Rescue of the Greeks by Christos Papoutsy gives us a good look at a short window, the events around Smyrna in September 1922 that culminated in the mass genocide of Greek and Arminian Christians. Additional writing of Ambassador Horton sheds further light on the atrocities encountered in those days. But this is a look at just a small part of this genocide.

While reviewing and compiling this data for this book, it becomes apparent that at the outset of World War I (July 28, 1914, to November 11, 1918) and going as far back as 1894, Christians in Asia Minor were being systematically displaced. Reading The Thirty-Year Genocide - Turkey's Destruction of its Christian Minorities, 1894 - 1924 it becomes clear that Christians (Greek, Arminian, and Kurds) became refugees to escape this Genocide and ran to other parts of the world. The acts of terrorism by these Muslims are described as the first Holocaust of the 20th century, commonly referred to as the Greek, Armenian, and Assyrian Genocide. The refugees of these acts, while escaping genocide, left their ethnic roots, heritage, and history that goes back beyond the Byzantine Empire; they became a people without a country[47] ; but to be sure, they retained and preserved their Church and their deep commitment and faith in God.

Finding themselves in new countries, they quietly kept to themselves while working as shoe blacks, cleaning clothing, storekeepers, tailors, grocers, farmers, and factory workers. This was so that they could preserve their Christian Faith and educate their children beyond the grade school educations that they so often did not have so that their children and grandchildren would not have to suffer or flee from religious persecution, genocide, and discrimination. To this end, they also promoted and encouraged military service to remain strong in protecting those freedoms that are protected by the Constitution of the United States of America.

---

[47] For more information on how these refugees lost their identity and their country, read the article entitle "The lost descendants of Hellenism: The Antiochian" appearing in the Ethno-Political Journal on February 2, 2012 and "The Birth of the Republic of Turkey and the story of the Pontian Muslim" appearing in the Ethno-Political Journal on March 3, 2013. Both can be found at

http://ethniki-epanastasi.blogspot.com/2012/02/lost-descendants-of-hellenism.html   and

http://ethniki-epanastasi.blogspot.com/2013/03/the-birth-of-republic-of-turkey-and.html , respectively. Here these acts of terrorism by the Muslims are described as the first Holocaust of the 20th century, commonly referred to as the Greek, Armenian, and Assyrian Genocides

The family trees, to the best of our ability, are presented in Appendix D to this book. Going forward it is my hope that these families will come to know each other again and maintain their Christian beliefs and a record of the expansion of these family trees.

CHAPTER TEN

Panayiotis is Reunited with his Siblings

I n 1962, after decades of being separated from his family, his father and mother having passed away, his brother Stavros passed away as a young man due to wounds he received fighting the Nazis in WW-II and his part in the urban gorilla resistance in Chania, Panayiotis decided that the time had come to travel to Chania to be reunited with his dear sister, Panayiota, and his brothers, Athanasios, Pantelis, and Minas. When he last saw them, Panayiota was a young woman, Athanasios was a twelve-year-old boy and Pantelis and Minas were young children. They had last been together on November 2, 1922, when they said goodbye to each other as Panayiotis was boarding the Italian passenger ship, SS Acropolis, at the Port of Pieria. At that time, they expected to be together again in a couple of years, now it was August 1962, almost forty years later.

Panayiotis had arrived at a point in his life where his family was financially secure. He owned Peter Planes Shoes which at that time had the main store in Coral Gables and a second store in North Miami. The North Miami store was operated by his son Frank. He owned the building that the Coral Gables store was located; Peter Planes Shoes occupied one of the five stores in the building, and he rented the other four stores out to other businesses. I had graduated high school and had completed my first two years of college at the University of Miami and was in the midst, at my mother's request, of transferring to Florida State University.   My mother Katherine and I would manage the Coral Gables Store while my father took a couple of weeks to travel to Greece to, after forty years, be reunited with his siblings. Maria had graduated high school in 1961 and in May of 1962 had just completed her first year of college. He decided that he would take his daughter Maria with him. He carefully selected the date for his visit to coincide with the Feast Day of the Dormition of the Theotokos, "Panayias", August 15 of each year. This is a very Holy Greek Orthodox Holiday and is also his and his sister's Name Day (Panayiotis and Panayiota) and the name day of his daughter, Maria. He wanted the occasion of this Feast Day of the Church and of the name day of his sister, daughter, and himself for all the family to be together once again after so many decades of separation.

Panayiotis did not know what to expect, but he wanted to see what remained of the family that had escaped genocide on September 12, 1922 and had suffered the cruelty of war in WW II, the family of his birth. He had left as a boy at fourteen and now will return as a fifty-five-year-old man, with his daughter accompanying him and a wife and two sons waiting for him to return to them in America.

As a surprise for Panayiotis, while away, my mother and I planned to remodel the Coral Gables store of Peter Planes Shoes, making changes that Panayiotis had talked about but had not found the opportunity to implement. Panayiotis was scheduled to return home the weekend before the back-to-school rush when children most often got new clothing, shoes, and school supply for the new school year. While over the years his children's shoe store catered to children with special orthopedic needs, the parents of those children began bringing their other children to Peter Planes Shoes for regular footwear as well. With this, the business had grown and the back-to-school time of year was extremely busy.

While not planned, while he was away, I had the opportunity to meet Jose Perez, a man who was fifty years old (a little younger than my father's age) that had arrived from Communist Cuba the day before he came to our store seeking work. He did not speak much English, but my father spoke passable Spanish. Jose had his own children's shoe store in Havana but earlier that week representatives of Fidel Castro came to his store, took the keys to his home and his store, and told him that the government had taken over his store and business and that he should leave Cuba, the country of his ancestors and his birth. Jose's family had previously left Cuba, so when he left his store, he packed a bag, went to the airport, and left the country to go to Miami. I hired Jose to be my father's assistant with the understanding that he would enroll in night school and learn English and that all were subject to my father's approval upon his return. Jose went to work immediately and help me and my mother with the remodeling of the store. Jose would work with my father till my father's retirement, then he would work with my brother for years; years after my father's death and my brother's leaving the business, Jose would purchase and own the store in Coral Gables.

Panayiotis and Maria were met at the Athens Airport by his brother Minas, his wife Nitsa (Eleni), and his two young children, Fotis M and Vassilis M Platanidis. What an experience, the last time he saw Minas, Minas was a small child, now, so many years had passed, and he appears at the airport as a grown man with his wife and two small children that were about the age of Pantelis and Minas the last he saw them. Minas and Panayiotis would spend a couple of days in Athens and then leave to travel to Chania. In Chania, Panayiotis would be reunited with his much-beloved sister Panayiota and his brothers Athanasios and Pantelis. He would also meet and spend time with the spouses of his siblings and his many nieces and nephews. This year they celebrated the Feast of Panayias and the name days of Panayiota, Panayiotis, and Maria together as one reunited family. My father gave thanks to Christ and the Theotokos for this opportunity given to him so many years later.

As he was greeted in Chania by Panayiota, he could see the years that had transpired, as in his mind he contrasted the 56-year-old woman that was in front of him to the young vibrant 15-year-old girl he left at the Port of Peoria in November 1922. The years had grown on her, she had a large family of her own and lived with her husband in a small house down by the limani in Chania. Athanasios was no longer the young boy and Pantelis was not the young child he left behind.

Now, their parents, Fotis and Kyriaki, having passed away, and their brother Stavros' life having passed away from wounds that he suffered at the hands of the Nazi's, these five siblings finally had the opportunity to celebrate as a family this Holy Feast Day of Panayias; sit and talk with one another; recall those heroine events that lead to their exodus from Alasehir (Philadelphia) in Asia Minor; their securing access to the USS Linchfield; the voyage from Smyrna to the Port of Piraeus; and the days that followed before Panayiotis would board the steamship with aunt Stella Tsalikidou to make the voyage to America.

While Panayiotis and his daughter were guests in the home of his brother Athanasios and his wife Marisa. They visited the home of Pantelis who now lived in the small house that Panayiotis had sent money for his father to purchase for the family. They visited the bombed-out ruins of what was their father's store down at the limani; bombed out by the Nazi's who were searching for their father as he had been a key member and organizer of the urban guerrilla resistance in Chania (an underground urban guerilla resistance that actively and aggressively resisted the Nazi occupation and fought back against the Gestapo). Panayiotis visited Pantelis at his barbershop and Pantelis gave his brother a haircut and a shave. These were small moments, small acts, but to these siblings who had been denied these small moments and acts over four decades, each was precious and was received with prayers of thanks to our Lord and Savior Jesus Christ and to the Holy Mother, the Theotokos.

Panayiotis wanted to help his family as much as he could. He had previously sponsored Panayiota's son, Andreas, to come to America. Andreas had graduated high school in Crete and came to America on August 29, 1957, to live with us and to begin his college education at the University of Miami. He, like my father, had ambitions to be a doctor. Andreas moved to Detroit Michigan where he continued his studies. Later, moving to Chicago Illinois he attended medical school. He graduated from Chicago College with a degree in Osteopathic Medicine; then continued his education and became a doctor in Obstetrics ("OBGYN"); taught medicine at the Kansas City College of Health and Science, and eventually established a practice as an OBGYN in Hollywood Florida. Today he is retired and maintains two homes, one in Chania and one in Hollywood Florida. His children were born in the United States and have given him an abundance of grandchildren. While Panayiotis gave him his initial start, he was determined, and over the years, regardless of what he encountered, he accomplished his objective.

Panayiotis was looking to see how he could help any of his nieces or nephews move ahead with their education. On this trip, he agreed to underwrite the education for a son of Pantelis and Artemisa, Fotis P. Platanidis. He agreed to provide the funds for him to attend a university in Italy where he would pursue his education and intended to become an engineer. Panayiotis believed that education was the best way to help move his family forward to a better way of life. Undoubting Faith fortified by Education were the necessary ingredients to lift the families up from their decades of suffering.

There was much that had happened in those many years that had passed. Much to discuss as they rented a car to go to Heraklion Crete to see the ruins of the Phoenicians that first settled Crete. Once back on the mainland, Minas and Panayiotis purchased a car that they used to go to visit various of the ruins of antiquity such as the Ancient Cities of Delphi and Corinth, The Temple of Poseidon at Cape Sounion, and the Parthenon in Athens. Panayiotis decided to leave the car with his brother to use and maintain once he left to return to America. Panayiotis explained that he would return and that the car would be there for him to travel and visit his family and to tour the many attractions of Greece.

Photographs on top starting on the left, Panayiotis and Maria viewing the valley of the olive trees from the ancient city of Delphi; Maria taking her own picture of our father, Panayiotis, at Delphi; Picture was taken by Minas at Meteora Holly Monastic area in Thessalia, Greece showing Panayiotis, his sister-in-law Eleni, Fotis the son of Minas and by the car, my sister Maria.

The photograph below is taken by Uncle Minas. From left to right my father Panayiotis, His brother (Uncle Pantelis), my sister Maria, my cousin Fotis (son of Minas), and Aunt Eleni (wife of Minas).

Panayiotis would make two more trips to Chania to visit and spend time with his siblings. He visited in 1964 with me, his son Billy. Then again in 1965 with Katherine and his daughter Maria. He enjoyed all these trips. Most of all he enjoyed sitting and visiting with his brothers and sister, talking with Athanasios about their childhood in Alasehir. On each of these trips to Chania, he would stay at the home of Athanasios. While he enjoyed these visits, down deep he also lamented the absence of his parents and his brother Stavros.

Time had separated them by decades in which they aged, but despite what was almost a lifetime that they were separated, their love for one another never faded and reminded paramount in their every movement regardless of if they were together or apart. Holding this all together was their common experience in escaping genocide at the hands of Kemal Ataturk and their deep and unshaken belief in Christ and the Holy Mother, the Theotokos. This Faith they had acquired from their father and mother, Fotis and Kyriaki.

When you look upon the life of Panayiotis' parents, Fotis and Kyriaki Platanidis, and reflect on the fact that they experienced suffered and survived the years of struggle with the Muslim radicals of the Ottoman Empire, WW-I; the Greco-Turkish War; and Kemal Ataturk's Genocide of Greek and Arminian Christians which included the loss of Kyriaki' brother, left dead in the streets of Smyrna as his sisters and brother fled for their lives. Then after leaving their home behind in Alasehir (Philadelphia, Asia Minor), they were confronted by WW-II and the occupation of Crete by the Nazis; and they lost their son, Stavros, by the wounds that he received at the hands of the Nazis. Anyone of these atrocities is beyond what one would suffer in one lifetime; they suffered all of this in their one lifetime. Reflecting on this, you begin to realize that the thread that carried them through all these atrocities was their Faith in Christ and the Holy Mother, the Theotokos. Panayiotis had acquired his practice of Prayer and deep Faith by the example that his parents set in their everyday lives in Alasehir and reinforced and confirmed in the face of death, destruction, and ruin. They, Fotis and Kyriaki, lead and taught their children by example.

CHAPTER ELEVEN

Subsequent Trips to Visit Family in Greece

In 1964 Panayiotis made a second trip to visit his family in Greece, this time he went with me, his son Billy. Earlier that year my father without saying anything to me, traveled by car from Coral Gables to Tallahassee. On arrival in Tallahassee, he came to my apartment and knocked on the door. I was surprised as I was not expecting him; he had never come to visit me at school. We embraced and he came in and explained that he was leaving in the morning but wanted to see me, so he drove up for a visit. We had dinner that evening and when we woke up in the morning, we made breakfast, after breakfast, I was off to class, and he was in the car traveling back to Coral Gables.

While visiting he asked me what my plans for the summer were, I told him I wanted to attend school through the two summer sessions. He asked me if I could attend school just part of the summer as he wanted to spend some time with me and thought that we would travel to New York, see the house that we had when I was a child, and visit family in New Jersey. Then he wanted to go to Greece, just the two of us, so he can introduce me to my uncles, aunts, and cousins. I did not hesitate, we agreed to take this trip.

As planned, I attended school the first half of the summer session that year returning home the second week of July. Dad and I had discussed our agenda for the trip. We would leave home and go to New Jersey to visit with the Johansson family for a couple of days, then go to New York City. We wanted to visit and see our former home on White Plains Road and my grandparent Venis' home on Sheridan Avenue, both in the Bronx. He also wanted to go to Manhattan to visit the site of Indian Walk Shoes Company on Park Avenue, Hospital for Special Surgery, and the Time Square Shoe Repair.

On the day that we were to leave for New York, my father handed me a $100.00 bill and told me to put it in my pocket and do not spend it for anything. I was surprised as in 1964 this was a lot of money and why have it in my pocket if I was not to spend it on anything? I asked him why he was giving me this money? His response was "…a man walks differently when he has money in his pocket so put it in your pocket, know that it is there, but you will not have to use it for anything as I have us all taken care of." I did as he told me, but also, over these many years, I have always carried some money with me without any intention of spending the money.

We found that many of the places he wanted to visit had changed from when they were part of his life. Our home on White Plains Road and the apartment house on Sheridan Avenue where my grandparents once lived seemed to be untouched by time, they were as we both remembered them. At our home on White Plains Road, we knocked on the door of the neighbor. The woman that answered had been one of my playmates as a child. She was living in the same house she grew up in, her parents were much older, Dad and I had a brief, but happy, visit with them.

Traveling to Manhattan we arrived at the site of the Indian Walk Shoe Company, I remembered his look of bewilderment as we stood on the sidewalk and looked up at a giant skyscraper that had been built at that site. The storefront of the shoe company was no more, but looking down at the sidewalk you can see an embedded logo and the words "The Indian Walk Shoe Company". "Yes," he exclaimed, "we have the right place, see the name and logo on the sidewalk". He wanted me to see these places; for me, it was interesting to see him having what was nothing less than a nostalgic trip as he visited places that had some significance in his life.

We traveled from New York to Athens, arriving at the airport and after going through customs, we were met by Uncle Minas and his family. They had come to the airport to greet us and to take us to the hotel, the King's Palace Hotel in Athens. My father was very happy to see his brother Minas and sister-in-law Eleni and his two nephews Fotis M Platanidis and Vasilis M Platanidis. We would stay in Athens for a few days before we would travel to Chania to see his sister and his other two brothers.

While in Athens Dad and I went shopping and came upon an art store. This was a store maintained by an artist, his name was Karras, he did oil paintings. My father saw one oil painting of an olive tree, it was truly nice and realistic. He wanted it for his dining room back home. The artist told him that he could ship it to him and that way he would not have to handle it, it was rather large. Dad decided to buy the painting but told the artist that he wanted to be sure that this was the painting that he would get, so he asked for a pen and signed his name on the back of the canvas, saying, this way I will remember that this is the painting that I pick.

The painting was shipped to our home in Coral Gables, when he unpacked it he showed my mother, Katherine, his signature on the back of the canvas and said, that he signed it to be sure he got the painting he picked out. Today I have that painting in my home and when I look at his signature on the back of the canvas, it reminds me that this is the painting he pick out when we were together in Athens. The painting is "The Olive Trees, by Nicholas Karras."

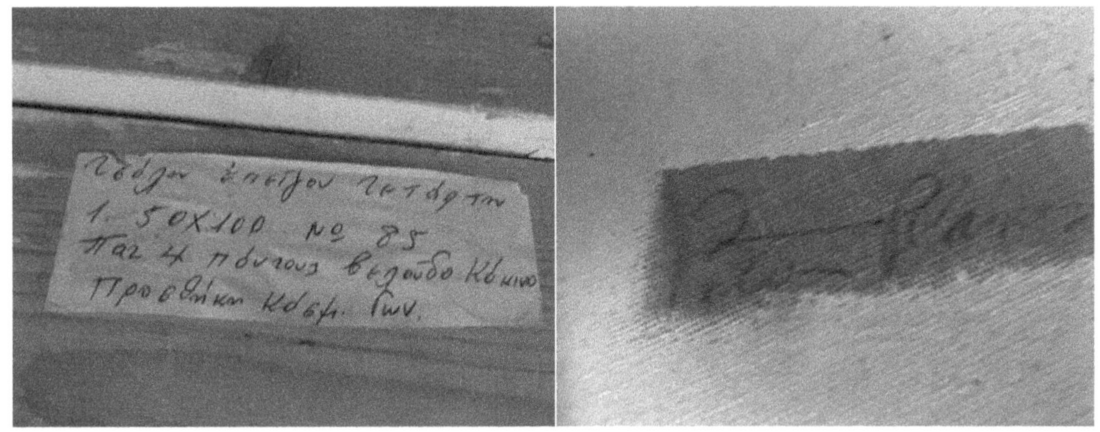

Above photographs of the label and Panayiotis signature on the back of the Oil painting by Nicholas Karras

From Athens, we traveled to Chania where we stayed at the home of my uncle Athanasios and his wife Maritsa. Their home was nice, and the love and hospitality in that home was immense. While staying there we would visit with his brothers Pantelis and his sister Panayiota and their families. Often meeting for lunch or dinner at a restaurant on the limani or on one of the beaches. On one of our days in Chania, my father drove me and my younger cousin, George, (son of Athanasios) to Heraklion where we visited the ruins of a Minoan palace.

Photograph, taken on August 15, 1964, by William P. Planes (Platanides) on the front porch of Uncle Athanasios' home in Chania Crete.   In the photo:

Standing: 1) Cousin Panayiota Tsalikidou (daughter of Demetrios Tsalikidis), 2) cousin Yoryos Tsalikidis (son of Demetrios Tsalkikidis), 3) Kiki (Kyriaki, daughter of Athanasios and Maritsa), 4) Uncle Pantelis, 5) Aunt Artemisia, 6) Despina (daughter of Pantelis and Artemisia).

Sitting: 1) the second wife of Demetrios Talikidis and mother to cousins Panayiota and Yoryos Tsalikidis, 2) my father Panayiotis 3) Aunt Maritsa.

Sitting on the floor: 1) Fotis (son of Minas), 2) Uncle Athanasios, 3) George (son of Athanasios).

Uncle Pantelis wanted us to visit his barbershop. We went to the barbershop on the limani. There my uncle gave me a shave and a haircut. While I had previously noticed that his hands would always shake when he put the razor or scissors in his hands and began the shave or the haircut, the trembling of his hands would completely disappear. The same thing happened whenever he would use his hands. It was only when his hand was at rest that they would tremble. I now realize that more than likely Uncle Pantelis may have been suffering from Parkinson's disease. The effects of the disease were apparent in his stiff gate and other mannerisms. Of course, in those days, very little was known about Parkinson's Disease. My shave and haircut were good, afterwards, we ordered a few cold beers and some Μεζεδάκια (Mezedakia, small snacks or appetizers) from the restaurant next door. This is one of the many memories I kept of this trip to visit my father's brothers and sister.

From Chania, we returned to the Kings Place Hotel in Athens. The then owner of the King's Palace was from Rhodes. He was returning to Rhodes for a couple of days and invited my father and I, to visit Rhodes and to be his guest. My father accepted but said that we would stay at a hotel and that we would stay for two days. As it turned out, we stayed a week. Reservations were made for us to go to Rhodes on an overnight boat and to stay at the Hibiscus Hotel.

The boat trip to Rhodes was pleasant. Upon arrival, we went to the hotel and checked into our room. The hotel was across the street from the beach. Nothing but the beach was on the beachside of the road, it was beautiful. When we met our host for lunch, he brought his wife and his daughter. His daughter was a few years younger than me, she was very attractive. She and I went site seeing while my father visited with her parents. The next day we went with her and her parents to "Πεταλούδες", in English "Butterflies" (the "Valley of the Butterflies"). I never saw so many butterflies in one place, it was beautiful. Upon returning from Petaloudes we later met them for dinner. That evening, after we returned to our hotel, my father explained to me that the man not only owned the King's Palace Hotel in Athens, but he had other holdings which included the Bank in Rhodes. He told me that they sought to offer their daughter and a very large dowery for me to marry her. We could live in Rhodes, Athens, and America. My father and I discussed this over the next few days. After a couple of days, my father explained to them that he and I discussed the marriage, but it was too soon for me to consider marriage. He explained that I had planned to finish my education and then would enter the US Marine Corp to serve my military obligation to the USA and that I felt strongly that I had to complete my education and my military service before I could consider marriage. A marriage contract was not made.

We stayed a few more days, then returned to Athens and were joined by Uncle Minas and his family. We would spend a considerable amount of time with Uncle Minas and Aunt Eleni. We traveled the mainland of Greece visiting many of the ruins of Greek Antiquity. We went to Delphi and spent a night at the hotel in Delphi, the hotel was built on the side of a cliff. Approaching the lobby, you were only able to see a one-story building, that being the lobby. The elevators from the lobby went down as the hotel floors were built on the side of a cliff. From our rooms we could see out across a large valley that led out to the sea, this was called the Valley of Olives as there was a blanket of olive trees extending from the mountains, down through the valley, and ending at the sea. We would also visit the Ancient Cities of Delphi and Corinth, The Temple of Poseidon at Cape Sounion, and the Parthenon in Athens. As our trip grew close to the time that we were to return home, we prepared and made our trip back across the Atlantic to return to our home in Coral Gables.

The photograph was taken in the home of Uncle Minas a couple of days before my father, and I, departed Greece to return home. Aunt Eleni (Nitsa) is sitting in front; From left to right standing are Uncle Minas, Maria and Chrysoula Spyridakis (daughters of Aunt Panayiota), Kyriaki (Koula, daughter of Uncle Pantelis), my father Panayiotis, Fotis P. Platanidis (son of Uncle Pantelis), and myself.

While making the journey back home, my father asked me if I could promise him that after he passed away, could I take it upon myself to stay in touch with my cousins and try to preserve these family ties. He knew that the younger generations would not have in common the events that he had with his sister and brothers as a child and later in life, but he sought comfort that one from his children would attempt to keep ties with the family in Greece. I promised him that I would.

At the time I made this promise to my father, I did not really understand how quickly the ties between family members going from generation to generation can be forgotten and lost. I know that now, and thus I seek to preserve the Panayiotis story and make tighter the ties between the generations that have followed and will follow.

In the years that follow my trip in 1964, I would make three more trips to Greece, but other than seeing Uncle Minas in September 1976, I would never see my Aunt Panayiota or Uncles Athanasios, Pantelis, and Minas again. All, but for Minas who passed away March 3. 1977, would pass away prior to this brief trip in 1976.

In 1965 my mother went with my father to Greece; my sister went with them. While it was not intended to be, this was my father's last trip to visit his family in Greece and my mother's only trip to meet my father's sister and three of his brothers.

On this trip, time was spent in Athens before going on to Chania. AHEPA's (American Hellenic Educational Progressive Association) International Convention that year was held in Athens Greece. My mother, having held a National Office of both AHEPA and the Greek Ladies' Philoptochos Society (the "Philoptochos") attended this convention with my father and sister. The convention afforded my father the opportunity to visit with his good friend, Archbishop Iakovos. Among my parent's belongings, I found a letter from Archbishop Iakovos addressed to my mother. In his letter, he acknowledges visiting with her at this convention and expresses his joy over the philanthropic work that she had and continued to do with the Greek Ladies Philoptochos Society.

The photograph on the left is of Maria with my father and mother, Panayiotis, and Katherine, outside the Grand Banquet of the 1965 AHEPA's (American Hellenic Educational Progressive Association) International Convention in Athens Greece.

The photograph on the right is, from left to right, Panayiotis, Katherine, Archbishop Iakovos of America and Exarch in America of the Patriarch Athenagoras in Constantinople and a person that I am not able to identify.

After the AHEPA convention, my parents and sister traveled to Chania for a week with my father's family. For the Platanidis family, this was a special reunion as after many years, they, for the first time would meet Katherine. The entire Platanidis family assembled for this reunion with Panayiotis and to meet Katherine. For the first time ever, all four brothers with their respective spouses with their sister and her spouse, and many of my father's nieces and nephews would sit to share a meal and visit with my mother, Katherine. Of all the cousins, only I and my brother Frank were not in Chania.

*The photograph was taken in **Chania Crete** on August 15, 1965, at the Holy Holiday gathering for the Dormition of the Holy Mother, the Theotokos, which is the name day of my father Panayiotis, my sister Maria, and aunt Panayiota. In the forefront of the picture at the head of the table is Uncle Athanasios; to his left and continuing on all the way around the table is my father Panayiotis, Uncle Pantelis, Aunt Artemisia, my sister Maria (covered), Cousins Katherine Spyridakis, Nikos Spyridakis, Marian Spyridakis and Chrisoula Spyridakis, Uncle Minas, a cousin I cannot identify perhaps is Koula or Despina, Cousin Fotis son of Pantelis, Uncle Ioannis Spyridakis, my mother Katherine, Aunt Panayiota, a sister to Ioannis Spyridakis, and Aunt Maritsa.*

For a week, each day there was an informal lunch at the edge of the sea. While tables were shoved together to attempt to put everyone at one long large table, a table long enough was not possible, thus beyond the main table, there were other tables that accommodated the cousins. It had taken forty-three years for Panayiotis to return home with his wife so that he could present in person his wife Katherine to all that remained of his family; and Katherine to what remained of his family. I found pictures of one such lunch among my mother's personal effects.

In retrospect, I wonder how my mother felt. Here she was, an adult woman, married to my father since November 25, 1934,[48] and has raised three children with her husband, she found herself going home to meet his family so many years later. Certainly, her going with Panayiotis to "meet the family" was like closing the barn door after the horses were out. Nonetheless, her meeting with Panayiotis' family was a great success. Through the years she had always been

---

[48] Panayiotis and Katherine applied for and were issued a marriage license on October 20, 1936 which they used in a Church Wedding on November 25, 1934.

mindful to write to them and exchange family news with them, never leaving them out of the "loop" because she had never met them. She made sure that she was at least "pen pals" with them, so it was not like they were meeting a stranger. My father was enthused as this was the first time, he was ever able to introduce his wife who he loved so much, face to face to his family.

Beyond the gatherings for lunch, there were other activities that included swimming at the beach, playing backgammon, site seeing, and dinners in the evening either at a restaurant or at the home of Uncle Athanasios and Aunt Maritsa. There were a lot of walks and conversations, recollections, and stories of home in Asia Minor. This was a good time, a time that a family that had been torn apart by acts of genocide and of war, welcomed to come together after so many decades of separation; a time to also come together to honor the memories of my grandparents, Fotis and Kyriaki Platanidis, my father's uncle Yoryos Tsalikidis, and my Uncle, Stavros F. Platanidis, all of which were an integral part of this immediate family unit but had long passed away in the name of Christ, **MAY THEIR MEMORY BE ETERNAL!!!**

This was my father's last trip to see his family, he and his brothers and sister would pass away. Today, only Aunt Eleni, wife of Mina, is still living. She is now ninety-five years old and was the youngest of all the family from that generation.

Photograph was taken in November 2021 of (from left to right) Avgi Platanidis (daughter of my cousin Fotis M. Platanidis), Fotis M. Platanidis, and his mother, my Aunt Eleni Platanidis (Thea Nitsa). This picture was taken at the home of Fotis' brother, William (Valsilis) M. Platanidis, in Athens Greece as they look at old family photographs and documents to send to me for this book.

The photograph was taken in October 2021 of (from left to right) my cousin Vasilios (William) M. Platanidis (son of Minas and Eleni Platanidis), Andreas Spyridakis (son of Ioannis and Panayiota Spyridakis), Thea Nitsa, Olga (wife of Vasilios M. Platanidis), and Fotis M. Platanidis. They were gathered to gather seeking information, old documents, and photographs to send me for this book.

Recently, by email, I received from my cousin Fotis M. Platanidis a copy of a letter he found among some old papers of his father, Minas. The letter was written in Greek in my fathers' hand on October 18, 1967, to his brother Minas and his wife Nitsa (Elaine). The letter starts out explaining his sadness to learn that his sister, Panayiota, had passed away.   He says:

"My beloved brother and sister Minas and Nitsa,

With great sadness, I received your letter that you wrote about the death of our sister.

Yesterday, I had just received a letter from Pantelis, where he also wrote me with great sadness with the news of our beloved sister Panayiota. I hope God will keep light the soil that covers her.

Now that I am writing to you, I cannot hold back my tears. May God keep all of you and all of the family of our beloved sister well, and life to you (Ζωή σε σας)…"

Later in the letter, he mentions that he and my brother, business-wise, are going their separate ways, that

"…on November 25, 1967, Maria will marry a twenty-nine years old doctor, who is a surgeon. Katherine is in bed with phlebitis. The Doctor will not allow her to get up…Vasilis…will be a father around December…Fotis and I separated our business…I am alone…"

My father's letter to Minas impresses me in that while he had good news regarding his upcoming retirement, the marriage of his daughter, and the upcoming birth of a grandchild, it was obvious that despite all that joy, at least at that moment, he was overcome with grief at the news regarding the death of his sister. As children they were close, and even having been separated by the events that unfolded because of the genocide of the Greek Christians by Kemal Ataturk, his love for her had stayed deeply seated in his heart as now expressed in this letter some forty-five years after the genocide. He has seen her for the last time in August 1965, now, in October 1967 she had passed to be with Christ. **MAY HER MEMORY BE ETERNAL!!!**

My father and brother, business-wise, went their separate ways. In the summer of 1968, my father retired, and my brother took over the business, paying my father's retirement each month in exchange for complete ownership of the business by my brother (previously the business was owned by my mother and father; the sale of the business to my brother allowed him ownership and monetize the values of the business in terms of retirement for my parents).

Now, so many years later, having seen this letter for the first time and seeing that among my father's expression he states "…I am alone." This saddens me deeply. I had returned from the service in March of 1967 and immediately moved to Fort Lauderdale as I wanted to be alone. My father and I shared a special bond in that while all his children were an important part of his life, it was I that he shared the most with, spent time with, and discussed life with. Having moved to Ft. Lauderdale to be alone, did I create a separation from him so that he felt "alone"? I hurt thinking that I may have contributed in any way to my father's feelings of being "alone".

In September 1976, I travelled to London England for two weeks, with my then-wife Marianthi, to meet with a client who was a member of the Lloyds Syndicate regarding my audit of their financial statements and operations in the United States. I took the intervening weekend to fly from London to Athens.   I made this trip specifically to see my Uncle Minas In Athens. Arriving on a Friday afternoon and leaving on Sunday afternoon I was able to meet and visit Uncle Minas. At that time Minas had been predeceased by all his brothers and his sister. I spent some time with him and commented to my wife that, while he was in his fifties he did not look well. Six months later we would receive news from my cousin Koula (Kyriaki, daughter of Pantelis) that Uncle Minas passed away on March 3, 1977. Now all the Fotis Platanidis family survivors of the 1922 genocide by Kemal Ataturk had passed away, leaving only the memory to be memorialized by their children, all of us being the First Generation of Survivors of Genocide at the hands of Kemal Ataturk.

I made two more trips to Greece to visit my cousins and my Aunt Eleni, each with my second wife, Regina.

On the trip we made to Chania in August 1998, we stayed at the Palatino Hotel on the limani. This is a small hotel that is located on Chania's limani. It has a wonderful view of the ancient Phoenician Harbor and boost of a great breakfast buffet. Each morning, Regina and I enjoyed the breakfast buffet while sitting outside and enjoying the view of the limani.

The above four photographs show the picturesque view of the Ancient Phoenician Harbor at the Limoni of Chania as seen from the Hotel Platina and the morning buffet that is included in the price of the rooms.

During this visit, my Aunt Maritsa opened up the living room and dining room of her home to have dinner with Regina and I, including all the cousins. I was told that this was the first time she opened her home to receive guests and have dinner with someone since the death of her husband, my Uncle Athanasios. Aunt Artemisa also had us for dinner at the home she shared with two of the four children that were born to her and my Uncle Pantelis, my cousins Koula (Kyriaki) and Stelios.

On the trip made in 2000, we traveled with our friends and business associate Steve and Joyce Palace (shorten from Palyocastridis, his family is from Asia Minor as well). At that time Steve was President of the private conglomerate. We would spend time with my cousins (Fotis

M, Fotis P and Despina, daughter of Uncle Pantelis), my aunt Eleni, who was living in Athens; and then, while Steve and Joyce went to the island of Samos, we went to Chania to visit with my cousins in Chania and my aunts Maritsa and Artemisa.

Since the trip in 2000, I have not returned to Greece. While my cousin Koula came to the United States in 1999 to attend my wedding to Regina, and from time to time I have had the opportunity to visit with my cousin Andrea who has a home in Hollywood Florida, I have not been able to visit any of the family in Greece. But I have kept in touch by email and by phone.

CHAPTER TWELVE

William and his Children

My father and grandfather, Panayiotis and Fotis, were confronted with several storms doing their lifetime, storms that defined their being and existence while offering them the challenge to progress through the "eye of the storm", their storms, in order to survive and emerge clear of the storm with their Faith stronger than before. To not traverse the storm would be an abandonment of their faith in Christ. While I, with my wife Regina, and our children have led a good life, we, like my father and grandfather, have experienced life's storms and have had to repeatedly look to and depend on our undoubting Faith in Christ and the Holy Mother, the Theotokos, to safely traverse through the "eye of the storm" and immerge with our spiritual and physical life intact and stronger than before.

My daughter Rhea (Αικατερίνη) and son Billy (Βασίλης) were born in my first marriage, marriage to Marianthi Liappas Planes. Rhea was born nine months after I returned from active duty in the US Navy. Her birth dealt me a hand that I did not see it coming. In December 1967, when Dr. Stratton ("Taki") Sterghos brought Rhea out of the delivery room and handed her to me, at that moment my life and purpose changed. There can be no greater moment in one's life than the moment you hold and see a new life, a new life that by God's Grace was brought into this world as a part of yourself.

At that moment, I knew I had to protect this child from the evils of this world and that it would be up to me to establish in her the religious Faith that my father and mother had instilled in me. I knew what evils there are in the world and that this child had no idea of the world about her as up to now her world was restricted to the space and environment inside her mother's womb.

In February 1970, my son Billy was born, I had the same feeling but this time those feelings were not new or a surprise as I had felt these feelings about 26 months prior when his sister was born. The feelings of having to provide, protect, support, educate, and instill an undoubting Faith in Christ in your child were strong and predominant at the birth of both my children. Adding to these feelings is the fact that, unlike many other people, I am the first generation of a survivor of genocide by Kemal Ataturk. As such my father had instilled in me the knowledge that these extreme forms of evil and cruelty are a reality of the world in which we live. These evils do not go away; they loom in the darkness of the world seeking the opportunity to deliver evil without any notice.

Upon returning from active duty in the Navy, I, with my wife, moved to Ft Lauderdale where both Rhea and Billy were born. Having just returned from the Navy, I did not want to stay in Miami, I wanted to be close enough to visit but far enough away to be alone. For whatever reason, my father seemed to understand my need to be apart yet not be away. In retrospect, while they did not have a name for it at that time, perhaps I was suffering from PTSD; years later I would be diagnosed with PTSD.

In Fort Lauderdale I purchased a two-bedroom bathhouse, it was small, but the monthly payments including principal, interest, taxes, and insurance was $99.00 a month. I opened a small office within walking distance from my home and established an accounting practice; and became an active member and a member of the Church Board at St. Demetrious Greek Orthodox Church. As my practice grew, I needed more space, so my father and I built a small office building and named it the Planes Professional Center. My father was proud of my efforts. After his 1968 retirement from Peter Planes Shoes, most weekdays, early in the morning, he would drive one hour North to the office, let himself into the office and prepare coffee for the staff. Then we would spend an hour or two sitting in my office, we both drank coffee while I worked. This went on over a couple of years till he took ill, it was a ritual, one that we both enjoyed.

Panayiotis enjoying swimming and diving in his pool at his home on the Coral Gables Deep Waterway after his retirement from Peter Planes Shoes

The home that Panayiotis and Katherine built on the Coral Gables Deep Waterway at 625 Villa Bella Avenue, Coral Gables, Florida.

Panayiotis passed away on December 3, 1971, **MAY HIS MEMORY BE ETERNAL!!!** I was devastated by the passing of my father. The day before the viewing at the funeral parlor, I called Fr. Mekras and borrowed the prayer book, the book that he used for funerals and memorial services, and went to the funeral home that night by myself. Without my mother or my siblings knowing, the funeral director allowed me to see my father in a private viewing room. There I said prayers for him from the prayer book, followed by prayers from my heart and ending with an hour in which I just knelt by his casket and talked to him, talk to him about many things, telling him what a great father he had been to me; thanking him for bringing me up to be a man, and telling him that I could only hope and pray that I would be as good a father to Rhea and Billy as he was to me. I told him that he left me a large pair of shoes to fill.

For two or three years after he passed, I would pick up the phone to call him only to be shocked back to reality when my mother would answer. When she answered I would quickly realize that he had passed. Not knowing what to say when my mother answered, I would engage her in conversation, but I never told her that the call was initiated to talk to my father. To be sure, while my father was a great father to me, my mother was likewise a great mother. A man could not be blessed more than I was to be born the son of these two Orthodox Christian parents.

In 1974, I merged my CPA firm with a national CPA firm and then transferred to the Miami Office as the Miami managing partner. Moving to Miami, I was closer to my mother and back attending Church at St. Sophia Greek Orthodox Cathedral, the Church in which I was raised. My children attended the same Sunday School that I did as a boy. My son's Sunday School teacher, Mary Venable, had been my Sunday School teacher. For decades she was the Sunday School Teacher for all the boys that served as altar boys with Fr. Mekras. I had served in the Holy Altar for ten years under the direction of Fr. Mekras. When he was old enough Billy was able to serve as an altar boy with Fr. Mekras.

Father Mekras had always told us that "…the Church on its very worst day is better than the world is on its very best day." He always stressed to me the importance of remaining in the Church and following the teachings of the Orthodox Christian Church. He stressed that we should never leave the Church. Returning to Miami gave me the opportunity to have my children be a part of St. Sophia Greek Orthodox Cathedral and be exposed to many things I was exposed to while growing up in the Church.

Rhea and Billy attended private school and we had a nice home in Pine Bay Estates. As my CPA practice progressed, In 1981 I had achieved a level of financial security that, at thirty-nine years old, I was able to retire. Retirement was a big mistake as I was too young to retire. What's more, once I retired, I realized that my wife was living two lives, one with me and one with other ideas and objectives.

Photograph of our home in Pine Bay Estates, Miami, Florida

At a point, the marriage was pushed into a divorce. My then-wife had discussed with her attorney the collectibles and jewelry we maintained in the home and in a wall safe at home. With this the attorney hired some men, three of whom came to the home with guns, gaining entry and physical struggle with me, they held me, Rhea, and Billy, at gunpoint; we were captives in our home for three days. I was the only thing standing in the way of a couple of gunmen and my two children. I had to keep the children safe and at the same time, I had to find a way to get a message to my attorney to let him know that I, with the two children, were being held captive while our captors systematically were attempting to remove all the items of value from the home. Eventually, without their knowledge, I was able to get a message to my attorney, Tom Lee, and he, with an emergency order from a Dade County Circuit Court Judge, brought an end to this ordeal[49].

As this divorce finalized, my only concern was retaining custody of Rhea and Billy, in this, I succeeded, I obtained sole custody. Not only did I have sole custody, but their mother's only visitation rights were to be under independent supervision as it had been determined that she was dangerous to herself and others. She not only sanctioned the armed break-in and looting at our home, but on one occasion she attempted to kill me and the two children. While the divorce provided, among other things, that I would pay her $1,000,000 over a period of five years, my attorney advised that I should pay it as quickly as possible as he expected that she would be back

---

[49] In subsequent Court proceedings, the three intruders would testify that they were hired by my then wife's attorney and that they had delivered the valuables to her attorney's home in Southwest Dade County. They testified that the last time that they saw these valuables were at that attorney's house and that the attorney and the wife were trying on and wearing our jewelry. None of the valuable were ever recovered.

seeking to modify the financial arrangement in order to seek more money. If I paid her out quickly and she subsequently attempted to get more, she would have to repay the early payments and she more than likely would have spent it, thus would not be able to seek additional funds. I paid her out in four months, all cash, and Tom was correct, two years later she was back for more, but could not repay the early payments thus was barred from any further claims.

After the court finalized the divorce, I remember sitting on the front step of our home with Rhea and Billy on each side of me watching the truck from a moving company driving off with most of the furniture and all the glasses, china, flatware, pots and pans that had been in our home. We were left with three-bedroom sets, the furniture in my den and the family room as well as one grandfather's clock and a Steinway baby grand piano. Rhea began to cry saying, "Daddy, she took everything, we do not even have a glass to drink water." I looked at her and with my arms wrapped around her and her brother, I said "she did not take everything, she left the most important things behind, and I have them and she does not." Rhea looked at me somewhat bewildered and said, "What did she leave behind?" and as I smiled at her and Billy I said, "you and your brother, I have what cannot be replaced and tonight the three of us will go shopping and in a couple of days, the house will be full of all that other stuff, and I will still have the two of you." I could see a strong smile come over both their faces. I was strong, so they knew it was all okay and that they were safe.

For the next couple of years, I played Mr. Mom, staying at home, not working, but caring for my children. The children and I split our time between the home in Pine Bay Estates and our horse ranch in Jupiter Farms Florida[50] . We raised horses, went to horse shows, and in general, spent a lot of time together. After a couple of years a friend of mind, Wisty Maytag[51], insisted that I take her to dinner. I consented but what I did not know was that she had made an arrangement with another lady to go to dinner with us. The dinner was an effort to introduce me to a lady, Regina, that was also in the process of divorcing.

---

[50] The ranch had a ranch house, a barn, lake, and several large pastures. It was about thirty acres and was contiguous to the Bert Reynolds Ranch. From there we would raise, and train horses and the children competed at county, reginal, state and national horse shows.

[51] I knew Wisty from my college days at Florida State, she had been married Bud Maytag, the owner of Maytag appliances and the President and controlling shareholder of National Airlines. Regina knew Wisty as they both were airline stewardess for National Airlines.

Photograph of my brother Frank, myself, and my sister Maria taken at my horse ranch in Jupiter Farms Florida

When I picked Wisty up for dinner, she asked if I could make a stop at her friend's, Regina, little did I know that her friend was expecting us and that we were picking her up as she was going to dinner as well. The three of us went to dinner and had an enjoyable evening. After we left Regina off at her home, while driving Wisty home, she asked what I thought of Regina. After my comments, she handed me Regina's phone number and suggested I call her and take her out, this time without a chaperone. I did call Regina and we went out to dinner again. We continued to see each other on a very frequent basis. Today we are married and have been together almost forty years.

At the time that I met Regina, she had two children, one was 2 ½ years old (David) and the other was six months old (Michael). With Rhea being 15 years old and Billy being 13 years old, the two sets of children did not mix well. Nonetheless, we attempted to combine all into one.

On August 21, 1999, Regina and I would be married. The wedding service was performed by Very Rev Father Typhon Theophilopoulos at St. Michael the Archangel Shrine in Tarpon Springs Florida. Regina, a faithful Roman Catholic, without my asking, decided to be Confirmed in the Greek Orthodox Church, Father Typhon performed the Chrismation, and his Presbytera, Helen Theophilopoulos was Regina's God Mother. From 1999 till her retirement in 2012, Regina (a Registered Nurse Practitioner) devoted her time to medical care for the elderly and the religious and academic education of children, especially those with Special Needs.

After high school, Rhea attended Florida State University, she stayed there two years and did not finish. Upon returning to Miami, she began to work selling durable medical equipment (DME). Eventually, she established her own company which she later merged into a larger DME where she stayed as an area manager for several years. Privately she also took on some clients to do their medical billings and to consult regarding Certifications of medical practices and clinical facilities. Rhea was good with numbers. Until Rhea was an adult, I did not realize that she was dyslectic, thus her difficulty in a formal school setting.

Rhea married Gerson Martinez at the St. Demetrious Greek Orthodox Church in Fort Lauderdale Florida. They had three children, Mathew, Andria, and Andrew. Eventually, she would divorce. After divorcing she opened her own cigar and tobacco store in Coral Gables. When she opened this shop, I gave her a picture to hang in her shop. It was a picture of my Grandfather, Fotis, outside of his tobacco shop in Chania. We laughed and said that it could not be a coincidence that the great-granddaughter of Fotis Platanidis, who owned and operated a shop in Chania, which among other things, sold tobacco, would likewise open and operate her own tobacco shop in Coral Gables. We mentioned and laughed that it must be in the DNA. Eventually, Rhea retired, selling her tobacco shop she moved to North Carolina where she remarried and now lives; owns her own horse ranch; and works as the manager of a medical company that provides outpatient mental health rehab. She and her husband Carlos are happy and enjoy their ranch.

Rhea remains close to her children, Mathew, Andria, and Andrew. All three were Baptized in the Greek Orthodox Church. Rhea's three children are now adults; they are not married, and to this day live together in their own house. They are contemplating moving to North Carolina to be close to their mother. Interestingly, both boys work for the same company with their father, a company that supplies Oxygen to hospitals and to those that are home-bound and need breathing machines. Andria was an elementary school teacher at a Catholic Parochial School.

Billy attended Stetson University and graduated with a degree in business. He eventually met his wife, Vivian (Βασιλική). Vivian was born in Cuba and as a child escaped the oppressive government of a communist dictator, Fidel Castro, with her father, mother, brother, and grandparents. Vivian, a Roman Catholic, is mindful of the cannons of the Greek Orthodox Church and follows them with Billy. They were married in the Greek Orthodox Church (Archangel Michael Shrine in Tarpon Springs) and live in South Miami Florida. They have one son, Adrian who was born on December 21, 2010. Both Billy and Vivian love Adrian; Adrian is the apple of Billy's eye. Adrian was Baptized in the Greek Orthodox Faith at St. Sophia Greek Orthodox Cathedral in Miami Florida.

One of the principal shareholders of the private conglomerate, James W. Keen, at Stetson University in Deland FL with me to see my son William P. Planes II graduate from college.

Billy became the President of the auto transport division of the private conglomerate that we built. Eventually, he wanted to establish his own company in real estate. Today Billy is active professionally as a Real Estate Broker, a CCIM, and the owner of the ReMax Realty franchise in Coral Gables Florida. He and Vivian are totally engaged in Adrian's life and education. Billy has a strong faith in Christ and tries to live his faith in every facet of his life.

CHAPTER THIRTEEN

A Gift from God

Both Rhea and Billy have a distinct feature to their intellect which I am certain that they are not fully aware of, this is a feature that was passed to me, my brother Frank and sister Maria, from our father, Panayiotis. I suspect that this trait is genetic and that Panayiotis, not having completed high school, had to acquire this trait from his father, Fotis, or his mother, Kyriaki.

Panayiotis had the ability to look at a list of numbers (perhaps 30-40 numbers in one column) that were various amounts; and by simply running his finger down the list, he could without hesitation tell you the total. He understood that numbers are an exact science and that all numbers have specific relations to each other that never changed. My brother Frank and my sister Maria inherited our father's orientation and abilities in math as have I. I know that while my brother may not have identified this as a unique ability, he utilized this gift in his day-to-day dealing. On the other hand, even though she obtained a Bachelor' Degree in Mathematics and a Master's Degree for teaching math, I doubt if my sister understands, developed, or utilized this gift that I am sure she inherited.

While neither Rhea nor Billy have recognized this unique mathematical orientation, I have observed them unconsciously drawing upon this ability and thus know that they possess this talent, however, they have not consciously undertaken the development and application of this talent in their business dealing. I also suspect that my brothers' children, especially Peter and Khristina, and my sister's daughters, especially Stephanie and Christina, are similarly oriented. To what degree they have cultivated and used this unique ability with math, I do not know.

When I was five years old Aunt Sophia, who was married to my mother's brother Thanasis Venis, was visiting us at Folly Beach South Carolina. It was a rainy summer day, and she was attempting to keep the children busy playing games. She had a stack of math flashcards that she was using with her son, my cousin Teddy. Trying to think of ways to entertain us she thought she would make a game out of the flashcards, taking the simpler flashcards and asking for us to provide the answers. As this progressed, she seemed surprised by my answers. She singled me out to sit down and review more of the flashcards. She began to drill me on the times tables (1 times 1 is 1, 2 times 1 is 2, etc.). As we progressed, she advanced to each of the times tables in succession from the ones table up to the twelves table. After an hour had passed, she was amazed as I, at five years old, could quickly give her the answer of any times table up to twelve without hesitating. By the end of her visit, she had me giving her answers to math addition, multiplication, and division problems off the top of my head. She and my mother thought that this was amazing, I did not understand why they were so excited at my recitations; on the other hand, my father simply smiled and said he was not surprised and that he was confident that I could do much more.

My Aunt Sophia, was the first to experience my Gift from God.
My Uncle Paul Karp is in the background

For years I did not understand my personal relationship with numbers. I can look at a number and my mind fills with permutations of that number; that number's significance by itself; and how that number affects every other number on into infinity. As a young person, my mind worked rapidly with numbers, so rapidly I would become angry or frustrated with others as I simply took it for granted that everyone had this ability and viewed numbers as I did, in the abstract, within my head, no pencil, paper or adding machine needed.

Every number is a constant and never changes. From the beginning of all time, "pi" has been and always will be 3.1415265 and the area of a circle is and always will be "pi r squared" and the circumference of a circle is and always will be "2 pi r", this is simply the way it is, it will never change in regard to "pi" or any other number in the universe. Each number is unique unto itself; and unique as it relates to all numbers into infinity. Numbers are an exact science, but most of the population does not understand or recognize this fact. My anger and frustration with other people, adversely affected my personal relationships, relationships that I regret losing.

At a point, my father addressed this with me and explained that what I experienced with numbers was unique and that most other persons not only did not experience this but had no foundation to even begin to understand. He taught me not to take it for granted that anyone, much less everyone, could look at a problem and view the problem from the perspective that I clearly saw without effort. He showed me how to apply this gift to our life's personal and business environment. While he did not have a name for it, he also taught me what I later came to understand was cybernetics[52]. My days of thinking that other people were lazy or stupid came to an end; my frustration with others ended. I realized that this was a gift that few had and even fewer even understood; and that combining my aptitude with math with cybernetics, I had a powerful and unique ability, one that very few would experience and know how to use it on a daily.

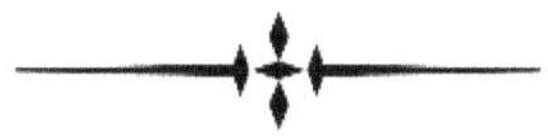

---

[52] Cybernetics is a transdisciplinary and "antidisciplinary" approach concerned with regulatory and purposive systems—their structures, constraints, and possibilities. The core concept of the discipline is circular causality or feedback—that is, where the outcomes of actions are taken as inputs for further action

CHAPTER FOURTEEN

Caesar wants what Caesar believes is Caesar's

Understanding my gift with numbers and combining this with cybernetics I began to use it to my advantage, creating business deals, evaluating economic trends and accessing their potential consequence, counter-balancing the economics of one industry against the economics of another so that a portfolio would be balanced so that an economic failure of one industry precipitated what would be the success of another; shielding hard assets from the effects of soft assets; evaluating risk against rewards; and capping the returns on income so that they would exponentially increase, thus several years later the asset could be sold at a substantial gain. Simply put, for every action, there is a reaction; and for any loss to occur, someone must make a gain.

As I put these formulae to work, I began to build a conglutinate, an organization that included many industries that normally would not be associated with one another (i.e. consulting, factoring [53], mortgage lending, medical receivables financing[54] , government contracting, HVAC sheet metal fabrication and installation, agriculture, long term acute care hospitals, nursing homes,

---

[53] Factoring it the purchasing of accounts receivable from companies that cannot afford to carry them, thus affording the seller a faster return on their working capital which lets them reinvest in more sales, thus supporting an increase of the sales growth and profit of the Seller.

[54] Medical Receivable Financing is different from Factoring in that it is a form of secured lending against amounts due from third party payors for medical services, principally services rendered from hospitals and other providers of medical care.

mental health hospital, assisted living facilities, auto transport, real estate holdings, real estate management, medical data processing, hospital and nursing home management companies, and others).

The concentration of my skills was such that I did not run the entities of the conglomerate; other officers and employees operated the companies in the conglomerate. I focused on using my gifted talent to look for other investments and opportunities; thus, I continued to use my mathematical gifts combined with the application of cybernetics. I spent my time looking for the product upon which I could utilize these talents and maximize a return on investment. I used all my efforts to find a product.

In seeking "product" (troubled companies that could be restructured to become profitable and then sold at a profit after they seasoned and contributed to the overall consolidated cash flow and return on investment for the parent company of this conglomerate) I needed some help. I actively sought help and considered several persons to bring on board to assist me in the search, evaluation, and management of "product". At a point in time Langfred W. White, Esq. agreed to come into the parent company of the conglomerate as Sr. Ex. Vice President and in-house legal counsel. This turned out to be a good fit. Langfred was well versed in creditor rights, the Uniform Commercial Code, Real Estate Law, knew how to document transactions, and most of all, while he did not know the specifics of my gift, he knew there was a specific aptitude0 and thus was an attentive thinker and gave considerable effort to knowing the ins and outs of each transaction. This was important as Langfred was given the responsibility of documenting and closing the purchases of the "product" as well as the eventual sales of the "product". Once a product was purchased it was assigned to others to implement the corrective actions needed to "right the ship" and prepare the product for resale in three to five years. Lan and I would observe management's progress and monitor when it was appropriate to convert the investment into a profit.

While Langfred and I would have what others would call arguments, we viewed and preferred to call them spirited discussions or our differences of opinion. Our spirited discussions never affected our friendship or our respect for one another as they always gave way to a better understanding of the important and necessary components of these transactions. These spirited discussions, for me, were a requirement as I used Lan's reactions to evaluate what I may expect from others as a reaction, in effect a test of the cybernetics related to the overall model of the transaction. At a point in time, our respect and trust in each other and each other's ability left us able to work separately and apart from each other knowing that each knew what needed to be done and how it should be accomplished. Today, Langfred is a Circuit Court Magistrate hearing case involving Pinellas County Building and Zoning, and a Board-Certified Arbitrator hearing case over the Eastern United States and Puerto Rico. He is also the Co-Trustee of the two Irrevocable Trusts set up by Regina and me on May 6, 2003. We both trust him implicitly.

In searching and finding "product", out of every 100 companies and opportunities that Lan and I would evaluate, we would isolate twenty-five for further consideration; from the twenty-five, we would further isolate four entities and from the four entities, we might pick one to consummate. The rule was we do not need to make a deal, but we would make a deal if it rang all the bells on our terms. This was a long process. Many times, I would get up from negotiation and advise everyone that I was finished, then turning to Lan I would simply state that I was taking the plane and going home and that if he wanted to stay I would send the plane back for him; but if he wasn't at the terminal to meet the plane upon its return the pilots would have instructions to leave and return home without him. I would leave Lan to haggle with sellers or buyers, being completely comfortable knowing that he understood what I wanted and what I needed to make this all happen. He knew that if he could not get what I had asked for, he was to simply get up and walk. My walking away and leaving them a ten-to-twelve-hour period to meet my terms with Lan was generally a good motivator for them to acquest to our terms. Walking away for us was as much a victory as closing a deal. Ultimately, we acquired and subsequently sold or discontinued operations for forty-seven companies, companies that maintained operations in eight states and employed hundreds of people. Through this process, we preserved and made secure the jobs of hundreds of people, preserved family income for them and their children, and at the same time, enjoyed the challenge and the effort of making it all happen. Many of these operations continue to operate successfully today.

While Regina and I were paid our salaries semi-monthly for my time and effort in securing products and her time and efforts put forth to further the operations of selected companies, we also received an annual bonus. The annual bonuses were paid to us and other key officers and employees on the last pay period of each year. These bonuses were based on the successes we were able to achieve for the companies during that year. Other than our salaries, healthcare insurance, 401K, and bonuses, our personal expenses, cars, car insurance, vacations, living expenses, entertainment, etc. were never paid for by any of the companies.

As the conglomerate grew and my income increased, each year I would redeposit my annual bonus directly back to the company as a noninterest-bearing loan; then, over the following year, the company repaid these loans as I utilized this money to assist the needs of Greek Orthodox Churches, philanthropic efforts, establishing three homes for orphans and abandoned children in Romania; and to assist children of special needs while teaching them the Orthodox Christian Faith. Fortunately, my wife, Regina was of a similar mine. She too turned back to the company her annual bonus and likewise, it was used with mine for these purposes. She devoted a large number of her efforts to the Orthodox Christian school that we founded for special needs children. This school accepted all children regardless of the child's race, creed, or color.

My gift with numbers is a gift from God. I could not use it for myself, as that would not honor our Lord for what was gifted to me by God. I was provided with what I needed to live a good and happy life as a Greek Orthodox Christian and a US citizen with my inalienable rights to be free and worship protected by the Constitution of the USA. Each year, the funds over and above my needs were used for the Lord's work, to support His Church, and for philanthropy.

2004 and 2005 did not find me active in the conglomerate, in 2004 I had withdrawn as President of the parent company but remained on the Board of Directors so I could concentrate predominately on my health. I may have been in the office, cumulatively, four to six weeks that entire year. 2005, while an active year, was centered around St. Nicholas Greek Orthodox Cathedral in Tarpon Springs, its 2006 Centennial Celebration, and the forthcoming visitation at the time of the Centennial Celebration of His All-Holiness, Archbishop of Constantinople-New Rome, and Ecumenical Patriarch Bartholomew I. The Church appointed me to organize and effect this Celebration and Visitation by the Patriarch schedule for five days with the arrival of the Patriarch on January 4, 2006, and his departure on January 8, 2006.

This was a tremendous undertaking[55]. While traditionally the Epiphany Celebration was held by St. Nicholas in Tarpon Springs, this year it would include participation from the Greek Orthodox Church of St. George (in New Port Richey FL), Holly Trinity (in Clearwater FL), St. Stephanos (in St. Petersburg FL), St. Barbara (in Sarasota FL), St. John (in Tampa FL) and St. Sophia (in Lakeland FL), all being churches that were seeded and founded from St. Nicholas in Tarpon Springs[56]. To organize these events the Very Reverend Father Sabastian Skordallos[57] oversaw the ecclesiastical aspects of the events and I oversaw the activities of the layette[58]. In organizing the committee, I had each of these seven churches provide a member of their respective church board of directors to be a member of the overall Centennial Committee. Each of these representatives along with myself, Fr. Skordallos[59], Harry Patsalidis, and Nikitas Manias became the Centennial Committee (ten members in all, four from St. Nicholas and one from each

---

[55] During 2005 and extending to April 2006 these activities were full time for me, thus I was not at the offices of the Conglomerate and not active in their day-to-day activities.

[56] St. Nicholas Greek Orthodox Church, founded in 1905, was the second Greek Orthodox Church established in America. The first is Holy Trinity Greek Orthodox Church funded in New Orleans, La. St. Nicholas until the 1950's was under the Bishop of Kalymnos. Subsequently it was placed under the Archdiocese of America. It has always had the largest celebration of Epiphany in the Americas.

[57] Father Skordallos was an archimandrite at the time of the Centennial. After the Centennial he was transferred to the Archdiocese of America to serve the Church under Archbishop Demetrios and was subsequently elevated to be a Bishop of the Greek Orthodox Church of America.

[58] These activities were supported by the effort of so many persons, it would be impossible to list them here, but to name a few there was Paul Aiello, Emmanuel Gombos, Nicholas Katsaras, Gorge Kouskoutis, George Psetas, Alec Veloudis, Dr. Theodore Vlahos MD, N. Michael Kouskoutis, Vasilie Faklis, Anthony Hatzeleris, Joanne Kambouris, Helen Katzaras, Dee Nicholaou, John Pantrelis, Regina Planes, Theo Samarkos, and Bessie Zamtopoulos.

[59] The Very Revered Fr. Skordallos has been since elevated to His Grace, Bishop Sabastian.

of the other six Tampa Bay Area Churches); the members from the area Churches had the additional responsibility for involving the members of their respective Churches in the preparation for and participation in these events. Additionally, there was an Executive Committed that included me, Very Reverend Fr. Skordallos , Harry Patsalidis, and Nikitas Manias. Beginning in January 2005, the Centennial Committee met once a week, the Executive Committee met two additional times a week. By September 2005 the Centennial Committee began meeting as often as twice a week while the Executive Committee had three additional meetings in the evenings each week.

These events, which would include religious ceremonies, luncheons, dinners, banquets, concerts. golf tournaments, etc., would span five days beginning with the welcoming ceremonies at the St. Petersburg Airport for the Patriarch on January 4, 2006, and ending with the Patriarch's departure from St. Petersburg Airport on January 8, 2006[60]. The planning and implementation for these events included countless meetings in New York at the Archdiocese with Archbishop Demetrious and his staff; in Atlanta at the Metropolis of Atlanta with Metropolitan Alexios and his staff; and locally with participants from all the area churches and all the sub-committees set up for each event that would be held over the five days that the Patriarch was here to be with us, the Faithful members of the Church here in Tampa Bay.

His All-Holiness, Archbishop of Constantinople-New Rome, and Ecumenical Patriarch Bartholomew I walks among the Faithful, greeting and Blessing them as they reach out to touch him and to receive His Blessing at St. Nicholas Greek Orthodox Cathedral in Tarpon Springs, Florida on the evening of January 4, 2006.

---

[60] At the generosity and expense of Alex and Faye Spanos (owners of the then San Diego Chargers) a private jet plane was provided to bring His All Holiness and other Hierarchs of the Church from Istanbul (Constantinople) to Florida and return them home safely.

The 2006 Centennial Celebration of St Nicholas, the 2006 Celebration of Epiphany, and the 2006 Visitation of the Patriarch to St. Nicholas were major events for Orthodox Christians in Tampa Bay. It would include Liturgies and other Ecclesiastical Events; these were major events for the Tampa Bay Area. The event itself, on the day of Epiphany, January 6, 2006, entailed the closing down of the City of Tarpon Springs to all vehicular traffic, the use of 300 members of law enforcement[61] , and the participation of over 80,000 persons that were either resident in or came into the City that day to celebrate and take part in the religious Liturgy, the procession to Spring Bayou and the religious service at Spring Bayou which included the Blessing of the Waters, the throwing and retrieval of the Cross and the Blessing of the diver that retrieved the cross that day (sixteen-year-old Jack Vasilaros). This event in and of itself was larger than a Super Bowl Game, with over 40,000 attending the ceremony at Spring Bayou with thousands of people lining the streets to see the procession from St. Nicholas Cathedral to Spring Bayou, all managed by the Church through its Centennial Committee and Centennial Executive Committee for which I was the Chairman.

His All-Holiness, Archbishop of Constantinople-New Rome, and Ecumenical Patriarch Bartholomew throwing the Cross after his Blessing of the Waters at Spring Bayou on January 6, 2006

---

[61] The composition of the law enforcement necessary of this event was principally supplied by the Pinellas County Sheriff's Department in cooperation of additional personal provided by the Hillsborough County Sheriff's Department as well as the City of Tarpon Springs Police Department. FBI, State Department Security, and Secret Service were also assigned to protect the Patriarch.

The Liturgy and Cross Ceremony on Epiphany Day and the Liturgy celebrating the Centennial anniversary of St. Nicholas in Tarpon Springs on Sunday, January 8, 2006, marked the first time that a Patriarch of the Greek Orthodox Church had ever been the Celebrant of the Liturgy in the United States. For the Orthodox Christians that were in Tarpon Springs and the Tampa Bay Area, these events that they would participate in would occur with the Celebrant being the 287th successor of the Apostle Andrew, His All-Holiness Archbishop of Constantinople-New Rome, and Ecumenical Patriarch Bartholomew I; their Patriarch. The opportunity to celebrate the Liturgy and receive Holy Communion at a service with His All-Holiness would be and was, for many, a lifetime experience. I am deeply thankful to Christ to have had the opportunity to assist and be part of bringing this Blessing to so many people in the Tampa Bay Area.

287th successor of the Apostle Andrew

His All-Holiness, Archbishop of Constantinople-New Rome, and Ecumenical Patriarch Bartholomew I at St. Nicholas Greek Orthodox Cathedral in Tarpon Springs, Florida, Epiphany 2006

Regarding the Liturgy and the religious event at Spring Bayou on January 6, 2006, these events were broadcasted live over various broad cast networks, including the US Armed forces Network, Reuters, and many others. This includes live stream availability reaching approximately

100 nations on earth with its central theme being "You do not need to be Greek to be Orthodox, you only need to accept Christ observing the Orthodox traditions". We were told that this religious broadcast was live on air in China for two hours. I, as an Archon of the Church, a member of St. Nicholas, and, most important, as a Baptized Orthodox Christian, was deeply and spiritually moved.

A page from the 2006 Centennial Album of St. Nicholas Greek Orthodox Cathedral, Tarpon Springs, FL.

The first photograph is of my father's family in Smyrna taken in 1913 or 1914. When this was originally published it was thought that the photo was taken in 1920, but since the family realized that it was taken before the birth of Panayiotis' brothers Stavros and Minas, and at the time of the Baptism of Panayiotis' brother Pantelis, thus the photo was taken in 1913 or 1914.

The second photograph was taken on January 5, 2006, at a private audience for the Platanides family with His All-Holiness Patriarch Bartholomew His All-Holiness Ecumenical Patriarch Bartholomew I of Constantinople during his visit to Tarpon Springs, Florida, for the 2006 Epiphany Celebration and the 2006 Centennial Celebration of the settlement of Greek Orthodox Faithfull and the establishment of the St. Nicholas

Greek Orthodox Cathedral in Tarpon Springs Florida. In this picture, you can see Katherine seated in a wheelchair in the center of the picture and standing (from left to right) Linda Johanson, my cousin Richard Johanson, myself, Regina Planes, His All-Holiness Ecumenical Patriarch Bartholomew I of Constantinople, my son William P Planes II (Billy), Metropolitan Alexios of Atlanta, my sister Maria Planes Maistrellis, Archbishop Demetrios of America, Vivian Planes (my son Billy's wife), and my cousin Andreas Spyridakis (son of my father's sister Panayiota).

Katherine exchanges greetings with His All-Holiness Ecumenical Patriarch Bartholomew I of Constantinople while her Godson Richard Johanson is wheeling her chair and others in the room are observing them. For my mother, Katherine, a lifelong Faithful and Devout Greek Orthodox Christian, to have the opportunity to meet and talk to His All-Holiness was worth all my work and efforts, it brought her immense joy.

The Great Seal of the State of Florida bestowed upon William P and Regina M Planes in January 2006 for Outstanding Community Service

My work with the Church and other philanthropic endeavors did not make the IRS happy. The Centennial Celebration of St. Nicholas and the Visitation of His All-Holiness cost $1.6M of which I provided $1.2M of these costs for the St. Nicholas   Centennial Celebration, the 2006 Epiphany Celebration, and the 2006 Visitation to St. Nicholas of His All-Holiness Ecumenical Patriarch Bartholomew I of Constantinople. In a meeting with me, IRS agents clearly stated that they cannot understand why I would give that money to the Church. Years later I would read entries in IRS's "ICS History Transcripts[62]" related to me and see that they not only expressed their disfavor of the money I spent and contributed to the Church, but they discussed sending an agent to meet and discuss this further with Father Michael Eaccarino who at that time was the Dean of St. Nicholas Greek Orthodox Cathedral in Tarpon Springs Florida. They sought to confirm directly with him that I was lying and that my generosity with the Church never happened.

Having made one mistake in my life for which I had to serve time, from the time I returned from serving my time (December 1985) and continuing into my old age, the IRS has focused on me, in an attempt to find something so that they could prosecute me for tax fraud (from 1985 to today a total of 37 years). Not having engaged in any such behavior they have never been able to find anything on which to bring charges and to prosecute me for tax fraud. An entry on April 24, 2006, in an IRS's ICS History Transcripts, an IRS Revenue Agent ("RO") wrote:

> *"Review of subcode 910[63] …We were trying to show that the money was available for payment of tax at the time of accrual and that Planes chose to not pay the tax and then used the money for his own personal benefit (emphasis added)…".*

Several months later the same RO made an additional entry stating:

> *"We were investigating him for fraud but so far our efforts have been* **unsuccessful" (Emphasis Added).**

In another set of ICS History Transcript entries by a different Revenue Agent ("RO") dated February 4, 2004, the RO states

"This case is successor corp of 'University Rehab Hospital' in New Orleans…there is no evidence that a 4180 interview was ever conducted…"

---

[62] ICS History Transcripts are "sensitive and confidential" records of the IRS maintained by the agents of the IRS in the ordinary daily course of business of the IRS. These transcripts are not available to the Taxpayer or the public but were produced to William Planes by way of proceeding sin Federal Court. While not part of the Court' files they are in the possession of this Taxpayer.

[63] The IRS subcode 910 indicates a matter being investigated for tax fraud.

On August 11, 2005, the RO confirms that as of that date that an interview form 4180 or a 433-A was not taken from Mr. Planes. The RO, on January 20, 2006, made an entry under general history in the ICS History Transcript stating:

> "…There has been extensive work done on this case by many different revenue officers over a number of years. The principal officers of this TP (taxpayer) live in Florida…"

Then on May 25, 2006, the RO by an entry in the ICS History Transcript, confirms that the RO is not able to summons the information for a 433-A

> "…because we do not have an underlying individual assessment against… them" (referring to myself and my wife);

the RO goes on to state

> "However, R/O has learned from our informant and the revenue officers in Florida[64] …that the Planes live in a multimillion-dollar house…have very expensive cars, and owns a yacht…indicating an ability to pay[65]".

Based on this statement the RO assess me approximately \$5.7M related to an entity that I did not own and for whom I had not been a director, officer, employee, or signature on the entity's bank accounts.

In a different proceeding, R/O sought to assess my taxes related to an entity that I did not own, was not an officer or director, and was not a signer on the entity's bank accounts. This R/O, in an effort to prove that I had both access and control over the entity and the entity's bank accounts, subpoenaed bank resolutions and signature cards of Bank One in the State of Louisiana. The R/O's entries into the ICS History Transcript states

---

[64] In several of the quotations taken directly from IRS Confidential and Sensitive transcripts maintained by IRS agents there are grammatical or spelling errors. There has been no attempt here to correct these grammatical and spelling errors as they are quoted verbatim from the IRS records in which they are stated.

[65] As part of legal proceeding brought by the government in November 2018 approximately 66,000 pages of IRS confidential records that are not normally available to taxpayers was produced. These included ICS History Transcripts going as far back as 1998. The name of the confidential informant along with the multiple written statements given by the confidential informant under oath and penalty of perjury was contained in these documents. In the deposition of this confidential informant the informant confirmed that IRS sought these sworn statement for the purpose of bring tax fraud charges against me;   that the informant had no knowledge of my personal financial resources; that I had never asked them to make false bookkeeping entries in the company's books and records; that I had never taken any money from the conglomerate for personal uses other than my salary and bonus; and that in exchange for the written statements of the informant the IRS had released the informant from three assessments and one pending assessment of taxes all of which totaled in excess of \$2.0M.

"Mr. Planes has not been shown to have been a signor on any of the 3 Bank One accounts in the name of…. specifically Operating Acct…Accounts Payable acct…and Payroll Acct…"

The R/O continues to state,

"I summonsed Bank One for information on the above accounts and was informed that there were no records located for those accounts…This seems to be very strange…This seems to be an attempt on the part of Mr. Planes and possibly Bank One to avoid acknowledging who had signature authority for these accounts…".

At that time, I knew nothing of the IRS's efforts to obtain this banking information. The R/O was so determined to attach tax fraud to me, she fantasized that I was controlling the behavior and responses of a National Banking Company, Bank One, in the State of Louisiana.

Christ said, "…Render therefore to Caesar the things that are Caesar's and to God the things that are God's" (Matthew 22:21-). That is what I have done, but apparently, Caesar is not happy and wants God to get less and for Caesar to get more than the tax code states that they are due.

IRS has not been successful in finding and bringing tax fraud charges against me; as I simply did my work, followed the rules, and took my deductions for contributions to the Church and other charitable works in which I was engaged. Our company books and our personal financial records along with the business and personal tax returns were prepared by qualified accountants and signed by Certified Public Accountants. At a point these Church and charitable contributions exceeded what was allowed under the Internal Revenue Code, thus, as provided in the IRC, the excess was carried over to be applied as deductions in future years, to this date the aggregate of these charitable contributions have not been fully utilized.

I humbly thank Christ for walking with me through the eye of this incessant storm with the IRS which commenced on or about 1998 and has continued till October 6, 2020 (the date that their last effort came to an abrupt stop); I truly believe that there were times that Christ was carrying me as the efforts of the IRS were overwhelming. It is not over yet; I expect that they will be back again.   For years I have prayed daily for Christ (and to the Theotokos for her intercession). My prayer is that the Will of Christ would allow him to continue to walk with me, give me the energy and wisdom for me to keep my family safe, and protect my family from this ongoing storm created by an evil that has sought to distort my good works and discredit me of who I am, a devout Orthodox Christian. I thank Christ for being born to such good Orthodox Christian parents and for all that I have experienced in life; and that I was able to live in a country that has freedom of religion, speech, and choice. I know that my life has been one in which Christ has always been with me, every step of the way.

For me, having grown old and experiencing failing health, I have Peace in the fact that both my children are Faithful Christians, they know, believe in, and practice daily Prayer. I am also comforted that Rhea and Billy know how to provide for their own needs as well as the needs of their children (my grandchildren Mathew, Andria, Andrew, and Adrian) and that they continually attempt and work to make my grandchildren faithful Christians and educated self-sufficient individuals. Both have been provided with encouragement to live their Faith every day. They, like their grandfather Panayiotis and I, start and end each day in prayer with unquestioning Faith that Christ loves them and watches over them and at no time gives them more to bear than they are capable of carrying. I remind them of what Fr. Mekras told us, "…never leave the Church."

CHAPTER FIFTEEN

The Mother Church and Living Life Through Good Works

s the Apostles and Disciples of Christ went forth into the world to deliver the news of Christ and His resurrection, the Church was formed. As the Church formed there were, from the beginning, three "Sees"; these established in the First Century were Rome, Antioch, and Alexandria. The See of Constantinople was added in the 4th century, and the See of Jerusalem was added in the 5th Century. Together these five Sees were recognized as the patriarchy of the Church by the Council of Ephesus in 431 AD. A Patriarchate is an ecclesiological term in Christianity, designating the office and jurisdiction of an ecclesiastical patriarch.

These five ancient patriarchates of the Pentarchy, were headed by patriarchs as the highest-ranking bishops in the Christian Church prior to the Great Schism. These were the patriarchates of Rome, Constantinople, Alexandria, Antioch, and Jerusalem. This Schism of East and West occurred on July 16, 1054, when the Ecumenical Patriarch of Constantinople, His All-Holiness Michael Cenulanus was excommunicated from the Christian Church by the Pope Leo IX of the Roman See; and likewise Pope Leo IX of the Roman See was excommunicated from the four remaining Sees; these mutual excommunications split the Latin-rite See of Rome from the four

Byzantine-rite Sees of the patriarchates in the East, resulting in the formation of the Roman Catholic and Eastern Orthodox Churches.

In 1965, in a simultaneous ceremony during a historic meeting of Patriarch Athenagoras I and Pope Paul VI at the Patriarchate of Jerusalem it was agreed that these excommunications decreed in 1054 would be revoked. Thus, on December 7, 1965, by way of statements simultaneously read in Rome by Pope Paul VI and at the Patriarchate in Istanbul by Patriarch Athenagoras I, the Sees of the Christian Church were reunited.

The four Eastern Orthodox patriarchates (Constantinople, Alexandria, Antioch, and Jerusalem), along with their Latin Catholic counterpart in the West, Rome, are distinguished as "senior" (Greek: πρεσβυγενή, presbygenē, "senior-born") or "ancient" (παλαίφατα, palèphata, "of ancient fame") and are among the apostolic Sees, having had one of the Apostles or Evangelists as their first bishop: Andrew, Mark, Peter, James, and Peter again, respectively. In the case of Constantinople, Apostle Andrew had visited the City of Byzantium in 38 AD, not Constantinople. It was not till 330 AD that the Roman Emperor Constantine the Great declared Constantinople as the new capital of the Roman Empire, Constantinople was established on the grounds of the former City of Byzantium. Apostle Andrew appointed Bishop Stachys, the Apostle who remained bishop in Byzantium until 54 AD. Therefore, the Apostolic See of Constantinople, which was earlier referenced as the See of Byzantium, appointed the Bishop (Patriarch) of Constantinople.

When it comes to living life through good works, we must reflect on the teaching of Christ, as they have been recorded in the Gospels of the Apostles Mathew, Mark, Luke, and John, the letters by the Apostles, and the writings and cannons of the Church as provided by the Hierarchs of the Church. The writings and cannons of the Church are immense, yet one can reduce them to a guide to apply to one's life. Of course, there are the Ten Commandments, the Nicene Creed, the Lord's Pray, the Psalms of David. Within the Gospels, there are many parables to read and learn from.

Today's society, for the most part, looks at a man and determines his success based on his financial net worth. How much money does he have in the bank; what properties does he own; how big is his house; what kind of cars does he drive, etc... But the teachings of Christ tell us that the measure of a man's life is not determined based on the abundance of his earthly riches. Let's be realistic, what you take with you when you pass from this world, is your sole, not your earthly riches, not even your body. The measure of a man is what he does with his life and how he utilities the assets made accessible to him by God in the support of his Church, the needy, the orphaned, the sick, and suffering; a man's "good works". It does no good to hold on to your wealth, but it does good to put it to work in religious and philanthropic works.

Christ told us **(Matthew 19:24**-) "Again I say to you it is easier for a camel to go through the eye of a needle than for a rich man to enter the Kingdom of God." This is clear and concise. I think this says a lot.

Notwithstanding the good works I have done, I am simply humbled cannot forget the life of my good friend, Very Rev. Father Tryfon Theophilopoulos. I had engaged in a lot of philanthropic works through him, always as an "anonymous" participant. While this made me feel good, I did not realize what a real philanthropist was till after Fr. Tryfon passed away. What I learned after his passing made me learn to be humble.

The Very Rev. Father Typhon K. Theophilopoulos, the Dean of St. Nicholas Greek Orthodox Cathedral in Tarpon Springs Florida for 30 years, stood out as a unifying leader in the Tarpon Springs community. While without a doubt a significant influence on the Church Community of St. Nicholas his love of the Church reached far beyond the doors of the Church. His light shone brightly as a husband, father, friend, and most importantly, a "Man of God".

As a "Man of God" and a friend, he inspired so many, including myself, to do good things for others. Not long after we became friends, I started working with him to help members of the St. Nicholas Church Community; reaching out with him to those who were in need. If someone had cancer and couldn't afford chemotherapy treatment, we paid for their treatment. If someone needed to have their electric or water utility bills paid, it was done. If they needed to have groceries, they got groceries. If they needed a friend, they had a friend. Some of my financial resources when to support these needs, either thorough Fr. Tryfon or the St. Nicholas Philoptochos.

Years ago, there were three children whose mom went missing and their father was in prison. The children were being raised by their grandparents who were in their mid to late 80's and lived on a fixed income. We helped support that family. Father Tryfon told them to go to the Acropolis Deli on Tarpon Avenue and to see Teddy. The Grandmother would go to Teddy's once a week and get meats, cheeses, and everything she needed for that week, she was never asked to pay as Teddy and I, at the request of Father Tryfon handled everything, we both shared the cost. Neither Teddy nor I sought recognition.

It was not the acts of kindness and good that were provided that influenced me, it was the way Father Tryfon went about providing these acts of kindness and good works which was important. There's an old Greek saying that says "Κάνε το καλό και ρίξτο στο γιαλό"; loosely translated to English it says, "Do a good deed and expect nothing in return." While my parents always stressed this to me as well as my brother and sister as we grew up, it was not till I saw Fr. Tryfon practice this as a part of his everyday life that I really realized its true meaning and importance.

Stepping forward to be kind and do good deeds should never be to gain recognition. Service to others should be from the heart without any request or expectation of recognition or reward. You do good works to serve others, not for recognition or reward from others. Father Tryfon was the embodiment of this saying, "Do a good deed and expect nothing in return."

After Fr. Tryfon passed away, a ledger book was found in his desk draw, a draw that he always kept locked. On one side of the ledger, he had chronologically entered all the gratuities he received for services he provided, be they house blessings, baptisms, weddings, etc... On the opposite page in the ledger, he recorded the disposition of these gratuities, all of which evidenced that he used the money to help people and not to help himself. This record went as far back as thirty years, the time he first arrived in Tarpon Springs, and assumed his assignment as the Dean of St. Nicholas Cathedral and the Spiritual Father to what would be decades of service to this Orthodox Christian community and the community of Tarpon Springs Florida.

As it turns out, he didn't keep any of the gratuities that he was given, but while never telling anyone he turned these gratuities into generosity and assistance to the many that he met and interacted with each day of his life that were in need. With these gratuities, Father Tryfon paid electric bills, bought food, and distributed turkeys on Thanksgiving Day and Christmas as well as among many other charitable acts to assist those in need. Fr. Tryfon brought joy and comfort to people, some of these people he knew and many he did not know; Fr. Tryfon did this to do good and never sought recognition. He took the generosity bestowed on him by others as gratuities and did not use them for himself but distributed these gratuities to those in need, never once asking or seeking recognition.

By knowing and understanding Father Tryfon's life and acts of kindness to all those around him, including strangers, we can learn what it truly means to be a Philanthropist, a truly great giver, unselfish caring, and loving person. It's not about the amount of money or time that you give but rather how much of yourself you give without expecting or asking for anything in return.

In January 2006, while not asking or expecting it, I was moved and happy that my wife Regina and I were the first recipients of the Very Rev. Father Tryfon Theophilopoulos Philanthropist of the Year" award. While we were named Philanthropist of the year, Fr. Tryfon was truly a Philanthropist as he taught us to give freely and without expectation of gain or recognition; Fr. Tryfon was the real Philanthropist as he always gave from whatever he had freely to those in need.

Fr. Tryfon's service to the Church and the Tarpon Springs Community made him a special person. I was fortunate to have him as a friend and for him to have been my spiritual advisor. I am Blessed to have participated in so many philanthropic acts of caring, kindness, love, and understanding with him.

An additional note, when I submitted my DNA to 23andMe, one of the DNA relatives that was revealed is a 4th cousin living in Amaliada Greece whose name is Michael Theofilopoulos. It says that we shared Grandparents four time removed. How or if he is related in anyway to my priest, very dear friend, and spiritual advisor for many years, Fr. Tryfon Theophilopoulos, is yet to be determined.

Reflecting upon doing good work, especially related to the younger generation, I think the most important thing for the younger generation to remember is that while serving others it is important to be humble. Whatever you may choose to do, whether you donate your time or resources, do not do it for recognition, do it with humility (leave any feeling of self-importance behind). What I have received throughout the years from helping others is private and comforting by having done these good works, this far exceeds any awards or articles written.

Remember, what you have, both physically and intellectually, is a gift bestowed upon you from God, you own nothing, it all belongs to him who has provided these gifts to you to do His works and His will. As such, one must utilize the gifts given to us by God unselfishly to help others. Utilizing God-given gifts to help others is the highest form of good works that one may achieve. Recognition and awards are not part of the package.

The End

APPENDIX A

Contribution from Fotis M. Platanidis

INTRODUCTION

I was invited by my elder cousin **William Planes,** son of **Peter** (Vasilios Platanidis, son of Panayiotis) who was brother to my late father **Minas,** to write about the ordeals and the struggles of the members of our family during World War II. As it is known, our family was established in Chania, Crete, Greece after the Genocide of the Greek population of Mikra Asia (Minor Asia) from the Turks. This is where the Great War found our family. The following testimony is written to be added in the book that William P. Planes is editing about the family history under the general title:

"ΠΛΑΤΑΝΙΔΗΣ (PLATANIDIS), through the eye of the storm...."

I am Fotios Platanidis, son of Minas. I was born in Athens, the capital of Greece in 1956. This is where my family was living because my father, Minas, was a military journalist and

Chief Editor of the monthly Journal of the Armed Forces of Greece under the name "ARIS" which had headquarters in the center of Athens, next to the Parliament.

My late father used to send me every summer to Chania in Crete island to pass the holiday time with our relatives. Sometimes he brought all the family there and we stayed in the houses of our relatives for the holiday, as they always did whenever they visited Athens where we were living. A family as a unity and the ancient rule of Greek Hospitality preserved!

I present this part of our family history following the testimonies of my late father **Minas Platanidis** son of **Fotios** mainly. Also, partially from my late uncles and aunts **Athanasios Platanidis** and his wife **Maritsa** and **Pantelis Platanidis** and his wife **Artemisia** whom I met and socialized with them in Chania of Crete many times since childhood.

Our cousin Professor **Andrew Spyridakis**, son of **Ioannis Spyridakis,** and our aunt **Panayiota Platanidis-Spyridakis**, added valuable information to my research and testimony. I do not recall token memories from his respectful parents because they passed away when I was a child.

A great help came from my nice **Joanna Platanidis**, daughter of **George Platanidis** and grand daughter of my uncle, **Athanasios**, providing me additive important documents for family history in this period, which she found in the archives-heritage of her grandfather and she remains the guard of our family grave in Agios Loukas Cemetery in Chania.

This testimony is based also on studying for years relevant historical books, family documents, and State Archives.

Of course, I listened to other testimonies from old people in Chania of Crete who lived within the facts of this War and survived from it, and of course they knew our family.

I never met our late uncle **Stavros Platanidis**, son of **Fotios** because he died at young age, just after the German Occupation of Crete. This happened due to war illnesses and the deterioration of his health, following the harsh conditions of living and fighting on the Northern Epirus - Albanian front where he served as a recruited soldier of the Greek Army. A similar fate had hundreds and finally thousands of his co-fighters of his Division. Additively, Stavros passed through a harsh interrogation in the hands of the notorious Gestapo during the German Occupation of Crete, as my father Minas have told me. Probably, this factor speeded up the decline of his health, too.

I never met my grandfather Fotios Platanidis son of Emmanuel and my grandmother Kiriaki Platanidis, coming from the Tsalikidis family.

They passed away in 1951 and 1953 accordingly. But I met them spiritually many times in my life, especially when I needed to borrow inspiration and courage from their stand in life.

Finally…as looks, relatives say that I am a 'copy' of my grandfather, Fotios!

In this appendix are included family documents that verify the following writing about the participation of our family in this historical and painful period.

WAR HITS PLATANIDIS FAMILY ONCE AGAIN

As we saw in the chapters before, Fotios Platanidis and his family escaped the Turkish Genocide of 1922 fleeing to main Greece. They remained for a period of almost 3 years in Refugee Camps in central Greece and Athens. Then, they were granted full Greek citizenship and they got permission to establish in Chania, Crete. This they did after the departure of their eldest son Panayiotis for America to study and become a doctor with the aid of the brother of our grandmother Kiriaki, **Pantelis Tsalikidis**.

He was established in the USA before the outbreak of the complete extermination of Hellenism in Mikra Asia (Minor Asia) by the guided by Germans, Turks. The suffering has started long before 1922, thus driving a lot of Greeks to immigrate before the complete catastrophe, including Pantelis Tsalikidis and his family. Here we have to mark that the ethnic cleansing of all Orthodox Christian populations of Mikra Asia had started in 1891 and again in 1909 with the Genocide of the Armenians and went on for Greeks and Assyrians later. The Germans under General Lehman von Sanders were organizing and the Turks were executing the mass crimes…. Life was unbearable for the Christian populations.

Our grandfather Fotios carried a family legend that a far ancestor of ours came from Crete. Possibly, that is why he was determined to establish in Crete. Thus, he avoided other propositions, like establishing in Athens. The truth is that in Crete, he felt -and all of us feel- like home as many of Platanidis family members carry the human type of a Cretan! Mysteries and questions for events through History…

During the peaceful period before World War II, the elder boys Athanasios, Pantelis, and Stavros had their military service done, in time for each one of them. Then, they remained in reserve, as all-male Greek citizens. Minas, the youngest one was growing to meet his military duty within the war days.

As it is known, fascist Italy declared war on Greece on 28th of October 1940, after the denial of Greece to allow Italian troops to enter and use for military purposes Greek territories and the State itself. Small Greece said "NO" to great Italy!! This is when Greece entered World War II.

Greece declared immediately mobilization to face the Italian attack. In this mobilization the remaining three elder sons of Fotios Platanidis, the **Athanasios, Pantelis,** and **Stavros** were called in arms and were recruited as they should. They joined the Cretan 5th Division of the Greek Army and accordingly they appeared in the 14th Chania Regiment of this Division. The war with Italians broke out on the Albanian frontier as the Italians invaded. They were stopped and turned back. Then the battles took place on the soil of Northern Epirus that was given to Albania from the Great Powers in 1914, although it was inhabited 100% by the Greek population... We have to mark here that the Albanian Regime collaborated with fascist Italy and took part in the attack on Greece! These were the main reasons that increased the passion of the officers and soldiers of the Greek Army who crushed the Italian strength, thus liberating a 3.000 years old part of Greece.

The 5th Cretan Division included recruited Athanasios and Stavros in the beginning and later on Pantelis. (Pantelis had a big vision problem -wearing thick glasses to the end of his life. So, he was not sent immediately to the front). The Cretan Division arrived at the end of November in Amyntaion of Makedonia by train and then they marched for 130 kilometers on the mountains by foot (!!!) in order to reach the front line. It was a hellish winter at that time and the Cretans coming from a Mediterranean +20 C temperature found a -20 C sometimes. They had to march within the snow and mud.

The Division took contact with the enemy on 29th of January 1941 and took the main effort at the deadliest battles of Klisoura, Trebesina, Sendeli, etc, where the Italian Army faced catastrophe and deterioration, humiliating Mussolinini's imperial arrogance!

The Cretan 5th Division paid the highest cost of casualties of all Greek Army during the Greek - Italian war and became famous for the heroism of its soldiers that struck accurately the Italian imperial Army and pride.

In these battles, **Athanasios** was hit on the head by a part of an Italian artillery shell. Semi-dead was captured prisoner of war by the Italians, who found him unconscious and gave him medical care for his severe wound thus saving his life. He was transferred to a Prisoners of War camp in Italy where he was cured. He remained there until the collapse and the surrender of fascist Italy to the Allies' Forces. In the chaos that came into Italy in September 1943, he escaped with others from the Prisoners of War camp and he fled to Switzerland, where he stayed till the end of the war in 1945. The family in Chania were under stress because of him because finally, they lost any contact with him not knowing if he survived under the chaotic circumstances of 1943. Switzerland was neutral in the War, but still, there was no communication with the occupied countries by the Nazi Germans...At the time, Athanasios was already married to Maritsa Glinouand they had a daughter who carried the name of our grandmother, Kiriaki.

Younger **Stavros**, not married, took part in the above-mentioned battles surviving from bullet wounds, as our cousin dc Andrew Spyridakis remembers. But in this continuous extremely cold and humid environment, staying without food for days sometimes, he got hard pneumonia that followed him and weakened him from then on and finally cost his life shortly. He died just after the German Occupation but he managed to see his beloved Crete and Greece free again.

As for **Pantelis**, we saw that he was not sent to the front in the first place probably due to his poor vision problem. Without glasses, he could not see..... Still, he volunteered and insisted to be sent on the front in exchange for Athanasios who was married and father of a child. Practically he offered his life in exchange for the life of his brother who had a family to support!! Pantelis at the time was not married, yet. Classic Greek family ethics of that time... Finally, his request was accepted and he was sent to the front. Unfortunately, his brother for whom he volunteered for exchange on the frontline was wounded and captured prisoner of war at the time that he arrived there. Pantelis shared the ordeals and the struggles of his fellow co-fighters and he was lucky not to be wounded on his body. But, he got tuberculosis due to the continuous lack of food supplies on the front, plus the deadly climate conditions. Tuberculosis and weakness, he carried to the end of his life.

Finally, the fascist Italian arrogant attack on Greece came to a dead end and the Greek troops liberated all Northern Epirus and were marching to dismantle all Albania. At this point Hitler took the decision to assist his Italian ally and attacked Greece from the north, using the Bulgarian Government's permit and aid for it. After a heroic resistance of the Greek Army on the Greek-Bulgarian frontier at the Forts of Metaxa, which was honored even by the German attackers, the Greek Army decided to stop the struggle and the bloodshed on two different fronts. A treaty was signed between the Greek and the German side where the officers and the soldiers of the Greek Army would be respected for their bravery and would not be treated as prisoners of war. So, at least **Stavros** and **Pantelis** were free to return to Crete after the dismantling of the Greek Army in Northern Greece. **Athanasios** remained a prisoner of war in Italy.

Most of the Cretan origin soldiers were anxious to find ways to return home and defend Crete since the King and the Government of Greece fled there to continue -as they said….- the struggle! Unfortunately, no measures were taken to transfer the Cretan 5th Division to the island... Thousands of soldiers without leadership had to walk all the way to southern Greece (1.000 kilometers) and try to find private solutions on how to return to their home island crossing the sea which was controlled strictly by air by the Germans. Many succeeded, including **Stavros** and **Pantelis,** but also many were lost... From the 20.000 more or less personnel of the Cretan Division, only 50% of them achieved, finally reached Crete. The majority of them achieved that after the Battle of Crete and the German bloody victory and occupation of the island.

The outcome of this historic and world-famous battle could be different if the Cretan 5th Division was transferred in time back to their home island of Crete to defend it, as many in Greece and worldwide historical writers accept...

PLATANIDIS FAMILY IN THE INFERNO OF THE BATTLE OF CRETE

As we saw, the heavy shadow of the German troops covered and occupied the main body of Greece. The Greek Government and King George fled to Crete as it was the last Greek free piece of land. In Crete gathered also the main body of the British Expeditionary Force included the British as well as Australians, New Zealanders and Greek Cypriots , and even Maoris from the British Commonwealth troops. They came to Greece in March of 1941. They were supposed to aid the Greek Army to stop the German advance, but most of them did not come in any contact with the enemy due to disagreements with the Greek Army Headquarters...

After a heroic resistance of the Greek Army on Metaxa's Forts, the Makedonian front collapsed and the British Expeditionary Force evacuated to Crete by all means. Along with them, followed parts of the dismantled Greek Army that had the will to continue the fight, ignoring the Treaty that was signed in Athens with the Germans for surrender and the end of hostilities. No measures were taken by the evacuating Government to transfer to Crete the heroic 5th Cretan Division, at least...

All sides -Greek and British- expressed the will to defend Crete with long speeches and proclamations, but no serious preparation was done for such a purpose.

The Germans organized Operation MERCURY (HERMES) in order to conquer and occupy Crete, in their efforts to capture or deport Allies' troops from the island. They needed the island for its strategic point towards North Africa and they wanted to create a safe zone against Allies' air raids on the valuable oil fields in Romania. These were supplying with fuels the war efforts of the 3rd Reich! For this strategic purpose, they did not want the air fields of Crete to be in the hands of the Allies...

Chania got the first taste of war on 29th of November 1940. A squadron of Italian bombers coming from the airport of occupied Rodos dropped bombs on Chania city and port. Rare damages were done and few casualties occurred. Some fell near Platanidis family house, but no damage was done on it.

The real horror came on the 14th of May 1941. The 8th German Air Fleet hit Crete with hundreds of bombers on military targets as well as on the cities of Chania, Rethymnon, and Heraklion aiming to terrorize the Cretan population. Whole parts of the 3 cities became rumble. Hundreds of peaceful civilians were killed and thousands were injured. Chania center and port became a pile of rumbles. Many historical constructions and buildings got totally destroyed or hurt inevitably. That was a preparation for the air assault that they were planning for the attack on Crete using mainly the famous German Para-troopers.

Fotios Platanidis family house is placed at Skoufon 43 street, within the old city which is surrounded by the medieval castle walls. In simple words, their house found itself in the middle of the bombing zone of the German air-bombers!! Three out of hundreds of photos follow to show how Chania looked like after these criminal air raids that targeted the civilian population.

Our family house had a German bomb falling next to it, destroying the neighbor building and causing severe damages to ours. One floor was fallen but the ground floor stood. This new disaster Fotios and his wife Kiriaki had to face alone.....

Their eldest son Panayiotis was in the US. Athanasios, Stavros, and Pantelis were sent to the Albanian front and the youngest Minas was recruited and was sent to the Centre for Army Training of Tripolis in Peloponnesus on 7th of April 1941. That was the day that the Germans hit Greece.

Their daughter Panayiota with her children was next to her husband, Ioannis Spyridakis, who was an officer of the Royal Peripheral Police and at the time was Chief of the Police Station of Ebrosneros, a mountain town some 40 kilometers away from Chania.

Somebody can imagine the feelings and the stress of Fotios and Kiriaki. They had 4 of their sons in the turmoil of the war fronts, not knowing if they are alive and now they had to survive in a semi fallen house surrounded by rumbles with utilities destroyed..... The building in which Fotios was operating a tobacco shop nearby the house did not fall, but the shop was destructed and remained a wreck for a long time. A photograph coming from the German Archives shows the condition of it a long time after the bombing of Chania and the Battle of Crete. (Somebody can see clearly the name ΠΛΑΤΑΝΙΔΗΣ marked on it in this photo. The Zundapp three-wheel motorcycle outside of it belongs to the German Feldgendarmerie-Military Police). As anybody can understand, the means of living were brought to zero, once more for the Platanidis family.

New tragedy and new ashes after Smyrna for Fotios and Kiriaki. They survived the Genocide of the Turks in 1922 plus the refugee life in poverty and diseases for three years and now they had to face the German Nazi barbarian actions in 1941 that were destroying everything. The lives and the survival of their four sons were uncertain....

Writing these lines I realize what they passed through and I wonder the size of their physical and psychological strength!!! What quality of people were they, these eternal Greeks???

We described previously what happened with Athanasios, Stavros, and Pantelis and why they were absent at the days of the Battle of Crete, serving on a different front. We will follow Minas trail, who took part in the events and battles that followed in Crete.

Minas, in 1939 applied to join the Military Academy of Greece in order to become an Officer of the Greek Army after graduating. He followed the dreams of his father, Fotios.

As I was told by relatives, he had a very good performance at the relevant exams. Still, he was cut due to the fact that he came from a family that were followers of the dreams of the known democrat Eleftherios Venizelos.

At the time in Greece were kept records of the political beliefs of the citizens. You should carry a 'certificate' of 'correct' political beliefs to progress to any direction...

Unfortunately, Greeks were divided between Democrats and Royalists. Since Greece was governed then by strict right-wing Royalist personnel led by Ioannis Metaxas, Minas got no chance to proceed... He kept no regret for this. In his mind, Greece was upon any divisive political beliefs.

Our family was not nationalists or fanatics of any kind. They were simply patriots that followed the dreams of Eleftherios Venizelos for the liberation from the Turks of all Greek populations and sacred soils since the ancient era... This is the 'stand in life' that we were taught by them.

Putting aside his disappointment, he appeared on 16th of October 1940 at the 14th Regiment of the 5th Cretan Division to serve his military duty. Fotios and Kiriaki finally were left with their daughter Panayiota only, next to them. Even her, she had to be with her children and her husband who was a serving officer of the Peripheral Police, with increased duties due to war.

As it is known, on 28th of October 1940 fascist Italy attacked Greece. The three elder brothers of Minas were recruited and sent to the Albanian Front. (Athanasios and Stavros immediately and Pantelis later on). Following the need for somebody to take care of the old parents that had already sent 3 sons to the front line, Minas was temporarily released on the 1st of December of 1940, according to the Military records.

Still, the needs of the Army increased further for more recruits after the heavy casualties on the Albanian Front and the prospective of a German attack. So, Minas was recruited again and sent and appeared to the Center of Military Training in Tripolis of Peloponnesus on 7th of April of 1941. That was the day that Hitlerite Germany declared war and attacked Greece.

Finally, Fotios and Kiriaki stayed alone! During the air raids of the 14th of May, Ioannis Spyridakis and our aunt Panayiota's house in Nea Chora of Chania received a harsh visit from the German bombs, and severe damages were done to it. The house could not be inhabited. This pushed Ioannis to take Panayiota and the children to Ebrosneros. He was afraid of further air raids. He took care and all along with other women and children of the town, he put them in some mountain caves, where the locals were hiding during the Turkish tyranny. As a Chief of the local Police station, he helped the population to be protected and not be in the battle zone. The men left the town to take part in the fight. Panayiota and her children were watching from above in some safety the drama that was going on at the lower places where the Germans were landing -as our cousin, Professor Andrew Spyridakis remembers being a child at the time.

Athanasios, prisoner of War wife, Maritsa with her daughter Kiriaki, found shelter in the village of Fre, where Maritsa's relatives received them and protect them.

So, Fotios and Kiriaki remained again alone. They thought that they had to stay and keep the family house in Chania! Having their children spread by the winds of the war, they probably felt that they should stay there as a duty to anyone of them that would survive from the storm and needed family and shelter to recover!

Just to keep the torch of hope lighted with no stop! The vital link for the re-unification of the family. They were almost sacrificed for this reason on the German air raids of 14th of May and the semi-destruction of their house...

As we know, after the collapse of the Macedonian Front, some separated units of the dismantled Greek Army that did not accept the Surrender Treaty, tried to follow the Government and the King to Crete. They participated in a last attempt to build up a defense and resistance stronghold to German aggression.

Mina's unit, of 8 battalions with untrained yet soldiers(!!) were asked from their commanders for their possible wish to follow since they were untrained for war. As Minas testified later, they all volunteered to continue the struggle by all means! They left the barracks in Tripoli in central Peloponnesus and following their officers marched by feet for days all the way down to the sea in Monemvasia some and Kalamata others hoping to find ships to transfer them to Crete. Despite the endless attacks of the German Air force and having few casualties by miracle, they achieved that. In the night the high seas were under the control of The Allies' fleet since the German Air Force could not operate. This situation helped them to reach Crete.

Mina's battalion was placed in Heraklion. As we described, on 14th of May 1941 they faced the massive air raids of the German Air Force. On 20th of May, the skies were filled with thousands of German parachute troops dropped by hundreds of Junger carriage planes and linked gliders coming from the airfields of occupied central Greece. The supreme force of Hitler's Army! The deadliest battles and fights took place in all sights of Northern Crete with the German paratroops that landed. The carnage reached beyond belief... Historians from all sides stand to prove the allegation...

Minas and his fellow soldiers faced the well-trained and fully equipped German paratroopers with the old type of arms -and lack of ammunition, sometimes! They put up strong defenses against the enemy. On the third day of the battle 22nd of May, Minas was wounded badly with penetrating trauma on the left lung and another penetrating one on the left arm. As he described later he was aiming at a German paratrooper at the same time that he was aiming at him. He understood that the German was also shot by him, but still, he made it for a second shot...

Due to the importance of the traumas -especially the lung one- Minas was hardly breathing, vomiting blood , and was kept in life due to his very strong organism. He was picked up by fellow soldiers and with about 15 other wounded Greeks, who trusted them to a retreating Allies unit in order to take them to a safe place and out of the battle zone. This was not done and the heavily wounded Greek soldiers were left at an agricultural house that had an underground cellar for the wines of the family that used to live there. At the time of the incident, the injured were received by an old Cretan lady that was in the house with two grandchildren of hers. With the aid of others, the injured were put in the underground cellar. The German front line was close...

To their bad luck Germans achieved to break defenses of the Greek soldiers and civilian volunteers temporarily in that area. Getting to the agriculture house and seeing the trails from the blood of the wounded soldiers, discovered their shelter. As they were furious from the very heavy casualties that they already suffered to the moment, they executed the old lady and her two grandchildren(!!!) and dropped several grenades in the wine cellar to kill also the injured that were lying there unarmed(!!!). Their legitimate soldier's uniforms were visible......

Anybody knowing the least from the Geneva Convention about the War rules and ethics of the civilized nations regarding Prisoners of War can understand in which wild animal level the Nazis transformed the German soldiers' ethics...

The result was that half of the about 16 wounded soldiers died immediately and some of the survivors later on. Next to Minas was lying a fellow soldier who absorbed the main blast of an explosion saving thus the life of Minas who suffered minor injuries on both of his legs and body. As he remembered at a glimpse of an eye the legs of his savior colleague next to him had 'disappeared'!!

Minas carried some pieces of the German grenades in legs and arms stuck on the bones for life.

Finally, at a new attack of the Greeks and the equal temporary retreat of the Germans from the area, the surviving injured of the wine storage cellar were rescued. Minas was carried and delivered to the **Pananion Hospital of Heraklion** on 23rd of May, where he stayed hospitalized for almost 5 months. He 'escaped' from the Hospital on the 4th of October 1941 although he was not totally cured, in very tense circumstances regarding his body safety and his freedom.

You see, the dark night of the German occupation had started in Crete, and collaborators of the enemy appeared..... At the time, Fotios and Kiriaki thought that Minas was killed in battle.

The good news for his survival came after they have done the ceremony of 40 days for his memory, by a co-fighter that he finally informed them that he survived wounded.

OCCUPATION-RESISTANCE-LIBERATION in Crete 1941-1945

Getting into this era of four difficult years, we follow the adventures of the three out of four brothers that after months would rejoin their family in Chania and start cooperation in order to survive within the new catastrophe. Athanasios was kept as a prisoner of war in Italy. The situation and their patriotic values taught by their father and mother pushed them finally to join the Resistance against the German occupation and help the Allies' efforts with their struggle.

As it is known and as the historians from all sides admit, there was not a serious preparation for the defense of Crete, the last free Greek piece of land. The reasons for it were various. Greek dividing politics and British hidden plans prepared the grounds for defeat and let Crete face the four years nightmare in the hands of the Hitlerites.

The Greek Government took no steps to repatriate the 5th Cretan Division to Crete. The British Air Force left Crete uncovered and the retreating British Expeditionary Force found itself even unarmed in cases..... They had left a massive amount of their arms and equipment on the main body of Greece's ports fleeing to Crete!

The well-trained and experienced (from the war in the Albanian Front) 20.000 fighters of the 5th Cretan Division could make it impossible for the Germans to conquer the island.

They were missing now...

An effective air cover of Crete from the Allies could make sure the option of Victory. This basic factor was missing, too.....

Only the British fleet that dared to operate in the nights, sank all the efforts of the Germans to land on Crete military aids to their paratrooper's units.

The German air assault on 20th of May 1941 engaged in battle by force the Allies' troops that were seriously thinking to flee to Egypt. They had to fight back. There were also the leftovers of the Greek Army. In a not well-organized defense environment an unexpected 'army' came for assistance. The civilian villagers of Crete carry primitive weaponry or agricultural tools sometimes!! ....you see, the Authorities and the British Command were reluctant to arm them to the last moment!!....

The Cretans following their fighting tradition from the years of the Turkish occupation voluntarily came in the struggle to defend the island against the Germans' attack and assist the

Greek and Allies' Forces. Historians wrote a lot for the heroism of the unexpected volunteer army of the Cretan civilians!

Pages of heroism were written also by stubborn Australians and brave New Zealanders. Maoris from New Zealand reassured their fame as bravest fighters!

After ten days of a Battle that shook the globe, Crete was occupied by the Germans. The victory was bitter for them! Their elite paratrooper's force had almost 50% of casualties (dead, wounded, and missing!!!). Hitler felt so disappointed that he ordered the dismantling of their units, forever!

Then, the Germans started violent reprisals against the population that resisted their attacking forces. Mass executions took place against the males from the age of 14 and on, up to elders of 70 and 80 years old. Villages were destroyed by explosives and arson. The Germans were looking for revenge for their heaviest casualties, with exploding wrath on the population.

In these circumstances, Minas was 'trapped' in Pananion Municipal Hospital of Heraklion due to his heavy battle wounds. This period of 5 months of hospitalizing he spend in continuous stress of a possible arrest and execution from the Germans. He decided to leave the hospital as soon as his wounds permit him. He was pushed to do this since a new factor came on...,

When the German occupation stabilized and controlled everything, collaborators and informants appeared among the impoverished population. They were few but accurate... There were also few educated pro-German intellectuals. Minas proved unlucky because a pro-German surgeon doctor of the Hospital supervised his case!! This person was expressing publicly his anger for "the barbarian village Cretans that slaughtered the gentle soldiers of the 3rd Reich".....

In October 1941 this 'doctor' signed an order for 'a further surgery action' on Minas legs. This surgeon had a cruel record of handicapped soldiers after his 'surgeries'...

At this point, Minas made his move. With the aid of certain personnel of the Hospital who were silent, but helping patriots left the Hospital in the night dressed in civilian clothes.

It took a few days since resistance connections brought him to the town of Vamos, close to Chania. There, he hides for two months under the care of **Ioannis Klonaris,** Headmaster of the High School of the area of Apokoronas. Minas was wanted because he deserted the hospital without permission. The German Army Headquarters in Heraklion were informed and were looking for him.....

The unforgettable **Ioannis Klonaris,** a brilliant personality of Chania and Crete and devoted patriot, happened to be the ex-professor of Minas in high school. Among them, there were strong soul ties, as their correspondence shows! He made it possible for Minas to hide and take further care of his serious wounds and so survive! May his memory be eternal!!

Under these circumstances, Minas joined the resistance efforts that have started among the Cretans within the first days of occupation. He stayed in Vamos until he stood well on his feet and purchased false identity documents supplied by the resistance circles. Then he made his first approach to Chania in April 1941 and finally met with his parents Fotios and Kiriaki, as well as his brothers Stavros and Pantelis. Later on, he met with his sister Panayiota and her family. That was one more miracle for the family.

As we described before, Stavros and Pantelis served at the Albanian Front as recruits of the 5th Cretan Division. After the attack of the Germans, the defeat and the surrender of the Greek Army, they were trapped in the main body of Greece. Reading the memories of other co-soldiers of Stavros and Pantelis in the 5th Division that they had survived and finally landed on Crete, we can presume the unbelievable details of their Odyssey... Unfortunately, Stavros died young and Pantelis left no written or verbal memories for this feat.

Pantelis seemed that he wanted to forget all the hard experiences of war and death. As soon as he managed to land on Crete and come back to our family house he got married and started a family with our aunt Artemisia. Soon, they had their children within the war. Kiriaki (Koula) was born in 1943 and Fotios in 1945. Later on, two more children followed, although the drama of civil war continued the flow of blood, sweat, and tears for the Greek people.

At the time, groups of Cretans fled on the high mountains of the island and formed armed guerilla groups in order to fight the occupying island German forces and take revenge for the losses of their beloved caused by them. The mountain villages offered them assistance in food and shelter at hard times. The Allies' Headquarters for the Middle East based in Cairo of Egypt encouraged the efforts of the guerilla groups. It was suitable for them to occupy Germans in conflicts within the occupied by them areas. The first fights started and German reprisals followed. All Cretan patriots put aside any political differences declared present in the call of duty. Everybody should offer according to what he could to the countless needs of the struggle.

Fotios and his sons' souls were in flames... They could not forget. The Germans who organized Kemal Ataturks' units and assist the plans for the ethnic cleansing and expel of the Greeks from their ancient lands in Mikra Asia were in front of them again, killing, destroying, and occupying. The feeling for resistance came spontaneously. Their situation put them at the post where they could serve better. Fotios was in his 64 years old, exhausted from the sufferings during the Genocide. Stavros and hiding Minas carried sensitive health due to the war ordeals and wounds. They could not follow the free guerillas on the steep high mountains of Crete that have harsh weather conditions. This would kill them quickly. They followed the dangerous path of the urban guerilla. The one that has the risk of life daily acting within the enemy lines. Pantelis carrying tuberculosis from the Albanian Front wanted to settle, but also helped!

Stavros, as a carpenter and builder, succeeded to reconstruct enough of the upper floor of the house that was destroyed by the German bombs. Pantelis and Artemisia, as soon as they got married, established in the family house, in Skoufon 43, on the restored by Stavros upper floor. The presence of a new family living with the parents of the groom and babies on the way provided later on a good cover for resistance activities...

Minas had already been in contact with the resistance organizations EAM and EOK. At the time all resistance organizations cooperated and synchronized their activities with the needs of the Allies' operations in the general Middle East. They secured for him false documents so he could move freely without the danger of immediate arrest by the Occupation Forces. Controls were strict and German Martial Law could send somebody easily in front of the firing squad.....

Our family house was used as one more base for hiding arms, correspondence of the organizations, and other essential materials needed to Resistance. Fotios was the supervisor and his sons were the active members of the participation in the resistance activities. Minas was the 'secret agent' of the family, Stavros was the soldier for difficult works, and Pantelis with his family and the elders was the cover of the operations! I remember our aunt Artemisia saying to me in her very old days: "....we were very lucky to survive during the Occupation when I remember what things and people Minas and Stavros were bringing in the house....". For activities like that the Germans held responsible the total family and their firing squad was waiting tirelessly for new victims.

Fotios with Minas used also his little shop at the Port of Chania as a meeting point for secret resistance people that were presented themselves as traders or interested clients that wanted to buy the broken by the air raids shop!

Finally, Minas purchased false papers where he appeared like a trader. Using those he managed to travel to Piraeus and Athens with a commercial barge type vessel and so help the transfer of correspondence and persons wanted by Germans under their nose. The covering reason was the transfer and trading of the carobs towards the starving population of the Greek capital, Athens. His experience with the sea brought further duties in front of him:

A big problem had occurred from the first day of the Occupation. A lot of British, Australian, New Zealander's officers, and soldiers that did not arrive in time at the embarkation points to flee to Egypt, were left behind. Some did not find space for them in the filled ships of evacuation. There were 3.000 approx., of them wandering around the island trying to avoid the captivity by the Germans. The hospitable Cretan villagers gave them shelter, food, and cover. This brought a headache to the Greek resistance because when the Germans found any hidden Allies' personnel arrested them and send them to Prisoners of War Camps. This did not count for the Cretan families that provided the strictly forbidden shelter with the death penalty. Many hospitable families that showed solidarity to the officers and soldiers of the Allies were exterminated. The Allies personnel should go and at the same time avoid captivity by the enemy.

In these circumstances, Minas was among the ring of trustee people that were selected to transfer smoothly groups of Allies' officers and soldiers to the south of Crete in the Sfakia region and then travel them by boat to salvation and freedom. Sfakia is placed on the Libyan sea and across North Africa. From there, using large fishing boats, he was traveling all night to cross the sea, bring his 'special guests' in Libya and Egypt, and lay them in the hands of Allies Forces. The night hours were not enough to cover all distance from Crete to the North Africa coast. They covered 2/3 of it. But with the first light of the day, they were protected under the wings of the Allied Air Force that was alerted every time for their arrival by the resistance networks.

Minas never referred extensively to his sons about these operations for reasons that my cousin William P. Platanidis, the author of this book explains..... So I cannot clearly describe who did what exactly... A few times that he talked about those times in front of us, I understood that all family members knew and were supporting these operations with more or less involvement in them. All families could join the German-made death row if something went wrong!! This is what I understood from rare faint references of other members of the family. Many of the details of this writing are taken from testimonies of other co-fighters of the Platanidis brothers that knew and cooperated with them.

In different circumstances, Athanasios being in the Prisoners of War Camp in North Italy prepared his own resistance to the Axis of the Fascists and Nazis. With some colleagues Greeks etc., they were preparing their escape from the Prison Camp. They found a good chance in September 1943 when the Mussolini regime collapsed and Italy asked for a Truce with the Allies. In this upside-down and before the Germans capture by their forces all Italy, Athanasios and some of his co-prisoners broke the Camp perimeter and fled to Switzerland which was neutral during the war, respected by all.

Still there he remained isolated and the good news did not travel to his family in Chania until the end of the War. As we referred before, he was counted missing on the Albanian Front and after a first censored letter that came to the family from the Prisoner's of War Camp, there was no communication at all. Not even Minas' high resistance connections with the Middle East could not supply some worthy information about Athanasios's fate. Our aunt Maritsa thought that she became a widow... Thankfully, God had other plans for Athanasios. A photo of his first and final censored letter appears in this edition.

Returning our view on Chania again, we see Minas getting in serious trouble in 1944. All these participations in operations and the exposure of his face to various persons finally brought the Gestapo on the trail of Minas activities. This happened to a number of his colleagues in resistance networks. Unfortunately, all along with heroes and patriots, appear traitors and volunteered slaves as well through History. They come from the darkest side of the human race. As a known Cretan politician wrote, "they rise from the sewer of society".....

Due to the aid of such persons, Gestapo (the Nazi German Secret Police) arrested a number of urban resistance fighters and commanders in the Chania Region. Minas was arrested, too. Many simple supporters were arrested along with them. It is possible that in this 'harvest' Stavros was taken too, as a suspect. My father Minas told me once that Stavros suffered from the consequences of the extreme weather conditions on the Albanian Front and the ordeals of the retreat. He added that his arrest and mistreatment in the hands of the notorious German Secret Police, his health condition became even worse and drove him to death a little bit later.

There are a few questions left for us. Putting the pieces together with logic we can make a clear clue since the elders were not talking a lot about their adventures in order to 'protect' the fantasy and the feelings of the young ones.....

Minas used false identity documents in the beginning, provided by the Resistance circles. It is possible that he carried them when he was arrested by Gestapo. In that case, somebody can understand why the Germans did not arrest the total Platanidis family. Given the fact that Minas stood bravely against the investigating methods of Gestapo and did not reveal his real identity, the family was protected. Stavros's case was probably in a different direction... Still, we lack information about what exactly happened to him. The sure thing is that the war campaign with its ordeals and the harsh German mistreatment drove him to an early death. He is another fallen for Homeland.

Minas after he did not 'talk' and refused cooperation with the Germans, was driven in front of the German Martial Court of Chania. This 'court' sentenced him with a **'twice in death'** penalty. Then he was driven to Agia Prison where patriots sentenced to death from all Cretan territories were forwarded to be executed. There he lived for a while awaiting execution along with several Chania personalities and citizens who shared with him the same fate.

Minas was lucky, finally. The German Commander of occupied Crete, General Brauer, was depressed from the continuous defeats of the German Army in the Eastern Front, and the landing of the Allies in Southern Italy. He understood that Germany was losing the war. He decided not to pull the rope around his neck further..... He ordered his subordinates to stop executions. On the 25th of March 1944, -the date that the Greeks celebrate the National Liberation Day from the Turks- he offered Amnesty for the persons convicted to death for 'political crimes'. Around one hundred or more executives of resistance and freedom fighters avoided execution and were set free! The death row stopped a few cells before Minas one... The happiness and relief in the humble house of Skoufon 43 was beyond belief. Kiriaki had done all possible prayers for the savior of the life of her youngest child. She felt happy as well as proud.

Proud Fotios M. Platanidis after and Athanasios return in 1945 saw one by one his sons coming back from death and covered with National Pride as they have done their duty to the homeland! He made them be like that and now he was paid with pride for all the efforts and sacrifices that their out bringing has taken!!

A Certificate of Gratitude signed by the Field-Marshal and Supreme Allied Commander of the Mediterranean Theater of War, Haig R. Alexander, was awarded to Minas as a recognition of his services to the Allies' cause and the salvation of many of their personnel entrapped in Crete. A copy of it is presented in this edition. This is a document that was saved and explains a lot to any interested party.

Minas received that after the end of WW II from General H. R. Alexander himself. He always thought that it came as a recognition for the struggle and sacrifices of all members of our family.

P.S

An additive testimony was given to me about Minas resistance and humanitarian activities, by Emilios Matalon, a Jewish Greek citizen, who was a close neighbor in Athens. He had settled there after the War. All of his relatives perished tragically in Auswitz Concentration Camp.

He was married to Mrs. Esther, after the Holocaust and at the end of the War. She and her two brothers only were rescued from their big family that perished as well tragically in the German Concentration Camps. My father and my mother kept company with them since they were old and had no children. They were both educated and interesting personalities.

Emilios appreciated very much my father Minas! He liked the company and the friendship of my parents and our intellectual and artistic social environment. Mr. Matalon has studied logistics and he was the cashier of a famous business enterprise of Athens in luxury fabrics called "EL GRECO", owned by the Tabah family.

This couple enjoyed very much the old romantic songs of Athens (kandata) and the music of Mikis Theodorakis and Manos Chatzidakis. Whenever we had people for dinner and joy time at home, they were invited and ate and sing with the friends of my parents. One day my mother made cookies that Mrs. Esther liked very much. She ordered me to take fresh-made cookies to her. I arrived at their apartment and accomplished my mother's wish. Then Mr. Emilios, lying in bed due to aches of age called me and expressed his best feelings for us and his gratitude for the general attitude of my parents towards them.

Before I left for home, Emilios held my hand and told me: "Fotis, I will tell you that, today: Your father Minas saved a Jewish family during the German Occupation! Remember that for life". I felt touched by this declaration and I went home and expected my father to return from his office and explain to me the testimony of Mr. Emilios.

My father as he usually did on matters about the Genocide and the War, avoided my questions..... Later on, I confirmed the testimony of our friend Mr. Emilios Matalon! Delegates of the families referred were present for the last salute at Minas Platanidis funeral in March 1977.....

THE EPILOGUE

Somewhere here ends the partial Odyssey of the Platanidis family during World War II.

It is known that the main body of the German Occupation Forces retreat from Greece in October 1944. This did not happen for 15.000 well-armed German troops in Crete. Somehow they were 'trapped'.(?) For sure, the Germans had no fleet to evacuate them.

After the Amnesty that General Brauer offered, Chania lived in a moratorium between the Germans and the strong Resistance Organizations that held strong positions on the nearby mountains. Still, the Germans continued hostilities in cases of conflicts with the guerillas, or conflicts of interest with civilians. Finally, all the German units in Crete concentrated in Chania Region.

These Germans came to an agreement straight with a delegation of British Officers from Allies Middle East Command, where:

1. They were allowed to keep their arms and weaponry and they continued to be responsible to enforce the law and keep the public order in Chania Region under the supervision of the Allies' Command of the Middle East Forces(!!!!!!).

2. This would stand until there would be found a way to leave as a whole untouched by the Local Authorities of Crete and Greece.

That was a great paradox within the Great War! The Greeks were sacrificed in this war. They should enjoy more respect from our Allies...

As we referred, the German troops withdrew (retreat) from Greece in October 1944. The 'trapped' in Crete German troops concentrated in a zone around Chania and its surrounding area on the north side of Crete. All the way till the middle days of August of 1945 (!!!) the Germans were occupying the above-mentioned territory under British order, armed and ruling. They were not under the control of the Greek Government that was already established in the rest of the country. They did not surrender to Greek Authorities, as they should be forced by the winning Allies. Greece was, supposedly, one of them...

Berlin was fallen in the first day of May 1945 and on the 9th of May, the World War II finished. But still, German troops were allowed to rule and impose 'law and order' in this part of northern Crete, up to the middle of August 1945. During the 6 months period since the German retreat from Greece, plus the 3 months period after the official end of the war, they were imposed by the Allies to exercise power in Chania territory and they came in fight several times with the guerilla freedom fighters and civilians, trying to eliminate them... The only 'change' that came was that their commanding officer was replaced by the blood-thirsty General Bendak. More victims of the German aggression were added to the long list that the Germans achieved to offer to Crete's population...

Platanidis family had to suffer this additive period, all along with the rest population of Chania the German rule and Occupation.

Then a catastrophic Civil War came for Greece, fueled by the Great Powers of the time. Cold War has started... Pantelis was recruited again for this and thankfully he survived! At the time that all peoples of Europe enjoyed Peace and Reconstruction since 1945, Greece had to bleed up to 1950!

Minas, after WW II and the Greek Civil War, as a military reporter, was touched by the struggle of the Greek Cypriots in the 1950es for the liberation from Colonialism and the Unification with Greece, led by Georgios Grivas - Digenis. The request of the Cypriots, who offered many of their children as soldiers to the British Commonwealth for WW II was denied by the British Crown. Oppression measures were taken.

Minas, as expected, supported this fair struggle by his articles on the press and God knows what else he did…. The 'silence code' to the young ones re-appeared for this case, too! We are left with some photos of him with Archbishop of Cyprus, Makarios, and the thankful writings of certain known Cypriots….

Minas, so disappointed the British Colonial Authorities committing even atrocities on the Cyprus population during the Cypriot Liberation Struggle and proceeded even sending several fighting children of Cyprus to the gallows pole...

All along with Minas, Athanasios, Stavros, and Pantelis were disappointed to see that Northern Epirus -that was liberated again by the Greek Army and their personal bloody efforts in 1940, still was given again to the artificial state of Albania, due to geopolitics interests of the Allies. At the time Northern Epirus held 400.000 persons of Greek population with at least 3.000 years proved presence in the area and all of the important cities carrying still their ancient Greek names!!

That was tragic for Fotios and his sons and all the Greek people. Such behavior was not expected to take place by the Allies with which we fought together against German totalitarianism and for the values of Democracy and Freedom. The Greek Nation offered so much blood, sweat, and tears in two World Wars.

Greece was supposed to be among the winners in the two World Wars, but still received ingratitude and no gains from Her involvement in common causes that cost holocausts.

Germany, -wealthy Germany of today- did not pay still the War Reparations to Greece for the catastrophes, the killings, and total damages that they have done to any aspect of life in this country, including the looting of the Greek Treasury using the known 'Forced Loan for the needs of War.' On the contrary, their banks were allowed to drive Greece of today in impoverishment. Probably, they take revenge for our Resistance against their dictator plans to rule the World….

Minas, my father, perished at the age of 58 years old, due to implications caused by the old war wounds.

Stavros perished in his 30 years due to war and German mistreatment.

Athanasios has gone up to 66 years. Without the war ordeals, he could reach 100 years old, easily!

Pantelis, despite tuberculosis and the continuous weakness after his participation in the war, reached 77years!!! Call it a miracle!! Panayiota reached 59 years only, carrying a big family and bringing up children in this full of turbulence period.

Fotios and Kiriaki reached 74 years, despite all the nightmares that they had to fight in life. For sure they could approach a century of life if they avoided all the ordeals that are described in this book by the Vampires of History like the Turkish barbarians and the German nationalists.

Their souls met with my late uncle Panayiotis in the Heavens!

May their Memory be Eternal!!

I thank from heart all the Americans and the Greek-Americans that will show the patience to read the details of Platanidis family struggles, ordeals, and sacrifices in World War II as part of the endless Greek Drama. I wish the last ones never to forget the roots of their origin and be proud of them!

Hellenism remains light for Humanity!

Fotios Platanidis, son of Minas   Athens 2021

P.S.

Greeks are clever people and know how to enjoy life. They proved once more best fighters for freedom and independence and as Winston Churchill declared for the heroism of the Greek Army in the Albanian Front:

"….from now and on we will not say that the Greeks fight like heroes. We have to say that heroes fight like the Greeks!!!"

…..it seems that these Greeks forget quickly the lessons of History and they trust words…..! They should be more wise and careful if they want to survive in the future world avoiding new tragedies…..

APPENDIX B

The Seven Churches in Revelations

According to Revelation 1:11, on the Greek island of Patmos, Jesus Christ instructs John of Patmos to: "Write on a scroll what you see and send it to the seven churches: to Ephesus, and to Smyrna, and to **Pergamum, and to Thyatira, and to Sardis, and to Philadelphia, and to Laodicea**." The churches in this context refers ... to the community or local congregations of Christians living in each city.

The seven churches

The seven churches are named for their locations. The Book of Revelation provides descriptions of each Church.

- Ephesus (Revelation 2:1-7): known for having labored hard and not fainted, and separating themselves from the wicked; admonished for having forsaken its first love (2:4)

- Smyrna (Revelation 2:8-11): admired for its tribulation and poverty; forecast to suffer persecution (2:10)

- Pergamum (Revelation 2:12-17): located where 'Satan's seat' is; needs to repent of allowing false teachers (2:16)

- Thyatira (Revelation 2:18-29): Known for its charity, whose "latter works are greater than the former"; tolerates the teachings of a false prophetess (2:20)

- Sardis (Revelation 3:1-6): admonished for - in contrast to its good reputation - being dead; cautioned to fortify itself and return to God through repentance (3:2-3)

- Philadelphia (Revelation 3:7-13): known as steadfast in the faith, keeping God's word, and enduring patiently (3:10)

- Laodicea, near Denizli (see Laodicean Church) (Revelation 3:14-22): called lukewarm and insipid (3:16)

What Do the 7 Churches in Revelation Represent? Summaries and Explanations

The Book of Revelation addresses seven letters to seven churches in Asia Minor. Each letter, as proclaimed by Jesus Christ and recorded by John the Apostle, declares the triumphs and failures of the recipient churches and warns each congregation to repent.

The advice in these letters is prophetic, forewarning present-day Christian communities of the snares that can lure us away from our faith.

Who Wrote Revelation?

Christian scholars from the **second century to date** have attributed the physical writing of Revelation to John the Apostle, son of Zebedee (**Mark 3:17**), and author of the Gospel and Epistles of John. Although John literally wrote Revelation, the Book makes it clear that the source of the **revelations** is Jesus (**Revelation 1:1-2**).

In the first century A.D., the Apostle John was exiled to the island of Patmos, a Roman penal colony near Asia Minor. John's "crime" was practicing Christianity. While in Patmos, John was seized by the Holy Spirit and received prophetic visions from Christ instructing him to: "Write on a scroll what you see and send it to the seven churches: to Ephesus, Smyrna, Pergamum, Thyatira, Sardis, Philadelphia, and Laodicea" (**Revelations 1:1-2**; 9-11).

Why Were These Seven Churches Chosen to Receive the Apocalyptic Message?

Revelation's seven churches were among several early Christian communities in Asia Minor. These particular seven churches may have been chosen to receive Christ's apocalyptic message because, geographically, the churches were located along an **established, circular trade**

route that brought together the most populous and influential parts of the province. Once the apocalyptic message was given to the churches in these prominent cities, the message would spread to the Christian communities in the rest of the province.

Although the seven letters in Revelation are tailored to the named churches, these churches and their stated deficiencies can symbolize all churches in one respect or another. The instruction given to Revelation's congregations, therefore, is valuable to Christian congregations today.

<u>Where Were the Seven Churches and What Do They Symbolize?</u>

1. Ephesus. The Church that Has Abandoned Its Love for Christ and His Teachings (Revelation 2:1-7)

Summary and Explanation: Ephesus was the prominent commercial and cultural center of Asia. Christ's letter to the Ephesian church praises the congregation for its "deeds...hard work...and perseverance," and for its rejection of false apostles (**Revelation 2:2-3**).

Despite its hard work and doctrinal integrity, Christ faults the community for having "forsaken the love [they] had at first" (**Revelation 2:4**). This "forsaken love" can mean that the Ephesians had become less devoted to Christ or that the work they did was no longer motivated by love for one another. The letter to the Ephesian church does offer the community hope if they repent and rekindle their love for Christian living (**Revelation 2:5-7**).

Significance Today: The lesson in the letter to Ephesus teaches that truth and love must go hand-in-hand. A church that upholds doctrinal purity at the expense of showing love is just as flawed as a church that upholds congregational harmony at the expense of truthful teachings. Instead, Jesus reveals that a church fashioned in His image must teach God's Truth in love.

2. Smyrna. The Church that Remains Faithful Amidst Persecution (Revelation 2:8-11)

Summary and Explanation: Smyrna was home to a large Jewish community hostile to Christians. The Bible notes that slanderous accusations by Jews against Christians had led to Christian persecution by Roman authorities (**Acts 14:2**, 19: **Acts 17:13**).

Christ's revelation to Smyrna commends the community for its material poverty but spiritual wealth and acknowledges its wrongful persecution (**Revelation 2:9**). Christ does not reprimand this church but warns of impending imprisonment for some of its members, urging them to remain faithful "even to the point of death" and remember the promise of their "victor's crown" (**Revelation 2:10**).

Significance Today: Like the church in Smyrna, Christians are persecuted worldwide in obvious and insidious ways. This letter warns all Christians that although we may suffer greatly, the length of **tribulation** will be short compared to the promise of eternal life.

3. Pergamum. The Church that Compromises Its Beliefs (Revelation 2:12-17)

Summary and Explanation: The city of Pergamum was renowned for its pagan practices. The letter to the church there lauds the congregation for upholding its faith despite the city's pervasive pagan influences (**Revelation 2:13**). The letter then addresses the church's sin by denouncing some of its members for following false teachings that brought about religious and moral compromise (**Revelation 2:14-15**).

The Lord calls on the community to repent or risk the judgment that will emanate from the "sword of [His] mouth" (**Revelation 2:16**). Those who repent will be given the "hidden manna" that is the grain of Heaven (**Psalm 78:24**), and a "white stone" or clean slate with a new identity in Christ (**Revelation 2:17**).

Significance Today: Like the Christians in Pergamum, it's easy to normalize the non-Christian behavior of those around us and allow that behavior to dilute our values (**1 Corinthians 15:33**). But the Bible urges us to "not conform to the pattern of this world" but be transformed by the renewal of our mind in accordance with God's Word (**Romans 12:2**).

4. Thyatira. The Church that Follows False Prophets (Revelation 2:18-29)

Summary and Explanation: Thyatira was a wealthy commercial city. Jesus' letter to Thyatira praises the church for having grown in faith and service (**Revelation 2:19**). The church's downfall was its devotion to a false prophet that led some members to commit idolatry and immorality (**Revelation 2:20**). Although the false prophet remained unrepentant, Jesus affirms that the congregation can still repent by turning away from the prophet's ways (**Revelation 2:21-22**).

The Lord reminds us in this revelation that He will repay each of us according to our deeds (**Revelation 2:23**). The payment for sin is death. Those who persevere in faith, however, will receive a share of Christ's messianic authority over all nations and triumph over death (**Revelation 2:26-28**).

Significance Today: Just as some in Thyatira's church were led astray by a false prophet, Christians today fall prey to cult leaders, occult practices, and other false teachings. To share in Christ's victory, we are to avoid these "so-called deep secrets" of Satan (**Revelation 2:24**) and hold firm to Christ's teachings.

5. Sardis. The Church that is Spiritually Dead (Revelation 3:1-6)

Summary and Explanation: Sardis was a city that had endured two surprise attacks despite its fortifications. Our Lord faults the church in Sardis for maintaining an outward appearance of being "alive," while actually being spiritually dead (**Revelation 3:1**). Alluding to the city's history of prior surprise attacks, Jesus warns the congregation to "wake up" and repent, lest he "come like a thief" to bestow His judgment (**Revelation 3:2-3**).

Those in Sardis who heed Christ's warning will be "dressed in white," a symbol of purity and victory, and will be acknowledged in Heaven's Book of Life (**Revelation 3:5**).

Significance Today: Today, Christians can fall into the trap that ensnared the church in Sardis if we merely go through the motions of practicing our faith without really feeding our spirit. We can avoid becoming "the living dead" by engaging in our faith through Bible study, prayer, and fellowship.

6. Philadelphia. The Church that Patiently Endured Despite Weaknesses (Revelation 3:7-13)

Summary and Explanation: Philadelphia was home to a synagogue community hostile to Christians. Christ praises the Philadelphians for remaining faithful in the face of trials despite their limited strength (**Rev. 3:8**).

Jesus does not reproach this congregation but condemns its persecutors. (**Revelation 3:9**). Christ promises that if Philadelphia's congregants remain faithful to Him, He will protect them from the "hour of trial" and make them pillars in God's heavenly temple (**Revelation 3:10-12**).

Significance Today: The message to Philadelphia shows us the blessings that come when we maintain our faith despite life's tribulations. In fact, those who persevere despite weaknesses will stand strong as pillars in Heaven.

7. Laodicea. The Church with a Lukewarm Faith (Revelation 3:14-22)

Summary and Explanation: Laodicea was a prosperous industrial and commercial center. Jesus' letter to this church wastes no time denouncing the congregation for its lukewarm faith, threatening to "spit" the congregation out of His mouth (**Revelation 3:16**).

Christ scolds this church for allowing its economic prosperity to cause its spiritual bankruptcy and reveals that, despite its economic wealth, only He can provide spiritual wealth (**Revelation**

3:17-18). Those in Laodicea's church who open the door to Christ will share in His Heavenly banquet and have the right to sit with Him on His throne (**Revelation 3:20-21**).

APPENDIX C

Article published in Ellopia Magazine Written by Nancy Horton

(Daughter of Consul George Horton)

Ellopia Magazine vol. 13, November-December 1992, p. 44-47 antibaro.gr (originally published in Greek, translated by Microsoft Word)

Most are usually interested in the political view of the events of Asia Minor. Since I was asked to write about my father's experiences, let me note that he had a mystical bond with Smyrna. How did a tenth-generation Yankee from a town in the north of New York State so much relate to a city on the coast of Asia Minor? As a child, his father read to him from the Bible, including the book of Revelation. Smyrna, as the last of the seven cities of the Apocalypse that survived, made a deep impression on him, that he kept it throughout his life and constantly mentioned it in his works. During his career he served in many other diplomatic posts, in places that were considered hot, but, as he said, Smyrna was the Mecca of his ambitions. It seems, therefore, that it was fatal to be present at the death of the Christians and the destruction of the city. Smyrna was his fate. He had closely linked the symbolism of the Apocalypse for the struggle between good on the one hand and darkness and greed on the other with the events he watched in Smyrna that led to its destruction.

Horton went to Smyrna during World War I and represented the interests of all allies until Turkey declared war on the United States as well. "For the first time in a hundred years," he said, "the American flag was taken down by the Consulate." Horton always commented, "we turn the other cheek to the Turks, for reasons known only to directors of large companies".

The victory of the Greeks during the Balkan Wars and the struggle for the liberation of Thessaloniki won the admiration of British politicians and especially of Lloyd George. It also became apparent that some territorial docts of Greece would be very important for Great Britain. So the British invited Venizelos to London. They wanted a base near the Adriatic: Argostoli of Kefalonia. In return, they said, Greece would take Cyprus. The Greeks, however, had not realized that Lloyd George was not always able to impose a policy that would not have the approval of the class that essentially ruled England.

In January 1915, the British Minister of Foreign Affairs, Sir Edward Gray, telegraphed to the British Ambassador in Athens and recommended that he offer Greece an important area on the coast of Asia Minor. In return, Greece would enter the war on the side of the Entente. "If Venizelos wants a specific promise, we will extract it without difficulty," the British leaders wrote at the time. Venizelos agreed to land allied troops in Thessaloniki. King Constantine and his supporters were against this violation of Greek neutrality*: Thus, two Greek governments were created (one pro-Venizelist in Thessaloniki and one pro-royalist in Athens).

In May 1919, in the last days of the Paris peace conference, Lloyd George and Venizelos decided that the Greek troops would occupy Smyrna, a decision that went against the advice of many political men. On May 14, allied detachments occupied the port of Smyrna, while the next day the Greek troops disembarked.

In August of the following year, the sultan signed the Treaty of Sèvres, which liberated certain Greek territories from the power of the Turks, while a large part of the empire came under the control of an International Committee. However, this treaty was never ratified, not only because it met with opposition from the Young Turks of Ankara, but also because France and Italy refused to sign, which considered the Treaty of Sèvres as a diplomatic victory for the British and Greece as their satellite. So they not only came to an understanding with Kemal but also left him lying to him war material from Asia Minor, even though they knew that it would be used against the Greeks. After these events, with the Turkish nationalist army active on the battlefield, only a victory of the Greek army could put the treaty into force. "The security of the oppressed minorities," according to Horton, "depended solely on it, but the old policy of economic imperialism among the allied powers made any constructive integration impossible."

When Kemal rejected the treaty of Sèvres, Venizelos decided to take back the lost ground with a well-organized military campaign. He telegraphed to Lloyd George announcing his decision and asking for military and financial assistance. In his dream for the realization of the Great Idea, Venizelos saw with the eyes of his imagination the occupation of Constantinople. A Greek delegation went to London to discuss the attack. It is amazing the extent to which England became involved in the deliberations on the Asia Minor War and how extensively the Greeks consulted them before taking any step. The British, however, did not promise anything concrete and the Greeks left with the feeling that they had already decided to make the campaign. Five days later the Greek army began the attack. When the Greeks landed in Smyrna, Horton wrote to the State Department: "This will be another Syracuse campaign", implying the Syracuse war in 413 BC, which led to the bankruptcy of the Athenian treasury and put an end to the hegemonic position of Athens.

In November 1920, the elections brought King Constantine back to power. When Venizelos saw the furious demonstrations of the Royals in Athens and realized that he was losing, he resigned. Horton, in a report to the State Department, commented: "The fall of Venizelos, this great defender of Greece in Europe and America and the restoration of the discredited king, is the beginning of the end."

The British did not abide by the agreement with Venizelos. Winston Churchill justifies as follows the attitude of Britain and the non-concession of Cyprus to Greece after the king's return: "He was a ruler, who, despite the interests and the will of his people, tried for personal or family reasons, to bring his country to the side of the enemy, who was ultimately the defeated side. For this reason, Constantine's return dispelled all allied faith and devotion to Greece and canceled all obligations, except for legal ones." Churchill even added at the end: "It doesn't happen that moral creditors are so convenient every day."

This change also had an impact on the army: the Venizelist officers were replaced by trusted royalists. With this change, many regiments were left without officers. Horton wrote to the State Department: "I am informed by reliable sources that until the last moment the Greek army could get back on its feet and save the situation, but even the officers who wanted to stay in their positions to fight and expressed their desire to do so, were ordered to resign." However, General Hadjianestis, who had assumed command of the Greek army in May 1922, failed.

Of course, I do not intend here to analyze the course of the Asia Minor campaign. However, at that time Horton began a series of telegrams to the U.S. Secretary of State, asking permission to mediate with the Government of Ankara for amnesty, which would allow the exit of the Greek forces, that is, to allow them to barge. "Refugees are flocking through the city and panic is increasing," he wrote and suggested, "In the name of humanity and for the safety of American interests, I implore you to allow efforts to be made to mediate, which may prevent a possible destruction of the city." His telegrams reached William Phillips, who appears to have been an active Foreign Minister. This inept diplomat saw things differently. Phillips wrote to President

Harding: "I have another message from Consul General Horton. I think it would be wiser to limit our activities to caring for the lives of Americans and American property. I don't think the situation allows us to take on the role of volunteer mediator." One can imagine how beneficial Horton's proposal would have had if it had been accepted.

On September 9, the people of Smyrna saw the main Greek forces — their only defense against the Turks — overtake the city and board Cesme to return to Greece.

A remarkable feature of the whole picture of the destruction of Smyrna was the presence of the warships of the Great Powers, which sailed indifferently in the port, in order to protect the lives of their citizens. On the fire and destruction of the city, Horton wrote: "A joint order from the commanders of the warships, a harmless shot over the Turkish part of the city, would stop the holocaust." The commanders of the allied fleet did not take such action. The causes lie in the decade before the destruction of Smyrna. In 1901 a German expert had ascertained that the oil fields of Mosul (then belonged to Turkey, today to Iraq) were among the richest in the world. Eight years later, the Turkish government granted the right to extract subsoil wealth and build rails on a strip two thousand four hundred miles long in Asia Minor. The strip covered a depth of twenty kilometers on either side of the railway line, with a total area of ninety-six thousand square miles. The relevant contracts provided for investments of 200-300 million US dollars (in 1924 dollars). It was estimated that this area contained ten billion in minerals and other natural sources of wealth and eight billion barrels of oil.

Historians also point to the fact that the United States did not declare war on Turkey. Writes one: "This attitude on the part of the Us government was calculated to benefit U.S. trade interests in Turkey. Among them, Admiral Chester's accomplices appear to have been the most favored." Colby Chester, a retired U.S. Navy admiral, negotiated for several years with Turkey to win some concessions to grant rights to mine subsoil wealth and build a railway line. Chester was assisted in his efforts by Admiral Bristol, commander of the U.S. fleet in Turkish waters and U.S. High Commissioner in Istanbul. A historian commented on this: "In the years 1919-1923, so crucial to the history of Asia Minor, two American officials stood out as incarnations of opposing forces in the foreign policy of the United States: the tendency of conscience on the one hand and pragmatism on the other." Those two officials were Horton and Bristol respectively. Throughout his career, Horton has been keen to advance American commercial interests. He managed to save the Company Standard Oil from thousands of dollars in illegal taxes, but he did not believe in neutrality in cases of great national importance, where lives were at risk. There are many testimonies in this regard from the Turks, whom Horton helped when there was a need. Bristol, however, saw it as his duty to persuade journalists not to cover up the barbaric treatment of Christians by the Turks. His purpose was to win the favor of the Turks in order to ratify the concessions mentioned. Orders of silence were issued against Horton and other eyewitnesses of the events when they returned to the United States. Without a doubt, Bristol, in his opinion, acted patriotically. Horton, in a letter to my mother, said, "We are a great and glorious Republic, but the American people, like all many, do not always learn the truth of things." He observed: "In this whole web of conflicting interests, the serious observer is impressed with one thing: the clarity of John Boole's insight (England) and the candor and perseverance with which he fought for his cause. He knew what he wanted and got it. There are abundant oil wells in Maidan 1 Naftun, not far from Basra, in the Persian Gulf, where the: British landed early, during my war. There are fields of oil wells in Mosul (today in Iraq). General Townsett was heading there when the Turks stopped him at Kut-el-Mara, but this did not kill cousin John.

The Italians, who from the beginning were opposed to the presence of the Greeks in the region of Smyrna, rushed to make secret agreements with Kemal in March 1921 in exchange for large economic concessions and the promise to withdraw from Antalya the Italian occupation troops. In October of the same year, the French agreed with Kemal to withdraw the French occupying troops from Cilicia and to provide the Turks tacitly with war material, for which they were bravely paid. Besides, France was the first European country to cultivate economic relations with the Ottoman Empire since 1535. And as the director of the French Commercial Office of Istanbul proudly mentioned (1922). "Our schools, charitable institutions, hospitals, nursing homes, orphans' asylums, and exhibits have been established in every part of the East. In every city of the interior, in all the important villages... there are schools and French teachers, people who teach children the glory of France, our language, our history." It goes without saying, therefore, that France was not prepared to renounce all its achievements, let alone its economic advantages.

The Turks, having settled their diplomatic relations with the Soviet Union, were now ready to organize a general counterattack against the Greeks, whom they had all abandoned. On September 8, 1922, the Turks entered Smyrna, while the Greeks had no other way out, but to fall into the sea.

When I was making speeches, I didn't usually mention the rescue work my father did, because I was thinking that this didn't suit a daughter. I finally wondered, why not? these are facts, why hide them? And even today, on the plane, in the grocery store, on the beach, people who hear the name Horton tell me how they or their relatives were saved from it. He acted mostly unofficially and even in some episodes he felt he was forced to keep them secret. Someone I met on a Greek island, told me how Horton put hundreds of American flags on fishing boats or any other boat and after consulting with a crowd of women and children to meet him secretly at one point, he put them on the boats and sent them to the islands opposite Smyrna.

When the Turks entered the city, they followed, as you know, indescribable atrocities. Rape, murder, and looting were the most common sight. Many reported seeing soldiers of the Turkish regular army throwing—ironically—rags dipped in oil to burn the U.S. consulate. When the building began to burn it was time for the American community to abandon it. Among them were many relatives, friends, and employees, not all of them American citizens. It is worth noting that several American charities also lost their buildings to the arson, among them Horton's house with all its belongings. But the buildings of Standard Oil survived. Only these were guarded by armed American sailors.

As the ship set sail for Athens, Horton wrote: "One of the most acute impressions I gained from Smyrna was the feeling of deep shame, because I belonged to the human race." He compared the destruction of Smyrna to the demolition of Carthage by the Romans and remarked: "In the destruction of Carthage there was no fleet of Christian warships to monitor a situation for which their governments were responsible." Various refugees have since told me that one of their most powerful memories was the sound of dance music arriving at the port from the Allied warships. An eyewitness to the final death of the Byzantine Empire, Horton continues: "And this presence of these warships in the port of Smyrna, the Sotirion year 1922, which watched powerlessly the last moments of the Christians in Turkey, was the saddest and most important element of the whole history."

However, despite Bristol's policy of overlooking the loss of life to advance his commercial ambitions, we must not overlook the efficiency with which some U.S. Navy officers have helped save lives. Sailors took refugees on board for two days, despite the policy of not intervening by the United States. It is also worth mentioning the attitude of the Japanese who threw the cargo into the water in order to be able to take the victims of the disaster to their ships.

When Horton arrived in Athens, he received several telegrams from the personnel of the American ships, in which they told him that they were sending refugees and asking for his help in disembarking them. After helping find food and shelter for the refugees, Horton went to Washington, where he testified at Congressional hearings and fought to pass a law allowing refugees to take their relatives and parents to America.

Also, little known, are the activities developed by Horton during the work of the Treaty of Loza-ni. He believed that this treaty should not be closed without including a homeland and safeguards for the Armenians, compensation for losses, including the losses of the Americans, an assurance that all Christian women, girls, and women, kidnapped during the hostilities would be freed, and a demand that the Turks admit and renounce their crimes. While the Lausanne conference was continuing, the American representative appealed for the country of the Armenians but abandoned it in the face of Turkish reaction. The private economic interests of the Great Powers that had or hoped to acquire investments in Asia Minor dictated to their representatives to take care to fully protect these interests. As one historian said, the soldiers who threw dice for Christ's garments were no more obscene than the emissaries who haggled for concessions. A Standard Oil envoy to Lausanne punched his fist on the table and said, "Have we come here for these cursed minorities or to take care of our interests?" Members of Admiral Chester's team were also present, but nothing happened in the end, because the British arrived first in Mosul. "You can imagine how important the issue of oil is," Horton wrote to my mother from Washington, "since ethicists say that U.S. domestic reserves will be enough for only twenty years, and our entire culture depends on it. Even our warships run on oil. I am prepared to admit that we need it, but I believe that we could have gained our share in less criminal ways. Oil will not burn well when mixed with a lot of blood, and when it smells strongly from the smoke of churches and Holy Scriptures that are burned. As for myself, a thought will comfort me for the rest of my life, and then, I hope: Whatever disadvantages I had, my hands were not stained with Christian blood, and I have never betrayed my Christ for thirty pieces of silver."

Horton continued to write and make efforts to change situations that he considered questionable during and after the signing of the treaty of Lausanne, things about which I know very little. He formed a lobby in Washington for Christian minorities and later published his book "The Curse of Asia" and other works, in the hope of leading to the imposition of justice. He traveled all over America giving lectures on the Middle East and fundraising orphans and other victims. He liked to close his lectures with the following words, while the audience saw a slide of the chandelier of the church of Pergamon: "Let's go with our thoughts back to the years of St. John and imagine a candle burning in everyone. Candles of the kind mentioned by Portia. So a good deed shines in an evil world." Let's imagine it all fading out one by one, for many years, and the last one burning shiny and stable until September 1922. It always ended by listing the cities — their names alone. He believed that they recall more magnificence than all the poetry of the world: Ephesus, Sardis, Philadelphia, Theatura, Laodicea, Pergamos, Smyrna.

Nancy Horton (daughter of US Consul in Izmir George Horton)

APPENDIX D

Family Trees for the families of

- Platanidis

- Tsalikedou

- Venis

- Donjobolou

APPENDIX D
Family Trees
for the families of

Platanidis
Tsalikedou
Venis
Donjobolou

Family Trees of:

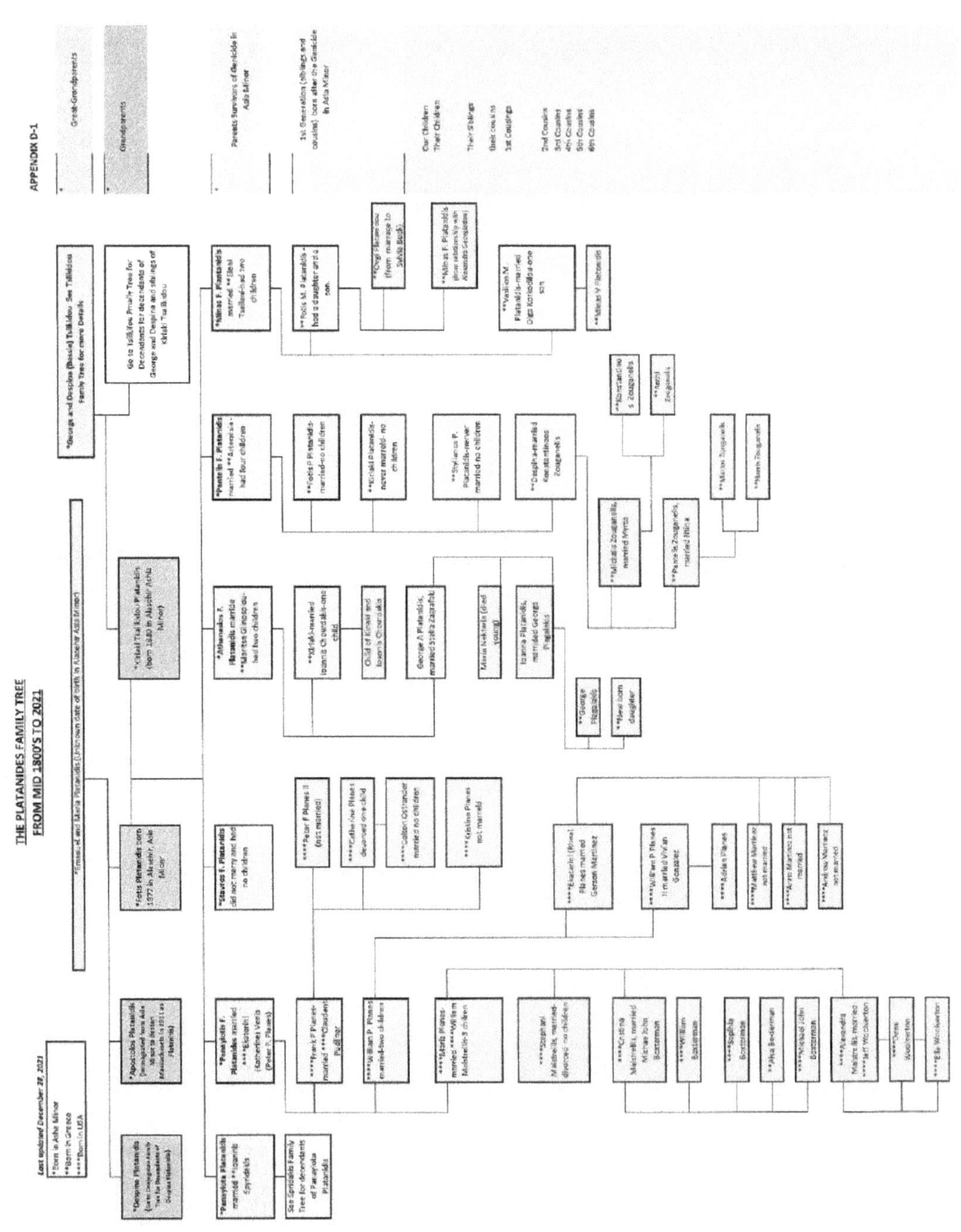

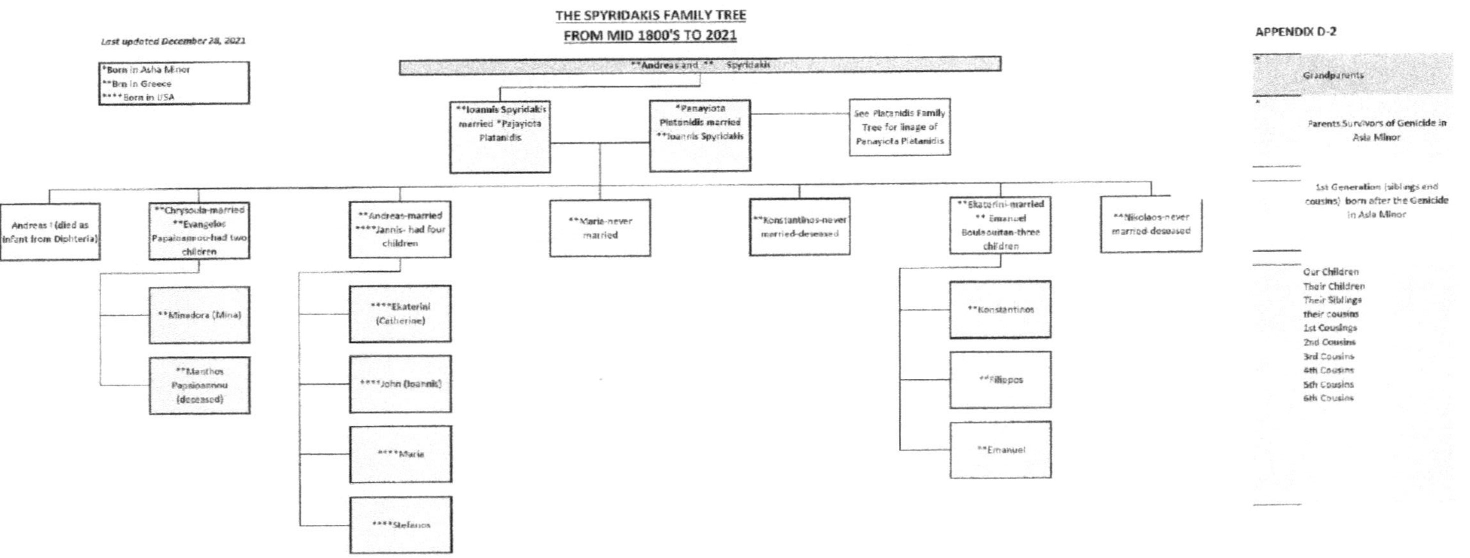
THE SPYRIDAKIS FAMILY TREE
FROM MID 1800'S TO 2021
Last updated December 28, 2021
*Born in Asia Minor
**Born in Greece
****Born in USA
**Andreas and ** Spyridakis
**Ioannis Spyridakis married *Panayiota Platanidis
*Panayiota Platanidis married **Ioannis Spyridakis
See Platanidis Family Tree for linage of Panayiota Platanidis
Andreas I (died as infant from Diphteria)
**Chrysoula-married **Evangelos Papaioannou-had two children
**Andreas-married ****Jannis- had four children
**Maria-never married
**Konstantinos-never married-deceased
**Ekaterini-married ** Emanuel Boutsourtan-three children
**Nikolaos-never married-deceased
**Minadora (Mina)
**Manthos Papaioannou (deceased)
****Ekaterini (Catherine)
****John (Ioannis)
****Maria
****Stefanos
**Konstantinos
**Filippos
**Emanuel
APPENDIX D-2
Grandparents
Parents Survivors of Genicide in Asia Minor
1st Generation (siblings and cousins) born after the Genicide in Asia Minor
Our Children
Their Children
Their Siblings
their cousins
1st Cousings
2nd Cousins
3rd Cousins
4th Cousins
5th Cousins
6th Cousins

Last updated December 28, 2021

THE NEW YORK-FLORODA VENIS FAMILY TREE
FROM MID 1800'S TO 2021

APPENDIX D-3

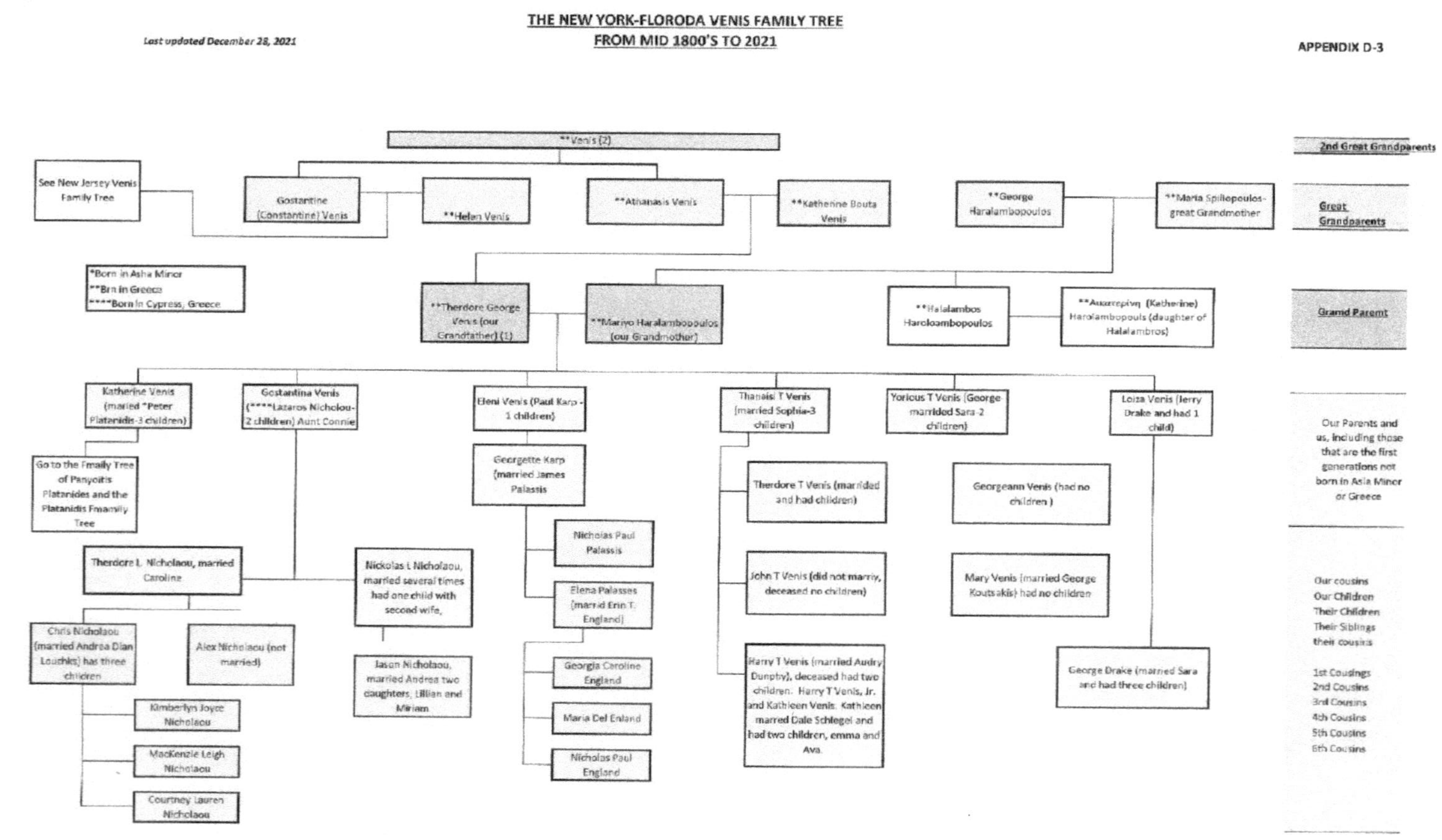

APPENDIX D-4

THE NEW JERSEY VENIS FAMILY TREE
FROM MID 1800'S TO 2021

Last updated December 28, 2021

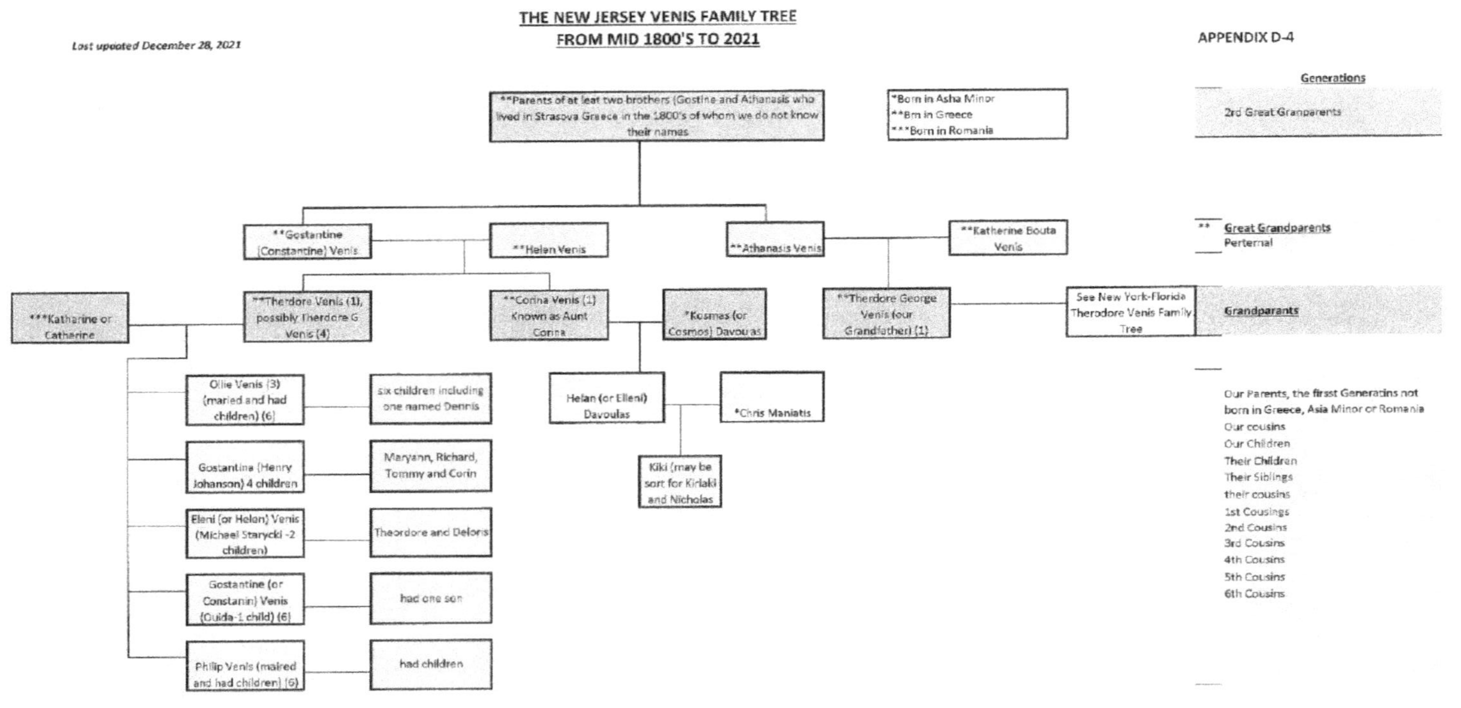

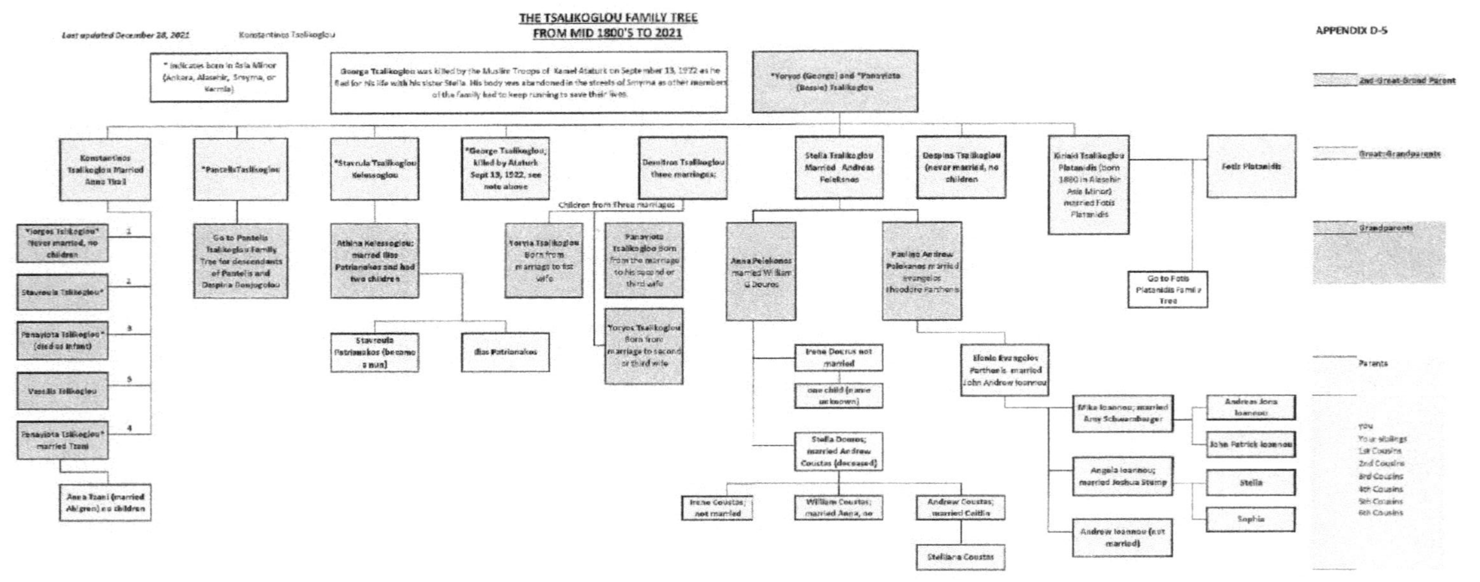

Last updated December 28, 2021
Konstantinos Tsalikoglou

THE TSALIKOGLOU FAMILY TREE
FROM MID 1800'S TO 2021

APPENDIX D-5

* Indicates born in Asia Minor (Ankara, Alasehir, Smyrna, or Vermia)

George Tsalikoglou was killed by the Muslim Troops of Kemal Ataturk on September 13, 1972 as he fled for his life with his sister Stella. His body was abandoned in the streets of Smyrna as other members of the family had to keep running to save their lives.

*Yoryos (George) and *Panayiota (Bessie) Tsalikoglou

Konstantinos Tsalikoglou Married Anna Tirol
*Pantelis Tsalikoglou
*Stavrula Tsalikoglou Kelessoglou
*George Tsalikoglou, killed by Ataturk Sept 13, 1922, see note above
Demitros Tsalikoglou three marriages;
Stella Tsalikoglou Married Andreas Felektsnos
Despina Tsalikoglou (never married, no children)
Kiriaki Tsalikoglou Platanidis (born 1880 in Alasehir Asia Minor) married Fotis Platanidis
Fotis Platanidis

1   *Yorgos Tsalikoglou* Never married, no children
2   Stavroula Tsalikoglou*
3   Panayiota Tsalikoglou* (died as infant)
5   Vasilis Tsalikoglou
4   Panayiota Tsalikoglou* married Tzani
Anna Tzani (married Ahlgren) no children

Go to Pantelis Tsalikoglou Family Tree for descendants of Pantelis and Despina Boujogolou

Athina Kelessoglou; married Ilias Patrianakos and had two children
Stavroula Patrianakos (became a nun)
Ilias Patrianakos

Children from three marriages
Yoryia Tsalikoglou Born from marriage to first wife
Panayiota Tsalikogloo Born from the marriage to his second or third wife
Yoryos Tsalikoglou Born from marriage to second or third wife

Anna Pelekonos married William G Douros
Paelino Andrew Pelekonos married Evangelos Theodoro Panthenis

Irene Douros not married
one child (name unknown)
Stella Douros; married Andrew Coustas (deceased)
Irene Coustas; not married
William Coustas; married Anna, no
Andrew Coustas; married Caitlin
Stelliana Coustas

Honia Evangelos Panthea is married John Andrew Ioannou
Efika Ioannou; married Amy Schwarzenberger
Andreas Jons Ioannou
John Patrick Ioannou
Angela Ioannou; married Joshua Stamp
Stella
Sophia
Andrew Ioannou (not married)

Go to Fotis Platanidis Family Tree

2nd-Great-Grand Parent
Great-Grandparents
Grandparents
Parents
You
Your siblings
1st Cousins
2nd Cousins
3rd Cousins
4th Cousins
5th Cousins
6th Cousins

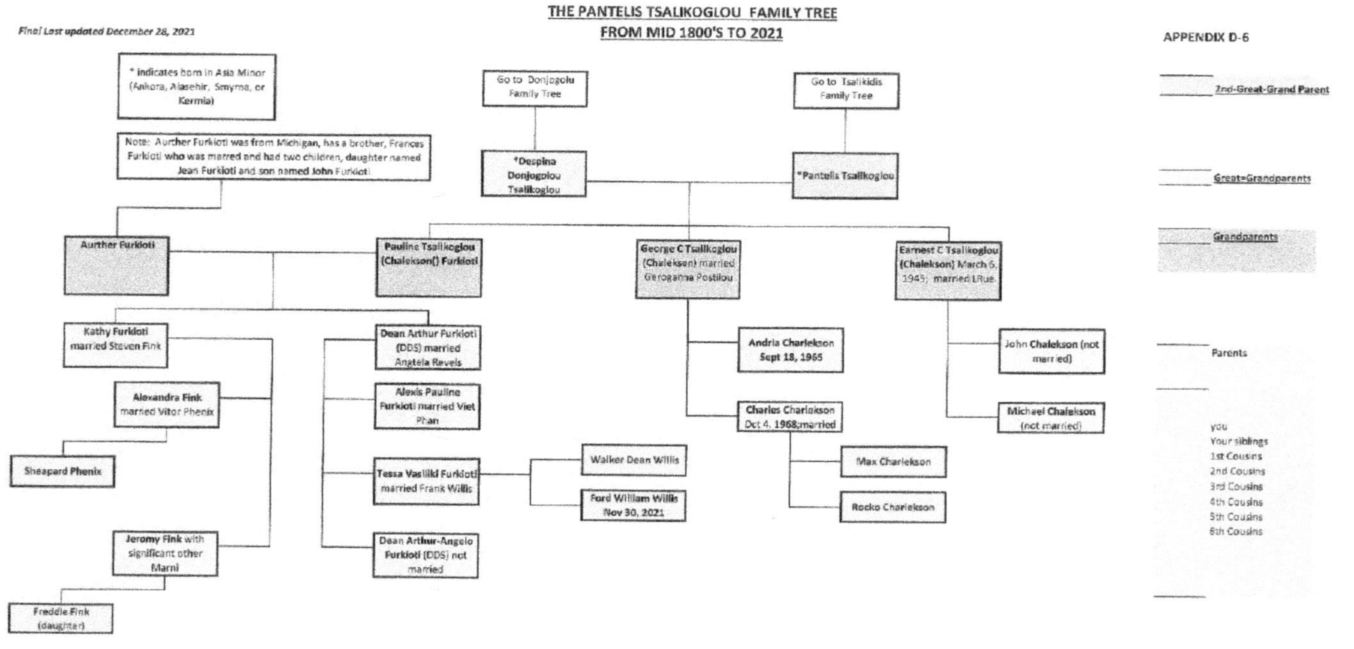
THE PANTELIS TSALIKOGLOU FAMILY TREE
FROM MID 1800'S TO 2021
APPENDIX D-6
Final Last updated December 28, 2021
* indicates born in Asia Minor (Ankora, Alasehir, Smyrna, or Kermia)
Note: Aurther Furkioti was from Michigan, has a brother, Frances Furkioti who was married and had two children, daughter named Jean Furkioti and son named John Furkioti.
Go to Donjogolu Family Tree
Go to Tsalikidis Family Tree
*Despina Donjogolou Tsalikoglou
*Pantelis Tsalikoglou
Aurther Furkioti
Pauline Tsalikoglou (Chalekson() Furkioti
George C Tsalikoglou (Chalekson) married Geroganna Postilou
Earnest C Tsalikoglou (Chalekson) March 6, 1945; married LRue.
Kathy Furkioti married Steven Fink
Dean Arthur Furkioti (DDS) married Angelia Revels
Andria Charlekson Sept 18, 1965
John Chalekson (not married)
Alexandra Fink married Vitor Phenix
Alexis Pauline Furkioti married Viet Phan
Charles Charlekson Oct 4, 1968;married
Michael Chalekson (not married)
Sheapard Phenix
Tessa Vasiliki Furkioti married Frank Willis
Walker Dean Willis
Max Charlekson
Ford William Willis Nov 30, 2021
Rocko Charlekson
Jeromy Fink with significant other Marni
Dean Arthur-Angelo Furkioti (DDS) not married
Freddie Fink (daughter)
2nd-Great-Grand Parent
Great=Grandparents
Grandparents
Parents
you
Your siblings
1st Cousins
2nd Cousins
3rd Cousins
4th Cousins
5th Cousins
6th Cousins

THE DONJOGULOU FAMILY TREE
FROM MID 1800'S TO 2021

Last updated December 28, 2021

APPENDIX D-7

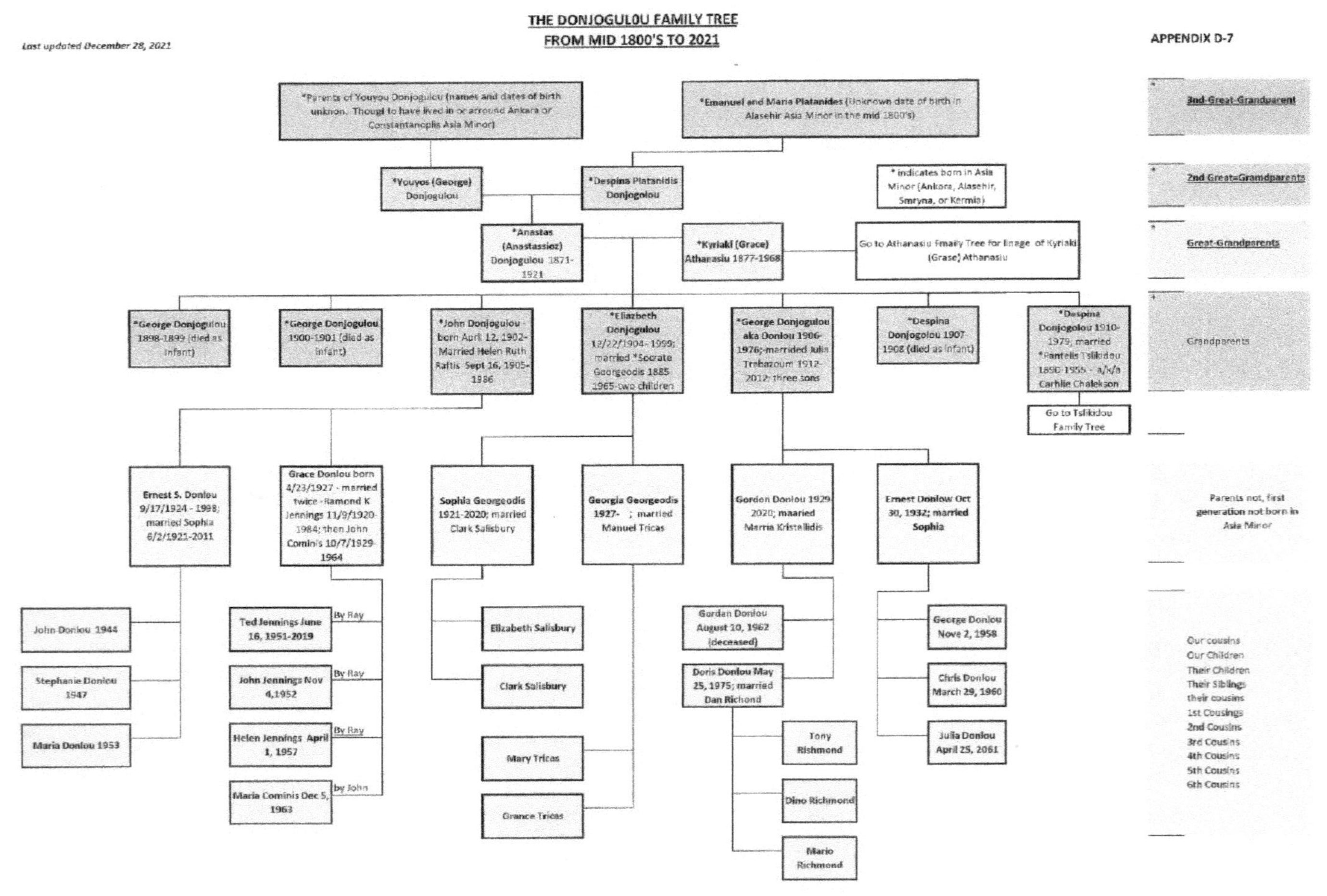

THE ATHANASIU FAMILY TREE
FROM MID 1800'S TO 2021

APPENDIX D-8

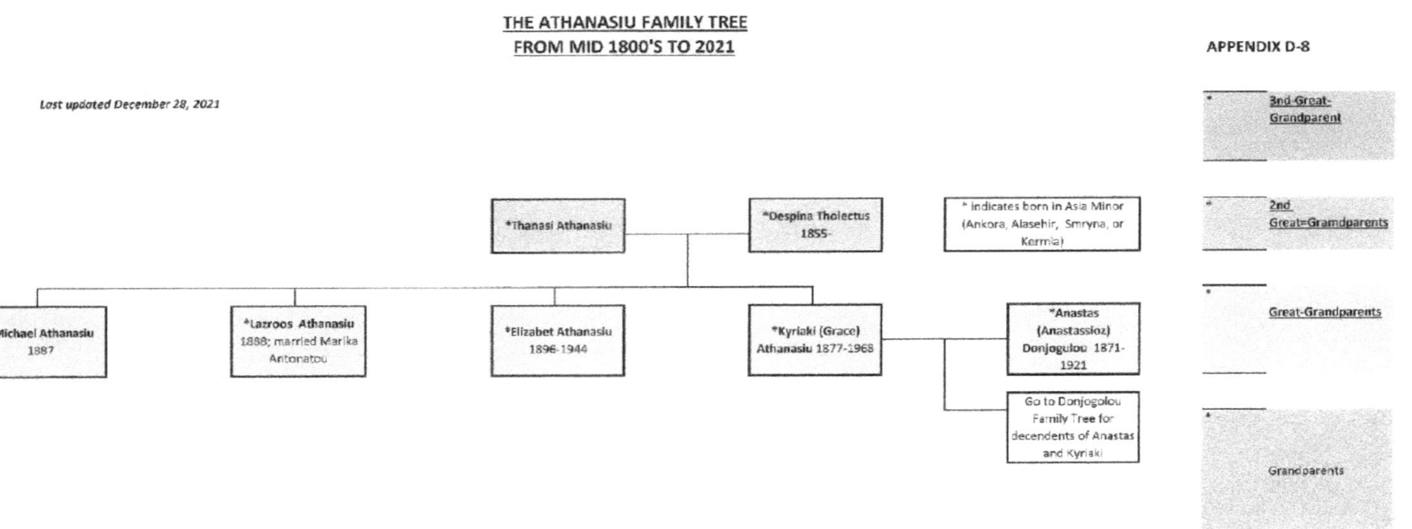

APPENDIX D-9
DNA Reletives of William P. Planes, Sr as reflected on 23andMe™

Display Name	Surname	Sex	Birth Year	Set Relationship	Predicted Relationship	Relative Range	Family Surnames	Family Locations
jane R		Female		5th Cousin	5th Cousin	3rd to Distant Cousin	Dzierzkowski, Jablonowski, Omencetter, Putkowski, Braun, Kollmyer, Kollmeier, Kohlmeyer, Seidensticker, Grau, Bryan, Ferreau, Strimple, Strempel, Burton, Adams, Mathis, Poulson, Sax	Warsaw, Poland. Bransk, VoivodeshipPodlaskie, CountyBielsk. Ovenstaedt, Westfalen, Prussia, Anspach, Hochtaunuskreis, WÃ¼rttemberg, Frankenhain, Germany;
Mary Kaloci	Kaloci	Female		5th Cousin	5th Cousin	3rd to Distant Cousin		
Stephanie Magoulas	Magoulas	Female	1975	5th Cousin	5th Cousin	3rd to Distant Cousin	Manninen, Mannila, Paatola, Kaukua, Olson, Hallam, Moilanen, Magnuson, Magoulas, Magoula, Koski, Raistakka	Finland; Trikala; Athens; Rosburg, WA; Varmland County, Sweden; Lysvik, Varmland County, Sweden; Taivalkoski, Finland; Chicago, Cook County, Illinois, United States
Tom Petropoulos	Petropoulos	Male	1971	4th Cousin	4th Cousin	3rd to 5th Cousin	Petropoulos, Panagopoulos	
Constantine Roumel	Roumel	Male		3rd Cousin	3rd Cousin	3rd to 5th Cousin		
Rosemary nee Kromidas Hendrix	Hendrix	Female	1934	5th Cousin	5th Cousin	3rd to Distant Cousin	Kromidas, Yiannasopoulos, Kosmas, Markopoulos, Hendrix	Messini, Veria, Michigan, Florida, Georgia
nicole keough	keough	Female		5th Cousin	5th Cousin	3rd to Distant Cousin		
Janet R Olson	Olson	Female		5th Cousin	5th Cousin	3rd to Distant Cousin	Rich, Riccio, Bagelos, Pappas, Olson	
Alessandro Genovese	Genovese	Male	1952	5th Cousin	5th Cousin	3rd to Distant Cousin	Spiropulos, Spiropulu, Genovese	
Mueser Shatku	Shatku	Female		5th Cousin	5th Cousin	3rd to Distant Cousin		Albania
Kathleen Heath	Heath	Female	1956	5th Cousin	5th Cousin	3rd to Distant Cousin	Egan, McCabe, Dickman, Heath	
Thomas Caulfield	Caulfield	Male		5th Cousin	5th Cousin	3rd to Distant Cousin		
Nick Kacprowski	Kacprowski	Male		5th Cousin	5th Cousin	3rd to Distant Cousin	Kacprowski, Richter, Antonopoulos, Syriopoulos	
Dasha Dasha	Dasha	Female		5th Cousin	5th Cousin	3rd to Distant Cousin	Babic, Srdic, Romic, Bogovac, Dasha	Belgrade, Sebia; Drvar, Bosnia; Zaglavica, Bosnia; Padjeni, Croatia; Knin, Croatia; Split, Croatia; Ivosevci, Croatia; Komiza, Croatia; Kistanje, Croatia; Frankfurt, Germany;
James Chukalas	Chukalas	Male		5th Cousin	5th Cousin	3rd to Distant Cousin	Chukalas, Tsoukalas, Missailidis	
Kimberly Harrison	Harrison	Female		4th Cousin	4th Cousin	3rd to 6th Cousin	Hatch, Sousa, Souza, Boblin, Gerbic, Grbic, Harrison	Austria, Yugoslavia (Croatia), England, Portugal, Canada (Alberta, British Columbia), United States (Massachussetts, Maine, Florida, California)
A Co	Co	Male		5th Cousin	5th Cousin	3rd to Distant Cousin		
MARTHA FOSTERI	FOSTERI	Female	1954	4th Cousin	4th Cousin	3rd to Distant Cousin	Fosteris, Daoudakis, FOSTERI	Chania-Crete, Amorgos, Athens
Stephanie Jones Labadie	Jones Labadie	Female	1984	5th Cousin	5th Cousin	3rd to Distant Cousin	Jones, Hodum, Manos, Manouilidis, Anagnostou, Jones Labadie	Watertown, MA; Pochahontas, TN
Elaine Ganas	Ganas	Female		5th Cousin	5th Cousin	3rd to Distant Cousin		Scotland, United Kingdom; Ireland; England, United Kingdom
Justin Landers	Landers	Male		5th Cousin	5th Cousin	3rd to Distant Cousin		
Stephen Janik	Janik	Male	1949	5th Cousin	5th Cousin	3rd to Distant Cousin	Janik, Rybska, JeleÅ„, Szkaradek, Kokosza, Baran, Hajduk, Szczepankiewicz, Policht, Dresza, WaÅ‚czyk, MrÃ³z, Nidecki, Galica, Kwasniowski, Koloczkowska, Wantell, Lesniocha, Pietrzyk, Dziedzic, Grzyb, Sikocolno, Smolek/Smoliuk/Smolukas, RadzeviÄius/Radziewicz/Rajavich, Valentukievich, Walukoniute, Lukashevich, Kasheta, Remizovska, Muchynski, Akscin, Kibirkshis	RoznÃ³w, Poland; ZagÃ³rze, Poland; Gierowa, Poland; Januszowa, Poland; Wojakowa, Poland; Radajowice, Poland; Gudeliai, Lithuania; Suwalki, Lithuania; Zheime, Lithuania; Kashety, Lithuania; Gailiunai, Lithuania; DuBois, Pennsylvania; Detroit, Michigan
IR		Male		5th Cousin	5th Cousin	3rd to Distant Cousin		
Michael Odai	Odai	Male	1971	5th Cousin	5th Cousin	3rd to Distant Cousin	Odai, Odaj, Tucci, Patane	Syracuse, New York, Bari, Italy; Tirana, Albania; Sulmona, Italy; Catania, Sicily, Italy

Marilyn Miller Wasbotten	Wasbotten	Female	5th Cousin	5th Cousin	3rd to Distant Cousin	Tilghman, Whitledge, Fugitt, Saunders, Sanders, Devonshire, Kabor, Holland, Jarman, Braxton, Hale, Roland, Blount, Deveraux, Knolleys, Boleyn, Carter, Pandreth, Lowen, Benson, Mannan, Manax, Dryden, Jones, Howard, Bramos, Wasbotten	Faversham, Kent, England, Peleponesus, Greece, Washington, DC, Hockerton, North Carolina, Virginia, Maryland, Plymouth, Mass.
Avraam Sekeroglou	Sekeroglou	Male	4th Cousin	4th Cousin	3rd to Distant Cousin	Sekeroglou	Serres GR, Athens GR, Aspra Spitia GR, Thessaloniki GR
Christopher Darke	Darke	Male	1958 5th Cousin	5th Cousin	3rd to Distant Cousin		
Nick Koukotas	Koukotas	Male	5th Cousin	5th Cousin	3rd to Distant Cousin	Koukotas Tsapenekas Pappanas Coulombis, Koukotas	
Alexi chip-v3 Papaleonardos	Papaleonardos	Male	5th Cousin	5th Cousin	3rd to Distant Cousin	boone thompson, papaleonardos, boone, thompson, ieoussis, Papaleonardos	Columbus, Ohio; Cincinnati, Ohio; Manhattan, NY; Greece
Ericka Lillis	Lillis	Female	1972 5th Cousin	5th Cousin	3rd to Distant Cousin	Stevens, Tipton, Peters, Yufon, Yupon, Storey, Hawkins, Howard, Lillis	New Orleans, LA; New York;
Josephine Sturgis	Sturgis	Female	5th Cousin	5th Cousin	3rd to Distant Cousin		
Arthur Johnson	Johnson	Male	3rd Cousin	3rd Cousin	3rd to 5th Cousin	Yannakopoulos, Dimitriades, Johnson	Cairo, Egypt; St Albans, England, UK; Magnesia, Asia Minor; Cyprus
Sotiris Mitropanopoulos	Mitropanopoulos	Male	5th Cousin	5th Cousin	3rd to Distant Cousin	Markoutsa, Mitropanopoulos, Iliopoulou	
Dimitris Papaleonardos	Papaleonardos	Male	5th Cousin	5th Cousin	3rd to Distant Cousin	Petritidis, Moire, Papaleonardos	
Dan PaÈ™oi	PaÈ™oi	Male	5th Cousin	5th Cousin	3rd to Distant Cousin		
Mircea PaÈ™oi	PaÈ™oi	Male	1987 5th Cousin	5th Cousin	3rd to Distant Cousin	Dogaru, PaÈ™oi	
CP		Male	5th Cousin	5th Cousin	3rd to Distant Cousin		
Stephanie DAula	DAula	Female	1990 5th Cousin	5th Cousin	3rd to Distant Cousin		
Elektra Cheliotis	Cheliotis	Female	1967 4th Cousin	4th Cousin	3rd to Distant Cousin	Cheliotis, Linari, Linaris, Pappala, Chouli, Tsatsaroni	
Matt Carnes	Carnes	Male	5th Cousin	5th Cousin	3rd to Distant Cousin	Carnes, White, Fletcher	
MB		Female	1964 5th Cousin	5th Cousin	3rd to Distant Cousin	Tic, Mincic	
Mark Jason Dillaberry	Dillaberry	Male	5th Cousin	5th Cousin	3rd to Distant Cousin	Dillaberry, Turner, Exline, Negrych	
Brigita Urbonas	Urbonas	Female	1993 5th Cousin	5th Cousin	3rd to Distant Cousin		
Adrienne Chauveau Zmiko	Chauveau Zmiko	Female	1987 5th Cousin	5th Cousin	3rd to Distant Cousin	Gilet, Braun, Rozek, Zmiko, Gaillot, Becka, Wojdyla, Chauveau Zmiko	France; KrzÄ™tÃ³w, Radomsko County, ÅÃ³dÅº Voivodeship, Poland; Creutzwald, Moselle, Grand Est, France; Petite-Rosselle, Moselle, Grand Est, France; Uzdolje, OpÄ‡ina Biskupija, Å ibenik-Knin County, Croatia; VÃ¶lklingen, Saarland, Germany; EstrÃ©e-Cauchy, Pas-de-Calais, Hauts-de-France, France
Thomas Burdine	Burdine	Male	5th Cousin	5th Cousin	3rd to Distant Cousin	Burdine, Chrones, Weber, Shaull, Davis, McDonald, Phillips, Drown, Bell, Blackwood, Matthews, Boren, Shrodes, Hess, Perin, Anderson, Updegraff, Hanna, Casey, Poole, Trego, Schall, Blue, Perrin, Gale, Dennis, Drowne, Aryers, Burnham, Benner, O'Nann, Moore, Livingstone, Beck, Chelsea, Hill	
Patricia S		Female	5th Cousin	5th Cousin	3rd to Distant Cousin	Barich, Vittone	
Pete Siaperas	Siaperas	Male	5th Cousin	5th Cousin	3rd to Distant Cousin		
Alyssa Varvarezos	Varvarezos	Female	1989 5th Cousin	5th Cousin	3rd to Distant Cousin		
Sokratis Frantzis	Frantzis	Male	5th Cousin	5th Cousin	3rd to Distant Cousin	Frantzis, Kallias, Bennoui, Sounigo, Nadjar	Italy
Kelsey Friedt	Friedt	Female	5th Cousin	5th Cousin	3rd to Distant Cousin		
Nicole Monson	Monson	Female	1981 5th Cousin	5th Cousin	3rd to Distant Cousin		
Panagiota (Penny) Kratimenos-Goncalves	Kratimenos-Goncalves	Female	1962 5th Cousin	5th Cousin	3rd to Distant Cousin		
Stephanie Flynn	Flynn	Female	4th Cousin	4th Cousin	3rd to Distant Cousin		
Nicholas Fotoples	Fotoples	Male	1981 5th Cousin	5th Cousin	3rd to Distant Cousin	Grevis, Young, Fotoples	
Yanicka de Nocker	de Nocker	Female	5th Cousin	5th Cousin	3rd to Distant Cousin		

Irene Moatsos	Moatsos	Female	5th Cousin	5th Cousin	3rd to Distant Cousin	Kangia, Perpignan, Moatsos	
james ocello	ocello	Male	5th Cousin	5th Cousin	3rd to Distant Cousin	Costoulas, Catsoulas, Katsoulis, ocello	Rochester, Monroe County, New York, United States
Vincent Episcopo	Episcopo	Male	2001 5th Cousin	5th Cousin	3rd to Distant Cousin	Seman, Episcopo, Patterson, Snyder	
Eva McMullan	McMullan	Female	4th Cousin	4th Cousin	3rd to Distant Cousin		
Mary Ann Patarino	Patarino	Female	1955 5th Cousin	5th Cousin	3rd to Distant Cousin		
ANTONY Stratis	Stratis	Male	4th Cousin	4th Cousin	3rd to 6th Cousin	Papadopoulos, Mastoris, Glynos, Glinos, Tiniakos, Skordos, Dapontis, Daponte, Dapontes, Vastardis, Stratis	
ANTONY Stratis	Stratis	Male	4th Cousin	4th Cousin	3rd to 6th Cousin	Papadopoulos, Mastoris, Glynos, Glinos, Tiniakos, Skordos, Dapontis, Daponte, Dapontes, Vastardis, Stratis	
Angelica Clark	Clark	Female	1947 5th Cousin	5th Cousin	3rd to Distant Cousin		
DAVID POURNARAS	POURNARAS	Male	1947 5th Cousin	5th Cousin	3rd to Distant Cousin		
Giorgio Mladjenovic	Mladjenovic	Male	1957 5th Cousin	5th Cousin	3rd to Distant Cousin		
Jacob Binley	Binley	Male	5th Cousin	5th Cousin	3rd to Distant Cousin	Binley, McDonnell	
Kristen Virmani	Virmani	Female	5th Cousin	5th Cousin	3rd to Distant Cousin	Knezevich, Malkovich, Virmani	
Vincent Russo	Russo	Male	5th Cousin	5th Cousin	3rd to Distant Cousin		
Barbara Wagner	Wagner	Female	5th Cousin	5th Cousin	3rd to Distant Cousin	Iwanski, Wagner	
Stanley Chamallas	Chamallas	Male	1954 5th Cousin	5th Cousin	3rd to Distant Cousin	Patsios, Sakalaris, Chamallas	
Polly Jenkins	Jenkins	Female	4th Cousin	4th Cousin	3rd to Distant Cousin		
Eric Bojonell	Bojonell	Male	1974 5th Cousin	5th Cousin	3rd to Distant Cousin	Bojonell, Bozonelis	
marketa matejcik	matejcik	Female	1971 5th Cousin	5th Cousin	3rd to Distant Cousin	Mysak, Lindner, Haas, Machala, matejcik	
Gia Agoritsas	Agoritsas	Female	5th Cousin	5th Cousin	3rd to Distant Cousin		
Maria Matua	Matua	Female	5th Cousin	5th Cousin	3rd to Distant Cousin	Matua, Munxuri	
Rachael Ellisor	Ellisor	Female	1984 5th Cousin	5th Cousin	3rd to Distant Cousin	Chalakias, Halkia, Ellisor	Greece
Kate Hoxha	Hoxha	Female	5th Cousin	5th Cousin	3rd to Distant Cousin		
S K	K	Male	5th Cousin	5th Cousin	3rd to Distant Cousin	Cizek, Kokonas, Gregory, Cordogan, Siavelis, K	
Flora Betea	Betea	Female	5th Cousin	5th Cousin	3rd to Distant Cousin		
Ewelina Rozalska	Rozalska	Female	5th Cousin	5th Cousin	3rd to Distant Cousin		
Elena Sarkissian	Sarkissian	Female	5th Cousin	5th Cousin	3rd to Distant Cousin		
Jennifer McHugh	McHugh	Female	1985 5th Cousin	5th Cousin	3rd to Distant Cousin	Kopsas, Jones, Lonis, Manion, Pritchett, Wolfe, Kastein, Klinger, Page, Fagg, Hillenburg, Robenson, Morphew, Kitchens, Crump, McHugh	Greece; Dinxperlo, Aalten, Gelderland, Netherlands; Gelderland, Netherlands; North Brabant, Netherlands
Vitalie Chetraru	Chetraru	Male	5th Cousin	5th Cousin	3rd to Distant Cousin	Haitu, paiu, bordeniuc, Bucur, Chetraru	Telenesti, Teleneşti District, Moldova
Katherine Vlahov	Vlahov	Female	5th Cousin	5th Cousin	3rd to Distant Cousin		
Dayna C		Female	5th Cousin	5th Cousin	3rd to Distant Cousin		Poland
Irene Papazicos	Papazicos	Female	5th Cousin	5th Cousin	3rd to Distant Cousin		
Tina Vulgaris	Vulgaris	Female	1959 4th Cousin	4th Cousin	3rd to Distant Cousin		
Tina Vulgaris	Vulgaris	Female	1959 4th Cousin	4th Cousin	3rd to Distant Cousin		
Shema Salim	Salim	Female	5th Cousin	5th Cousin	3rd to Distant Cousin		
Elizabeth Godwin	Godwin	Female	5th Cousin	5th Cousin	3rd to Distant Cousin	Bisulca, Calcagno, Biddera, Giuseppa, Doutney, Post, Partch, McEwen, Hoyt, Smith, Capada, Stoppard, Jackson, Parke, Munson, Moss, Lothropp, Ludlum, Cool, Kool, De Forest, Obe, DeForest, VanFlaesbeck, Godwin	
Amy C		Female	4th Cousin	4th Cousin	3rd to Distant Cousin	Kenner, Odom, pease, papaelias	
Michelle Alonso	Alonso	Female	5th Cousin	5th Cousin	3rd to Distant Cousin	Eaton, LeBay, DeNullo, Alonso	
Jonathan Walion	Walion	Male	5th Cousin	5th Cousin	3rd to Distant Cousin		
vivian quinones	quinones	Female	5th Cousin	5th Cousin	3rd to Distant Cousin		
Donna MacDonald	MacDonald	Female	5th Cousin	5th Cousin	3rd to Distant Cousin		
Caleb D'Antonio	D'Antonio	Male	5th Cousin	5th Cousin	3rd to Distant Cousin		
Chris Apostolopoulos	Apostolopoulos	Male	5th Cousin	5th Cousin	3rd to Distant Cousin		
Luke Spalj	Spalj	Male	5th Cousin	5th Cousin	3rd to Distant Cousin		

Name	Surname	Sex				Associated names	Location
John Kapetanis	Kapetanis	Male	1958 5th Cousin	5th Cousin	3rd to Distant Cousin	Kapetanakis, Kapetanis	
Antonia Mennis	Mennis	Female	5th Cousin	5th Cousin	3rd to Distant Cousin		
Nicholas Bradley	Bradley	Male	1984 5th Cousin	5th Cousin	3rd to Distant Cousin		
Frances H Kapsalis	Kapsalis	Female	1934 5th Cousin	5th Cousin	3rd to Distant Cousin	Hinos, Hinou, Bakopoulos, Lagios, Charalambopoulos, Kapsalis	
Candy Campus	Campus	Female	5th Cousin	5th Cousin	3rd to Distant Cousin		
Thor Wasbotten	Wasbotten	Male	5th Cousin	5th Cousin	3rd to Distant Cousin		
Diane Johnson	Johnson	Female	4th Cousin	4th Cousin	3rd to Distant Cousin		
Constance Nicholas	Nicholas	Female	5th Cousin	5th Cousin	3rd to Distant Cousin	Geekas, Demos, Lambropolous, Nicholas	Detroit, MI; Dracut, MA; Georgetown Sparta, Greece; Chora, Peloponnisos Dytiki Ellada ke Ionio, Greece
Tracie Keglic	Keglic	Female	5th Cousin	5th Cousin	3rd to Distant Cousin		
helen Zalokosta	Zalokosta	Female	1955 5th Cousin	5th Cousin	3rd to Distant Cousin	Zalokosta Varsos Koutsoupias, Zalokosta	Greece
Katherine Kokkos	Kokkos	Female	1954 5th Cousin	5th Cousin	3rd to Distant Cousin	Steen Locke Kokkos, Kokkos	
Alexandra Tsioutsioulas	Tsioutsioulas	Female	1947 5th Cousin	5th Cousin	3rd to Distant Cousin		
Jessica Siegel	Siegel	Female	1988 5th Cousin	5th Cousin	3rd to Distant Cousin	Sanders, Siegel	
donna pierson	pierson	Female	5th Cousin	5th Cousin	3rd to Distant Cousin	Piontek, Bilicki, pierson	
CH		Male	2001 5th Cousin	5th Cousin	3rd to Distant Cousin	Hanna, Van Winkle, Coley, Evanoff, Jackman	Arkansas, United States; Bulgaria
Samantha Early	Early	Female	5th Cousin	5th Cousin	3rd to Distant Cousin		
Rodger Polychronis	Polychronis	Male	1948 4th Cousin	4th Cousin	3rd to Distant Cousin		
Lyndsay Stednitz	Stednitz	Female	1991 4th Cousin	4th Cousin	3rd to Distant Cousin		
Cherie Luna	Luna	Female	1976 5th Cousin	5th Cousin	3rd to Distant Cousin		
JULIANNE MATARAGAS	MATARAGAS	Female	5th Cousin	5th Cousin	3rd to Distant Cousin	Marciano, Hermatoa, MATARAGAS	Romiri, Greece
erica D'Amico	D'Amico	Female	5th Cousin	5th Cousin	3rd to Distant Cousin		
Mike Ioanou	Ioanou	Male	1978 2nd Cousin, Once Removed	2nd Cousin, Once Removed		Ioanou, Parthanis	
Frank Kostopoulos	Kostopoulos	Male	1997 5th Cousin	5th Cousin	3rd to Distant Cousin		
jeremiah hanes	hanes	Male	1997 5th Cousin	5th Cousin	3rd to Distant Cousin	Hanes, hanes	
Megan Belica	Belica	Female	5th Cousin	5th Cousin	3rd to Distant Cousin		
Janina (Jasha) Skousbol	Skousbol	Female	5th Cousin	5th Cousin	3rd to Distant Cousin	Anna Klucznik, Stefania Markowski, Stefania Bor, Antoni Bor and wife Katarzyna Bor, Victor Klucznik, Stefan Markowski, Skousbol	
Ross Talis	Talis	Male	5th Cousin	5th Cousin	3rd to Distant Cousin	Talitsicas, Dalitsikas, Shinas, Dreliozis, Trapalis, Routsis, Rouches, Niketopoulos, Spiliotis, Dedopoulos, Drelles, Schinas, Talis	Milwaukee, Milwaukee County, Wisconsin, United States
Johanna Korantzopoulou	Korantzopoulou	Female	5th Cousin	5th Cousin	3rd to Distant Cousin		
Kristen Cordiello	Cordiello	Female	1991 5th Cousin	5th Cousin	3rd to Distant Cousin		
Olive Byrne	Byrne	Female	1953 5th Cousin	5th Cousin	3rd to Distant Cousin	Brady, Cowley, Byrne	Longford, County Longford, Ireland
Alexia Conger	Conger	Female	5th Cousin	5th Cousin	3rd to Distant Cousin	Weston, Triffonopoulos, Fotopoulos, Skandros, Skondras, Conger	
Andrew Budendorf	Budendorf	Male	5th Cousin	5th Cousin	3rd to Distant Cousin		
Caryl Antalis	Antalis	Female	1950 4th Cousin	4th Cousin	3rd to Distant Cousin	Gallanis, Kyriazoglou, Bobis, Antalis	
Valerie Janssens	Janssens	Female	1961 4th Cousin	4th Cousin	3rd to 5th Cousin		
dia mundle	mundle	Female	5th Cousin	5th Cousin	3rd to Distant Cousin	nouragas, zorbas, mundle	
AL		Female	5th Cousin	5th Cousin	3rd to Distant Cousin		
Dianna Lowe	Lowe	Female	5th Cousin	5th Cousin	3rd to Distant Cousin	Brown, Clark, Walker, Lowe	
Marc Legnard	Legnard	Male	5th Cousin	5th Cousin	3rd to Distant Cousin		
Blaine Swanzy	Swanzy	Female	5th Cousin	5th Cousin	3rd to Distant Cousin		
PA		Female	1972 5th Cousin	5th Cousin	3rd to Distant Cousin	Tassoff, Tasso, Tountas	
Turkmen Tari	Tari	Male	5th Cousin	5th Cousin	3rd to Distant Cousin		
Ingrid Campochiaro	Campochiaro	Female	1943 5th Cousin	5th Cousin	3rd to Distant Cousin	Gronki, Preiss, Petersen, Koch, Campochiaro	
Jessica Fittoria	Fittoria	Female	1992 5th Cousin	5th Cousin	3rd to Distant Cousin	Rosales, Fittoria	
Anthi Georgakopoulos	Georgakopoulos	Female	5th Cousin	5th Cousin	3rd to Distant Cousin		

Pamela Ajango	Ajango	Female	1974	5th Cousin	5th Cousin	3rd to Distant Cousin	Paras, Karellas, Teinfeld, Wilhelmson, Ajango	
Andrea Petratos (Tabor)	Petratos (Tabor)	Female	1966	5th Cousin	5th Cousin	3rd to Distant Cousin		
Chris Lagos	Lagos	Male	1969	5th Cousin	5th Cousin	3rd to Distant Cousin	Lagos, Pappas	
Konstantine Karantasis	Karantasis	Male	1980	5th Cousin	5th Cousin	3rd to Distant Cousin	Giavis, Sismanis, Kladakis, Karantasis	Ano Symi, Greece
katy reeder	reeder	Female		5th Cousin	5th Cousin	3rd to Distant Cousin		
Chloe Hoff	Hoff	Female	1993	4th Cousin	4th Cousin	3rd to 6th Cousin		
Christa Molloy	Molloy	Female		5th Cousin	5th Cousin	3rd to Distant Cousin	Micklitz, Scholz, Schwarzer, Brazzel, Bowers, Fielder, Touhey, Rosenquist, Molloy	Ballynakill, County Galway, Ireland; County Kerry, Ireland; FÃ¼rth, Middle Franconia, Bavaria, Germany; Cork, County Cork, Ireland; Waterford, County Waterford, Ireland
A Van Gilder	Van Gilder	Male	1951	5th Cousin	5th Cousin	3rd to Distant Cousin		
Blendi Hasa	Hasa	Male		5th Cousin	5th Cousin	3rd to Distant Cousin		
Heleni Lewis	Lewis	Female		5th Cousin	5th Cousin	3rd to Distant Cousin	Foulos, Kontonis, Xalepa, Lewis	Romania; Greece
Kristina Mentakis	Mentakis	Female		5th Cousin	5th Cousin	3rd to Distant Cousin		
Jennifer Broge Voss	Broge Voss	Female		5th Cousin	5th Cousin	3rd to Distant Cousin	Broge, Klunge, Murphy, Leonard, Schrader, McLean, Broge Voss	Ireland; Germany
Cemal O	O	Male		5th Cousin	5th Cousin	3rd to Distant Cousin		
Sydney Barron	Barron	Female	2000	5th Cousin	5th Cousin	3rd to Distant Cousin		
Ken Schuster	Schuster	Male		5th Cousin	5th Cousin	3rd to Distant Cousin		
Roseanne Shefferman	Shefferman	Female	1953	5th Cousin	5th Cousin	3rd to Distant Cousin		
Chris T	T	Male	1937	5th Cousin	5th Cousin	3rd to Distant Cousin		Italy
Joann Patterson	Patterson	Female		5th Cousin	5th Cousin	3rd to Distant Cousin		
Svetoslav BOJILOV	BOJILOV	Male	1965	5th Cousin	5th Cousin	3rd to Distant Cousin	Isov, Bokov, Surlekov, BOJILOV	
Adonis Stassinopoulos	Stassinopoulos	Male		5th Cousin	5th Cousin	3rd to Distant Cousin	Sakalis, Smirli, Stassinopoulos	
Terry Bowden	Bowden	Male	1946	5th Cousin	5th Cousin	3rd to Distant Cousin	Heath, Soper, Kearney, Winsor, Squire, Gruitt, Mountjoy, Baker, Lakeman, Robinson, Hiscox, Rowe, Sawford, Williams, Tinney, Rowden, Kelly, Bowden	County Kerry, Ireland; Devon, England, United Kingdom; Nelson, Nelson, New Zealand
sandra cosmopoulos	cosmopoulos	Female	1960	5th Cousin	5th Cousin	3rd to Distant Cousin		Athens, Greece; Greece
Melissa Lake	Lake	Female		5th Cousin	5th Cousin	3rd to Distant Cousin	Avgerinos, Lake	
Alexandria Doing	Doing	Female	1982	5th Cousin	5th Cousin	3rd to Distant Cousin	Masterson, Armstrong, Doing	
Tim Cumuze	Cumuze	Male		5th Cousin	5th Cousin	3rd to Distant Cousin		
Edmond Deci	Deci	Male		5th Cousin	5th Cousin	3rd to Distant Cousin		
IOANNIS LEMPIDAKIS	LEMPIDAKIS	Male	1937	5th Cousin	5th Cousin	3rd to Distant Cousin	Vassilakis, Stratigakis, Kourmoulis, LEMPIDAKIS	
Giannis Piperis	Piperis	Male	1975	5th Cousin	5th Cousin	3rd to Distant Cousin		
Kara G		Female		5th Cousin	5th Cousin	3rd to Distant Cousin	Tierney, Curry, Mcneill, LoRe, Bagley	
William Basso	Basso	Male		4th Cousin	4th Cousin	3rd to 6th Cousin		
Ryan Gladney	Gladney	Male		5th Cousin	5th Cousin	3rd to Distant Cousin		
Krystle Herrera	Herrera	Female		5th Cousin	5th Cousin	3rd to Distant Cousin		
Irene Kambos	Kambos	Female		5th Cousin	5th Cousin	3rd to Distant Cousin		
Hugh McLaurin	McLaurin	Male	1954	5th Cousin	5th Cousin	3rd to Distant Cousin		
Benjamin Brugh	Brugh	Male	1983	5th Cousin	5th Cousin	3rd to Distant Cousin	Cordone, Lindsay, Hall, Williams, Brugh, Malatesta, Osborne	
Dimitri Gerontis	Gerontis	Male		4th Cousin	4th Cousin	3rd to 6th Cousin		
Harry Cosmos	Cosmos	Male	1952	4th Cousin	4th Cousin	3rd to 5th Cousin	Gretsis, Treatafeles, Demetre, Yaglagoulo, Cosmos	
Penny Richardson	Richardson	Female	1949	5th Cousin	5th Cousin	3rd to Distant Cousin	Stutzman, Richardson	
Eleanor Luopa	Luopa	Female		5th Cousin	5th Cousin	3rd to Distant Cousin	Jones, Saari, Luopa	
James Katches	Katches	Male		5th Cousin	5th Cousin	3rd to Distant Cousin		
Elena Economou	Economou	Female		5th Cousin	5th Cousin	3rd to Distant Cousin		
Hanna Wiegers	Wiegers	Female		5th Cousin	5th Cousin	3rd to Distant Cousin		
Ashlee Vlahos	Vlahos	Female		3rd Cousin	3rd Cousin	3rd to 4th Cousin		
Nikoleta Exis	Exis	Female		5th Cousin	5th Cousin	3rd to Distant Cousin		
Nicole Secic	Secic	Female	2003	5th Cousin	5th Cousin	3rd to Distant Cousin		

Name	Surname	Gender	Year	Relationship	Relationship	Range	Surnames	Locations
George M		Male	1944	5th Cousin	5th Cousin	3rd to Distant Cousin		
William Sanacore	Sanacore	Male	1966	5th Cousin	5th Cousin	3rd to Distant Cousin		Greece
Jean Marie Poster	Poster	Female		5th Cousin	5th Cousin	3rd to Distant Cousin		
Shirley Tephly	Tephly	Female		5th Cousin	5th Cousin	3rd to Distant Cousin		
Cary Jordahl	Jordahl	Male	1970	4th Cousin	4th Cousin	3rd to 6th Cousin		
Amanda Gluck	Gluck	Female	1989	5th Cousin	5th Cousin	3rd to Distant Cousin		
nicholas semedalas	semedalas	Male	1962	5th Cousin	5th Cousin	3rd to Distant Cousin		
Vicki Peterson	Peterson	Female	1966	5th Cousin	5th Cousin	3rd to Distant Cousin		
George Hios	Hios	Male	1966	4th Cousin	4th Cousin	3rd to 6th Cousin	Stratakos, Hios	Greece
AM		Male		5th Cousin	5th Cousin	3rd to Distant Cousin		
Marina Petersen	Petersen	Female		5th Cousin	5th Cousin	3rd to Distant Cousin	Poulos, Cleotelis, Samonte, Petersen, Napoles, Napolis	Greece; Philippines; Denmark; Mitilini, Greece
Nicholas Kasimatis	Kasimatis	Male	1983	5th Cousin	5th Cousin	3rd to Distant Cousin		
Phaidon Petropoulos	Petropoulos	Male	2002	5th Cousin	5th Cousin	3rd to Distant Cousin		
Demetris Papaioannou	Papaioannou	Male	1987	5th Cousin	5th Cousin	3rd to Distant Cousin		
George Carafa	Carafa	Male	1970	5th Cousin	5th Cousin	3rd to Distant Cousin	Danzeisen, Carafa, Hornsby, Bartlett	
Windy Mclane	Mclane	Female	1990	5th Cousin	5th Cousin	3rd to Distant Cousin		
Nikki Garner	Garner	Female	1965	5th Cousin	5th Cousin	3rd to Distant Cousin		
Agim Mazreku	Mazreku	Male	1996	5th Cousin	5th Cousin	3rd to Distant Cousin		
jennifer judson	judson	Female	1974	5th Cousin	5th Cousin	3rd to Distant Cousin	Hernandez, Stavec, Lally, Hendricks, judson	Slovenia; Germany; Dublin, County Dublin, Ireland
Pamela Rambus	Rambus	Female	1971	5th Cousin	5th Cousin	3rd to Distant Cousin		
Jonjon T	T	Male	2000	5th Cousin	5th Cousin	3rd to Distant Cousin		
Elexia Freeman	Freeman	Female		5th Cousin	5th Cousin	3rd to Distant Cousin		
Debra Davallou	Davallou	Female		5th Cousin	5th Cousin	3rd to Distant Cousin		
Katerina Stylla	Stylla	Female		4th Cousin	4th Cousin	3rd to 5th Cousin		
MV		Female		5th Cousin	5th Cousin	3rd to Distant Cousin		
Anthony Santillo	Santillo	Male	1964	5th Cousin	5th Cousin	3rd to Distant Cousin		
Stefana Jovanovska	Jovanovska	Female		5th Cousin	5th Cousin	3rd to Distant Cousin		
M Sak	Sak	Male		5th Cousin	5th Cousin	3rd to Distant Cousin		
Maria Lucco	Lucco	Female		4th Cousin	4th Cousin	3rd to 6th Cousin	Makris, Lucco	Peloponnese, Greece
William Bergner	Bergner	Male	1942	5th Cousin	5th Cousin	3rd to Distant Cousin	Paukovitz, Bergner	
Helen Dimitratos	Dimitratos	Female		5th Cousin	5th Cousin	3rd to Distant Cousin		
LINDA LEWIS	LEWIS	Female	1954	4th Cousin	4th Cousin	3rd to 6th Cousin	Boblin, Karlzen, Gerbic, Wunderink, LEWIS	
Jennifer Cina	Cina	Female	1977	5th Cousin	5th Cousin	3rd to Distant Cousin		
Caitlin Conry	Conry	Female		5th Cousin	5th Cousin	3rd to Distant Cousin		
Tegan Kimball	Kimball	Female		4th Cousin	4th Cousin	3rd to 6th Cousin		
Petros Kouretsos	Kouretsos	Male		5th Cousin	5th Cousin	3rd to Distant Cousin		
Nikos Chatzipetros	Chatzipetros	Male		5th Cousin	5th Cousin	3rd to Distant Cousin		
Renee Demars	Demars	Female	1965	5th Cousin	5th Cousin	3rd to Distant Cousin		
Suzanne Dangler	Dangler	Female		5th Cousin	5th Cousin	3rd to Distant Cousin	driscoll, sak, st germaine, canon, Dangler	
Pauline Fox	Fox	Female		5th Cousin	5th Cousin	3rd to Distant Cousin	Clothakis, Petrogeorge (Petrogeorgakis), Pappadakis, Beys, Mavrakis, Fox	Kalamitsi Amigdali, Greece; Litsarda, Greece; Mournies, Greece; Chania, Greece
Kathy Obdzhanyan	Obdzhanyan	Female		5th Cousin	5th Cousin	3rd to Distant Cousin	Ovsepyan, Najaryan, Obdzhanyan, Bakhchedzhyan	
Vedran Jelinovic	Jelinovic	Male	1950	5th Cousin	5th Cousin	3rd to Distant Cousin		
Ajla Hosic	Hosic	Female	1997	5th Cousin	5th Cousin	3rd to Distant Cousin	Berilo, Velić, Fajic, Hosic	
aziz hammad	hammad	Male		5th Cousin	5th Cousin	3rd to Distant Cousin		
Maria Pelekanos	Pelekanos	Female		5th Cousin	5th Cousin	3rd to Distant Cousin	Bertsekas, Dardani, Markopoulos, Pelekanos	
Logan Weeks	Weeks	Male		5th Cousin	5th Cousin	3rd to Distant Cousin	Papageorgopolous, Bullard, Pappas, Casaregala, Baker, Weeks	Kalavrita, Greece; Kleitoria, Greece
A Roumell, Sr.	Roumell, Sr.	Male	1949	5th Cousin	5th Cousin	3rd to Distant Cousin	Roumeliotis, Roumell, Sr.	
Jason C		Male		5th Cousin	5th Cousin	3rd to Distant Cousin		
Helen Kontis	Kontis	Female		4th Cousin	4th Cousin	3rd to 6th Cousin		Mt Lebanon,Pa; Baltimore,MD; Ft.Lauderdale,Fla; Titusville,Fla

Name	Surname	Gender	Year	Relationship	Relationship	Relationship	Surnames	Location
Bujar Ibrahimi	Ibrahimi	Male	1981	5th Cousin	5th Cousin	3rd to Distant Cousin	Shehu, Mustafa, Leka, Ibrahimi	Albania; Pogradec, Pogradec District, KorÃ§Ã« County, Albania
Arabela Barbu	Barbu	Female	1994	5th Cousin	5th Cousin	3rd to Distant Cousin		
Stelian Damu	Damu	Male		5th Cousin	5th Cousin	3rd to Distant Cousin		
Brian A		Male	1960	5th Cousin	5th Cousin	3rd to Distant Cousin		
Arietta Tetreault	Tetreault	Female	1995	5th Cousin	5th Cousin	3rd to Distant Cousin	Rigopoulos, Baimas, Philibotte, Royal, Bozicas, Tzanetis, Dinelle, Tetreault	Lagkadia, Greece; Quebec, Canada
Stephanie Engman	Engman	Female		4th Cousin	4th Cousin	3rd to 6th Cousin		
TL		Male	1958	5th Cousin	5th Cousin	3rd to Distant Cousin	Nardi, Marr, Saracco	
Yolanda Tkachyk	Tkachyk	Female		5th Cousin	5th Cousin	3rd to Distant Cousin	Panagiotopoulos, Tkachyk	
Jack Wright	Wright	Male	1994	5th Cousin	5th Cousin	3rd to Distant Cousin		
Juan AyllÃ³n	AyllÃ³n	Male	1973	5th Cousin	5th Cousin	3rd to Distant Cousin	AyllÃ³n, Alonso, Colmenar, Mouton	
Frances Costanzi	Costanzi	Female	1958	5th Cousin	5th Cousin	3rd to Distant Cousin	Waldron, Martell, Milano, Pendergast, Palmieri, Qualtieri, Wagner, Wing, Costanzi	
Brittany Roginson	Roginson	Female	1989	5th Cousin	5th Cousin	3rd to Distant Cousin		
Patrice Gaydos	Gaydos	Female		5th Cousin	5th Cousin	3rd to Distant Cousin		
Jason Nicholaou	Nicholaou	Male		1st Cousin, Once Removed	1st Cousin, Once Removed		Nicholaou, Lawson, Venis	
Andy Johnson	Johnson	Male		5th Cousin	5th Cousin	3rd to Distant Cousin		
Stephanie Kopsas	Kopsas	Female		5th Cousin	5th Cousin	3rd to Distant Cousin		
George Pavlakis	Pavlakis	Male	2002	5th Cousin	5th Cousin	3rd to Distant Cousin		
Jennifer Knight	Knight	Female		5th Cousin	5th Cousin	3rd to Distant Cousin	Burris, Mickelsen, Walthall, Knight	
Karlana Talbert	Talbert	Female		5th Cousin	5th Cousin	3rd to Distant Cousin		
Nikola Bjelos	Bjelos	Male		5th Cousin	5th Cousin	3rd to Distant Cousin	Grbic, Brujic, Manojlovic, Bjelos	
nikolaos kozanitis	kozanitis	Male		5th Cousin	5th Cousin	3rd to Distant Cousin		
Christina Halm	Halm	Female		5th Cousin	5th Cousin	3rd to Distant Cousin		
Dean Mastoris	Mastoris	Male		5th Cousin	5th Cousin	3rd to Distant Cousin		
Melina Canas	Canas	Female		5th Cousin	5th Cousin	3rd to Distant Cousin		
Renee Caldwell	Caldwell	Female		5th Cousin	5th Cousin	3rd to Distant Cousin	Bates, Beach, Capron, Crouch, Diehl, Endris, Foerster, Geitmann, Graff, Grimmer, Haesselbart, Heffel, Heinze, Janing, Jahning, KÃ¶ster, Langhofer, Luebeck, Makepeace, Meier, Neumann, Proband, Rand, Reinhart, Reinwald, Savage, Schrade, Schuber, Siegel, Sokolowsky, Steinle, Strecker, Weber, Weir, Caldwell	Waldau; Waldow; Sachsen; Baden; Ergenzingen; GroÃŸ Tessin; Warin; Mecklenburg-Schwerin; Mecklenburg; Manitowoc; Kaukauna; Outagamie; Wisconsin; Kansas; Virginia; Russell; New York; Hermansdorff; Volga; Dreispitz; Saratov; Russia; Montgomery County, Virginia; Illinois; Germany;
Ryan Shekell	Shekell	Male		5th Cousin	5th Cousin	3rd to Distant Cousin		
Vasilis Scaltsas	Scaltsas	Male		5th Cousin	5th Cousin	3rd to Distant Cousin		
Mila Petkovic	Petkovic	Female		5th Cousin	5th Cousin	3rd to Distant Cousin		
Harrietta Christodoulos	Christodoulos	Female		5th Cousin	5th Cousin	3rd to Distant Cousin	kapsalis, Tzitzifianos, Bakopoulos, hinos, lagios, Christodoulos	
Brian Torres	Torres	Male	1981	5th Cousin	5th Cousin	3rd to Distant Cousin		
Angela Sarkissian	Sarkissian	Female		5th Cousin	5th Cousin	3rd to Distant Cousin	Assimacopoulos, Manos, Maras, Marasoglou, Hanemoglou, Manusiotis, Sarkissian	Asia Minor, Chicago, Illinois, Yioryitsi, Sparta/Greece; Ä°zmir, Ä°zmir, Turkey; Ä°stanbul, Ä°stanbul, Turkey
Atanaska Sitnova	Sitnova	Female		5th Cousin	5th Cousin	3rd to Distant Cousin	Penev, Stoicevi, Dobrevi, Sitnova	
Maria Melignano	Melignano	Female	1930	5th Cousin	5th Cousin	3rd to Distant Cousin	Buhlinger, Maruggio, Melignano	
Amanda Johnson	Johnson	Female		5th Cousin	5th Cousin	3rd to Distant Cousin		
C balon	balon	Female	1967	5th Cousin	5th Cousin	3rd to Distant Cousin	bogosavljevic, balon	Bosnia and Herzegovina
Beverly Radish	Radish	Female	1991	5th Cousin	5th Cousin	3rd to Distant Cousin		
Voula Hodgins	Hodgins	Female		5th Cousin	5th Cousin	3rd to Distant Cousin		
alexander schwappach	schwappach	Male	1992	5th Cousin	5th Cousin	3rd to Distant Cousin	Schwappach, Monde, schwappach	
Patricia H		Female	1943	5th Cousin	5th Cousin	3rd to Distant Cousin		
Cole Anagnost	Anagnost	Male		5th Cousin	5th Cousin	3rd to Distant Cousin		
Amal S	S	Female		4th Cousin	4th Cousin	3rd to Distant Cousin	Unknown Armenian Name, S	
Jessica Aden	Aden	Female	1978	5th Cousin	5th Cousin	3rd to Distant Cousin	Dillenburg, Koehler, Aden	

George Kontis	Kontis	Male	1945 4th Cousin	4th Cousin	3rd to 6th Cousin	Kontaridis, Kontis, Mikelis, Mikelopoulos, Comninos, Pateas, Zekos	Izmir, Turkey; Limnos Greece; Himadion (Retendou)Pirgos Greece; Pittsburgh, Pa
MH		Female	5th Cousin	5th Cousin	3rd to Distant Cousin		
Nicolette Dennis	Dennis	Female	1955 5th Cousin	5th Cousin	3rd to Distant Cousin	Limperes, Mavragiannis, Stilanidou, Stavros, Limperopoulos, Koudanis, Hasiotis, Delfakis, Nagus, Lyberopoulos, Koudani, Morris (Americanized Mavragiannis), Stevens (Americanized Stilanidou), Dennis	Ostrov, Ostrov, ConstanĉEa County, Romania; Ampelonas, Greece
Georgia Kilpatrick	Kilpatrick	Female	1937 4th Cousin	4th Cousin	3rd to 6th Cousin	Gamalis, Katsimalis, Froelich, Buckweitz, Kilpatrick	
John Tanzer	Tanzer	Male	5th Cousin	5th Cousin	3rd to Distant Cousin		
Judy Garvin	Garvin	Female	5th Cousin	5th Cousin	3rd to Distant Cousin	Rizzo, Difiore, Garvin	
Gemma Paquet	Paquet	Female	1993 5th Cousin	5th Cousin	3rd to Distant Cousin	collin, babacos, paquet, papathanasiou, pouliot, tanguay, pelletier, vallÃ©e, roy, gagnon, Paquet	
Doug Galletti	Galletti	Male	1967 5th Cousin	5th Cousin	3rd to Distant Cousin		
Adrian Chetraru	Chetraru	Male	5th Cousin	5th Cousin	3rd to Distant Cousin	Haitu, Bordeniuc, Paiu, Bucur, Chetraru	
Suzanne Hutchison	Hutchison	Female	5th Cousin	5th Cousin	3rd to Distant Cousin	Alimissis, Spiru, Hutchison	Butte, Silver Bow County, Montana, United States; Los Angeles, Los Angeles County, California, United States
Nikos Foundas	Foundas	Male	4th Cousin	4th Cousin	3rd to Distant Cousin		
alyssa Pappert	Pappert	Female	1983 4th Cousin	4th Cousin	3rd to Distant Cousin	Andricopoulos, Obrien, Pappert	
Chelsie Andersen	Andersen	Female	5th Cousin	5th Cousin	3rd to Distant Cousin	Harmon, Andersen	
Fae Houck	Houck	Female	1948 5th Cousin	5th Cousin	3rd to Distant Cousin	Moan, Hall, Stevens, Phelan, Hiram Moan, Elbridge Moan, Carl Stevens, Frederick Hall, Elinor Hand Hall, Thomas George Hand, Emma Moody Hand, George Valentine Hand, Patricia Morey Hall, Ralph Thomas Moan, Lucy Lake Pettit, Houck	
Victoria Craig	Craig	Female	5th Cousin	5th Cousin	3rd to Distant Cousin	Zukoski, Fisher, Gilmore, Mcknight, Stouch, Craig	
Maria Avdelas	Avdelas	Female	1966 5th Cousin	5th Cousin	3rd to Distant Cousin	Kalogiannis, Avdelas	
AT		Male	5th Cousin	5th Cousin	3rd to Distant Cousin		
Nick Goncalves	Goncalves	Male	5th Cousin	5th Cousin	3rd to Distant Cousin		
Darnell Nelson	Nelson	Male	5th Cousin	5th Cousin	3rd to Distant Cousin		
Tricia Young	Young	Female	1989 5th Cousin	5th Cousin	3rd to Distant Cousin		
Georgia Provence	Provence	Female	5th Cousin	5th Cousin	3rd to Distant Cousin		
George Solandros	Solandros	Male	1938 5th Cousin	5th Cousin	3rd to Distant Cousin		
Harry Cordatos	Cordatos	Male	1968 5th Cousin	5th Cousin	3rd to Distant Cousin		
Frances Aycock Kiker	Kiker	Female	5th Cousin	5th Cousin	3rd to Distant Cousin	Aycock, Myatt, Barnes, Wellons, Perry, Turner, Marshall, Mendenhall, Dillon, Hunter, Renfrow, Peelle, Reveile, Kiker	Smithfield (Johnston Co), NC; Raleigh, NC, Thomasville, NC, Greensboro, NC, Chester, PA; England; Staffordshire, Middlesex, Northhamptonshire, Kent, Derbyshire, Southhampton.
ELENI GILLA	GILLA	Female	4th Cousin	4th Cousin	3rd to 6th Cousin	Eleni George, Gilla, Dimitropoulos, Fotios, Athanasios, GILLA	
Constantin Antonie	Antonie	Male	1970 5th Cousin	5th Cousin	3rd to Distant Cousin	Antonie, Ochialbi	
Kristina Russo	Russo	Female	1986 5th Cousin	5th Cousin	3rd to Distant Cousin	Michaels, Skeans, De Palo, Russo	
Slagana Zugic	Zugic	Female	1977 5th Cousin	5th Cousin	3rd to Distant Cousin	Lakicevic, Zugic	
Vivian Kranenburg	Kranenburg	Female	1943 5th Cousin	5th Cousin	3rd to Distant Cousin		
Kimberly Stanford	Stanford	Female	1992 5th Cousin	5th Cousin	3rd to Distant Cousin	Wiles, Schonbok, Stanford	
george christopher	christopher	Male	4th Cousin	4th Cousin	3rd to Distant Cousin		
jill ferris	ferris	Female	1966 5th Cousin	5th Cousin	3rd to Distant Cousin	Mahoney, Thompson, Davidson, ferris	
Roxie Hiett	Hiett	Female	5th Cousin	5th Cousin	3rd to Distant Cousin		
Dimitrios Papageorgiou	Papageorgiou	Male	1963 5th Cousin	5th Cousin	3rd to Distant Cousin	Galanopoulos, Marinopoulos, Papageorgiou	
Wes Shofstahl	Shofstahl	Male	5th Cousin	5th Cousin	3rd to Distant Cousin		
Mirta Martinez	Martinez	Female	5th Cousin	5th Cousin	3rd to Distant Cousin		

Name	Surname	Sex	Year	Cousin	Cousin	Relationship	Aliases	Territory
Sharry Shekell	Shekell	Male		5th Cousin	5th Cousin	3rd to Distant Cousin		
Ozlem Jenkins	Jenkins	Female		5th Cousin	5th Cousin	3rd to Distant Cousin	Turan, Ã¶ÃYdÃn, Jenkins	
Athena Pelekanos	Pelekanos	Female		5th Cousin	5th Cousin	3rd to Distant Cousin	Dardani, Bertseka, Pelekanos	
Didra Kirschner	Kirschner	Female	1943	5th Cousin	5th Cousin	3rd to Distant Cousin		
Brady Brand	Brand	Male		5th Cousin	5th Cousin	3rd to Distant Cousin		
Gina Phelps	Phelps	Female		5th Cousin	5th Cousin	3rd to Distant Cousin	Casselio, Stella, Corvo, Phelps	
Yorgos K		Male	1985	5th Cousin	5th Cousin	3rd to Distant Cousin		
Elgi Haxhimanka	Haxhimanka	Male		5th Cousin	5th Cousin	3rd to Distant Cousin		
George Manos	Manos	Male	1957	5th Cousin	5th Cousin	3rd to Distant Cousin	Panagopolous, Karamanos, Bowman, Manos	
Martha Makkas	Makkas	Female		5th Cousin	5th Cousin	3rd to Distant Cousin		
Cynthia Vlahos Palmer	Vlahos Palmer	Female	1967	3rd Cousin	3rd Cousin		Vlahos, Geranios, Vlahos Palmer	
Liana Mellow	Mellow	Female		4th Cousin	4th Cousin	3rd to Distant Cousin	Toptschan, Parkhani, Mellow	
Sarah Fazio	Fazio	Female	1997	5th Cousin	5th Cousin	3rd to Distant Cousin		
E Waggoner	Waggoner	Female	2005	5th Cousin	5th Cousin	3rd to Distant Cousin		
Mark Kundid	Kundid	Male	1968	5th Cousin	5th Cousin	3rd to Distant Cousin		
Jordan Garr	Garr	Male	1984	4th Cousin	4th Cousin	3rd to Distant Cousin	harnack, garr, Garr	
Jeffery Bazzy	Bazzy	Male		5th Cousin	5th Cousin	3rd to Distant Cousin		
JD		Male	1983	5th Cousin	5th Cousin	3rd to Distant Cousin	Elkurd, Alkurd, Elkurdi, Alkurdi, Ghafari	Palestinian Territory
Frank Carabetta	Carabetta	Male		5th Cousin	5th Cousin	3rd to Distant Cousin		
Larry Tarabicos	Tarabicos	Male	1960	5th Cousin	5th Cousin	3rd to Distant Cousin		
Amy Upton	Upton	Female	1979	5th Cousin	5th Cousin	3rd to Distant Cousin		
Mary Drineas	Drineas	Female		4th Cousin	4th Cousin	3rd to 5th Cousin		
Mary Drineas	Drineas	Female		4th Cousin	4th Cousin	3rd to 5th Cousin		
KONSTANTINOS KANTOUTSIS	KANTOUTSIS	Male	1988	5th Cousin	5th Cousin	3rd to Distant Cousin	Pekos, Kantoutsis, Kolitsopoulos, Drakopoulos, Serelis, Kalampokis, Stavropoulos, Stabropoulos, Gountoumis, Gkountoumis, Goudoumis, Gkoudoumis, Dedousis, Dethousis, Thethousis, Thedousis, Nikolopoulos, Regoukos, Regkoukos, Mpitsikos, Bitsikos, Tsapepas, KANTOUTSIS	
Nensi Leka	Leka	Female	1986	5th Cousin	5th Cousin	3rd to Distant Cousin		
Joanne Peal	Peal	Female		5th Cousin	5th Cousin	3rd to Distant Cousin		
Diane Tollefson	Tollefson	Female		5th Cousin	5th Cousin	3rd to Distant Cousin	Gevan, Mc Conville, Schwappach, Schmauder, Lavery, Gevas, Mietz, Stathopoulas, Tollefson	
Charles Warburton	Warburton	Male		5th Cousin	5th Cousin	3rc to Distant Cousin		
Kathleen Alumbaugh	Alumbaugh	Female		5th Cousin	5th Cousin	3rd to Distant Cousin	Pensa, Pennza, Savastano, Pasto, DiNicola, Benedetto, Licursi, Pistillo, Alumbaugh	
Zinovia Cheliotis	Cheliotis	Female		4th Cousin	4th Cousin	3rd to Distant Cousin		
Joanna Wysocka	Wysocka	Female	1968	5th Cousin	5th Cousin	3rd to Distant Cousin		
Hristina Bakalova	Bakalova	Female	1988	5th Cousin	5th Cousin	3rd to Distant Cousin		
Robert Milovski	Milovski	Male	1994	5th Cousin	5th Cousin	3rd to Distant Cousin		
Tyler Hutchison	Hutchison	Male	1995	5th Cousin	5th Cousin	3rd to Distant Cousin		
Charissa Gianos	Gianos	Female		5th Cousin	5th Cousin	3rd to Distant Cousin	Diamantopoulos, Kanellopoulos, Katzaveilos, Agnastopoulos, Gianos	
HC		Female		5th Cousin	5th Cousin	3rd to Distant Cousin		
Leonard Vladi	Vladi	Male		5th Cousin	5th Cousin	3rd to Distant Cousin	Vladi.papa.dusha.deliu, Vladi	
Spero Michailidis	Michailidis	Male	1973	5th Cousin	5th Cousin	3rd to Distant Cousin		
Connie Ross	Ross	Female	1972	5th Cousin	5th Cousin	3rd to Distant Cousin	Vassilopoulos, Kounavis, Patsou, Leloutha, Ross	
Helen Plias	Plias	Female	1976	5th Cousin	5th Cousin	3rd to Distant Cousin	Trendos, Navakos, Plias	
Jennifer Prushan	Prushan	Female	1996	5th Cousin	5th Cousin	3rd to Distant Cousin		
Alexander Nicholas	Nicholas	Male		4th Cousin	4th Cousin	3rd to Distant Cousin		
Melanie Barnes	Barnes	Female	1999	5th Cousin	5th Cousin	3rd to Distant Cousin	Vincent, Barnes	
Paula Cho	Cho	Female		4th Cousin	4th Cousin	3rd to Distant Cousin		
Alicia Hemphill	Hemphill	Female	1968	5th Cousin	5th Cousin	3rd to Distant Cousin		

Name	Surname	Sex	Year			Relationship	Associated surnames	Location
Constantina Tzilos	Tzilos	Female	1957	5th Cousin	5th Cousin	3rd to Distant Cousin		
tom ranglas	ranglas	Male		5th Cousin	5th Cousin	3rd to Distant Cousin		
Matthew Vavoukakis	Vavoukakis	Male		5th Cousin	5th Cousin	3rd to Distant Cousin		
Jeff Montieth	Montieth	Male		5th Cousin	5th Cousin	3rd to Distant Cousin		
James Bowden	Bowden	Male	1988	4th Cousin	4th Cousin	3rd to 6th Cousin		
Mark Helm	Helm	Male		5th Cousin	5th Cousin	3rd to Distant Cousin	Risse, Schwanke, Helm, Shvannunska, Burke, Matson	
Demetrius Kilgore	Kilgore	Male		5th Cousin	5th Cousin	3rd to Distant Cousin		
Musa Methasani	Methasani	Male	1947	5th Cousin	5th Cousin	3rd to Distant Cousin		
Paige Labuda	Labuda	Female	2000	5th Cousin	5th Cousin	3rd to Distant Cousin		
Allison Spellicy	Spellicy	Female		5th Cousin	5th Cousin	3rd to Distant Cousin	Long, Bredemeyer, Spellicy	
Melia Ross	Ross	Female		4th Cousin	4th Cousin	3rd to Distant Cousin		
Patrick G		Male		5th Cousin	5th Cousin	3rd to Distant Cousin		
Paul J. Bales	Bales	Male	1958	5th Cousin	5th Cousin	3rd to Distant Cousin	Favier, Bales	
Shannon Charbonneau	Charbonneau	Female	1976	5th Cousin	5th Cousin	3rd to Distant Cousin	Johnston, Kaminsky, Lalonde, Longtin, Charbonneau	
V Goldman	Goldman	Male		5th Cousin	5th Cousin	3rd to Distant Cousin		
Ethan Canas	Canas	Male		5th Cousin	5th Cousin	3rd to Distant Cousin		
Vickie Soupos	Soupos	Female	1972	5th Cousin	5th Cousin	3rd to Distant Cousin	Colovos, Maniatis, Soupos	
Stephanie Torrey	Torrey	Female		5th Cousin	5th Cousin	3rd to Distant Cousin		
Kristina Bonnet	Bonnet	Female		5th Cousin	5th Cousin	3rd to Distant Cousin		
Manvel Solakian	Solakian	Male	1964	5th Cousin	5th Cousin	3rd to Distant Cousin		
Mary Michalopoulos	Michalopoulos	Female		5th Cousin	5th Cousin	3rd to Distant Cousin		
Denise Shekerjian	Shekerjian	Female		5th Cousin	5th Cousin	3rd to Distant Cousin		
Dimitri Daskalakis	Daskalakis	Male	2001	4th Cousin	4th Cousin	3rd to 6th Cousin		
Geo Kopoulos	Kopoulos	Female		5th Cousin	5th Cousin	3rd to Distant Cousin		
Emma Stavropoulos	Stavropoulos	Female		5th Cousin	5th Cousin	3rd to Distant Cousin		
Marek Pearse	Pearse	Male		5th Cousin	5th Cousin	3rd to Distant Cousin		
MK		Male	2004	5th Cousin	5th Cousin	3rd to Distant Cousin	Kouvarakis, Lagoudakis, Stamatakis, Vangopoulos, Mourlas	
Victoria Sideris	Sideris	Female	1968	5th Cousin	5th Cousin	3rd to Distant Cousin	Sideris, Knight	
Antonio Santillo	Santillo	Male	1938	5th Cousin	5th Cousin	3rd to Distant Cousin		
Gina Jenkins	Jenkins	Female		5th Cousin	5th Cousin	3rd to Distant Cousin		
Antonios Bardoutsos	Bardoutsos	Male		5th Cousin	5th Cousin	3rd to Distant Cousin		
CB		Male	1961	5th Cousin	5th Cousin	3rd to Distant Cousin	Beattie, Huth, Long, Neate	Scotland, United Kingdom
Tysha Harris	Harris	Female		5th Cousin	5th Cousin	3rd to Distant Cousin		
LB		Female		4th Cousin	4th Cousin	3rd to 6th Cousin		
Samuel Losasso	Losasso	Male	1995	5th Cousin	5th Cousin	3rd to Distant Cousin	Marinos, Deneris, Souliotis, Dizikes, Diantzikis, Haraka, Anastasopoulos, Losasso	Argos, Greece; Pireas, Greece; Volos, Greece; Corinth, Greece; Sparti, Greece
Martha Hobbs	Hobbs	Female		5th Cousin	5th Cousin	3rd to Distant Cousin	Theofilis, Hobbs	
Alexis J		Female	1991	5th Cousin	5th Cousin	3rd to Distant Cousin		
Edward Kraverotis	Kraverotis	Male		5th Cousin	5th Cousin	3rd to Distant Cousin		
Yvonne Poster	Poster	Female	1957	5th Cousin	5th Cousin	3rd to Distant Cousin	Martino, Martone, Statella, Salvador, Poster	Valencia, Valencia, Valencian Community, Spain; Barcelona, Barcelona, Catalonia, Spain; Sicily, Italy; Naples, Metropolitan City of Naples, Campania, Italy
Soteria Georgiadis	Georgiadis	Female		5th Cousin	5th Cousin	3rd to Distant Cousin		
Andrea Sacchetto	Sacchetto	Female		5th Cousin	5th Cousin	3rd to Distant Cousin		
Ivica Prgonjic	Prgonjic	Male	1963	5th Cousin	5th Cousin	3rd to Distant Cousin	Veres, Njezic, Preradovic, Hlavaty, Prgonjic	
Aubrey Lutz	Lutz	Female	2003	5th Cousin	5th Cousin	3rd to Distant Cousin		
Jana Reyer	Reyer	Female		5th Cousin	5th Cousin	3rd to Distant Cousin	Pirog, Reyer	
Apostolia Schiza	Schiza	Female	1978	5th Cousin	5th Cousin	3rd to Distant Cousin	[illegible], Schiza	
Theodore Stamas	Stamas	Male		4th Cousin	4th Cousin	3rd to 6th Cousin		
Milica Bosnjak	Bosnjak	Female		5th Cousin	5th Cousin	3rd to Distant Cousin		
Martha Rudnick	Rudnick	Female		5th Cousin	5th Cousin	3rd to Distant Cousin		
Nicholas Demetry	Demetry	Male		5th Cousin	5th Cousin	3rd to Distant Cousin	Demetry, Tuntas, Alatsa, Georgiadis, Hatzidimitriou	

Cindy Koutsovasili	Koutsovasili	Female		5th Cousin	5th Cousin	3rd to Distant Cousin	
Chris Santillo	Santillo	Male	1992	5th Cousin	5th Cousin	3rd to Distant Cousin	
Langston Wright	Wright	Female		5th Cousin	5th Cousin	3rd to Distant Cousin	Langston, Sparkman, Guzman, Velasquez, McCabe, Wright
THRASYVOULOS KIPOURGOS	KIPOURGOS	Male	1990	5th Cousin	5th Cousin	3rd to Distant Cousin	Thomas, Kalentzotis, Pantazopoulos, Fotis, KIPOURGOS
Kimberly Anderson	Anderson	Female	1970	5th Cousin	5th Cousin	3rd to Distant Cousin	
ALEXANDROS GIANNOULAKIS	GIANNOULAKIS	Male	1969	5th Cousin	5th Cousin	3rd to Distant Cousin	
S.W. D	D	Male		5th Cousin	5th Cousin	3rd to Distant Cousin	
nathaniel rogic	rogic	Male		5th Cousin	5th Cousin	3rd to Distant Cousin	
Pamela Conry	Conry	Female	1948	5th Cousin	5th Cousin	3rd to Distant Cousin	
Scott Evans	Evans	Male	1982	5th Cousin	5th Cousin	3rd to Distant Cousin	Evans, Haslam, Robinson, Limb, Perkins, Zabriskie, Sanders, Johnson, Lewis, Lang, Hart, Dewing, Reynolds, Higbee, Sidebottom, Porcker, McRae, Stewart, Smith, Schooler, Cooke, Rees, Quigg, Dougherty, Skidmore, Martineau, Asay, Fisher, Allred, Cox, Lefevre, Broadhead, Fausett, Tolman, Rice, Hackley, Walker, Jones, String, Morgan, Bybee; Cedar City, Iron County, Utah, United States; Virgin, Washington County, Utah, United States; Salt Lake City, Salt Lake County, Utah, United States
Arbera Muriqi	Muriqi	Female		5th Cousin	5th Cousin	3rd to Distant Cousin	
Kate Cobb	Cobb	Female		5th Cousin	5th Cousin	3rd to Distant Cousin	
Jennifer Perry	Perry	Female	1965	5th Cousin	5th Cousin	3rd to Distant Cousin	
Vasoula Brown	Brown	Female		5th Cousin	5th Cousin	3rd to Distant Cousin	
Jordan Losea	Losea	Female	1986	5th Cousin	5th Cousin	3rd to Distant Cousin	
Kody Doerschel	Doerschel	Male		5th Cousin	5th Cousin	3rd to Distant Cousin	
Joy White	White	Female		5th Cousin	5th Cousin	3rd to Distant Cousin	
Holly Hauser	Hauser	Female		5th Cousin	5th Cousin	3rd to Distant Cousin	
Claudine Cottini	Cottini	Female		5th Cousin	5th Cousin	3rd to Distant Cousin	
Olga Mandalas	Mandalas	Female	1954	5th Cousin	5th Cousin	3rd to Distant Cousin	Mandrapilias, Hios, Kokkoros, Tsamblinas, Mandalas
Tom Papadatos	Papadatos	Male		5th Cousin	5th Cousin	3rd to Distant Cousin	Lagousakos, Kouzounas, Laskaris, Papadatos, Gigantes, Bouranis
Srdjan Vujosevic	Vujosevic	Male		5th Cousin	5th Cousin	3rd to Distant Cousin	
Stere Mergeani	Mergeani	Male	1979	5th Cousin	5th Cousin	3rd to Distant Cousin	Mergeani, Pitu, Teja, Maca, Mergiani, Mergeane; Gramos, Greece; Tulcea, Tulcea, Tulcea County, Romania; Charlotte, Mecklenburg County, North Carolina, United States; Meehden, Silistra, Bulgaria; Serres, Greece
John Nolan	Nolan	Male	1981	5th Cousin	5th Cousin	3rd to Distant Cousin	O'Hullian, Nolan
Rose Ciniti	Ciniti	Female		5th Cousin	5th Cousin	3rd to Distant Cousin	
George Karalekas	Karalekas	Male	1939	5th Cousin	5th Cousin	3rd to Distant Cousin	Spheris, Saccogenis, Karalekas
George Stevens	Stevens	Male	1957	5th Cousin	5th Cousin	3rd to Distant Cousin	
Donald Noland III	Noland III	Male		5th Cousin	5th Cousin	3rd to Distant Cousin	
Theano Kazagli Wales	Kazagli Wales	Female	1974	5th Cousin	5th Cousin	3rd to Distant Cousin	Phillips, Noland, Noland III; Spiropoulos, Giorgantas, Kontopoulos, Kazaglis, Kazagli Wales; Zatouna, Greece; Elliniko, Greece; Markos, Greece; Atsicholos, Greece
William Chakalos	Chakalos	Male		5th Cousin	5th Cousin	3rd to Distant Cousin	
Veli Rexhepi	Rexhepi	Male		5th Cousin	5th Cousin	3rd to Distant Cousin	
Andrene Johnson	Johnson	Female	1952	5th Cousin	5th Cousin	3rd to Distant Cousin	Wingard, Patterson, Bringolf, Casey, Johnson
Alaine Parnas (Pamutsoglou) Fitzgerald	Parnas (Pamutsoglou) Fitzgerald	Female		4th Cousin	4th Cousin	3rd to 5th Cousin	Miktoniatis, Pamutsoglou, Becht, Brunger, Miller, Parnas (Pamutsoglou) Fitzgerald
Stan Keathly	Keathly	Male	1969	4th Cousin	4th Cousin	3rd to Distant Cousin	Uher, West, McCoy, Kowalski
Ana Antonie	Antonie	Female		5th Cousin	5th Cousin	3rd to Distant Cousin	Vakratsi, Petrardi, Kervanidoy, Manioti, Kamitsis, Karalis
Mike Kowalski	Kowalski	Male	1981	5th Cousin	5th Cousin	3rd to Distant Cousin	
Lida Mamoti	Mamoti	Female	1985	5th Cousin	5th Cousin	3rd to Distant Cousin	

Name	Surname	Gender	Year	Cousin	Cousin	Range	Associated Names	Location
Mary Salinske	Salinske	Female		5th Cousin	5th Cousin	3rd to Distant Cousin		
Lydia Root	Root	Female	1999	5th Cousin	5th Cousin	3rd to Distant Cousin	Root, Dagli	
Robert Gardner	Gardner	Male		5th Cousin	5th Cousin	3rd to Distant Cousin		
Maria Vouros	Vouros	Female	1958	4th Cousin	4th Cousin	3rd to 5th Cousin		
Maria Maloupis	Maloupis	Female	1959	5th Cousin	5th Cousin	3rd to Distant Cousin	Varkaroli, Tsatsaros, Athanasiou, Antonopoulos, Petreidis, Maloupis	Kampos, Greece
Ion Grigore	Grigore	Male	1921	5th Cousin	5th Cousin	3rd to Distant Cousin		
Lidia Spaho	Spaho	Female		5th Cousin	5th Cousin	3rd to Distant Cousin		
Bijan Davallou	Davallou	Male		5th Cousin	5th Cousin	3rd to Distant Cousin		
Jordanka Sitnova Mulligan	Sitnova Mulligan	Female		4th Cousin	4th Cousin	3rd to 6th Cousin		
Michael Tjilos	Tjilos	Male		5th Cousin	5th Cousin	3rd to Distant Cousin		
George Papazicos	Papazicos	Male		4th Cousin	4th Cousin	3rd to Distant Cousin		
Regina Harrigan	Harrigan	Female	1946	5th Cousin	5th Cousin	3rd to Distant Cousin	Bobancz, Harrigan	
Alexander Zidros	Zidros	Male		5th Cousin	5th Cousin	3rd to Distant Cousin		
JORDAN KESTRANEK	KESTRANEK	Female	1990	5th Cousin	5th Cousin	3rd to Distant Cousin		
Kathy Lambert	Lambert	Female		5th Cousin	5th Cousin	3rd to Distant Cousin		
Kristina Robertson	Robertson	Female		5th Cousin	5th Cousin	3rd to Distant Cousin		
John Johnson	Johnson	Male		5th Cousin	5th Cousin	3rd to Distant Cousin		
Elizabeth Poulos	Poulos	Female	1954	5th Cousin	5th Cousin	3rd to Distant Cousin		
Ronald Vaughn	Vaughn	Male		4th Cousin	4th Cousin	3rd to Distant Cousin	English, Roman, Vaughn	
Elliot C		Male	1985	5th Cousin	5th Cousin	3rd to Distant Cousin	Williamson	
Steven Panagos	Panagos	Male		4th Cousin	4th Cousin	3rd to Distant Cousin		
John Papas	Papas	Male	1951	3rd Cousin	3rd Cousin	3rd to 4th Cousin		
URBAN STUDER	STUDER	Male	1948	5th Cousin	5th Cousin	3rd to Distant Cousin	Schwartzmiller, Green, Hertzer, Studer, STUDER	Grand Est, France
Troy Higgins	Higgins	Male	1974	5th Cousin	5th Cousin	3rd to Distant Cousin	Huggins, Higgins	
Sandy Jarkas	Jarkas	Female	1994	5th Cousin	5th Cousin	3rd to Distant Cousin		
Susan Chekouras	Chekouras	Female		5th Cousin	5th Cousin	3rd to Distant Cousin		
B Riggle	Riggle	Male	1976	5th Cousin	5th Cousin	3rd to Distant Cousin		
gregory Panomitros	Panomitros	Male		5th Cousin	5th Cousin	3rd to Distant Cousin		
Mary Fishman-Glennan	Fishman-Glennan	Female		5th Cousin	5th Cousin	3rd to Distant Cousin		
Elma Tuzovic Beqaj	Tuzovic Beqaj	Female		5th Cousin	5th Cousin	3rd to Distant Cousin		
Maringlen Borici	Borici	Male		5th Cousin	5th Cousin	3rd to Distant Cousin		
Nicholas Pavlakis	Pavlakis	Male	2001	5th Cousin	5th Cousin	3rd to Distant Cousin		
Chris Trahiotis	Trahiotis	Male	2003	5th Cousin	5th Cousin	3rd to Distant Cousin	Trahiotis	
Anastasios Kapsalis	Kapsalis	Male		5th Cousin	5th Cousin	3rd to Distant Cousin	Veremis, Kapsalis	
Lynn Kota	Kota	Female	1970	5th Cousin	5th Cousin	3rd to Distant Cousin		
Angelo Tsakopoulos	Tsakopoulos	Male	1936	5th Cousin	5th Cousin	3rd to Distant Cousin		
Bekzod Tadjibaev	Tadjibaev	Male		5th Cousin	5th Cousin	3rd to Distant Cousin		Uzbekistan
David Warfield	Warfield	Male		5th Cousin	5th Cousin	3rd to Distant Cousin	Rees, Campbell, Partin, Prichard, Hubbs, Sharp, Terrell, Grant, Warfield	
Kevin Albers	Albers	Male		5th Cousin	5th Cousin	3rd to Distant Cousin	Albers, Spero	
sophia klopas	klopas	Female		5th Cousin	5th Cousin	3rd to Distant Cousin	kapernekas, galamas, klopas	
Anthony Bulldis	Bulldis	Male		5th Cousin	5th Cousin	3rd to Distant Cousin	Englert, Builldis, Owens, Doan, Gawrys, Oczhowski, Mozgawa, Stolzman	Balıkesir Province, Turkey
Panagiotis Koboudis	Koboudis	Male		5th Cousin	5th Cousin	3rd to Distant Cousin		
Alex Arvanitidis	Arvanitidis	Male		5th Cousin	5th Cousin	3rd to Distant Cousin		
james andrews	andrews	Male		5th Cousin	5th Cousin	3rd to Distant Cousin		
Nicole Allison	Allison	Female		5th Cousin	5th Cousin	3rd to Distant Cousin	Papadimitropoulos, Kagiannas, Allison	
Robin Parker	Parker	Female	1954	5th Cousin	5th Cousin	3rd to Distant Cousin		
A X	X	Female		5th Cousin	5th Cousin	3rd to Distant Cousin		
Bryar Balon	Balon	Male		5th Cousin	5th Cousin	3rd to Distant Cousin		
Evangelos Tambassis	Tambassis	Male		4th Cousin	4th Cousin	3rd to 6th Cousin		
Denise Hodge	Hodge	Female		5th Cousin	5th Cousin	3rd to Distant Cousin		
Kristie White	White	Female		5th Cousin	5th Cousin	3rd to Distant Cousin		Poplar Bluff, MO
Karen Haight-Selling	Haight-Selling	Female	1968	5th Cousin	5th Cousin	3rd to Distant Cousin		
Paul Sebesta	Sebesta	Male		5th Cousin	5th Cousin	3rd to Distant Cousin	Ciccone Brown, Sebesta	Italy

Name	Surname	Gender	Year	Relationship			Surnames	Location
Christopher Karabats	Karabats	Male	1946	5th Cousin	5th Cousin	3rd to Distant Cousin		
Maya Dias	Dias	Female	1987	5th Cousin	5th Cousin	3rd to Distant Cousin		
Karsten Loukides	Loukides	Male	1992	4th Cousin	4th Cousin	3rd to 5th Cousin		
Marta Mendizabal	Mendizabal	Female		5th Cousin	5th Cousin	3rd to Distant Cousin		
Panos Makkas	Makkas	Male		5th Cousin	5th Cousin	3rd to Distant Cousin		
Jessica Brooks	Brooks	Female		5th Cousin	5th Cousin	3rd to Distant Cousin	Ipjian, Pierre, Brooks	
Kristian Kellems	Kellems	Female		3rd Cousin	3rd Cousin	3rd to 5th Cousin		
Lisi Powers	Powers	Female		5th Cousin	5th Cousin	3rd to Distant Cousin	Powers, Cravero, varvaro	
Alexis Furkioti	Furkioti	Female		2nd Cousin, 3x Removed	2nd Cousin, 3x Removed		Furkioti, Revels, Chalekson	
AP		Male	1972	5th Cousin	5th Cousin	3rd to Distant Cousin	Tsokos, Kosma, Kretsi	
Pat Glavas	Glavas	Female		5th Cousin	5th Cousin	3rd to Distant Cousin		
VF		Female		5th Cousin	5th Cousin	3rd to Distant Cousin		
Valentin M		Male	1964	4th Cousin	4th Cousin	3rd to 6th Cousin	Mihov, Kaloyanov	
MARY RUSS	RUSS	Female		5th Cousin	5th Cousin	3rd to Distant Cousin	Kessinger, Marth, Brown, Pelzman, Logsdon, RUSS	
Grant Collins	Collins	Male		5th Cousin	5th Cousin	3rd to Distant Cousin	Evans, Collins, Beall, Elliott, Renshaw, Baldwin, Nowlan, Beaumont, Witherspoon	
Valentin Mihov	Mihov	Male		4th Cousin	4th Cousin	3rd to 6th Cousin		
Djordje Djordje	Djordje	Male	1938	5th Cousin	5th Cousin	3rd to Distant Cousin		
Olivia Espey	Espey	Female		5th Cousin	5th Cousin	3rd to Distant Cousin		
Agapios Kyritsis	Kyritsis	Male		5th Cousin	5th Cousin	3rd to Distant Cousin	kyritsis, Kyritsis	
Brankica Lazoroska	Lazoroska	Female		5th Cousin	5th Cousin	3rd to Distant Cousin		
Shaylene Schmidt	Schmidt	Female		5th Cousin	5th Cousin	3rd to Distant Cousin		
Hillary Pelukas	Pelukas	Female		5th Cousin	5th Cousin	3rd to Distant Cousin	Krolik, Menghini, Shattock, Pelukas	
Koray G		Male		5th Cousin	5th Cousin	3rd to Distant Cousin	Musa, Alptekin, Kucukarslan	Baghdad, Baghdad Governorate, Iraq; Kirkuk, Kirkuk, Kirkuk Governorate, Iraq
Robert Giokas	Giokas	Male		4th Cousin	4th Cousin	3rd to Distant Cousin		
stella marinos	marinos	Female		5th Cousin	5th Cousin	3rd to Distant Cousin	Marinos, Zogopolos, Paraskevopoulos, Baker, Fekas, Violiotis, Andrikopolos, Chiochios, Kapogeannis, marinos	San Francisco Bay Area, California, Manchester, NH, Newark, NJ, Kendriko, Kalamata, Greece, Karlovasi, Samos Greece,
Steven Cika Sr.	Cika Sr.	Male	1949	5th Cousin	5th Cousin	3rd to Distant Cousin		
Aurelia Alamariu	Alamariu	Female		5th Cousin	5th Cousin	3rd to Distant Cousin	Iordache, Anghel, Alamariu	
Joan Harn	Harn	Female	1951	5th Cousin	5th Cousin	3rd to Distant Cousin	Maat, McLellan, Harn	Scotland, United Kingdom
Karyn Peabody	Peabody	Female	1973	5th Cousin	5th Cousin	3rd to Distant Cousin	Bazis, Vosler, Peabody	
Michael Nikolov	Nikolov	Male		5th Cousin	5th Cousin	3rd to Distant Cousin		
Jennifer Digiulio	Digiulio	Female	1994	5th Cousin	5th Cousin	3rd to Distant Cousin	Depaolo, Harris, Bisenga, Palleschi, Digiulio	
Laurie Radojevich	Radojevich	Female		5th Cousin	5th Cousin	3rd to Distant Cousin		
Georgiean Dovellos	Dovellos	Female	1964	5th Cousin	5th Cousin	3rd to Distant Cousin		
Daniel Bazzy-Schmidt	Bazzy-Schmidt	Male		5th Cousin	5th Cousin	3rd to Distant Cousin		
Robert Rodopoulos	Rodopoulos	Male	1968	5th Cousin	5th Cousin	3rd to Distant Cousin		
Valeria Martinovic	Martinovic	Female	1963	5th Cousin	5th Cousin	3rd to Distant Cousin	GaÅjpar, BaÄiÄ‡, Martinovic	
Rebecca Missios	Missios	Female		5th Cousin	5th Cousin	3rd to Distant Cousin		
EIRENE BURNETTE	BURNETTE	Female		4th Cousin	4th Cousin	3rd to 5th Cousin		
Peter Chandrinos	Chandrinos	Male	1963	4th Cousin	4th Cousin	3rd to Distant Cousin		
Chrissy P	P	Female		4th Cousin	4th Cousin	3rd to Distant Cousin		
Antonios Angelikopoulos	Angelikopoulos	Male		4th Cousin	4th Cousin	3rd to Distant Cousin		Izmir, Ä°zmir, Turkey; Cairo, Cairo Governorate, Egypt
John Simso	Simso	Male	1969	5th Cousin	5th Cousin	3rd to Distant Cousin	Walbon, Deangelo, Lee, Hanssen, Simso	Norway; Italy
Gent Bitincka	Bitincka	Male		5th Cousin	5th Cousin	3rd to Distant Cousin		
Cassandra Diamond	Diamond	Female	1987	4th Cousin	4th Cousin	3rd to Distant Cousin	Hudgins, Henderson, Diamond	
Vicki Cobb	Cobb	Female	1948	4th Cousin	4th Cousin	3rd to Distant Cousin	Syriopoulos, Shereopoulos, Shereos, Anagnostopoulos, Christacakos, Christos, Cobb	Sioux City, Woodbury County, Iowa, United States; Chicago, Cook County, Illinois, United States
E. Niko Mourgelas	Mourgelas	Male		5th Cousin	5th Cousin	3rd to Distant Cousin		
Antony Robertson	Robertson	Male		5th Cousin	5th Cousin	3rd to Distant Cousin	Robertson, Escobar, Marshal, Basurto	
Sophia Verros	Verros	Female	1975	5th Cousin	5th Cousin	3rd to Distant Cousin	Anagnostopoulos, Gountanis, Verros	

Name	Surname	Gender				Surnames	Location
Nick Kogkas	Kogkas	Male	1993 4th Cousin	4th Cousin	3rd to 6th Cousin		
Jacqueline Crandell Gregerich	Crandell Gregerich	Female	1950 5th Cousin	5th Cousin	3rd to Distant Cousin	Crandell, Parker, Best, Josephson, Fassett, White, Campbell, Nolte, Andrus, Schultz, Oldham, Woodward/Woodard, Murphy, Thomas, Powell, Foote, Rockwell, Eggleston, Rasmussen, Hartman, Hart, Wenn, Crandell Gregerich	
Trevor B		Male	5th Cousin	5th Cousin	3rd to Distant Cousin		
Adrienne Barris	Barris	Female	1951 4th Cousin	4th Cousin	3rd to Distant Cousin		
Andrea Gioulis	Gioulis	Female	5th Cousin	5th Cousin	3rd to Distant Cousin		
Jim Cerasani	Cerasani	Male	4th Cousin	4th Cousin	3rd to Distant Cousin		
LAMBRINI VLAGOS	VLAGOS	Female	5th Cousin	5th Cousin	3rd to Distant Cousin	Roumbos, Papaxristou, VLAGOS	Kandila, Greece
Tihomir Matijasevic	Matijasevic	Male	5th Cousin	5th Cousin	3rd to Distant Cousin		
Joseph Gad	Gad	Male	5th Cousin	5th Cousin	3rd to Distant Cousin		
Larry Kilpatrick	Kilpatrick	Male	4th Cousin	4th Cousin	3rd to 6th Cousin		
HZ		Female	1958 5th Cousin	5th Cousin	3rd to Distant Cousin	Aggelopoulos, Anagnostopoulos, Andranopoulos, Anagnos, Koakouzelis	
Costas Rakitzis-Poulos	Rakitzis-Poulos	Male	5th Cousin	5th Cousin	3rd to Distant Cousin	Vouloumanos, Rakitzis-Poulos	; Sparti, Peloponnisos Dytiki Ellada ke Ionio, Greece
Maria Provatas	Provatas	Female	1997 5th Cousin	5th Cousin	3rd to Distant Cousin	Provatas, Spanos, Apostoleris, Kefalas, Keramidas	
Michal Skolnik	Skolnik	Male	1983 5th Cousin	5th Cousin	3rd to Distant Cousin		
Austyn Plumlee	Plumlee	Female	5th Cousin	5th Cousin	3rd to Distant Cousin		
Arthur Vandenplas	Vandenplas	Male	1951 5th Cousin	5th Cousin	3rd to Distant Cousin	Vandenplas, Fauconier, Heris, Renard, Skibbe, Radzom, Hunecke, Curth, Linnemann, Preusser, Kelly, Pfau	Ireland; France; Germany
Jennifer McGarity	McGarity	Female	5th Cousin	5th Cousin	3rd to Distant Cousin		Japan; Italy; Spain; Switzerland
Barbara Zerfoss	Zerfoss	Female	4th Cousin	4th Cousin	3rd to 6th Cousin	Paravantis, Dvorsky, Pulos, Zerfoss	
Steve Kor	Kor	Male	1952 5th Cousin	5th Cousin	3rd to Distant Cousin	Cordogan, Siavelis, Kokonas, Gregory, Kor	
Kathrine Chromy	Chromy	Female	5th Cousin	5th Cousin	3rd to Distant Cousin		
Elaine Latto	Latto	Female	5th Cousin	5th Cousin	3rd to Distant Cousin	Demitroloulo, Apostolatou, Papaxaralambou, Potamiano, Latto	
Nedelcho Sitnov	Sitnov	Male	1975 5th Cousin	5th Cousin	3rd to Distant Cousin		
Stavroula Challoumi	Challoumi	Female	5th Cousin	5th Cousin	3rd to Distant Cousin		
Catherine Sternfeld	Sternfeld	Female	1960 5th Cousin	5th Cousin	3rd to Distant Cousin	Milios, Rokas, Sideratos, Stavrou, Manoli, Marini, Sternfeld	Greece
Jennifer Horner	Horner	Female	5th Cousin	5th Cousin	3rd to Distant Cousin		
Christine Connell	Connell	Female	1989 5th Cousin	5th Cousin	3rd to Distant Cousin	Pennacchini, Matyus, Connell	
Sofia Kangas	Kangas	Female	5th Cousin	5th Cousin	3rd to Distant Cousin	Kangas, Koken, Constantinou, Christofidou, Bouboulis	
Despina Papadakis	Papadakis	Female	5th Cousin	5th Cousin	3rd to Distant Cousin	Papadakis, Grigoraki, Soter, Sotirakopoulou, Georgeopoulos	
Mark Morley	Morley	Male	5th Cousin	5th Cousin	3rd to Distant Cousin		
Tasha Dalessandro	Dalessandro	Female	1982 5th Cousin	5th Cousin	3rd to Distant Cousin	Tremblay, Dalessandro	
Anastasia Franklin	Franklin	Female	2002 5th Cousin	5th Cousin	3rd to Distant Cousin		
Bill Maniatis	Maniatis	Male	1988 5th Cousin	5th Cousin	3rd to Distant Cousin		
Joanne Hudson	Hudson	Female	1970 5th Cousin	5th Cousin	3rd to Distant Cousin	Tzamtzi, Tzamtzis, Hudson	
Sofia Bachiloglu Ruminot	Bachiloglu Ruminot	Female	2000 4th Cousin	4th Cousin	3rd to 6th Cousin	Bachiloglu, Cuevas, Ruminot, Bachiloglu Ruminot	
Jessica Jackson	Jackson	Female	1991 5th Cousin	5th Cousin	3rd to Distant Cousin	Jackson, McMillan, Beard, Noble, Arnold (biological grandmother - my mother was adopted)., Brown, Kyle, Newberry. Abernathy, Richardson, Hanna, Sory, Holley, Parsons, Sessions, Powell, Davis(via Lacey daughter marriage), Williams(via Noble daughter marriage), Lacy/Lacey	Arizona, Texas, Colorado; Virginia, United States; South Carolina, United States
anna A		Female	5th Cousin	5th Cousin	3rd to Distant Cousin		

Name	Surname	Gender		Cousin	Relationship	Surnames	Location
Stavroula Kizis	Kizis	Female		4th Cousin	4th Cousin	3rd to 6th Cousin	Alexandros, Euagelos, Stavroula, Grigorios, Ermioni, Kizis	Alexandria, Alexandria Governorate, Egypt
LORI DINOVO	DINOVO	Female		5th Cousin	5th Cousin	3rd to Distant Cousin		
George Bokas	Bokas	Male	1975	5th Cousin	5th Cousin	3rd to Distant Cousin		
Cathy tsakopoulos	tsakopoulos	Female	1964	5th Cousin	5th Cousin	3rd to Distant Cousin	Tsurekidis, Gitzas, Papaerifrimiadou, Tsavdaroglou, Tsakopoulos, tsakopoulos	EskiÅŸehir, EskiÅŸehir, Turkey
frances matsis	matsis	Female		5th Cousin	5th Cousin	3rd to Distant Cousin	Mallas, Pleotis, Tzoris, matsis	
Cheyenne Maxwell	Maxwell	Female		5th Cousin	5th Cousin	3rd to Distant Cousin		
Lily Sanborn	Sanborn	Female		5th Cousin	5th Cousin	3rd to Distant Cousin		
Rachelle Geary	Geary	Female		5th Cousin	5th Cousin	3rd to Distant Cousin	Piersanti, Howe, Geffas, Swenson, Hyde, Geary	Italy; Greece
roseanne spano swider	spano swider	Female	1954	5th Cousin	5th Cousin	3rd to Distant Cousin	spano, poveromo, dionisio, crocitto, spano swider	
jordan kravette	kravette	Male		4th Cousin	4th Cousin	3rd to Distant Cousin		
Taylor Swanzy	Swanzy	Female	1999	5th Cousin	5th Cousin	3rd to Distant Cousin	Swanzy, Annastas, Harris, Malaoula	
Martha Deffenbaugh	Deffenbaugh	Female	1953	5th Cousin	5th Cousin	3rd to Distant Cousin		
Bonnie Triche	Triche	Female	1958	5th Cousin	5th Cousin	3rd to Distant Cousin	Rayha, Soos, Gresik, Triche	
Nick Anagnostopoulos	Anagnostopoulos	Male	1968	4th Cousin	4th Cousin	3rd to Distant Cousin	Seremitis, Bakarezos, Anagnostopoulos	
Kathleen Williams	Williams	Female		5th Cousin	5th Cousin	3rd to Distant Cousin		
Cheryl Smith Styron	Smith Styron	Female	1962	3rd Cousin	3rd Cousin		Brown, Breeding, Smith, Griffith, Venis, Benis, Ogden, Carlisle, Kolhoun, Donovan, Wells, Walls, Fountain, Smith Styron	
Betsey Porterfield	Porterfield	Female		5th Cousin	5th Cousin	3rd to Distant Cousin		
Nikolas Mastandrea	Mastandrea	Male		5th Cousin	5th Cousin	3rd to Distant Cousin	Viglas, Bazos, Levear, Mastandrea	Scotland, United Kingdom; Australia
Corinne Michels	Michels	Female		5th Cousin	5th Cousin	3rd to Distant Cousin	Amodeo, Sicari, Ferlazzo, Michels	
Bernice Giamundo	Giamundo	Female		5th Cousin	5th Cousin	3rd to Distant Cousin	Masciandaro, Flaccavento, Giamundo	
Chelsea Gillingham	Gillingham	Female	1989	5th Cousin	5th Cousin	3rd to Distant Cousin	Pappas, Gillingham	Crete Region, Greece
Maria Koken	Koken	Female		3rd Cousin	3rd Cousin	3rd to 5th Cousin		
Nancy Dorsey	Dorsey	Female	1972	5th Cousin	5th Cousin	3rd to Distant Cousin	Greco, Sabella, Zucchero, Dorsey	
TK		Female		5th Cousin	5th Cousin	3rd to Distant Cousin		
Cassidy K		Female		5th Cousin	5th Cousin	3rd to Distant Cousin		
Emma Bruno	Bruno	Female		5th Cousin	5th Cousin	3rd to Distant Cousin		
Guiseppa Barcia	Barcia	Female	1920	5th Cousin	5th Cousin	3rd to Distant Cousin		
Stephanie Ansolabehere	Ansolabehere	Female		5th Cousin	5th Cousin	3rd to Distant Cousin		
Sarah Stark	Stark	Female	1986	5th Cousin	5th Cousin	3rd to Distant Cousin	Swain, Lewis, Stark	
Taffin Lampis	Lampis	Female	1962	5th Cousin	5th Cousin	3rd to Distant Cousin	Eleftheriou, Black, Trierscheidt, Offut, Sarris, Mitchell, Ballantyne, Clegg, Easom, Lampis	Austria; Ireland; Galveston, Galveston County, Texas, United States
Vasiliki Kovalengou	Kovalengou	Female		5th Cousin	5th Cousin	3rd to Distant Cousin		
Michael Bailey	Bailey	Male	1955	4th Cousin	4th Cousin	3rd to Distant Cousin		
Erica Green	Green	Female	1988	5th Cousin	5th Cousin	3rd to Distant Cousin	Pappas, Burgoyne, Rogers, Gilfedder, Scully, Green	Sicily, Italy; Clinton County, New York, United States
Suzanne Chapman	Chapman	Female		5th Cousin	5th Cousin	3rd to Distant Cousin	Gillespie, Bargoil, Durham, Saxon, Chapman, Bargoiloski	
Sofia Lykos	Lykos	Female		5th Cousin	5th Cousin	3rd to Distant Cousin	Chevalier, Mamali, Jette, Lykos	
Christina S		Female		5th Cousin	5th Cousin	3rd to Distant Cousin	Sarras, Zineli, Tagiou	Ä°zmir, Ä°zmir, Turkey; Andros, Greece
Kathryn Hanson	Hanson	Female		4th Cousin	4th Cousin	3rd to Distant Cousin	Antalis, Kauffman, Gallanis, Hanson	
Jon Antonopoulos	Antonopoulos	Male		5th Cousin	5th Cousin	3rd to Distant Cousin		
Cathie Pappas	Pappas	Female		5th Cousin	5th Cousin	3rd to Distant Cousin	Mavrakis, Petrogeorge, Pappas	Kalamitsi, Greece
Maria Georgakopoulos	Georgakopoulos	Female		5th Cousin	5th Cousin	3rd to Distant Cousin		
Georgia Ruocco	Ruocco	Female		5th Cousin	5th Cousin	3rd to Distant Cousin	Barron, Edwards, Tsafaras, Rodopoulos, Coleman, Woodward, Davis, Pelletier, Tucker, Petronas, Tsafarras, Tsaffaras, Ruocco	
Elena Apostolopoulos	Apostolopoulos	Female		5th Cousin	5th Cousin	3rd to Distant Cousin		
Randi Hanis	Hanis	Female	1981	5th Cousin	5th Cousin	3rd to Distant Cousin	Beaty, Boulahanis, Blue, boree, Giardina, Hanis	

david roger anthony	anthony	Male	5th Cousin	5th Cousin	3rd to Distant Cousin	Taradjka, Tempelhof, Jakubovitz, Weiss, Hollander, Antoniades, Amaxapoulos, Vassiliades, Cala, anthony	
Daphne Giltner	Giltner	Female	2005 5th Cousin	5th Cousin	3rd to Distant Cousin	Androniki Ntanga, Apostolos Ntangas, Eileen Marrs, Michael Giltner, Panagiota Pashou, Aristotelis Pashos, Panagiota Ntanga, Dimitris Ntangas, Giltner	Greece; Texas, United States
Emmanuel Athans	Athans	Male	5th Cousin	5th Cousin	3rd to Distant Cousin	Athanasiou, Klapsinos, Athans	
Thiago Alves da Costa	Alves da Costa	Male	5th Cousin	5th Cousin	3rd to Distant Cousin		
Jesse Ymer	Ymer	Male	1981 5th Cousin	5th Cousin	3rd to Distant Cousin		
Jean-Pierre Ratusz	Ratusz	Male	1954 5th Cousin	5th Cousin	3rd to Distant Cousin	Gizycki, Ratusz	
Lauren Kirk	Kirk	Female	1984 5th Cousin	5th Cousin	3rd to Distant Cousin	Kyriakos, Kyriacopulous, Bruget, Ramos, Kirk	
Katia Takaziadou	Takaziadou	Female	4th Cousin	4th Cousin	3rd to Distant Cousin		Cairo Governorate, Egypt
Spiros Tsiatas	Tsiatas	Male	1982 5th Cousin	5th Cousin	3rd to Distant Cousin	Lappas, Papamastorakis, Leventis, Mavrogenis, Tsiatas	
Camille Hatch	Hatch	Female	5th Cousin	5th Cousin	3rd to Distant Cousin		
Kim Bazzy	Bazzy	Female	5th Cousin	5th Cousin	3rd to Distant Cousin	Lightfoot, Swartz, Bazzy, Mansour, Coffman, Kauffman	
Mia Kagehiro	Kagehiro	Female	5th Cousin	5th Cousin	3rd to Distant Cousin		
Melissa Storkson	Storkson	Female	1979 5th Cousin	5th Cousin	3rd to Distant Cousin	Kettlewell, Smith, Sexton, Emery, Storkson	
Harry Peart	Peart	Male	1927 5th Cousin	5th Cousin	3rd to Distant Cousin		
Christina Plessas	Plessas	Female	5th Cousin	5th Cousin	3rd to Distant Cousin	Gilbert, Donner, Fisher, Kotsakis, Plessas	Alonistaina, Greece
Robin Rozycki	Rozycki	Female	5th Cousin	5th Cousin	3rd to Distant Cousin	Sutter, Smigiel, Rozycki, Klidy	
Melina Megaridis	Megaridis	Female	5th Cousin	5th Cousin	3rd to Distant Cousin	Clute, Sewell, Megaridis	
Andrew Weidhaas	Weidhaas	Male	5th Cousin	5th Cousin	3rd to Distant Cousin		
Cassandra Chapman	Chapman	Female	5th Cousin	5th Cousin	3rd to Distant Cousin	Chapman, Cruickshank, Tserghanos, Papadopoulos.	
Tracy Gilbert	Gilbert	Female	5th Cousin	5th Cousin	3rd to Distant Cousin		
Scott Hofer	Hofer	Male	5th Cousin	5th Cousin	3rd to Distant Cousin		
Dragica Zdraveska	Zdraveska	Female	5th Cousin	5th Cousin	3rd to Distant Cousin		
Katharine Reynolds	Reynolds	Female	1981 5th Cousin	5th Cousin	3rd to Distant Cousin		
michelle haines (Kamberos)	haines (Kamberos)	Female	5th Cousin	5th Cousin	3rd to Distant Cousin	Lewis, Bennis, Kamberos, Brinker, Smith, haines (Kamberos)	
Catherine Garza	Garza	Female	1938 5th Cousin	5th Cousin	3rd to Distant Cousin	Dedes, Franko, Pomaiba, Garza	
Erin Staiger (Salb)	Staiger (Salb)	Female	1980 4th Cousin	4th Cousin	3rd to Distant Cousin		Greece
Anastasia Williams	Williams	Female	1984 5th Cousin	5th Cousin	3rd to Distant Cousin	Cretekos, Johnson, Youngman, Landry, Koutsogiannopoulos, Askounis, Giannakis, Williams	
serkan bayraktar	bayraktar	Male	1976 5th Cousin	5th Cousin	3rd to Distant Cousin	Cucevic, Bayraktar, Denizci, bayraktar	
FANI KALAKOS	KALAKOS	Female	1965 4th Cousin	4th Cousin	3rd to 6th Cousin	MPOTINI, BOTINI, [illegible], [illegible], KARIOTIS, HAIDOGIANNOY, [illegible], KALAKOS	Sicily, Italy; Mani, Greece
Kris Radkov	Radkov	Male	5th Cousin	5th Cousin	3rd to Distant Cousin		
Evangelos Masellas	Masellas	Male	5th Cousin	5th Cousin	3rd to Distant Cousin	Plakidis, Marsellos, Masellas, Nouros, Maselos	İzmir, Turkey; Metropolitan City of Venice, Veneto, Italy; Sicily, Italy
Vistian Bortes	Bortes	Male	5th Cousin	5th Cousin	3rd to Distant Cousin	BORTES, JUIRJ, Bortes	
Breanna Cole	Cole	Female	4th Cousin	4th Cousin	3rd to Distant Cousin		
Carlo Cukon	Cukon	Male	1961 5th Cousin	5th Cousin	3rd to Distant Cousin		
Jamie Tufanio	Tufanio	Male	1992 5th Cousin	5th Cousin	3rd to Distant Cousin		
Nick Diogenes	Diogenes	Male	5th Cousin	5th Cousin	3rd to Distant Cousin		
John Brown	Brown	Male	5th Cousin	5th Cousin	3rd to Distant Cousin		
Jay Photoglou	Photoglou	Male	5th Cousin	5th Cousin	3rd to Distant Cousin	Sandoval, Seraph, Photoglou	
Amanda Sideris	Sideris	Female	1985 5th Cousin	5th Cousin	3rd to Distant Cousin	Knight, Sideris	Greece; Poland; Germany; United Kingdom; Ireland; Italy
Elaine Demopolis	Demopolis	Female	1995 5th Cousin	5th Cousin	3rd to Distant Cousin	Demopolis, Demopoulos	
Danielle Hill	Hill	Female	5th Cousin	5th Cousin	3rd to Distant Cousin		

Name	Surname	Gender	Year	Cousin	Cousin	Relationship	Surnames	Locations
Jane Stover	Stover	Female		5th Cousin	5th Cousin	3rd to Distant Cousin		
Georgios Blandos	Blandos	Male		5th Cousin	5th Cousin	3rd to Distant Cousin	Blandos, Piperas	
Mariane Pearse	Pearse	Female		5th Cousin	5th Cousin	3rd to Distant Cousin		
C K S	S	Female		5th Cousin	5th Cousin	3rd to Distant Cousin	Sullivan, Alverado, Rosales, Egger, Von Greiner, Von Gerenver, Gottlieb & Therese Von Greiner, S	Ottawa, Ill, San Luis Potsi Mexico, Monterrey, Mexico,; Turners Falls, Mass.,Castletown Beara, Ireland, Obervillach, Austria
Paraskevi Mouzakiti	Mouzakiti	Female	1999	5th Cousin	5th Cousin	3rd to Distant Cousin	Mouzakiti, Parry	Greece; United Kingdom
Chris Spady	Spady	Male		5th Cousin	5th Cousin	3rd to Distant Cousin		
George Kavgic	Kavgic	Male	1963	5th Cousin	5th Cousin	3rd to Distant Cousin		
Adrian Nazario Valdez	Nazario Valdez	Male	1997	5th Cousin	5th Cousin	3rd to Distant Cousin		
Zoe Tsamitis	Tsamitis	Female		5th Cousin	5th Cousin	3rd to Distant Cousin		
Alexis Pence	Pence	Female		4th Cousin	4th Cousin	3rd to Distant Cousin		
John Gianoukos	Gianoukos	Male		3rd Cousin	3rd Cousin	3rd to 5th Cousin		
John Gianoukos	Gianoukos	Male		3rd Cousin	3rd Cousin	3rd to 5th Cousin		
Natalie Kaduri	Kaduri	Female	1996	5th Cousin	5th Cousin	3rd to Distant Cousin	Gadgeva, Gadjeva, Gadzheva, Kaduri	
Robert Coates	Coates	Male	1947	5th Cousin	5th Cousin	3rd to Distant Cousin	Coates, Schultz, Teske, Dreger, Ellison, Grafer, Wackernagel, Gruening, Kroneberg, Anderson, Reid, Denure, Greb/Graeb, Robinson	Yorkshire, Northern Ireland, Picardie, Thuringen, Erfurt, Volhynia, Kraft and Muller in Russia-Saratov region
Tom Englezos	Englezos	Male	1943	5th Cousin	5th Cousin	3rd to Distant Cousin		
Danielle Novak	Novak	Female		5th Cousin	5th Cousin	3rd to Distant Cousin		
Joseph Saponaro	Saponaro	Male	1964	5th Cousin	5th Cousin	3rd to Distant Cousin	Saponaro, Sarangelo, Marzano, Rini	
SF		Female	1970	5th Cousin	5th Cousin	3rd to Distant Cousin		
Ioanna Katsigiannis	Katsigiannis	Female		4th Cousin	4th Cousin	3rd to Distant Cousin		
Eleni Vogas	Vogas	Female		5th Cousin	5th Cousin	3rd to Distant Cousin		
Joanne (De Pierre) (Wolfe) Babey	(De Pierre) (Wolfe) Babey	Female	1964	4th Cousin	4th Cousin	3rd to Distant Cousin		
Dimitria Costello	Costello	Male	1941	5th Cousin	5th Cousin	3rd to Distant Cousin		
Diane Kapuranis	Kapuranis	Female		5th Cousin	5th Cousin	3rd to Distant Cousin		
Kristina German	German	Female	1989	4th Cousin	4th Cousin	3rd to Distant Cousin	Morris, Manganelli, Monos, German	
Milos Lalic	Lalic	Male	1982	5th Cousin	5th Cousin	3rd to Distant Cousin	Rackov, IliÄ‡, MiloÅ¡eviÄ‡, Lalic	
Ryan Glenn	Glenn	Male	1979	5th Cousin	5th Cousin	3rd to Distant Cousin	Knezevich, Malkovich, Hahn, Glenn	
Anastasia Tatsis / Gale	Tatsis / Gale	Female		5th Cousin	5th Cousin	3rd to Distant Cousin	Barbatsoufis, Ballis, Boudrogianni, Tatsis, Tatsis / Gale	
Diane Rhodes	Rhodes	Female		5th Cousin	5th Cousin	3rd to Distant Cousin	Chrisoheri, Altinzi, Rhodopoulou, Trakakis, Goulermos, Rhodes	
Lindsey Melendez	Melendez	Female		4th Cousin	4th Cousin	3rd to Distant Cousin		
Diane Kacprowski	Kacprowski	Female		4th Cousin	4th Cousin	3rd to Distant Cousin		
Will Raum	Raum	Male		5th Cousin	5th Cousin	3rd to Distant Cousin	Cox, Raum	
Jacqueline Haag	Haag	Female	1951	5th Cousin	5th Cousin	3rd to Distant Cousin		
Andreas Apostolopoulos	Apostolopoulos	Male	1951	5th Cousin	5th Cousin	3rd to Distant Cousin		
Deborah Dantonio	Dantonio	Female		5th Cousin	5th Cousin	3rd to Distant Cousin		
Sherban Sarbu	Sarbu	Male	2005	5th Cousin	5th Cousin	3rd to Distant Cousin		
K Connor	Connor	Female	1977	5th Cousin	5th Cousin	3rd to Distant Cousin	Pelletier, Jess, Connor	
Joseph Di Donna	Di Donna	Male		4th Cousin	4th Cousin	3rd to Distant Cousin		Greece; Italy
Erdugan Gashi	Gashi	Male	1996	5th Cousin	5th Cousin	3rd to Distant Cousin		
Joseph Pirozek	Pirozek	Male		5th Cousin	5th Cousin	3rd to Distant Cousin	marino, Zurlo, Pirozek	
Melanie Choe	Choe	Female	1998	5th Cousin	5th Cousin	3rd to Distant Cousin	Choe, Koukotas	
LYNN MOHR	MOHR	Female		5th Cousin	5th Cousin	3rd to Distant Cousin		
Peter Constantopoulos	Constantopoulos	Male		4th Cousin	4th Cousin	3rd to Distant Cousin		
Silvio Kustera	Kustera	Male	1975	5th Cousin	5th Cousin	3rd to Distant Cousin	PrpiÄ‡, KuÅ¡tera, Kustera	
Alexandra Nannas	Nannas	Female		5th Cousin	5th Cousin	3rd to Distant Cousin		
Maria Skiadelli	Skiadelli	Female	1970	5th Cousin	5th Cousin	3rd to Distant Cousin		
James Golden	Golden	Male		5th Cousin	5th Cousin	3rd to Distant Cousin	Smith, Benivendo, Henry, Golden	
Michael Deluca	Deluca	Male		5th Cousin	5th Cousin	3rd to Distant Cousin		
SS		Female	1950	5th Cousin	5th Cousin	3rd to Distant Cousin		

Name	Surname	Gender	Year	Relationship	Relationship	Category	Related Surnames	Location
Dominique Troehler	Troehler	Female		4th Cousin	4th Cousin	3rd to Distant Cousin	Adams, Tunda, Troehler	
Dimitrios Papavasiliou	Papavasiliou	Male	1951	5th Cousin	5th Cousin	3rd to Distant Cousin		
Vaso Chatzi	Chatzi	Female		5th Cousin	5th Cousin	3rd to Distant Cousin		
Morgan Hinzmann	Hinzmann	Female		5th Cousin	5th Cousin	3rd to Distant Cousin		
barbara sardarov	sardarov	Female	1948	5th Cousin	5th Cousin	3rd to Distant Cousin	srdrev, hakala, picinich, jonovich, sardarov	
Jerry Crawford	Crawford	Male		5th Cousin	5th Cousin	3rd to Distant Cousin		
Joel Deming	Deming	Male		4th Cousin	4th Cousin	3rd to Distant Cousin		
Antonette Psaila	Psaila	Female	1943	5th Cousin	5th Cousin	3rd to Distant Cousin		
Justin Hedges	Hedges	Male	1993	5th Cousin	5th Cousin	3rd to Distant Cousin		
Athanasios Koulias	Koulias	Male		5th Cousin	5th Cousin	3rd to Distant Cousin	Tsichloglannis, Mpousias, Koulias	
Georgia BOWDEN	BOWDEN	Female	1957	4th Cousin	4th Cousin	3rd to 6th Cousin		
yiannis katsiris	katsiris	Male	1968	5th Cousin	5th Cousin	3rd to Distant Cousin		
Michael Stamas	Stamas	Male	1965	5th Cousin	5th Cousin	3rd to Distant Cousin	Stamatopoulos, Fortier, Durand, Gamache, Brassard, Gauthier, Korovesis, Stamas	QuÃ©bec City, CommunautÃ©-Urbaine-de-QuÃ©bec, QuÃ©bec, Canada; Normandy, France
Julianne Triphon	Triphon	Female	1989	5th Cousin	5th Cousin	3rd to Distant Cousin	Fronimakis, Triphonopoulos, Mosconitsiotou, Asimakopoulos, Econopoulos, Triphon	
Dionne Myers	Myers	Female		5th Cousin	5th Cousin	3rd to Distant Cousin	Stanley, Vodicka, Manos, Myers	
Tina Vacalopoulos	Vacalopoulos	Female		5th Cousin	5th Cousin	3rd to Distant Cousin	Lagonikos, Papadopoulos, Vacalopoulos	
Alexandra Parliaors	Parliaors	Female		5th Cousin	5th Cousin	3rd to Distant Cousin	Parliaros, Parliaors	
Lisa K		Female	1941	4th Cousin	4th Cousin	3rd to 6th Cousin	Ramos, Chronis, Chronopoulos	
Lirim Turkaj	Turkaj	Male		5th Cousin	5th Cousin	3rd to Distant Cousin	Hasanaj, Kennedy, Chesnutt, Joyner, Turkaj	Albania; Kosovo; Garfield, Emanuel County, Georgia, United States; Vero Beach, Indian River County, Florida, United States; Gainesville, Alachua County, Florida, United States; Assawoman, Accomack County, Virginia, United States; Macon, Bibb County, Georgia, United States; Oklahoma, United States
Louise Ganas	Ganas	Female		5th Cousin	5th Cousin	3rd to Distant Cousin		
Malcolm Dean	Dean	Male		5th Cousin	5th Cousin	3rd to Distant Cousin		
Jade Burruezo	Burruezo	Female		5th Cousin	5th Cousin	3rd to Distant Cousin		
Suzanne Martikas	Martikas	Female		4th Cousin	4th Cousin	3rd to 6th Cousin	Houndros, Huntalas, Martikas	
Marshal Eagle	Eagle	Male	1976	5th Cousin	5th Cousin	3rd to Distant Cousin		
Paraskeve Frances Pantelides	Pantelides	Female		5th Cousin	5th Cousin	3rd to Distant Cousin	Panterlis, Hegoumenakis, Halabalakis, Glinos, Galanaki, Pantelides	Turkey
Esin Saribatir	Saribatir	Female		5th Cousin	5th Cousin	3rd to Distant Cousin		
Matthew Wittig	Wittig	Male		5th Cousin	5th Cousin	3rd to Distant Cousin	Caldararu, Bitu, Wittig	
Jenni Rein	Rein	Female		4th Cousin	4th Cousin	3rd to Distant Cousin		
Claudia Elbert	Elbert	Female	1974	5th Cousin	5th Cousin	3rd to Distant Cousin		
Gabrielle A		Female		5th Cousin	5th Cousin	3rd to Distant Cousin		
Michelle Stephanoff	Stephanoff	Female		5th Cousin	5th Cousin	3rd to Distant Cousin	Stephanoff, Hagotta, Ajovich, Ivan, Nestorova, Kadis, Kadieff, Nedelko, Nickoff	
Julija Zubac	Zubac	Female		5th Cousin	5th Cousin	3rd to Distant Cousin		
Lidia Janeska	Janeska	Female		5th Cousin	5th Cousin	3rd to Distant Cousin		
Ahnna Escobedo	Escobedo	Female		5th Cousin	5th Cousin	3rd to Distant Cousin		
Linda Murray	Murray	Female		5th Cousin	5th Cousin	3rd to Distant Cousin	Demetriades, Tsaffaras, Saffaras, Zounes, Murray	
Margo H		Female	1951	5th Cousin	5th Cousin	3rd to Distant Cousin		
George Hadjigeorgiou	Hadjigeorgiou	Male	1975	4th Cousin	4th Cousin	3rd to 5th Cousin		
Tina Panas	Panas	Female	1928	5th Cousin	5th Cousin	3rd to Distant Cousin		
Elaine Ioanou	Ioanou	Female	1954	2nd Cousin	2nd Cousin			
Peter Wood	Wood	Male		5th Cousin	5th Cousin	3rd to Distant Cousin	Kiritsis, Chekouras, Koletas, Wood	
Eric Jeffers	Jeffers	Male	1988	5th Cousin	5th Cousin	3rd to Distant Cousin	Palm, Jeffers	
Ben Brown	Brown	Male		5th Cousin	5th Cousin	3rd to Distant Cousin		
Lori Sarabian	Sarabian	Female	1963	5th Cousin	5th Cousin	3rd to Distant Cousin		

Name	Surname	Gender				Associated Surnames	Location
Hanna Furmanski	Furmanski	Female	5th Cousin	5th Cousin	3rd to Distant Cousin		
Dimitri Glavas	Glavas	Male	5th Cousin	5th Cousin	3rd to Distant Cousin		
Kathy Brandt	Brandt	Female	1958 5th Cousin	5th Cousin	3rd to Distant Cousin		
Joanna Zanopoulo	Zanopoulo	Female	5th Cousin	5th Cousin	3rd to Distant Cousin	Zanopoulo, Michailidis, Iliadis, Chrystodoulou	
Jessica Ebanks	Ebanks	Female	5th Cousin	5th Cousin	3rd to Distant Cousin	Thomas, Olivo, Ebanks	
Andreanna L		Female	5th Cousin	5th Cousin	3rd to Distant Cousin		
Lesley Wylie	Wylie	Female	5th Cousin	5th Cousin	3rd to Distant Cousin	Lawhorn, Leamons, Murray, Wylie	
Triantafillos Katsoudas	Katsoudas	Male	5th Cousin	5th Cousin	3rd to Distant Cousin	Kontoulas, Katsoudas	
Alexandra Williams	Williams	Female	4th Cousin	4th Cousin	3rd to Distant Cousin	Joe Radosta, Anthony Williams, Athena Birbilis, Valerie Apton, Williams	
Lydia Gil	Gil	Female	5th Cousin	5th Cousin	3rd to Distant Cousin		
Preston Plumlee	Plumlee	Male	5th Cousin	5th Cousin	3rd to Distant Cousin		
Avrelia Palivos	Palivos	Female	4th Cousin	4th Cousin	3rd to Distant Cousin		
Justin Kotlarz	Kotlarz	Male	5th Cousin	5th Cousin	3rd to Distant Cousin		
John A Lenic	Lenic	Male	5th Cousin	5th Cousin	3rd to Distant Cousin	Rogish, Lenic	
Jeffrey White	White	Male	1949 5th Cousin	5th Cousin	3rd to Distant Cousin	Elliott, Lewis, Noland, White	
John Kellems	Kellems	Male	1992 3rd Cousin	3rd Cousin	3rd to 4th Cousin	kellems, vlahos, bishop, Kellems	
Teresa Alvanitakis Sunnergren	Alvanitakis Sunnergren	Female	5th Cousin	5th Cousin	3rd to Distant Cousin	Alvanitakis, Mullen, Gurdo, Alvanitakis Sunnergren	
Constantino Anezinos	Anezinos	Male	4th Cousin	4th Cousin	3rd to Distant Cousin	kafkalakis, argira, tsiridanis, Anezinos	Crete, Greece; Lesvos, Greece; San Francisco, CA; Athens, Greece; Sfakia,Greece; Venice, Italy
Oana Nikulin	Nikulin	Female	5th Cousin	5th Cousin	3rd to Distant Cousin	Purja, Tutuianu, Nikulin	
Samantha Dauer	Dauer	Female	1999 5th Cousin	5th Cousin	3rd to Distant Cousin	dauer, krzenski, vukelich, Dauer	
Sheila Jacobs	Jacobs	Female	1954 5th Cousin	5th Cousin	3rd to Distant Cousin	lee, Jacobs	
Victoria Melignano	Melignano	Female	5th Cousin	5th Cousin	3rd to Distant Cousin	Maruggio, Melignano, Catuosco, Burhlinger	
Antonia Garner	Garner	Female	4th Cousin	4th Cousin	3rd to Distant Cousin		
Kathy Gioulis	Gioulis	Female	5th Cousin	5th Cousin	3rd to Distant Cousin		
Bessie Sergides	Sergides	Female	5th Cousin	5th Cousin	3rd to Distant Cousin		
Edmond Gerveni	Gerveni	Male	1973 5th Cousin	5th Cousin	3rd to Distant Cousin	Gerveni, Mustafaraj, KarÃ§ini, Pleshti	
Abby Alter	Alter	Female	1968 Distant Cousin	Distant Cousin		I am adopted. I know some info on my birth mother but not my birth father. I am looking for him., Alter	Looking for relatives from NY five boroughs)
AP		Male	1986 4th Cousin	4th Cousin	3rd to 6th Cousin	Gountanis, Tyrovolis, Kanatselos, Virvilos, Sideris, Tithis	Valtetsi, Greece; Mani, Greece
David Pennell	Pennell	Male	1985 4th Cousin	4th Cousin	3rd to Distant Cousin		
Mary Maragos	Maragos	Female	1957 5th Cousin	5th Cousin	3rd to Distant Cousin	Kasimatis, Crealese, Gillig, DeBartolo, Maragos	
George Sandlin	Sandlin	Male	1975 5th Cousin	5th Cousin	3rd to Distant Cousin		
Dena Karigan	Karigan	Female	5th Cousin	5th Cousin	3rd to Distant Cousin	Loukakos, Papaspiridis, Papaspiridi, Karigan	
Alkis Gotovos	Gotovos	Male	1987 5th Cousin	5th Cousin	3rd to Distant Cousin	Giannakopoulos, Gotovos	
Jennifer Papandreou	Papandreou	Female	5th Cousin	5th Cousin	3rd to Distant Cousin		
Brendan Arar	Arar	Male	5th Cousin	5th Cousin	3rd to Distant Cousin		
Suzanne Glencairn-Campbell	Glencairn-Campbell	Female	1974 5th Cousin	5th Cousin	3rd to Distant Cousin	Glencairn-Campbell, Voss smith, Pratt, Campbell, Sloane, Muecke	
Haley Chrystie Bise	Chrystie Bise	Female	4th Cousin	4th Cousin	3rd to 6th Cousin		
Jacob Johnson	Johnson	Male	5th Cousin	5th Cousin	3rd to Distant Cousin		
Aybike Sahin	Sahin	Female	5th Cousin	5th Cousin	3rd to Distant Cousin	Mutluoglu, Aytok, Sahin	
Matthew Thomson	Thomson	Male	1973 4th Cousin	4th Cousin	3rd to 6th Cousin		
Michael Theofilopoulos	Theofilopoulos	Male	1950 4th Cousin	4th Cousin	3rd to 5th Cousin	stathopoulou, theofilopoulos, Theofilopoulos	Amaliada, Greece
Brandie Kopsas-Kingsley	Kopsas-Kingsley	Female	1982 5th Cousin	5th Cousin	3rd to Distant Cousin		
Maria Beikos	Beikos	Female	5th Cousin	5th Cousin	3rd to Distant Cousin	Bezanis, Bessios, Bakou, Beikou, Beikos	
Nicholas Lampros	Lampros	Male	5th Cousin	5th Cousin	3rd to Distant Cousin		
Eleni Karytinou	Karytinou	Female	1986 5th Cousin	5th Cousin	3rd to Distant Cousin		
PETER FLOROS	FLOROS	Male	4th Cousin	4th Cousin	3rd to Distant Cousin		

Name	Surname	Gender				Related surnames	Location
Michael Ferentinos	Ferentinos	Male	4th Cousin	4th Cousin	3rd to 5th Cousin		
Wilbert Rhodes	Rhodes	Male	1934 5th Cousin	5th Cousin	3rd to Distant Cousin		
Franciscus Loukrezis	Loukrezis	Male	5th Cousin	5th Cousin	3rd to Distant Cousin	Vouvakis, Loukrezis	
Dorth Beilo	Beilo	Female	1971 5th Cousin	5th Cousin	3rd to Distant Cousin		
John Chiesa	Chiesa	Male	1960 4th Cousin	4th Cousin	3rd to Distant Cousin		
Monica Noble	Noble	Female	1965 5th Cousin	5th Cousin	3rd to Distant Cousin		
Hannah Bohlsen	Bohlsen	Female	5th Cousin	5th Cousin	3rd to Distant Cousin	Bohlsen, Laganas	
Gustavo Espada	Espada	Male	5th Cousin	5th Cousin	3rd to Distant Cousin		
Yildiz Onal	Onal	Female	4th Cousin	4th Cousin	3rd to Distant Cousin		
Michael Muldoon, Sr.	Muldoon, Sr.	Male	5th Cousin	5th Cousin	3rd to Distant Cousin		
Kristina Koci	Koci	Female	5th Cousin	5th Cousin	3rd to Distant Cousin		
Ruth Dickson	Dickson	Female	1933 5th Cousin	5th Cousin	3rd to Distant Cousin		
Ekrem Ramadan	Ramadan	Male	1983 5th Cousin	5th Cousin	3rd to Distant Cousin		
Matthew Conrad	Conrad	Male	1985 5th Cousin	5th Cousin	3rd to Distant Cousin	vasiloff, conrad, johnston, Conrad	
MD		Female	5th Cousin	5th Cousin	3rd to Distant Cousin	Hollman, Poolos	Greece
Star Kahn	Kahn	Female	5th Cousin	5th Cousin	3rd to Distant Cousin	Theodos, Fenichel, Hoffman, Kirangelos, Kahn	
Alexandra Pislaru	Pislaru	Female	1997 5th Cousin	5th Cousin	3rd to Distant Cousin	Enache, Istvan, Beleni, Pislaru	
Nancy Falb	Falb	Female	4th Cousin	4th Cousin	3rd to 5th Cousin		
Christopher Anagnost	Anagnost	Male	5th Cousin	5th Cousin	3rd to Distant Cousin		
Artemis Gregory	Gregory	Female	5th Cousin	5th Cousin	3rd to Distant Cousin	Asprogiannis, Galatas, Tsipras, Toumaras, Gregory	
Taylor Troehler	Troehler	Female	5th Cousin	5th Cousin	3rd to Distant Cousin		
Justin Adcock	Adcock	Male	1971 5th Cousin	5th Cousin	3rd to Distant Cousin		
Irini Aleksi	Aleksi	Female	5th Cousin	5th Cousin	3rd to Distant Cousin		
Maria Helena Segri	Segri	Female	5th Cousin	5th Cousin	3rd to Distant Cousin		
Lindsey Johnson	Johnson	Female	5th Cousin	5th Cousin	3rd to Distant Cousin		
David Carlin	Carlin	Male	1981 5th Cousin	5th Cousin	3rd to Distant Cousin	Carlin, Santomieri	
Eve Anders	Anders	Female	5th Cousin	5th Cousin	3rd to Distant Cousin		
George Tzimas	Tzimas	Male	1968 5th Cousin	5th Cousin	3rd to Distant Cousin	Basounas, Pappas, Oikonomou, Papathimios, Tzimas	
Richard navis	navis	Male	1966 5th Cousin	5th Cousin	3rd to Distant Cousin	Stoyko, navis	
George Economy	Economy	Male	1958 5th Cousin	5th Cousin	3rd to Distant Cousin		
Demetrios Parliaros	Parliaros	Male	1983 5th Cousin	5th Cousin	3rd to Distant Cousin		
Constantina Petropoulos	Petropoulos	Female	1964 5th Cousin	5th Cousin	3rd to Distant Cousin		
Izzy Fakhreddine	Fakhreddine	Female	5th Cousin	5th Cousin	3rd to Distant Cousin		
Ronnie Nagler	Nagler	Female	5th Cousin	5th Cousin	3rd to Distant Cousin		
Kelsey Wheeler	Wheeler	Male	4th Cousin	4th Cousin	3rd to Distant Cousin	Bruce, Rufle, Wheeler, White, Stipple, Ruffle, King, Rice, Vassall, Loring, Couch, James, Smith, Demichele, De michele, Martinello, Hagerman	Italy; Switzerland; Holyoke, Hampden County, Massachusetts, United States; Cleveland, Cuyahoga County, Ohio, United States; Ontario, Canada; Fitchburg, Worcester County, Massachusetts, United States; Plainfield, Hampshire County, Massachusetts, United States; Westminster, Worcester County, Massachusetts, United States; Lee, Berkshire County, Massachusetts, United States; Amherst, Hampshire County, Massachusetts, United States; Sudbury, Middlesex County, Massachusetts, United States; Cranfield, Central Bedfordshire, England, United Kingdom; Leiden, Leiden, South Holland, Netherlands; Devon, England, United Kingdom; Woodham Mortimer, Essex, England, United Kingdom; Bedford, England, United Kingdom
Neil Stanar	Stanar	Male	1976 5th Cousin	5th Cousin	3rd to Distant Cousin		

Name	Surname	Sex	Year			Related Surnames	Locations
Cheryl LaMore	LaMore	Female	1974 5th Cousin	5th Cousin	3rd to Distant Cousin		
Vasileios Gianoukos	Gianoukos	Male	5th Cousin	5th Cousin	3rd to Distant Cousin		Arkadia Greece
Alexis Harrington	Harrington	Female	5th Cousin	5th Cousin	3rd to Distant Cousin		
Ioannis Papadopoulos	Papadopoulos	Male	1974 5th Cousin	5th Cousin	3rd to Distant Cousin	Papadopoulos, Aronis, Bouranis, Georgiou, Vlavianos	
Nick Sakaleros	Sakaleros	Male	1975 5th Cousin	5th Cousin	3rd to Distant Cousin		
Bryan Ortiz	Ortiz	Male	4th Cousin	4th Cousin	3rd to Distant Cousin		
Dianne Chilingerian	Chilingerian	Female	5th Cousin	5th Cousin	3rd to Distant Cousin	Bahadourian, Sarajian, Poonarian, Memleketian, Chilingerian	Diyarbakir, Adana, Gurun, Turkey, Boston, New York, New Jersey, Virginia
Paula Jo Triche	Triche	Female	5th Cousin	5th Cousin	3rd to Distant Cousin		
Nick Pachnos	Pachnos	Male	5th Cousin	5th Cousin	3rd to Distant Cousin	Christopoulos, Leva, Pachnos	
Maria Walsh	Walsh	Female	5th Cousin	5th Cousin	3rd to Distant Cousin		
Dennis Gerbino	Gerbino	Male	5th Cousin	5th Cousin	3rd to Distant Cousin		
Shayne Zroback	Zroback	Male	1975 5th Cousin	5th Cousin	3rd to Distant Cousin		
Tressa J		Female	1969 5th Cousin	5th Cousin	3rd to Distant Cousin	Fales, Garrett, Duncan, Janos, Stratinos, Perchikes, Stephens, Catsaros, Katsaros, Corbitt	
Anna DeFreitas	DeFreitas	Female	5th Cousin	5th Cousin	3rd to Distant Cousin		
jimmy matragos	matragos	Male	1948 4th Cousin	4th Cousin	3rd to 5th Cousin		
jeffery Mccabe	Mccabe	Male	4th Cousin	4th Cousin	3rd to Distant Cousin	McCabe, DeSanto, Mccabe	
Rebecca Davis	Davis	Female	1958 5th Cousin	5th Cousin	3rd to Distant Cousin	Foy, Legleitner, Hufford, Johnson, Troup, Davis	Germany; Ireland
LN		Male	5th Cousin	5th Cousin	3rd to Distant Cousin	Toufexis, Stavridis, Titis, Armentsoudis, Papaioannou, Stefas, Mitsiobounas, Pallas, Gkantsidis, Dimou, Zois, Chotos	
Lisa Brennan	Brennan	Female	5th Cousin	5th Cousin	3rd to Distant Cousin		
Annamarie Yerkes	Yerkes	Female	1990 5th Cousin	5th Cousin	3rd to Distant Cousin		
Robert Sclafani	Sclafani	Male	5th Cousin	5th Cousin	3rd to Distant Cousin	basta, montalbano, quartararo, caprista, mancuso, friscia, larocca, Sclafani	New York, Pennsylvania, Sicily, Calabria
DIAS HARALAMBOPOULOS	HARALAMBOPOULOS	Male	4th Cousin	4th Cousin	3rd to 6th Cousin	Haralambopoulos, Kourtessis, Haralambous, Pachis, Zenellis, HARALAMBOPOULOS	Peloponnisos-Greece, Attika-Greece
Vanna Potter	Potter	Female	5th Cousin	5th Cousin	3rd to Distant Cousin		
Efrosine Gianoukos Katsoufis	Gianoukos Katsoufis	Female	5th Cousin	5th Cousin	3rd to Distant Cousin	Gianoukos, Gianoukos Katsoufis	Somerville, MA; Winchester, MA; Belmont, MA; Glenview, IL; Chicago, IL; Athens, Greece;
N A	A	Male	1995 5th Cousin	5th Cousin	3rd to Distant Cousin		
Stella Olympic	Olympic	Female	5th Cousin	5th Cousin	3rd to Distant Cousin		
EM		Female	1978 5th Cousin	5th Cousin	3rd to Distant Cousin	Methasani, Molla, Musabelli, Seferi	
Jessica Stratton	Stratton	Female	1997 5th Cousin	5th Cousin	3rd to Distant Cousin		
Nalan Turan	Turan	Female	5th Cousin	5th Cousin	3rd to Distant Cousin	Oral, Ecker, Wichmann, Turan	
kosta peleti	peleti	Male	5th Cousin	5th Cousin	3rd to Distant Cousin		
Jill Evert	Evert	Female	5th Cousin	5th Cousin	3rd to Distant Cousin	Limberios, Borsick, Trautman, Slocum, Evert	
Milena Brown	Brown	Female	4th Cousin	4th Cousin	3rd to Distant Cousin		
Teodora Udrea	Udrea	Female	5th Cousin	5th Cousin	3rd to Distant Cousin		
Christine Brett	Brett	Female	1988 5th Cousin	5th Cousin	3rd to Distant Cousin		
Mike Panagakos	Panagakos	Male	1953 5th Cousin	5th Cousin	3rd to Distant Cousin		
Mehrnaz Dehghan-Nayeri	Dehghan-Nayeri	Female	1993 5th Cousin	5th Cousin	3rd to Distant Cousin		
Katherine Tsakopoulos	Tsakopoulos	Female	5th Cousin	5th Cousin	3rd to Distant Cousin		
Christopher Martin	Martin	Male	1984 5th Cousin	5th Cousin	3rd to Distant Cousin	Martin, Gonzales, Vinson, Brizes, Adams, Townsend	Lithuania; Scotland, United Kingdom; Spain
Viken Manoukian	Manoukian	Male	5th Cousin	5th Cousin	3rd to Distant Cousin		
Mary Ann Gibus	Gibus	Female	4th Cousin	4th Cousin	3rd to 5th Cousin		
C Garner	Garner	Female	1996 4th Cousin	4th Cousin	3rd to Distant Cousin	Stoddard, Lange, Barlos, Vlachogiannopoulos, Garner	
Maria Papadopoulos	Papadopoulos	Female	1978 5th Cousin	5th Cousin	3rd to Distant Cousin	Papadopoulos, Katsiglanis, Farasopoulos, Raptakis	Agrafa, Grekiska fastlandet, Thessalia Sterea Ellada, Greece

Name	Alt	Sex	Col1	Col2	Col3	Names	Places
Christina DiSalvo	DiSalvo	Female	1977 5th Cousin	5th Cousin	3rd to Distant Cousin	Lena Bustemante, David Ralph Barr, Jack Di Salvo, Jenny Di Salvo, DiSalvo	
JOHN GALLANIS	GALLANIS	Male	5th Cousin	5th Cousin	3rd to Distant Cousin		
PAMELA-DON MONAGHAN	MONAGHAN	Female	5th Cousin	5th Cousin	3rd to Distant Cousin		
Angelos Varagiannis	Varagiannis	Male	5th Cousin	5th Cousin	3rd to Distant Cousin		
Maria Carson	Carson	Female	5th Cousin	5th Cousin	3rd to Distant Cousin		
Isabella Mourgelas	Mourgelas	Female	5th Cousin	5th Cousin	3rd to Distant Cousin		
Alex Levy	Levy	Male	1994 5th Cousin	5th Cousin	3rd to Distant Cousin		
Susan Branch	Branch	Female	1956 5th Cousin	5th Cousin	3rd to Distant Cousin	Novosel, Cernich, Eskra, Branch	
Efthimios Tserotas	Tserotas	Male	5th Cousin	5th Cousin	3rd to Distant Cousin		
Thomas Tye	Tye	Male	1956 5th Cousin	5th Cousin	3rd to Distant Cousin		
Stanislaw Markowski	Markowski	Male	1923 5th Cousin	5th Cousin	3rd to Distant Cousin	Bor, Antoni Bor, Markowski	
Kristina Lefteri	Lefteri	Female	5th Cousin	5th Cousin	3rd to Distant Cousin		
Jorge Salazar	Salazar	Male	5th Cousin	5th Cousin	3rd to Distant Cousin		
Bert Bradley	Bradley	Male	4th Cousin	4th Cousin	3rd to Distant Cousin		
Venitia Caudill	Caudill	Female	1926 4th Cousin	4th Cousin	3rd to Distant Cousin	Coniaris, Polychronopoulos, Caudill	
Stephanie Rondos	Rondos	Female	5th Cousin	5th Cousin	3rd to Distant Cousin	Rondos, Salem, Siliano	Italy
Gregory Paras	Paras	Male	4th Cousin	4th Cousin	3rd to 6th Cousin	Chaiko, Hussey, Paras, Mennon	
Samantha Leone	Leone	Female	5th Cousin	5th Cousin	3rd to Distant Cousin		
George Tjilos	Tjilos	Male	1964 3rd Cousin	3rd Cousin	3rd to 4th Cousin	Tjilos, Tsilos, Tzilos, Gelos, Gilos, Palazis, Stamboulis, Stoyou, Stouyou	Peloponisos, Greece; Peloponesos, Greece; Rhodes, Greece; Rodos, Greece
Spiros Katsanis	Katsanis	Male	4th Cousin	4th Cousin	3rd to 5th Cousin		
C Genis Murray	Genis Murray	Female	4th Cousin	4th Cousin	3rd to 5th Cousin		
Mike T		Male	4th Cousin	4th Cousin	3rd to 5th Cousin		
AP		Male	4th Cousin	4th Cousin	3rd to 6th Cousin		
S Marshall	Marshall	Male	4th Cousin	4th Cousin	3rd to 6th Cousin		
leah bizoumis	bizoumis	Female	1963 4th Cousin	4th Cousin	3rd to 6th Cousin	glynou, kiriazi, dallue, katsiferi, bizoumis	
Dimitrios Zarafopoulos	Zarafopoulos	Male	4th Cousin	4th Cousin	3rd to 6th Cousin		
Peter Ellis	Ellis	Male	4th Cousin	4th Cousin	3rd to 6th Cousin		
PRISCILLA T		Female	4th Cousin	4th Cousin	3rd to 6th Cousin	Andreson, Androutsopoulos, Spelios, Speliopoulos, Coulopoulos, Latchis, Rigopoulos, Patterson, Papandricopoulos, Latsis, Paul	
HB		Male	4th Cousin	4th Cousin	3rd to 6th Cousin		
Ria L	L	Female	4th Cousin	4th Cousin	3rd to 6th Cousin		
Stelyana Baleva	Baleva	Female	4th Cousin	4th Cousin	3rd to 6th Cousin		
JS		Male	4th Cousin	4th Cousin	3rd to 6th Cousin		
Rebecca Mitchell	Mitchell	Female	4th Cousin	4th Cousin	3rd to 6th Cousin		
spero theros	theros	Male	1946 4th Cousin	4th Cousin	3rd to 6th Cousin	Theros, Theoderakolpous, theoderakolpous, theros	
DC		Male	4th Cousin	4th Cousin	3rd to 6th Cousin		
Richard Rizzo	Rizzo	Male	1970 4th Cousin	4th Cousin	3rd to 6th Cousin		
Michel Karkour	Karkour	Male	1990 4th Cousin	4th Cousin	3rd to 6th Cousin		
MT		Female	4th Cousin	4th Cousin	3rd to 6th Cousin		
Stephanie S		Female	4th Cousin	4th Cousin	3rd to Distant Cousin		
Leland McAllister	McAllister	Male	4th Cousin	4th Cousin	3rd to Distant Cousin		
M Beers	Beers	Female	4th Cousin	4th Cousin	3rd to Distant Cousin	Serafini, Stanford, Mason, Leonard, Beers	Quincy, MA; Weymouth, MA; England, Supino, Italy
JG		Male	4th Cousin	4th Cousin	3rd to Distant Cousin	KOTIS, PANOUTSOS, GERANIOS, KLEASON	Greece; Tripoli, Greece
Joan Farmer	Farmer	Female	1945 4th Cousin	4th Cousin	3rd to Distant Cousin	Nash, Koutikas, Marinos, Gummersbach, Farmer	
Aikaterini Dimopoulou	Dimopoulou	Female	4th Cousin	4th Cousin	3rd to Distant Cousin		
Peggie McHugh	McHugh	Female	4th Cousin	4th Cousin	3rd to Distant Cousin		
M Morrell	Morrell	Female	1988 4th Cousin	4th Cousin	3rd to Distant Cousin	Morrell, Vakos	
DP		Female	4th Cousin	4th Cousin	3rd to Distant Cousin		
William Candiloros	Candiloros	Male	4th Cousin	4th Cousin	3rd to Distant Cousin		
RV		Male	1970 4th Cousin	4th Cousin	3rd to Distant Cousin	Bussell	

Name	Surname	Gender	Year				Other names	Location
nicholas B		Male		4th Cousin	4th Cousin	3rd to Distant Cousin	bastounes, elliott, anton	
Veronica Iossifova	Iossifova	Female		4th Cousin	4th Cousin	3rd to Distant Cousin		
G Jenkins	Jenkins	Female		4th Cousin	4th Cousin	3rd to Distant Cousin		
Dharini Shukla	Shukla	Female		4th Cousin	4th Cousin	3rd to Distant Cousin		
P Angelikopoulos	Angelikopoulos	Male		4th Cousin	4th Cousin	3rd to Distant Cousin	kotarinos, angelikopoulos, Angelikopoulos	Egypt
Eric Newcomb	Newcomb	Male		4th Cousin	4th Cousin	3rd to Distant Cousin		
Corin Ross	Ross	Male		4th Cousin	4th Cousin	3rd to Distant Cousin		
PK		Female		4th Cousin	4th Cousin	3rd to Distant Cousin		Turkey; Italy
Jamie L		Female		4th Cousin	4th Cousin	3rd to Distant Cousin		
Anthony Langenstein	Langenstein	Male		4th Cousin	4th Cousin	3rd to Distant Cousin		
JT		Male		4th Cousin	4th Cousin	3rd to Distant Cousin		
Philip Spelson	Spelson	Male		4th Cousin	4th Cousin	3rd to Distant Cousin		
LA		Female		4th Cousin	4th Cousin	3rd to Distant Cousin		
Thomas Markandonis	Markandonis	Male		4th Cousin	4th Cousin	3rd to Distant Cousin		
Harry P		Male		4th Cousin	4th Cousin	3rd to Distant Cousin		
Patrick George Gleason	Gleason	Male		4th Cousin	4th Cousin	3rd to Distant Cousin		
EP		Female		4th Cousin	4th Cousin	3rd to Distant Cousin		
AR		Female	1972	4th Cousin	4th Cousin	3rd to Distant Cousin	Mottillo, Anthony	
Alexandra V		Female		5th Cousin	5th Cousin	3rd to Distant Cousin		
Miglena Asadurova	Asadurova	Female		5th Cousin	5th Cousin	3rd to Distant Cousin		
ZL		Male		5th Cousin	5th Cousin	3rd to Distant Cousin		
Joanna Howard	Howard	Female		5th Cousin	5th Cousin	3rd to Distant Cousin		
PK		Male		5th Cousin	5th Cousin	3rd to Distant Cousin		
AE		Female		5th Cousin	5th Cousin	3rd to Distant Cousin		
Evan Crikis	Crikis	Male		5th Cousin	5th Cousin	3rd to Distant Cousin		Tennessee, United States; Greece
Paul S		Male		5th Cousin	5th Cousin	3rd to Distant Cousin		
SV		Female		5th Cousin	5th Cousin	3rd to Distant Cousin		
John Lynch	Lynch	Male		5th Cousin	5th Cousin	3rd to Distant Cousin		
J		Male		5th Cousin	5th Cousin	3rd to Distant Cousin		
glenn blanford	blanford	Male		5th Cousin	5th Cousin	3rd to Distant Cousin	halliday, glenn, blanford	
CC		Male		5th Cousin	5th Cousin	3rd to Distant Cousin		
Diagoras Nicolaides	Nicolaides	Male		5th Cousin	5th Cousin	3rd to Distant Cousin		
George T		Male		5th Cousin	5th Cousin	3rd to Distant Cousin		
Carol Burdine	Burdine	Female		5th Cousin	5th Cousin	3rd to Distant Cousin		
J neece	neece	Female		5th Cousin	5th Cousin	3rd to Distant Cousin		
D Marsh	Marsh	Female		5th Cousin	5th Cousin	3rd to Distant Cousin	Brei, Brunner, Marsh	
Evan Cvitanovic	Cvitanovic	Male		5th Cousin	5th Cousin	3rd to Distant Cousin		
Vito Cotrone	Cotrone	Male		5th Cousin	5th Cousin	3rd to Distant Cousin		
PV		Female		5th Cousin	5th Cousin	3rd to Distant Cousin		
Helene Koenig	Koenig	Female		5th Cousin	5th Cousin	3rd to Distant Cousin		
ZK		Female		5th Cousin	5th Cousin	3rd to Distant Cousin		
Timothy S		Male		5th Cousin	5th Cousin	3rd to Distant Cousin		
George Canas	Canas	Male		5th Cousin	5th Cousin	3rd to Distant Cousin		
Trisha Gentile	Gentile	Female		5th Cousin	5th Cousin	3rd to Distant Cousin		
Brick Cullum	Cullum	Male	1996	5th Cousin	5th Cousin	3rd to Distant Cousin		
Dimitrios Leventopoulos	Leventopoulos	Male		5th Cousin	5th Cousin	3rd to Distant Cousin	Leventopoulos, Contuzzi, Georgopoulos	Agios Nikolaos Kalavryton (Peloponnese), Izmir, Kerkyra (Ionian islands)
Chris K		Male		5th Cousin	5th Cousin	3rd to Distant Cousin		
Costa Troupakis	Troupakis	Male		5th Cousin	5th Cousin	3rd to Distant Cousin		
Maria Ousley	Ousley	Female	1960	5th Cousin	5th Cousin	3rd to Distant Cousin	Kutuvinis, Ousley	
Taylor Beasley	Beasley	Female		5th Cousin	5th Cousin	3rd to Distant Cousin		
K M	M	Male		5th Cousin	5th Cousin	3rd to Distant Cousin		
Panagiotis Kourakos	Kourakos	Male	1986	5th Cousin	5th Cousin	3rd to Distant Cousin	Kourakos	
Daniela Baleva	Baleva	Female		5th Cousin	5th Cousin	3rd to Distant Cousin		
Helen Biliouris	Biliouris	Female		5th Cousin	5th Cousin	3rd to Distant Cousin		
TP		Male		5th Cousin	5th Cousin	3rd to Distant Cousin		
Johnny Kleitches	Kleitches	Male	1958	5th Cousin	5th Cousin	3rd to Distant Cousin	Kleitches, Kanos	Greece

Name	Surname	Gender	Year				Surnames	Places
ST		Male		5th Cousin	5th Cousin	3rd to Distant Cousin		
P Tolev	Tolev	Male		5th Cousin	5th Cousin	3rd to Distant Cousin		
Dmitry R		Male	1966	5th Cousin	5th Cousin	3rd to Distant Cousin		
George L		Male		5th Cousin	5th Cousin	3rd to Distant Cousin		
FB		Male		5th Cousin	5th Cousin	3rd to Distant Cousin		
IS		Female		5th Cousin	5th Cousin	3rd to Distant Cousin		Andros, Greece
Sueanna Masterson	Masterson	Female	1965	5th Cousin	5th Cousin	3rd to Distant Cousin	Mastoras, Niehaus, Tonjas, Rich, Masterson	
Genta H		Female		5th Cousin	5th Cousin	3rd to Distant Cousin		
B Blanks	Blanks	Male		5th Cousin	5th Cousin	3rd to Distant Cousin	Blanks, Nichols, Photopoulos, Rue, Nelson	
N Kenny	Kenny	Male		5th Cousin	5th Cousin	3rd to Distant Cousin		
GW		Female		5th Cousin	5th Cousin	3rd to Distant Cousin		
WK		Female	1972	5th Cousin	5th Cousin	3rd to Distant Cousin		
HA		Female		5th Cousin	5th Cousin	3rd to Distant Cousin		
Tom D		Male		5th Cousin	5th Cousin	3rd to Distant Cousin		
Georgia Apostolopoulou	Apostolopoulou	Female		5th Cousin	5th Cousin	3rd to Distant Cousin	Apostolopoulou, Christodoulou, Lignos, Argyropoulou	Larnia, Athens, Ikaria, Santorini, Salamina
JS		Female		5th Cousin	5th Cousin	3rd to Distant Cousin		
Emilia Knezevic	Knezevic	Female		5th Cousin	5th Cousin	3rd to Distant Cousin		
Nomiki Kastanas	Kastanas	Female		5th Cousin	5th Cousin	3rd to Distant Cousin	Papamichael, Zakas, Avdanas, Kastanas	
LB		Female		5th Cousin	5th Cousin	3rd to Distant Cousin		
Karleen Steinle	Steinle	Female		5th Cousin	5th Cousin	3rd to Distant Cousin		
Melody P		Female		5th Cousin	5th Cousin	3rd to Distant Cousin		Manitoba, Canada; Nova Scotia, Canada; Ontario, Canada; England, United Kingdom; Scotland, United Kingdom; Iceland; Ukraine
CP		Female		5th Cousin	5th Cousin	3rd to Distant Cousin	Bourounis, Karapanagos, Giannakopoulos	Tropaia, Greece; Viziki, Greece
Stephan Schmidt	Schmidt	Male		5th Cousin	5th Cousin	3rd to Distant Cousin		
KO		Female		5th Cousin	5th Cousin	3rd to Distant Cousin		
David Caras	Caras	Male		5th Cousin	5th Cousin	3rd to Distant Cousin		
Kaedyn S		Female		5th Cousin	5th Cousin	3rd to Distant Cousin		
Ramiz Silava	Silava	Male		5th Cousin	5th Cousin	3rd to Distant Cousin		
Mathew Crum	Crum	Male		5th Cousin	5th Cousin	3rd to Distant Cousin		
Kalliroe Tasios	Tasios	Female	1976	5th Cousin	5th Cousin	3rd to Distant Cousin	Asprogiannis, Makkas, Galatas, Tsipras, Giannopoulos, Toumaras, Lainis, Tasios	
Terry Geary	Geary	Female		5th Cousin	5th Cousin	3rd to Distant Cousin		
Amanda Cutting	Cutting	Female	1987	5th Cousin	5th Cousin	3rd to Distant Cousin		
NC		Male		5th Cousin	5th Cousin	3rd to Distant Cousin		
DM		Female		5th Cousin	5th Cousin	3rd to Distant Cousin	Mehmetaj, Dautaj	
Tatiana S		Female		5th Cousin	5th Cousin	3rd to Distant Cousin		
Kris M		Female		5th Cousin	5th Cousin	3rd to Distant Cousin		
AL		Female		5th Cousin	5th Cousin	3rd to Distant Cousin	Lazic, Dobricic, Velemir, Milivojevic, Nikitovic	Croatia (Sinj, Tijarica), Serbia (multiple places)
Marie Pantazi	Pantazi	Female		5th Cousin	5th Cousin	3rd to Distant Cousin		
Tyler Heathcote	Heathcote	Male		5th Cousin	5th Cousin	3rd to Distant Cousin		
EH		Female		5th Cousin	5th Cousin	3rd to Distant Cousin		
Ani Apfelbacher	Apfelbacher	Female		5th Cousin	5th Cousin	3rd to Distant Cousin		
TC		Male	1964	5th Cousin	5th Cousin	3rd to Distant Cousin		
Brian Chenes	Chenes	Male		5th Cousin	5th Cousin	3rd to Distant Cousin		
CS		Female		5th Cousin	5th Cousin	3rd to Distant Cousin		
VC		Female		5th Cousin	5th Cousin	3rd to Distant Cousin		
Eric Sullivan	Sullivan	Male		5th Cousin	5th Cousin	3rd to Distant Cousin		
Nicole Terracciano	Terracciano	Female		5th Cousin	5th Cousin	3rd to Distant Cousin		
Paulina Tarr	Tarr	Female		5th Cousin	5th Cousin	3rd to Distant Cousin		
PV		Female	1947	5th Cousin	5th Cousin	3rd to Distant Cousin	Beykos or Belkos, Hall	
Bruce Williams	Williams	Male		5th Cousin	5th Cousin	3rd to Distant Cousin		
Patricia Franzoni	Franzoni	Female	1977	5th Cousin	5th Cousin	3rd to Distant Cousin		
Melissa Livanos	Livanos	Female	1981	5th Cousin	5th Cousin	3rd to Distant Cousin		
Eric Hall	Hall	Male		5th Cousin	5th Cousin	3rd to Distant Cousin		

Name	Surname	Gender	Year	Rel.	Rel.	Rel.	Names	Places
Scott N		Male		5th Cousin	5th Cousin	3rd to Distant Cousin		
Sophia C		Female		5th Cousin	5th Cousin	3rd to Distant Cousin		
Steve K		Male		5th Cousin	5th Cousin	3rd to Distant Cousin		
Eljon N		Male	1985	5th Cousin	5th Cousin	3rd to Distant Cousin	Celo, Nace, Naco, Natsis	
Sarah Williamson	Williamson	Female		5th Cousin	5th Cousin	3rd to Distant Cousin		
MC		Male		5th Cousin	5th Cousin	3rd to Distant Cousin		Sicily, Italy
JP		Male		5th Cousin	5th Cousin	3rd to Distant Cousin		
Via Tziagas	Tziagas	Female		5th Cousin	5th Cousin	3rd to Distant Cousin		
Stacy Camp	Camp	Female	1970	5th Cousin	5th Cousin	3rd to Distant Cousin		
NK		Female		5th Cousin	5th Cousin	3rd to Distant Cousin	Stamboulis	Alexandria, Egypt, Athens, Greece, Washington, DC
Tricia Louras	Louras	Female	1996	5th Cousin	5th Cousin	3rd to Distant Cousin	Louras, Karvouniaris, Ambathiotakis, Christopulos, Trahalakis, Tsiolis	
TT		Female		5th Cousin	5th Cousin	3rd to Distant Cousin		
Gustavo Ramirez-Garcia	Ramirez-Garcia	Male		5th Cousin	5th Cousin	3rd to Distant Cousin		
Hilmi Baric	Baric	Male		5th Cousin	5th Cousin	3rd to Distant Cousin		
WL		Male		5th Cousin	5th Cousin	3rd to Distant Cousin		
Marc Leighton	Leighton	Male		5th Cousin	5th Cousin	3rd to Distant Cousin		
Anne Liskey	Liskey	Female		5th Cousin	5th Cousin	3rc to Distant Cousin		
kosta vlagos	vlagos	Male		5th Cousin	5th Cousin	3rd to Distant Cousin		
EP		Female	1959	5th Cousin	5th Cousin	3rd to Distant Cousin		
CF		Male		5th Cousin	5th Cousin	3rd to Distant Cousin		timisoara, romania
Chris S		Male		5th Cousin	5th Cousin	3rd to Distant Cousin		DC, Alexandria Egypt, Volos Greece, Izmir/Smyrna Turkey, Urla/Vourla Turkey
A Ward	Ward	Female		5th Cousin	5th Cousin	3rd to Distant Cousin		
Vicki T		Female		5th Cousin	5th Cousin	3rd to Distant Cousin	Fouriaris, Apostolopoulos	
Gerald Heathcote	Heathcote	Male	1954	5th Cousin	5th Cousin	3rd to Distant Cousin	Heathcote, Rose, Pohto, Jones, Hacker, Rantilla, Smiley, Smith	Napa Ca, South Tahoe Ca, Warren, Ohio, Fairport Harbor, Ohio, Detroit, Michigan Ylistaro, Finland, Lancaster,Penn. Maryland, England,
AJ		Female		5th Cousin	5th Cousin	3rd to Distant Cousin		
MM		Female		5th Cousin	5th Cousin	3rd to Distant Cousin		
G Fileas	Fileas	Male		5th Cousin	5th Cousin	3rd to Distant Cousin		
VB		Female		5th Cousin	5th Cousin	3rd to Distant Cousin		
AP		Female	1962	5th Cousin	5th Cousin	3rd to Distant Cousin	Pasic, Pezic	
Eleni Kounalakis	Kounalakis	Female		5th Cousin	5th Cousin	3rd to Distant Cousin		
GP		Male		5th Cousin	5th Cousin	3rd to Distant Cousin		
Florence Paras	Paras	Female		5th Cousin	5th Cousin	3rd to Distant Cousin		
Christo K		Male	1988	5th Cousin	5th Cousin	3rd to Distant Cousin	Kolovos, Korellis, Korelis, Tourogiannis, Kakouros	
KV		Female		5th Cousin	5th Cousin	3rd to Distant Cousin	bournias, bournas, pifer, kallins, kallinteri, whompler	
DA		Male		5th Cousin	5th Cousin	3rd to Distant Cousin		
MS		Female		5th Cousin	5th Cousin	3rd to Distant Cousin		
K FISK	FISK	Female		5th Cousin	5th Cousin	3rd to Distant Cousin	Scrace, Joynt, Stephens, McKenzie, Turner, Skelly, McIntyre, Blundell, O'Shaughnessy, FISK	
Lisa Fazio	Fazio	Female		5th Cousin	5th Cousin	3rd to Distant Cousin		
Suhendan Tuncer	Tuncer	Female		5th Cousin	5th Cousin	3rd to Distant Cousin		
TH		Male		5th Cousin	5th Cousin	3rd to Distant Cousin		
CA		Male	1972	5th Cousin	5th Cousin	3rd to Distant Cousin		
Lauren Eager	Eager	Female		5th Cousin	5th Cousin	3rd to Distant Cousin	Eager, Klaassen	
EK		Female		5th Cousin	5th Cousin	3rd to Distant Cousin		Erzigian, Pontos; Kastoria, Greece; Thessaloniki, Greece; Canton, Ohio; Greece; Turkey;
MR		Female		5th Cousin	5th Cousin	3rd to Distant Cousin	Bramos	
Sondra Burden	Burden	Female		5th Cousin	5th Cousin	3rd to Distant Cousin	Burden, Steilberg, Willoughby, Jones	Louisville, KY; Naples, FL

Name	Surname	Gender		Relationship	Relationship	Relationship	Associated Names	Location
Louisa Conis	Conis	Female		5th Cousin	5th Cousin	3rd to Distant Cousin		
Carol C		Female		5th Cousin	5th Cousin	3rd to Distant Cousin		
KG		Female	1991	5th Cousin	5th Cousin	3rd to Distant Cousin		Ireland; Poland; Greece
J Greg	Greg	Female		5th Cousin	5th Cousin	3rd to Distant Cousin		
Vesko Georgiev	Georgiev	Male		5th Cousin	5th Cousin	3rd to Distant Cousin		
KZ		Female		5th Cousin	5th Cousin	3rd to Distant Cousin		
MK		Male		5th Cousin	5th Cousin	3rd to Distant Cousin	Gdula, Horvath, Kuzoff	
Alex P		Male	1989	5th Cousin	5th Cousin	3rd to Distant Cousin		
UW		Male		5th Cousin	5th Cousin	3rd to Distant Cousin	Odening, Ulbricht	
Gina H		Female		5th Cousin	5th Cousin	3rd to Distant Cousin		
Elias M		Male		5th Cousin	5th Cousin	3rd to Distant Cousin	Makos, Martiris	Montreal, Quebec, Canada; Epiros, Greece
MR		Female		5th Cousin	5th Cousin	3rd to Distant Cousin		
Vickie Sarelas Egan	Sarelas Egan	Female		5th Cousin	5th Cousin	3rd to Distant Cousin	Sarelas, Panagopoulos, Smyrniotis, Mouzakes, Sarelas Egan	
Lisa Dedvukaj	Dedvukaj	Female		5th Cousin	5th Cousin	3rd to Distant Cousin		
Robert Jovalis	Jovalis	Male		5th Cousin	5th Cousin	3rd to Distant Cousin	Jovalis, Perry, Lutz	
L Vournelis	Vournelis	Male		5th Cousin	5th Cousin	3rd to Distant Cousin		
Melanie Jones Parker	Jones Parker	Female		5th Cousin	5th Cousin	3rd to Distant Cousin	Jones, Manos, Anagnostou, Glidewell, Hodum, Jones Parker	
Nikoleta Koupa	Koupa	Female		5th Cousin	5th Cousin	3rd to Distant Cousin		
John Macias	Macias	Male	2000	5th Cousin	5th Cousin	3rd to Distant Cousin		
LV		Female		5th Cousin	5th Cousin	3rd to Distant Cousin		
Steve L		Male		5th Cousin	5th Cousin	3rd to Distant Cousin	Deluca, Burd	
Mina G		Female		5th Cousin	5th Cousin	3rd to Distant Cousin	Centala, Schad, Drembar, Gorak	
JM		Male		5th Cousin	5th Cousin	3rd to Distant Cousin		
JK		Male		5th Cousin	5th Cousin	3rd to Distant Cousin		
LC		Female		5th Cousin	5th Cousin	3rd to Distant Cousin		
JM		Female		5th Cousin	5th Cousin	3rd to Distant Cousin		
Andrew Ambrosino	Ambrosino	Male	1992	5th Cousin	5th Cousin	3rd to Distant Cousin	Plouffe, Ambrosino	
EC		Female		5th Cousin	5th Cousin	3rd to Distant Cousin		
MP		Female		5th Cousin	5th Cousin	3rd to Distant Cousin		
William Miller	Miller	Male		5th Cousin	5th Cousin	3rd to Distant Cousin		
Marguerite Ruminski	Ruminski	Female		5th Cousin	5th Cousin	3rd to Distant Cousin		
MJ		Female		5th Cousin	5th Cousin	3rd to Distant Cousin		
KD		Female		5th Cousin	5th Cousin	3rd to Distant Cousin		
elana D'Amico	D'Amico	Female		5th Cousin	5th Cousin	3rd to Distant Cousin		
Iskren Chernev	Chernev	Male		5th Cousin	5th Cousin	3rd to Distant Cousin	Chernev, Popovska	Varna, Bulgaria; Shumen, Bulgaria
Christina W		Female		5th Cousin	5th Cousin	3rd to Distant Cousin		
Lisa Gilbert	Gilbert	Female		5th Cousin	5th Cousin	3rd to Distant Cousin		
Antoinette Bonno	Bonno	Female		5th Cousin	5th Cousin	3rd to Distant Cousin	tomasino, Bonno	
Ivy E		Female		5th Cousin	5th Cousin	3rd to Distant Cousin		
Audrey Burger	Burger	Female	1993	5th Cousin	5th Cousin	3rd to Distant Cousin		
Georgia Rhodes	Rhodes	Female	1959	5th Cousin	5th Cousin	3rd to Distant Cousin		
LOUIS B		Male		5th Cousin	5th Cousin	3rd to Distant Cousin		
Therese DeGrace	DeGrace	Female		5th Cousin	5th Cousin	3rd to Distant Cousin	Mario Medaglia, Giosina Medaglia, Giovanni Siciliano, Annuziata Siciliano., Theresa Bouchard, Hector DeGrace, DeGrace	Calabria, Italy
Jerry Hamilton	Hamilton	Male		5th Cousin	5th Cousin	3rd to Distant Cousin		
Zachary Dunn	Dunn	Male		5th Cousin	5th Cousin	3rd to Distant Cousin		
AS		Male		5th Cousin	5th Cousin	3rd to Distant Cousin	Petzetakis, Karydis	
Frannie M		Female		5th Cousin	5th Cousin	3rd to Distant Cousin		
AS		Female		5th Cousin	5th Cousin	3rd to Distant Cousin		
Jennifer E		Female		5th Cousin	5th Cousin	3rd to Distant Cousin	Olivo, Thomas	
Alexandra Papageorge	Papageorge	Female		5th Cousin	5th Cousin	3rd to Distant Cousin		
Sheryl Marchuk	Marchuk	Female		5th Cousin	5th Cousin	3rd to Distant Cousin		
Craig West	West	Male		5th Cousin	5th Cousin	3rd to Distant Cousin		
Megan Shapiro	Shapiro	Female		5th Cousin	5th Cousin	3rd to Distant Cousin		

Name	Surname	Sex	Birth	Rel. 1	Rel. 2	Rel. 3	Surnames / Aliases	Location
J Amato	Amato	Male		5th Cousin	5th Cousin	3rd to Distant Cousin	Amato, Anderson	
JW		Male		5th Cousin	5th Cousin	3rd to Distant Cousin		
Penagiotis Dallis	Dallis	Male		5th Cousin	5th Cousin	3rd to Distant Cousin		
AJ		Male		5th Cousin	5th Cousin	3rd to Distant Cousin		
Michelle Odai	Odai	Female		5th Cousin	5th Cousin	3rd to Distant Cousin		
Kristian Szobi	Szobi	Male		5th Cousin	5th Cousin	3rd to Distant Cousin	Kolar, Rehorova, Szobi	Hungary
B M	M	Male		5th Cousin	5th Cousin	3rd to Distant Cousin	Mala, Ilias, Aliaj, Malaj, M	
Katherine P		Female		5th Cousin	5th Cousin	3rd to Distant Cousin		
Dimitris Pavlakis	Pavlakis	Male		5th Cousin	5th Cousin	3rd to Distant Cousin	Pavlakis	
Claudia L		Female	1974	5th Cousin	5th Cousin	3rd to Distant Cousin	Lira, Galvan, Meraz, Vasquez, Perez	Chihuahua, Mexico; Durango, Mexico; New Mexico, Texas, California
JL		Male		5th Cousin	5th Cousin	3rd to Distant Cousin		
GP		Male		5th Cousin	5th Cousin	3rd to Distant Cousin		
AS		Male		5th Cousin	5th Cousin	3rd to Distant Cousin		
Carolin Haines	Haines	Female		5th Cousin	5th Cousin	3rd to Distant Cousin	Langsch, Zawadzky, Pauldrach, Haines	
Eva Barbara	Barbara	Female		5th Cousin	5th Cousin	3rd to Distant Cousin		
Deanna C		Female		5th Cousin	5th Cousin	3rd to Distant Cousin	Maternal - Lalonde, Longtin, Paternal - Johnston, Pat Grandmother - Kominski	
Jama Siegel	Siegel	Female		5th Cousin	5th Cousin	3rd to Distant Cousin		
Mark Buscemi	Buscemi	Male		5th Cousin	5th Cousin	3rd to Distant Cousin		
M Witgenstein	Witgenstein	Male		5th Cousin	5th Cousin	3rd to Distant Cousin		
Arthur S		Male		5th Cousin	5th Cousin	3rd to Distant Cousin		
ER		Female	1954	5th Cousin	5th Cousin	3rd to Distant Cousin	Metaxas, Mariatos	Argostolion, Ionian Islands, Peloponnisos Dytiki Ellada ke Ionio, Greece
Alexandra Stamou	Stamou	Female	1973	5th Cousin	5th Cousin	3rd to Distant Cousin		
Nikolaos K		Male	1968	5th Cousin	5th Cousin	3rd to Distant Cousin		
WP		Male		5th Cousin	5th Cousin	3rd to Distant Cousin	Putkowski, Jablonowski, Omencetter, Braun, Kollmyer, Kollmeier, Kohlmeyer, Seidensticker, Grau, Bryan, Ferreau, Strimple, Strempei, Burton, Adams, Mathis, Poulson, Sax, Stout, Dzierzkowski, Czarnecki, waleri, Valeri	Warsaw, Poland. Bransk, VoivodeshipPodlaskie, CountyBielsk.; Ovenstaedt, Westfalen, Prussia, Anspach, Hochtaunuskreis, WÃ¼rttemberg, Frankenhain, Germany;
Sara Hedjever	Hedjever	Female	1987	5th Cousin	5th Cousin	3rd to Distant Cousin		
Alexandros Anastasopoulos	Anastasopoulos	Male	1980	5th Cousin	5th Cousin	3rd to Distant Cousin		
Ashleigh Stewart	Stewart	Female		5th Cousin	5th Cousin	3rd to Distant Cousin		
John Dower	Dower	Male		5th Cousin	5th Cousin	3rd to Distant Cousin		
GA		Female		5th Cousin	5th Cousin	3rd to Distant Cousin		
Maria Jacob	Jacob	Female		5th Cousin	5th Cousin	3rd to Distant Cousin		
Angie (Angelica) Singleton	Singleton	Female	2001	5th Cousin	5th Cousin	3rd to Distant Cousin	Velasquez, Stoicich, Singleton	
Alisher Saydalikhodjayev	Saydalikhodjayev	Male	1986	5th Cousin	5th Cousin	3rd to Distant Cousin	Saydalikhodjayev, saidalikhodjaev, saidalihodjaev, bokserman, boxerman	Tashkent
Alexandros Eleftheriadis	Eleftheriadis	Male	1967	5th Cousin	5th Cousin	3rd to Distant Cousin		
ES		Female		5th Cousin	5th Cousin	3rd to Distant Cousin		Czech Republic
Vjollca Bato Gjinolli	Bato Gjinolli	Female		5th Cousin	5th Cousin	3rd to Distant Cousin	Sulejmani, Baki, Batoja, Yseni, Bato Gjinolli	
DD		Female		5th Cousin	5th Cousin	3rd to Distant Cousin		
JR		Male		5th Cousin	5th Cousin	3rd to Distant Cousin		
Judah Contreras	Contreras	Male		5th Cousin	5th Cousin	3rd to Distant Cousin		
Sara Kennedy	Kennedy	Female		5th Cousin	5th Cousin	3rd to Distant Cousin		
steven DAntonio	DAntonio	Male		5th Cousin	5th Cousin	3rd to Distant Cousin		
Nick S		Male		5th Cousin	5th Cousin	3rd to Distant Cousin		
Chiara Kennedy	Kennedy	Female		5th Cousin	5th Cousin	3rd to Distant Cousin		
SM		Female		5th Cousin	5th Cousin	3rd to Distant Cousin		
Michael Gailas	Gailas	Male		5th Cousin	5th Cousin	3rd to Distant Cousin		
Konstantina Merikas	Merikas	Female		5th Cousin	5th Cousin	3rd to Distant Cousin		
Sabahnur Erdemli	Erdemli	Female		5th Cousin	5th Cousin	3rd to Distant Cousin		
Elena Barmpopoulou	Barmpopoulou	Female		5th Cousin	5th Cousin	3rd to Distant Cousin		
Roula Fokas Sheha	Fokas Sheha	Female		5th Cousin	5th Cousin	3rd to Distant Cousin		

Name	Surname	Gender	Year	Relationship	Relationship	Relationship	Associated surnames	Locations
Nicole V		Female		5th Cousin	5th Cousin	3rd to Distant Cousin		
EN		Female		5th Cousin	5th Cousin	3rd to Distant Cousin		
MA		Female		5th Cousin	5th Cousin	3rd to Distant Cousin		
JG		Male		5th Cousin	5th Cousin	3rd to Distant Cousin		
W Fortier	Fortier	Male		5th Cousin	5th Cousin	3rd to Distant Cousin		
MA		Male		5th Cousin	5th Cousin	3rd to Distant Cousin		
Peter Romas	Romas	Male	1990	5th Cousin	5th Cousin	3rd to Distant Cousin		
costa sakellariou	sakellariou	Male	1959	5th Cousin	5th Cousin	3rd to Distant Cousin	greek on my father's side - his father a sakellariou from ag. petros kynouria, his mother a samiotou from athens/koropi, my mother is anneke van kirk, her father harold van kirk from hudson mi, also harrow, her mother was gertrude weaver, also dom, sakellariou	ag. petros kynouria, athens,; hudson mi, doylestown pa
HD		Female		5th Cousin	5th Cousin	3rd to Distant Cousin		
Susan Wilmoth	Wilmoth	Female	1971	5th Cousin	5th Cousin	3rd to Distant Cousin		
Kevin Maliszewski	Maliszewski	Male	1986	5th Cousin	5th Cousin	3rd to Distant Cousin	Mieszanek, Maliszewski, Tarabek, Mitchell, Matysek	
Benjamin Friedman	Friedman	Male	1995	5th Cousin	5th Cousin	3rd to Distant Cousin		
Esmeralda Kaiteris	Kaiteris	Female		5th Cousin	5th Cousin	3rd to Distant Cousin		Constantinople, athens, lesbos, Mikras asias.
Penelope Tsinaridis	Tsinaridis	Female		5th Cousin	5th Cousin	3rd to Distant Cousin		
Lila Owens	Owens	Female		5th Cousin	5th Cousin	3rd to Distant Cousin		
F Sohaie	Sohaie	Female		5th Cousin	5th Cousin	3rd to Distant Cousin		
Anthony Dracopoulos	Dracopoulos	Male		5th Cousin	5th Cousin	3rd to Distant Cousin	Dracopoulos, Balafoutis, Drakopoulos	Evangelismos, Greece; Shinolaka, Greece; Montreal, Canada;
Jamie Clum	Clum	Female		5th Cousin	5th Cousin	3rd to Distant Cousin		
Flor Veseli	Veseli	Male		5th Cousin	5th Cousin	3rd to Distant Cousin		
Mitchell Sturevski	Sturevski	Male	1997	5th Cousin	5th Cousin	3rd to Distant Cousin		
Ford Jung	Jung	Male		5th Cousin	5th Cousin	3rd to Distant Cousin	Ford, Mumma, Harral, Clark, Cobby, Ahrens, Jung	
Raquel Segri Ferreira	Segri Ferreira	Female		5th Cousin	5th Cousin	3rd to Distant Cousin		
John Christopher	Christopher	Male		5th Cousin	5th Cousin	3rd to Distant Cousin		
Catherine DiVincenzo	DiVincenzo	Female		5th Cousin	5th Cousin	3rd to Distant Cousin		
Jeanette Lynam	Lynam	Female		5th Cousin	5th Cousin	3rd to Distant Cousin		
Cleopatra Milionis	Milionis	Female		5th Cousin	5th Cousin	3rd to Distant Cousin		
Varvara Leventopoulou	Leventopoulou	Female	1962	5th Cousin	5th Cousin	3rd to Distant Cousin	Leventopoulos, Kandilakis, Tsagkaris, Zaharopoulos, Economopoulos, Constantopoulos, Contuzzi, Akrivopoulos, Varvatsoulis, Georgakalos, Thanopoulos, Prapopoulos, Georgopoulos, Leventopoulou	Athens; Corfu; Izmir; Istanbul; Zatouna; Dimitsana; Siatista; Kalavryta; Sifnos; Georgioupolis, Crete
Angeliki Markaki	Markaki	Female		5th Cousin	5th Cousin	3rd to Distant Cousin		
Adela Mirtaj	Mirtaj	Female	1994	5th Cousin	5th Cousin	3rd to Distant Cousin		
Alicia Barlow	Barlow	Female	1969	5th Cousin	5th Cousin	3rd to Distant Cousin	Weinand, Zanglia, Breidenbach, Barlow	
Isis Sartin	Sartin	Female		5th Cousin	5th Cousin	3rd to Distant Cousin		
T Demopolis	Demopolis	Female		5th Cousin	5th Cousin	3rd to Distant Cousin		
Alaina Stacey	Stacey	Female		5th Cousin	5th Cousin	3rd to Distant Cousin		
Jordan Stacey	Stacey	Male		5th Cousin	5th Cousin	3rd to Distant Cousin		
A M		Male		5th Cousin	5th Cousin	3rd to Distant Cousin		
NZ		Male		5th Cousin	5th Cousin	3rd to Distant Cousin		
Paul Jarosz	Jarosz	Male		5th Cousin	5th Cousin	3rd to Distant Cousin	Lancmańska, Jarosz	

s svec	svec	Female	5th Cousin	5th Cousin	3rd to Distant Cousin	Ashall, Bramblet, Bright, Burney, Burton, Cokroft, Conway, Coulson, Cox, Durham, Frizzel, Gye, Hardee, Hardy, Holt, Jones (Tamar), Knight, Mckay, Mills, Mote, Nickolls, Pettit, Poynter, Price, Shrewsberry, Spencer, Stellav, Stewart, Waters, Witherington, Rowe, Frazier, Shelton, Reed, Shook, Crawford, hunter, svec	
Sandra E		Female	5th Cousin	5th Cousin	3rd to Distant Cousin	Chininis, Elanges, Koufou, Hadjeleas	
Michael Elanges	Elanges	Male	5th Cousin	5th Cousin	3rd to Distant Cousin	Strang, Elanges	
Danielle P		Female	5th Cousin	5th Cousin	3rd to Distant Cousin		
LT		Male	5th Cousin	5th Cousin	3rd to Distant Cousin		
C Martell	Martell	Female	1961 5th Cousin	5th Cousin	3rd to Distant Cousin		
EA		Male	5th Cousin	5th Cousin	3rd to Distant Cousin		
Brian P		Male	5th Cousin	5th Cousin	3rd to Distant Cousin		
MJ		Male	5th Cousin	5th Cousin	3rd to Distant Cousin		
Ventsyslav Raikov	Raikov	Male	5th Cousin	5th Cousin	3rd to Distant Cousin	Raikov, Kostov, Bandilov	
EP		Male	5th Cousin	5th Cousin	3rd to Distant Cousin	Pashalis, Toris	Greece, Athens, Volos, Almiros, Umnos, Melbourne, Australia, USA, New York
Alex Kennedy	Kennedy	Male	5th Cousin	5th Cousin	3rd to Distant Cousin		
K Andrea	Andrea	Male	5th Cousin	5th Cousin	3rd to Distant Cousin	Andrea, Adhami, Ndreu, Dindi, Titka	

Display Name	Surname	Sex	Birth Year	Set Relatio	Predicted F	Relative Range	Family Surnames	Family Locations
jane R		Female		5th Cousin	5th Cousin	3rd to Distant Cousin	Dzierzkowski, Jablonowski, Omencetter, Putkowski, Braun, Kollmyer, Kollmeier, Kohlmeyer, Seidensticker, Grau, Bryan, Ferreau, Strimple, Strempel, Burton, Adams, Mathis, Poulson, Sax	Warsaw, Poland. Bransk, VoivodeshipPodlaskie. CountyBielsk. Ovenstaedt, Westfalen, Prussia, Anspach, Hochtaunuskreis, WÃ¼rttemberg, Frankenhain, Germany;
Mary Kaloci	Kaloci	Female		5th Cousin	5th Cousin	3rd to Distant Cousin		
Stephanie Magoulas	Magoulas	Female	1975	5th Cousin	5th Cousin	3rd to Distant Cousin	Manninen, Mannila, Paatola, Kaukua, Olson, Hallam, Moilanen, Magnuson, Magoulas, Magoula, Koski, Raistakka	Finland; Trikala; Athens; Rosburg, WA; Varmland County, Sweden; Lysvik, Varmland County, Sweden; Taivalkoski, Finland; Chicago, Cook County, Illinois, United States
Tom Petropoulos	Petropoulos	Male	1971	4th Cousin	4th Cousin	3rd to 5th Cousin	Petropoulos, Panagopoulos	
Constantine Roumel	Roumel	Male		3rd Cousin	3rd Cousin	3rd to 5th Cousin		
Rosemary nee Kromidas Hendrix	Hendrix	Female	1934	5th Cousin	5th Cousin	3rd to Distant Cousin	Kromidas, Yiannasopoulos, Kosmas, Markopoulos, Hendrix	Messini, Veria, Michigan, Florida, Georgia
nicole keough	keough	Female		5th Cousin	5th Cousin	3rd to Distant Cousin		
Janet R Olson	Olson	Female		5th Cousin	5th Cousin	3rd to Distant Cousin	Rich, Riccio, Bagelos, Pappas, Olson	
Alessandro Genovese	Genovese	Male	1952	5th Cousin	5th Cousin	3rd to Distant Cousin	Spiropulos, Spiropulu, Genovese	
Mueser Shatku	Shatku	Female		5th Cousin	5th Cousin	3rd to Distant Cousin		Albania
Kathleen Heath	Heath	Female	1956	5th Cousin	5th Cousin	3rd to Distant Cousin	Egan, McCabe, Dickman, Heath	
Thomas Caulfield	Caulfield	Male		5th Cousin	5th Cousin	3rd to Distant Cousin		
Nick Kacprowski	Kacprowski	Male		5th Cousin	5th Cousin	3rd to Distant Cousin	Kacprowski, Richter, Antonopoulos, Syriopoulos	
Dasha Dasha	Dasha	Female		5th Cousin	5th Cousin	3rd to Distant Cousin	Babic, Srdic, Romic, Bogovac, Dasha	Belgrade, Sebia; Drvar, Bosnia; Zaglavica, Bosnia; Padjeni, Croatia; Knin, Croatia; Split, Croatia; Ivosevci, Croatia; Komiza, Croatia; Kistanje, Croatia; Frankfurt, Germany;
James Chukalas	Chukalas	Male		5th Cousin	5th Cousin	3rd to Distant Cousin	Chukalas, Tsoukalas, Missailidis	
Kimberly Harrison	Harrison	Female		4th Cousin	4th Cousin	3rd to 6th Cousin	Hatch, Sousa, Souza, Boblin, Gerbic, Grbic, Harrison	Austria, Yugoslavia (Croatia), England, Portugal, Canada (Alberta, British Columbia), United States (Massachussetts, Maine, Florida, California)
A Co	Co	Male		5th Cousin	5th Cousin	3rd to Distant Cousin		
MARTHA FOSTERI	FOSTERI	Female	1954	4th Cousin	4th Cousin	3rd to Distant Cousin	Fosteris, Daoudakis, FOSTERI	Chania-Crete, Amorgos, Athens
Stephanie Jones Labadie	Jones Labadie	Female	1984	5th Cousin	5th Cousin	3rd to Distant Cousin	Jones, Hodum, Manos, Manouilidis, Anagnostou, Jones Labadie	Watertown, MA; Pochahontas, TN
Elaine Ganas	Ganas	Female		5th Cousin	5th Cousin	3rd to Distant Cousin		Scotland, United Kingdom; Ireland; England, United Kingdom
Justin Landers	Landers	Male		5th Cousin	5th Cousin	3rd to Distant Cousin		
Stephen Janik	Janik	Male	1949	5th Cousin	5th Cousin	3rd to Distant Cousin	Janik, Rybska, JeleÅ„, Szkaradek, Kokosza, Baran, Hajduk, Szczepankiewicz, Policht, Dresza, WaÅ‚czyk, MrÃ³z, Nidecki, Galica, Kwasniowski, Koloczkowska, Wantek, Lesniocha, Pietrzyk, Dziedzic, Grzyb, Sikocolno, Smolek/Smoliuk/Smolukas, RadzeviÄius/Radziewicz/Rajavich, Valentukievich, Walukoniute, Lukashevich, Kasheta, Remizovska, Muchynski, Akscin, Kibirkshis	RoznÃ³w, Poland; ZagÃ³rze, Poland; Gierowa, Poland; Januszowa, Poland; Wojakowa, Poland; Radajowice, Poland; Gudeliai, Lithuania; Suwalki, Lithuania; Zheime, Lithuania; Kashety, Lithuania; Gailiunai, Lithuania; DuBois, Pennsylvania; Detroit, Michigan
IR		Male		5th Cousin	5th Cousin	3rd to Distant Cousin		
Michael Odai	Odai	Male	1971	5th Cousin	5th Cousin	3rd to Distant Cousin	Odai, Odaj, Tucci, Patane	Syracuse, New York; Bari, Italy; Tirana, Albania; Sulmona, Italy; Catania, Sicily, Italy

Vanicka de Nocker	de Nocker	Female		5th Cousin 5th Cousin 3rd to Distant Cousin	Kangia, Perpignan, Moatsos	
Irene Moatsos	Moatsos	Female		5th Cousin 5th Cousin 3rd to Distant Cousin	Costoulas, Catsoulas, Katsoulis, ocello	
James ocello	ocello	Male		5th Cousin 5th Cousin 3rd to Distant Cousin		Rochester, Monroe County, New York, United States
Vincent Episcopo	Episcopo	Male	2001	5th Cousin 5th Cousin 3rd to Distant Cousin	Seman, Episcopo, Patterson, Snyder	
Eva McMullan	McMullan	Female		4th Cousin 4th Cousin 3rd to Distant Cousin		
Mary Ann Patarino	Patarino	Female	1955	5th Cousin 5th Cousin 3rd to 6th Cousin		
ANTONY Stratis	Stratis	Male		4th Cousin 4th Cousin 3rd to 6th Cousin	Papadopoulos, Mastoris, Ghynos, Glinos, Tiniakos, Skordos, Dapontis, Daponte, Dapontes, Vastardis, Stratis	
ANTONY Stratis	Stratis	Male		4th Cousin 4th Cousin 3rd to 6th Cousin	Papadopoulos, Mastoris, Ghynos, Glinos, Tiniakos, Skordos, Dapontis, Daponte, Dapontes, Vastardis, Stratis	
Angelica Clark	Clark	Female	1947	5th Cousin 5th Cousin 3rd to Distant Cousin		
DAVID POURNARAS	POURNARAS	Male	1947	5th Cousin 5th Cousin 3rd to Distant Cousin		
Giorgio Mladjenovic	Mladjenovic	Male	1957	5th Cousin 5th Cousin 3rd to Distant Cousin		
Jacob Binley	Binley	Male		5th Cousin 5th Cousin 3rd to Distant Cousin	Binley, McDonnell	
Kristen Virmani	Virmani	Female		5th Cousin 5th Cousin 3rd to Distant Cousin	Knezevich, Malkovich, Virmani	
Vincent Russo	Russo	Male		5th Cousin 4th Cousin 3rd to Distant Cousin		
Barbara Wagner	Wagner	Female		5th Cousin 5th Cousin 3rd to Distant Cousin	Iwanski, Wagner	
Stanley Chamalias	Chamalias	Male	1954	5th Cousin 5th Cousin 3rd to Distant Cousin	Patsios, Sakalaris, Chamalias	
Polly Jenkins	Jenkins	Female		4th Cousin 4th Cousin 3rd to Distant Cousin		
Eric Bojonell	Bojonell	Male	1974	5th Cousin 5th Cousin 3rd to Distant Cousin	Bojonell, Bozonelis	
marketa matejcik	matejcik	Female	1971	5th Cousin 5th Cousin 3rd to Distant Cousin	Mysak, Lindner, Haas, Machala, matejcik	
Gia Agoritsas	Agoritsas	Female		5th Cousin 5th Cousin 3rd to Distant Cousin		
Maria Matua	Matua	Female		5th Cousin 5th Cousin 3rd to Distant Cousin	Matua, Munxuri	
Rachael Ellisor	Ellisor	Female	1984	5th Cousin 5th Cousin 3rd to Distant Cousin	Chalakias, Halkia, Ellisor	
Kate Hoxha	Hoxha	Female		5th Cousin 5th Cousin 3rd to Distant Cousin		Greece
S K	K	Male		5th Cousin 5th Cousin 3rd to Distant Cousin	Cizek, Kokonas, Gregory, Cordogan, Siavelis, K	
Flora Betea	Betea	Female		5th Cousin 5th Cousin 3rd to Distant Cousin		
Ewelina Rozalska	Rozalska	Female		5th Cousin 5th Cousin 3rd to Distant Cousin		
Elena Sarkissian	Sarkissian	Female		5th Cousin 5th Cousin 3rd to Distant Cousin		
Jennifer McHugh	McHugh	Female	1985	5th Cousin 5th Cousin 3rd to Distant Cousin	Kopsas, Jones, Lonis, Manion, Pritchett, Wolfe, Kastein, Klinger, Page, Fagg, Hillenburg, Robenson, Morphew, Kitchens, Crump, McHugh	Greece; Dimxperlo, Aalten, Gelderland, Netherlands; Gelderland, Netherlands; North Brabant, Netherlands
Vitalie Chetraru	Chetraru	Male		5th Cousin 5th Cousin 3rd to Distant Cousin	Haitu, paiu, bordeniuc, Bucur, Chetraru	Telenesti, Telenești District, Moldova
Katherine Vlahov	Vlahov	Female		5th Cousin 5th Cousin 3rd to Distant Cousin		
Dayna C		Female		5th Cousin 5th Cousin 3rd to Distant Cousin		Poland
Irene Papazicos	Papazicos	Female		5th Cousin 4th Cousin 3rd to Distant Cousin		
Tina Vulgaris	Vulgaris	Female	1959	4th Cousin 4th Cousin 3rd to Distant Cousin		
Tina Vulgaris	Vulgaris	Female	1959	4th Cousin 4th Cousin 3rd to Distant Cousin		
Sherna Salim	Salim	Female		5th Cousin 5th Cousin 3rd to Distant Cousin		
Elizabeth Godwin	Godwin	Female		5th Cousin 5th Cousin 3rd to Distant Cousin	Bisulca, Calcagno, Biddera, Giuseppa, Dcutncy, Post, Partch, McEwen, Hoyt, Smith, Capada, Stoppard, Jackson, Parke, Munson, Moss, Lothropp, Ludlum, Cool, Kool, De Forest, Obe, DeForest, VanFlaesbeck, Godwin	
Amy C		Female		4th Cousin 4th Cousin 3rd to Distant Cousin	Kenner, Odom, pease, papaelias	
Michelle Alonso	Alonso	Female		5th Cousin 5th Cousin 3rd to Distant Cousin	Eaton, LeBay, DeNullo, Alonso	
Jonathan Wallon	Wallon	Male		5th Cousin 5th Cousin 3rd to Distant Cousin		
vivian quinones	quinones	Female		5th Cousin 5th Cousin 3rd to Distant Cousin		
Donna MacDonald	MacDonald	Female		5th Cousin 5th Cousin 3rd to Distant Cousin		

Name	Surname	Sex	Year				Related Surnames	Location
Ingrid Campochiaro	Campochiaro	Female	1943	5th Cousin	5th Cousin	3rd to Distant Cousin	Gronki, Preiss, Petersen, Koch, Campochiaro	
Jessica Fittoria	Fittoria	Female	1992	5th Cousin	5th Cousin	3rd to Distant Cousin	Rosales, Fittoria	
Anthi Georgakopoulos	Georgakopoulos	Female		5th Cousin	5th Cousin	3rd to Distant Cousin		
Pamela Ajango	Ajango	Female	1974	5th Cousin	5th Cousin	3rd to Distant Cousin	Paras, Karellas, Teinfeld, Wilhelmson, Ajango	
Andrea Petratos (Tabor)	Petratos (Tabor)	Female	1966	5th Cousin	5th Cousin	3rd to Distant Cousin		
Chris Lagos	Lagos	Male	1969	5th Cousin	5th Cousin	3rd to Distant Cousin	Lagos, Pappas	
Konstantine Karantasis	Karantasis	Male	1980	5th Cousin	5th Cousin	3rd to Distant Cousin	Giavis, Sismanis, Kladakis, Karantasis	Ano Symi, Greece
katy reeder	reeder	Female		5th Cousin	5th Cousin	3rd to Distant Cousin		
Chloe Hoff	Hoff	Female	1993	4th Cousin	4th Cousin	3rd to 6th Cousin		
Christa Molloy	Molloy	Female		5th Cousin	5th Cousin	3rd to Distant Cousin	Micklitz, Scholz, Schwarzer, Brazzel, Bowers, Fielder, Touhey, Rosenquist, Molloy	Ballynakill, County Galway, Ireland; County Kerry, Ireland; FÃ¼rth, Middle Franconia, Bavaria, Germany; Cork, County Cork, Ireland; Waterford, County Waterford, Ireland
A Van Gilder	Van Gilder	Male	1951	5th Cousin	5th Cousin	3rd to Distant Cousin		
Blendi Hasa	Hasa	Male		5th Cousin	5th Cousin	3rd to Distant Cousin		
Heleni Lewis	Lewis	Female		5th Cousin	5th Cousin	3rd to Distant Cousin	Foulos, Kontonis, Xalepa, Lewis	Romania; Greece
Kristina Mentakis	Mentakis	Female		5th Cousin	5th Cousin	3rd to Distant Cousin		
Jennifer Broge Voss	Broge Voss	Female		5th Cousin	5th Cousin	3rd to Distant Cousin	Broge, Klunge, Murphy, Leonard, Schrader, McLean, Broge Voss	Ireland; Germany
Cemal O	O	Male		5th Cousin	5th Cousin	3rd to Distant Cousin		
Sydney Barron	Barron	Female	2000	5th Cousin	5th Cousin	3rd to Distant Cousin		
Ken Schuster	Schuster	Male		5th Cousin	5th Cousin	3rd to Distant Cousin		
Roseanne Shefferman	Shefferman	Female	1953	5th Cousin	5th Cousin	3rd to Distant Cousin		Italy
Chris T	T	Male	1937	5th Cousin	5th Cousin	3rd to Distant Cousin		
Joann Patterson	Patterson	Female		5th Cousin	5th Cousin	3rd to Distant Cousin		
Svetoslav BOJILOV	BOJILOV	Male	1965	5th Cousin	5th Cousin	3rd to Distant Cousin	Isov, Bokov, Surlekov, BOJILOV	
Adonis Stassinopoulos	Stassinopoulos	Male		5th Cousin	5th Cousin	3rd to Distant Cousin	Sakalis, Smirli, Stassinopoulos	
Terry Bowden	Bowden	Male	1946	5th Cousin	5th Cousin	3rd to Distant Cousin	Heath, Soper, Kearney, Winsor, Squire, Gruitt, Mountjoy, Baker, Lakeman, Robinson, Hiscox, Rowe, Sawford, Williams, Tinney, Rowden, Kelly, Bowden	County Kerry, Ireland; Devon, England, United Kingdom; Nelson, Nelson, New Zealand
sandra cosmopoulos	cosmopoulos	Female	1960	5th Cousin	5th Cousin	3rd to Distant Cousin		Athens, Greece; Greece
Melissa Lake	Lake	Female		5th Cousin	5th Cousin	3rd to Distant Cousin	Avgerinos, Lake	
Alexandria Doing	Doing	Female	1982	5th Cousin	5th Cousin	3rd to Distant Cousin	Masterson, Armstrong, Doing	
Tim Cumuze	Cumuze	Male		5th Cousin	5th Cousin	3rd to Distant Cousin		
Edmond Deci	Deci	Male		5th Cousin	5th Cousin	3rd to Distant Cousin		
IOANNIS LEMPIDAKIS	LEMPIDAKIS	Male	1937	5th Cousin	5th Cousin	3rd to Distant Cousin	Vassilakis, Stratigakis, Kourmoulis, LEMPIDAKIS	
Giannis Piperis	Piperis	Male	1975	5th Cousin	5th Cousin	3rd to Distant Cousin		
Kara G		Female		5th Cousin	5th Cousin	3rd to Distant Cousin	Tierney, Curry, Mcneill, LoRe, Bagley	
William Basso	Basso	Male		4th Cousin	4th Cousin	3rd to 6th Cousin		
Ryan Gladney	Gladney	Male		5th Cousin	5th Cousin	3rd to Distant Cousin		
Krystle Herrera	Herrera	Female		5th Cousin	5th Cousin	3rd to Distant Cousin		
Irene Kambos	Kambos	Female		5th Cousin	5th Cousin	3rd to Distant Cousin		
Hugh McLaurin	McLaurin	Male	1954	5th Cousin	5th Cousin	3rd to Distant Cousin		
Benjamin Brugh	Brugh	Male	1983	5th Cousin	5th Cousin	3rd to Distant Cousin	Cordone, Lindsay, Hall, Williams, Brugh, Malatesta, Osborne	
Dimitri Gerontis	Gerontis	Male		4th Cousin	4th Cousin	3rd to 6th Cousin		
Harry Cosmos	Cosmos	Male	1952	4th Cousin	4th Cousin	3rd to 5th Cousin	Gretsis, Treatafeles, Demetre, Yaglagoulo, Cosmos	
Penny Richardson	Richardson	Female	1949	5th Cousin	5th Cousin	3rd to Distant Cousin	Stutzman, Richardson	
Eleanor Luopa	Luopa	Female		5th Cousin	5th Cousin	3rd to Distant Cousin	Jones, Saari, Luopa	

Name	Surname	Gender	Year	Relationship	Associated Surnames	Locations
Maria Pelekanos	Pelekanos	Female		5th Cousin 5th Cousin 3rd to Distant Cousin	Bertsekas, Dardani, Markopoulos, Pelekanos	
Logan Weeks	Weeks	Male		5th Cousin 5th Cousin 3rd to Distant Cousin	Papageorgopolous, Bullard, Pappas, Casaregala, Baker, Weeks	Kalavrita, Greece; Kleitoria, Greece
A Roumell, Sr.	Roumell, Sr.	Male	1949	5th Cousin 5th Cousin 3rd to Distant Cousin	Roumeliotis, Roumell, Sr.	
Jason C		Male		5th Cousin 5th Cousin 3rd to Distant Cousin		
Helen Kontis	Kontis	Female		4th Cousin 4th Cousin 3rd to 6th Cousin		Mt Lebanon,Pa; Baltimore,MD; Ft.Lauderdale,Fla; Titusville,Fla
Bujar Ibrahimi	Ibrahimi	Male	1981	5th Cousin 5th Cousin 3rd to Distant Cousin	Shehu, Mustafa, Leka, Ibrahimi	Albania; Pogradec, Pogradec District, KorÃ§Ã« County, Albania
Arabela Barbu	Barbu	Female	1994	5th Cousin 5th Cousin 3rd to Distant Cousin		
Stelian Damu	Damu	Male		5th Cousin 5th Cousin 3rd to Distant Cousin		
Brian A		Male	1960	5th Cousin 5th Cousin 3rd to Distant Cousin		
Arietta Tetreault	Tetreault	Female	1995	5th Cousin 5th Cousin 3rd to Distant Cousin	Rigopoulos, Baimas, Philibotte, Royal, Bozicas, Tzanetis, Dinelie, Tetreault	Lagkadia, Greece; Quebec, Canada
Stephanie Engman	Engman	Female		4th Cousin 4th Cousin 3rd to 6th Cousin		
TL		Male	1958	5th Cousin 5th Cousin 3rd to Distant Cousin	Nardi, Marr, Saracco	
Yolanda Tkachyk	Tkachyk	Female		5th Cousin 5th Cousin 3rd to Distant Cousin	Panagiotopoulos, Tkachyk	
Jack Wright	Wright	Male	1994	5th Cousin 5th Cousin 3rd to Distant Cousin		
Juan AyllÃ³n	AyllÃ³n	Male	1973	5th Cousin 5th Cousin 3rd to Distant Cousin	AyllÃ³n, Alonso, Colmenar, Mouton	
Frances Costanzi	Costanzi	Female	1958	5th Cousin 5th Cousin 3rd to Distant Cousin	Waldron, Martell, Milano, Pendergast, Palmieri, Qualtieri, Wagner, Wing, Costanzi	
Brittany Roginson	Roginson	Female	1989	5th Cousin 5th Cousin 3rd to Distant Cousin		
Patrice Gaydos	Gaydos	Female		5th Cousin 5th Cousin 3rd to Distant Cousin		
Jason Nicholaou	Nicholaou	Male		1st Cousin, 1st Cousin, Once Removed	Nicholaou, Lawson, Venis	
Andy Johnson	Johnson	Male		5th Cousin 5th Cousin 3rd to Distant Cousin		
Stephanie Kopsas	Kopsas	Female		5th Cousin 5th Cousin 3rd to Distant Cousin		
George Pavlakis	Pavlakis	Male	2002	5th Cousin 5th Cousin 3rd to Distant Cousin		
Jennifer Knight	Knight	Female		5th Cousin 5th Cousin 3rd to Distant Cousin	Burris, Mickelsen, Walthall, Knight	
Karlana Talbert	Talbert	Female		5th Cousin 5th Cousin 3rd to Distant Cousin		
Nikola Bjelos	Bjelos	Male		5th Cousin 5th Cousin 3rd to Distant Cousin	Grbic, Brujic, Manojlovic, Bjelos	
nikolaos kozanitis	kozanitis	Male		5th Cousin 5th Cousin 3rd to Distant Cousin		
Christina Halm	Halm	Female		5th Cousin 5th Cousin 3rd to Distant Cousin		
Dean Mastoris	Mastoris	Male		5th Cousin 5th Cousin 3rd to Distant Cousin		
Melina Canas	Canas	Female		5th Cousin 5th Cousin 3rd to Distant Cousin		
Renee Caldwell	Caldwell	Female		5th Cousin 5th Cousin 3rd to Distant Cousin	Bates, Beach, Capron, Crouch, Diehl, Endris, Foerster, Geitmann, Graff, Grimmer, Haesselbart, Heffel, Heinze, Janing, Jahning, KÃ¶ster, Langhofer, Luebeck, Makepeace, Meier, Neumann, Proband, Rand, Reinhart, Reinwald, Savage, Schrade, Schuber, Siegel, Sokolowsky, Steinle, Strecker, Weber, Weir, Caldwell	Waldau; Waldow; Sachsen; Baden; Ergenzingen; GroÃŸ Tessin; Warin; Mecklenburg-Schwerin; Mecklenburg; Manitowoc; Kaukauna; Outagamie; Wisconsin; Kansas; Virginia; Russell; New York; Hermansdorff; Volga; Dreispitz; Saratov; Russia; Montgomery County, Virginia; Illinois; Germany;
Ryan Shekell	Shekell	Male		5th Cousin 5th Cousin 3rd to Distant Cousin		
Vasilis Scaltsas	Scaltsas	Male		5th Cousin 5th Cousin 3rd to Distant Cousin		
Mila Petkovic	Petkovic	Female		5th Cousin 5th Cousin 3rd to Distant Cousin		
Harrietta Christodoulos	Christodoulos	Female		5th Cousin 5th Cousin 3rd to Distant Cousin	kapsalis, Tzitzifianos, Bakopoulos, hinos, Iagios, Christodoulos	
Brian Torres	Torres	Male	1981	5th Cousin 5th Cousin 3rd to Distant Cousin		
Angela Sarkissian	Sarkissian	Female		5th Cousin 5th Cousin 3rd to Distant Cousin	Assimacopoulos, Manos, Maras, Marasoglou, Hanemoglou, Manusiotis, Sarkissian	Asia Minor, Chicago, Illinois, Yioryitsi, Sparta/Greece; Ã°zmir, Ã°zmir, Turkey; Ã°stanbul, Ã°stanbul, Turkey
Atanaska Sitnova	Sitnova	Female		5th Cousin 5th Cousin 3rd to Distant Cousin	Penev, Stoicevi, Dobrevi, Sitnova	
Maria Melignano	Melignano	Female	1930	5th Cousin 5th Cousin 3rd to Distant Cousin	Buhlinger, Maruggio, Melignano	
Amanda Johnson	Johnson	Female		5th Cousin 5th Cousin 3rd to Distant Cousin		

Name	Surname	Sex	Year	Rel 1	Rel 2	Rel 3	Associated Surnames	Region
Kristina Russo	Russo	Female	1986	5th Cousin	5th Cousin	3rd to Distant Cousin	Michaels, Skeans, De Palo, Russo	
Slagana Zugic	Zugic	Female	1977	5th Cousin	5th Cousin	3rd to Distant Cousin	Lakicevic, Zugic	
Vivian Kranenburg	Kranenburg	Female	1943	5th Cousin	5th Cousin	3rd to Distant Cousin		
Kimberly Stanford	Stanford	Female	1992	5th Cousin	5th Cousin	3rd to Distant Cousin	Wiles, Schonbok, Stanford	
george christopher	christopher	Male		4th Cousin	4th Cousin	3rd to Distant Cousin		
jill ferris	ferris	Female	1966	5th Cousin	5th Cousin	3rd to Distant Cousin	Mahoney, Thompson, Davidson, ferris	
Roxie Hiett	Hiett	Female		5th Cousin	5th Cousin	3rd to Distant Cousin		
Dimitrios Papageorgiou	Papageorgiou	Male	1963	5th Cousin	5th Cousin	3rd to Distant Cousin	Galanopoulos, Marinopoulos, Papageorgiou	
Wes Shofstahl	Shofstahl	Male		5th Cousin	5th Cousin	3rd to Distant Cousin		
Mirta Martinez	Martinez	Female		5th Cousin	5th Cousin	3rd to Distant Cousin		
Sharry Shekell	Shekell	Male		5th Cousin	5th Cousin	3rd to Distant Cousin		
Ozlem Jenkins	Jenkins	Female		5th Cousin	5th Cousin	3rd to Distant Cousin	Turan, Ã¶Ã¥dÃ¼n, Jenkins	
Athena Pelekanos	Pelekanos	Female		5th Cousin	5th Cousin	3rd to Distant Cousin	Dardani, Bertseka, Pelekanos	
Didra Kirschner	Kirschner	Female	1943	5th Cousin	5th Cousin	3rd to Distant Cousin		
Brady Brand	Brand	Male		5th Cousin	5th Cousin	3rd to Distant Cousin		
Gina Phelps	Phelps	Female		5th Cousin	5th Cousin	3rd to Distant Cousin	Cassello, Stella, Corvo, Phelps	
Yorgos K		Male	1985	5th Cousin	5th Cousin	3rd to Distant Cousin		
Elgi Haxhimanka	Haxhimanka	Male		5th Cousin	5th Cousin	3rd to Distant Cousin		
George Manos	Manos	Male	1957	5th Cousin	5th Cousin	3rd to Distant Cousin	Panagopolous, Karamanos, Bowman, Manos	
Martha Makkas	Makkas	Female		5th Cousin	5th Cousin	3rd to Distant Cousin		
Cynthia Vlahos Palmer	Vlahos Palmer	Female	1967	3rd Cousin	3rd Cousin		Vlahos, Geranios, Vlahos Palmer	
Liana Mellow	Mellow	Female		4th Cousin	4th Cousin	3rd to Distant Cousin	Toptschan, Parkhani, Mellow	
Sarah Fazio	Fazio	Female	1997	5th Cousin	5th Cousin	3rd to Distant Cousin		
E Waggoner	Waggoner	Female	2005	5th Cousin	5th Cousin	3rd to Distant Cousin		
Mark Kundid	Kundid	Male	1968	5th Cousin	5th Cousin	3rd to Distant Cousin		
Jordan Garr	Garr	Male	1984	4th Cousin	4th Cousin	3rd to Distant Cousin	harnack, garr, Garr	
Jeffery Bazzy	Bazzy	Male		5th Cousin	5th Cousin	3rd to Distant Cousin		
JD		Male	1983	5th Cousin	5th Cousin	3rd to Distant Cousin	Elkurd, Alkurd, Elkurdi, Alkurdi, Ghafari	Palestinian Territory
Frank Carabetta	Carabetta	Male		5th Cousin	5th Cousin	3rd to Distant Cousin		
Larry Tarabicos	Tarabicos	Male	1960	5th Cousin	5th Cousin	3rd to Distant Cousin		
Amy Upton	Upton	Female	1979	5th Cousin	5th Cousin	3rd to Distant Cousin		
Mary Drineas	Drineas	Female		4th Cousin	4th Cousin	3rd to 5th Cousin		
Mary Drineas	Drineas	Female		4th Cousin	4th Cousin	3rd to 5th Cousin		
KONSTANTINOS KANTOUTSIS	KANTOUTSIS	Male	1988	5th Cousin	5th Cousin	3rd to Distant Cousin	Pekos, Kantoutsis, Kolitsopoulos, Drakopoulos, Serelis, Kalampokis, Stavropoulos, Stabropoulos, Gountoumis, Gkountoumis, Goudoumis, Gkoudoumis, Dedousis, Dethousis, Thethousis, Thedousis, Nikolopoulos, Regoukos, Regkoukos, Mpitsikos, Bitsikos, Tsapepas, KANTOUTSIS	
Nensi Leka	Leka	Female	1986	5th Cousin	5th Cousin	3rd to Distant Cousin		
Joanne Peal	Peal	Female		5th Cousin	5th Cousin	3rd to Distant Cousin		
Diane Tollefson	Tollefson	Female		5th Cousin	5th Cousin	3rd to Distant Cousin	Gevan, Mc Conville, Schwappach, Schmauder, Lavery, Gevas, Mietz, Stathopoulas, Tollefson	
Charles Warburton	Warburton	Male		5th Cousin	5th Cousin	3rd to Distant Cousin		
Kathleen Alumbaugh	Alumbaugh	Female		5th Cousin	5th Cousin	3rd to Distant Cousin	Pensa, Pennza, Savastano, Pasto, DiNicola, Benedetto, Licursi, Pistillo, Alumbaugh	
Zinovia Cheliotis	Cheliotis	Female		4th Cousin	4th Cousin	3rd to Distant Cousin		
Joanna Wysocka	Wysocka	Female	1968	5th Cousin	5th Cousin	3rd to Distant Cousin		
Hristina Bakalova	Bakalova	Female	1988	5th Cousin	5th Cousin	3rd to Distant Cousin		
Robert Milovski	Milovski	Male	1994	5th Cousin	5th Cousin	3rd to Distant Cousin		
Tyler Hutchison	Hutchison	Male	1995	5th Cousin	5th Cousin	3rd to Distant Cousin		

Name	Surname	Sex	Year				Surnames	Locations
Yvonne Poster	Poster	Female	1957	5th Cousin	5th Cousin	3rd to Distant Cousin	Martino, Martone, Statella, Salvador, Poster	Valencia, Valencia, Valencian Community, Spain; Barcelona, Barcelona, Catalonia, Spain; Sicily, Italy; Naples, Metropolitan City of Naples, Campania, Italy
Soteria Georgiadis	Georgiadis	Female		5th Cousin	5th Cousin	3rd to Distant Cousin		
Andrea Sacchetto	Sacchetto	Female		5th Cousin	5th Cousin	3rd to Distant Cousin		
Ivica Prgonjic	Prgonjic	Male	1963	5th Cousin	5th Cousin	3rd to Distant Cousin	Veres, Njezic, Preradovic, Hlavaty, Prgonjic	
Aubrey Lutz	Lutz	Female	2003	5th Cousin	5th Cousin	3rd to Distant Cousin		
Jana Reyer	Reyer	Female		5th Cousin	5th Cousin	3rd to Distant Cousin	Pirog, Reyer	
Apostolia Schiza	Schiza	Female	1978	5th Cousin	5th Cousin	3rd to Distant Cousin	Ιξιτ[illegible], [illegible], Schiza	
Theodore Stamas	Stamas	Male		4th Cousin	4th Cousin	3rd to 6th Cousin		
Milica Bosnjak	Bosnjak	Female		5th Cousin	5th Cousin	3rd to Distant Cousin		
Martha Rudnick	Rudnick	Female		5th Cousin	5th Cousin	3rd to Distant Cousin		
Nicholas Demetry	Demetry	Male		5th Cousin	5th Cousin	3rd to Distant Cousin	Demetry, Tuntas, Alatsa, Georgiadis, Hatzidimitriou	
Cindy Koutsovasili	Koutsovasili	Female		5th Cousin	5th Cousin	3rd to Distant Cousin		
Chris Santillo	Santillo	Male	1992	5th Cousin	5th Cousin	3rd to Distant Cousin		
Langston Wright	Wright	Female		5th Cousin	5th Cousin	3rd to Distant Cousin	Langston, Sparkman, Guzman, Velasquez, McCabe, Wright	
THRASYVOULOS KIPOURGOS	KIPOURGOS	Male	1990	5th Cousin	5th Cousin	3rd to Distant Cousin	Thomas, Kalentzotis, Pantazopoulos, Fotis, KIPOURGOS	
Kimberly Anderson	Anderson	Female	1970	5th Cousin	5th Cousin	3rd to Distant Cousin		
ALEXANDROS GIANNOULAKIS	GIANNOULAKIS	Male	1969	5th Cousin	5th Cousin	3rd to Distant Cousin		
S.W. D	D	Male		5th Cousin	5th Cousin	3rd to Distant Cousin		
nathaniel rogic	rogic	Male		5th Cousin	5th Cousin	3rd to Distant Cousin		
Pamela Conry	Conry	Female	1948	5th Cousin	5th Cousin	3rd to Distant Cousin		
Scott Evans	Evans	Male	1982	5th Cousin	5th Cousin	3rd to Distant Cousin	Evans, Haslam, Robinson, Limb, Perkins, Zabriskie, Sanders, Johnson, Lewis, Lang, Hart, Dewing, Reynolds, Higbee, Sidebottom, Porcker, McRae, Stewart, Smith, Schooler, Cooke, Rees, Quigg, Dougherty, Skidmore, Martineau, Asay, Fisher, Allred, Cox, Lefevre, Broadhead, Fausett, Tolman, Rice, Hackley, Walker, Jones, String, Morgan, Bybee	Cedar City, Iron County, Utah, United States; Virgin, Washington County, Utah, United States; Salt Lake City, Salt Lake County, Utah, United States
Arbera Muriqi	Muriqi	Female		5th Cousin	5th Cousin	3rd to Distant Cousin		
Kate Cobb	Cobb	Female		5th Cousin	5th Cousin	3rd to Distant Cousin		
jennifer Perry	Perry	Female	1965	5th Cousin	5th Cousin	3rd to Distant Cousin		
Vasoula Brown	Brown	Female		5th Cousin	5th Cousin	3rd to Distant Cousin		
Jordan Losea	Losea	Female	1986	5th Cousin	5th Cousin	3rd to Distant Cousin		
Kody Doerschel	Doerschel	Male		5th Cousin	5th Cousin	3rd to Distant Cousin		
Joy White	White	Female		5th Cousin	5th Cousin	3rd to Distant Cousin		
Holly Hauser	Hauser	Female		5th Cousin	5th Cousin	3rd to Distant Cousin		
Claudine Cottini	Cottini	Female		5th Cousin	5th Cousin	3rd to Distant Cousin		
Olga Mandalas	Mandalas	Female	1954	5th Cousin	5th Cousin	3rd to Distant Cousin	Mandrapilias, Hios, Kokkoros, Tsambiras, Mandalas	
Tom Papadatos	Papadatos	Male		5th Cousin	5th Cousin	3rd to Distant Cousin	Lagousakos, Kouzounas, Laskaris, Papadatos, Gigandes, Bouranis	
Srdjan Vujosevic	Vujosevic	Male		5th Cousin	5th Cousin	3rd to Distant Cousin		
Stere Mergeani	Mergeani	Male	1979	5th Cousin	5th Cousin	3rd to Distant Cousin	Mergeani, Pitu, Teja, Maca, Mergiani, Mergeane	Gramos, Greece; Tulcea, Tulcea, Tulcea County, Romania; Charlotte, Mecklenburg County, North Carolina, United States; Mezhden, Silistra, Bulgaria; Serres, Greece
John Nolan	Nolan	Male	1981	5th Cousin	5th Cousin	3rd to Distant Cousin	O'nullian, Nolan	
Rose Criniti	Criniti	Female		5th Cousin	5th Cousin	3rd to Distant Cousin		

Name	Surname	Sex	Year	Relationship	Associated Surnames	Location
David Warfield	Warfield	Male		5th Cousin 5th Cousin 3rd to Distant Cousin	Rees, Campbell, Partin, Prichard, Hubbs, Sharp, Terrell, Grant, Warfield	
Kevin Albers	Albers	Male		5th Cousin 5th Cousin 3rd to Distant Cousin	Albers, Spero	
sophia klopas	klopas	Female		5th Cousin 5th Cousin 3rd to Distant Cousin	kapernekas, galamas, klopas	
Anthony Bulldis	Bulldis	Male		5th Cousin 5th Cousin 3rd to Distant Cousin	Englert, Bulldis, Owens, Doan, Gawrys, Oczhowski, Mozgawa, Stolzman	Balıkesir Province, Turkey
Panagiotis Koboudis	Koboudis	Male		5th Cousin 5th Cousin 3rd to Distant Cousin		
Alex Arvanitidis	Arvanitidis	Male		5th Cousin 5th Cousin 3rd to Distant Cousin		
james andrews	andrews	Male		5th Cousin 5th Cousin 3rd to Distant Cousin		
Nicole Allison	Allison	Female		5th Cousin 5th Cousin 3rd to Distant Cousin	Papadimitropoulos, Kagiannas, Allison	
Robin Parker	Parker	Female	1954	5th Cousin 5th Cousin 3rd to Distant Cousin		
A X	X	Female		5th Cousin 5th Cousin 3rd to Distant Cousin		
Bryar Balon	Balon	Male		5th Cousin 5th Cousin 3rd to Distant Cousin		
Evangelos Tambassis	Tambassis	Male		4th Cousin 4th Cousin 3rd to 6th Cousin		
Denise Hodge	Hodge	Female		5th Cousin 5th Cousin 3rd to Distant Cousin		
Kristie White	White	Female		5th Cousin 5th Cousin 3rd to Distant Cousin		Poplar Bluff, MO
Karen Haight-Selling	Haight-Selling	Female	1968	5th Cousin 5th Cousin 3rd to Distant Cousin		
Paul Sebesta	Sebesta	Male		5th Cousin 5th Cousin 3rd to Distant Cousin	Ciccone Brown, Sebesta	Italy
Christopher Karabats	Karabats	Male	1946	5th Cousin 5th Cousin 3rd to Distant Cousin		
Maya Dias	Dias	Female	1987	5th Cousin 5th Cousin 3rd to Distant Cousin		
Karsten Loukides	Loukides	Male	1992	4th Cousin 4th Cousin 3rd to 5th Cousin		
Marta Mendizabal	Mendizabal	Female		5th Cousin 5th Cousin 3rd to Distant Cousin		
Panos Makkas	Makkas	Male		5th Cousin 5th Cousin 3rd to Distant Cousin		
Jessica Brooks	Brooks	Female		5th Cousin 5th Cousin 3rd to Distant Cousin	Ipjian, Pierre, Brooks	
Kristian Kellems	Kellems	Female		3rd Cousin 3rd Cousin 3rd to 5th Cousin		
Lisi Powers	Powers	Female		5th Cousin 5th Cousin 3rd to Distant Cousin	Powers, Cravero, varvaro	
Alexis Furkioti	Furkioti	Female		2nd Cousin 2nd Cousin, 3x Removed	Furkioti, Revels, Chalekson	
AP		Male	1972	5th Cousin 5th Cousin 3rd to Distant Cousin	Tsokos, Kosma, Kretsi	
Pat Glavas	Glavas	Female		5th Cousin 5th Cousin 3rd to Distant Cousin		
VF		Female		5th Cousin 5th Cousin 3rd to Distant Cousin		
Valentin M		Male	1964	4th Cousin 4th Cousin 3rd to 6th Cousin	Mihov, Kaloyanov	
MARY RUSS	RUSS	Female		5th Cousin 5th Cousin 3rd to Distant Cousin	Kessinger, Marth, Brown, Pelzman, Logsdon, RUSS	
Grant Collins	Collins	Male		5th Cousin 5th Cousin 3rd to Distant Cousin	Evans, Collins, Beall, Elliott, Renshaw, Baldwin, Nowlan, Beaumont, Witherspoon	
Valentin Mihov	Mihov	Male		4th Cousin 4th Cousin 3rd to 6th Cousin		
Djordje Djordje	Djordje	Male	1938	5th Cousin 5th Cousin 3rd to Distant Cousin		
Olivia Espey	Espey	Female		5th Cousin 5th Cousin 3rd to Distant Cousin		
Agapios Kyritsis	Kyritsis	Male		5th Cousin 5th Cousin 3rd to Distant Cousin	kyritsis, Kyritsis	
Brankica Lazoroska	Lazoroska	Female		5th Cousin 5th Cousin 3rd to Distant Cousin		
Shaylene Schmidt	Schmidt	Female		5th Cousin 5th Cousin 3rd to Distant Cousin		
Hillary Pelukas	Pelukas	Female		5th Cousin 5th Cousin 3rd to Distant Cousin	Krolik, Menghini, Shattock, Pelukas	
Koray G		Male		5th Cousin 5th Cousin 3rd to Distant Cousin	Musa, Alptekin, Kucukarslan	Baghdad, Baghdad Governorate, Iraq; Kirkuk, Kirkuk, Kirkuk Governorate, Iraq
Robert Giokas	Giokas	Male		4th Cousin 4th Cousin 3rd to Distant Cousin		
stella marinos	marinos	Female		5th Cousin 5th Cousin 3rd to Distant Cousin	Marinos, Zogopolos, Paraskevopoulos, Baker, Fekas, Violiotis, Andrikopolos, Chiochios, Kapogeannis, marinos	San Francisco Bay Area, California, Manchester, NH, Newark, NJ, Kendriko, Kalamata, Greece, Karlovasi, Samos Greece,
Steven Cika Sr.	Cika Sr.	Male	1949	5th Cousin 5th Cousin 3rd to Distant Cousin		
Aurelia Alamariu	Alamariu	Female		5th Cousin 5th Cousin 3rd to Distant Cousin	Iordache, Anghel, Alamariu	
Joan Harn	Harn	Female	1951	5th Cousin 5th Cousin 3rd to Distant Cousin	Maat. McLellan, Harn	Scotland, United Kingdom
Karyn Peabody	Peabody	Female	1973	5th Cousin 5th Cousin 3rd to Distant Cousin	Bazis, Vosler, Peabody	
Michael Nikolov	Nikolov	Male		5th Cousin 5th Cousin 3rd to Distant Cousin		
Jennifer Digiulio	Digiulio	Female	1994	5th Cousin 5th Cousin 3rd to Distant Cousin	Depaolo, Harris, Bisenga, Palleschi, Digiulio	
Laurie Radojevich	Radojevich	Female		5th Cousin 5th Cousin 3rd to Distant Cousin		

Name	Surname	Gender	Year				Surnames	Location
Jennifer Horner	Horner	Female		5th Cousin	5th Cousin	3rd to Distant Cousin		
Christine Connell	Connell	Female	1989	5th Cousin	5th Cousin	3rd to Distant Cousin	Pennacchini, Matyus, Connell	
Sofia Kangas	Kangas	Female		5th Cousin	5th Cousin	3rd to Distant Cousin	Kangas, Koken, Constantinou, Christofidou, Bouboulis	
Despina Papadakis	Papadakis	Female		5th Cousin	5th Cousin	3rd to Distant Cousin	Papadakis, Grigoraki, Soter, Sotirakopoulou, Georgeopoulos	
Mark Morley	Morley	Male		5th Cousin	5th Cousin	3rd to Distant Cousin		
Tasha Dalessandro	Dalessandro	Female	1982	5th Cousin	5th Cousin	3rd to Distant Cousin	Tremblay, Dalessandro	
Anastasia Franklin	Franklin	Female	2002	5th Cousin	5th Cousin	3rd to Distant Cousin		
Bill Maniatis	Maniatis	Male	1988	5th Cousin	5th Cousin	3rd to Distant Cousin		
Joanne Hudson	Hudson	Female	1970	5th Cousin	5th Cousin	3rd to Distant Cousin	Tzamtzi, Tzamtzis, Hudson	
Sofia Bachiloglu Ruminot	Bachiloglu Ruminot	Female	2000	4th Cousin	4th Cousin	3rd to 6th Cousin	Bachiloglu, Cuevas, Ruminot, Bachiloglu Ruminot	
Jessica Jackson	Jackson	Female	1991	5th Cousin	5th Cousin	3rd to Distant Cousin	Jackson, McMilian, Beard, Noble, Arnold (biological grandmother - my mother was adopted)., Brown, Kyle, Newberry, Abernathy, Richardson, Hanna, Sory, Holley, Parsons, Sessions, Powell, Davis(via Lacey daughter marriage), Williams(via Noble daughter marriage), Lacy/Lacey	Arizona, Texas, Colorado; Virginia, United States; South Carolina, United States
anna A		Female		5th Cousin	5th Cousin	3rd to Distant Cousin		
Stavroula Kizis	Kizis	Female		4th Cousin	4th Cousin	3rd to 6th Cousin	Alexandros, Euagelos, Stavroula, Grigorios, Ermioni, Kizis	Alexandria, Alexandria Governorate, Egypt
LORI DINOVO	DINOVO	Female		5th Cousin	5th Cousin	3rd to Distant Cousin		
George Bokas	Bokas	Male	1975	5th Cousin	5th Cousin	3rd to Distant Cousin		
Cathy tsakopoulos	tsakopoulos	Female	1964	5th Cousin	5th Cousin	3rd to Distant Cousin	Tsurekidis, Gitzas, Papaerifrimiadou, Tsavdaroglou, Tsakopoulos, tsakopoulos	EskiÅŸehir, EskiÅŸehir, Turkey
frances matsis	matsis	Female		5th Cousin	5th Cousin	3rd to Distant Cousin	Mallas, Pleotis, Tzoris, matsis	
Cheyenne Maxwell	Maxwell	Female		5th Cousin	5th Cousin	3rd to Distant Cousin		
Lily Sanborn	Sanborn	Female		5th Cousin	5th Cousin	3rd to Distant Cousin		
Rachelle Geary	Geary	Female		5th Cousin	5th Cousin	3rd to Distant Cousin	Piersanti, Howe, Geffas, Swenson, Hyde, Geary	Italy; Greece
roseanne spano swider	spano swider	Female	1954	5th Cousin	5th Cousin	3rd to Distant Cousin	spano, poveromo, dionisio, crocitto, spano swider	
jordan kravette	kravette	Male		4th Cousin	4th Cousin	3rd to Distant Cousin		
Taylor Swanzy	Swanzy	Female	1999	5th Cousin	5th Cousin	3rd to Distant Cousin	Swanzy, Annastas, Harris, Malaoula	
Martha Deffenbaugh	Deffenbaugh	Female	1953	5th Cousin	5th Cousin	3rd to Distant Cousin		
Bonnie Triche	Triche	Female	1958	5th Cousin	5th Cousin	3rd to Distant Cousin	Rayha, Soos, Gresik, Triche	
Nick Anagnostopoulos	Anagnostopoulos	Male	1968	4th Cousin	4th Cousin	3rd to Distant Cousin	Seremitis, Bakarezos, Anagnostopoulos	
Kathleen Williams	Williams	Female		5th Cousin	5th Cousin	3rd to Distant Cousin		
Cheryl Smith Styron	Smith Styron	Female	1962	3rd Cousin	3rd Cousin		Brown, Breeding, Smith, Griffith, Venis, Benis, Ogden, Carlisle, Kolhoun, Donovan, Wells, Walls, Fountain, Smith Styron	
Betsey Porterfield	Porterfield	Female		5th Cousin	5th Cousin	3rd to Distant Cousin		
Nikolas Mastandrea	Mastandrea	Male		5th Cousin	5th Cousin	3rd to Distant Cousin	Viglas, Bazos, Levear, Mastandrea	Scotland, United Kingdom; Australia
Corinne Michels	Michels	Female		5th Cousin	5th Cousin	3rd to Distant Cousin	Amodeo, Sicari, Ferlazzo, Michels	
Bernice Giamundo	Giamundo	Female		5th Cousin	5th Cousin	3rd to Distant Cousin	Masciandaro, Flaccavento, Giamundo	
Chelsea Gillingham	Gillingham	Female	1989	5th Cousin	5th Cousin	3rd to Distant Cousin	Pappas, Gillingham	Crete Region, Greece
Maria Koken	Koken	Female		3rd Cousin	3rd Cousin	3rd to 5th Cousin		
Nancy Dorsey	Dorsey	Female	1972	5th Cousin	5th Cousin	3rd to Distant Cousin	Greco, Sabella, Zucchero, Dorsey	
TK		Female		5th Cousin	5th Cousin	3rd to Distant Cousin		
Cassidy K		Female		5th Cousin	5th Cousin	3rd to Distant Cousin		
Emma Bruno	Bruno	Female		5th Cousin	5th Cousin	3rd to Distant Cousin		
Guiseppa Barcia	Barcia	Female	1920	5th Cousin	5th Cousin	3rd to Distant Cousin		
Stephanie Ansolabehere	Ansolabehere	Female		5th Cousin	5th Cousin	3rd to Distant Cousin		

Name	Surname	Gender	Year / Relationship	Associated Surnames	Locations
michelle haines (Kamberos)	haines (Kamberos)	Female	5th Cousin 5th Cousin 3rd to Distant Cousin	Lewis, Bennis, Kamberos, Brinker, Smith, haines (Kamberos)	
Catherine Garza	Garza	Female	1938 5th Cousin 5th Cousin 3rd to Distant Cousin	Dedes, Franko, Pomaiba, Garza	
Erin Staiger (Salb)	Staiger (Salb)	Female	1980 4th Cousin 4th Cousin 3rd to Distant Cousin		Greece
Anastasia Williams	Williams	Female	1984 5th Cousin 5th Cousin 3rd to Distant Cousin	Cretekos, Johnson, Youngman, Landry, Koutsogiannopoulos, Askounis, Giannakis, Williams	
serkan bayraktar	bayraktar	Male	1976 5th Cousin 5th Cousin 3rd to Distant Cousin	Cucevic, Bayraktar, Denizci, bayraktar	
FANI KALAKOS	KALAKOS	Female	1965 4th Cousin 4th Cousin 3rd to 6th Cousin	MPOTINI, BOTINI, Îšî†îjî†î†ï₩î†îàî†—Îε, îœî†ÎVÎàî†ï₩î†î—Îε, KARIOTIS, HAIDOGIANNOY, Î§î†ï₩î†ÎVî†ï₩î†ÎïÎYÎ¥, KALAKOS	Sicily, Italy; Mani, Greece
Kris Radkov	Radkov	Male	5th Cousin 5th Cousin 3rd to Distant Cousin		
Evangelos Masellas	Masellas	Male	5th Cousin 5th Cousin 3rd to Distant Cousin	Plakidis, Marsellos, Masellas, Nouros, Maselos	Ä°zmir, Turkey; Metropolitan City of Venice, Veneto, Italy; Sicily, Italy
Vistian Bortes	Bortes	Male	5th Cousin 5th Cousin 3rd to Distant Cousin	BORTES, JUIRJ, Bortes	
Breanna Cole	Cole	Female	4th Cousin 4th Cousin 3rd to Distant Cousin		
Carlo Cukon	Cukon	Male	1961 5th Cousin 5th Cousin 3rd to Distant Cousin		
Jamie Tufanio	Tufanio	Male	1992 5th Cousin 5th Cousin 3rd to Distant Cousin		
Nick Diogenes	Diogenes	Male	5th Cousin 5th Cousin 3rd to Distant Cousin		
John Brown	Brown	Male	5th Cousin 5th Cousin 3rd to Distant Cousin		
Jay Photoglou	Photoglou	Male	5th Cousin 5th Cousin 3rd to Distant Cousin	Sandoval, Seraph, Photoglou	
Amanda Sideris	Sideris	Female	1985 5th Cousin 5th Cousin 3rd to Distant Cousin	Knight, Sideris	Greece; Poland; Germany; United Kingdom; Ireland; Italy
Elaine Demopolis	Demopolis	Female	1995 5th Cousin 5th Cousin 3rd to Distant Cousin	Demopolis, Demopoulos	
Danielle Hill	Hill	Female	5th Cousin 5th Cousin 3rd to Distant Cousin		
Jane Stover	Stover	Female	5th Cousin 5th Cousin 3rd to Distant Cousin		
Georgios Blandos	Blandos	Male	5th Cousin 5th Cousin 3rd to Distant Cousin	Blandos, Piperas	
Mariane Pearse	Pearse	Female	5th Cousin 5th Cousin 3rd to Distant Cousin		
C K S	S	Female	5th Cousin 5th Cousin 3rd to Distant Cousin	Sullivan, Alvarado, Rosales, Egger, Von Greiner, Von Gerenver, Gottlieb & Therese Von Greiner, S	Ottawa, Ill, San Luis Potsi Mexico, Monterrey, Mexico,; Turners Falls, Mass.,Castletown Beara, Ireland, Obervillach, Austria
Paraskevi Mouzakiti	Mouzakiti	Female	1999 5th Cousin 5th Cousin 3rd to Distant Cousin	Mouzakiti, Parry	Greece; United Kingdom
Chris Spady	Spady	Male	5th Cousin 5th Cousin 3rd to Distant Cousin		
George Kavgic	Kavgic	Male	1963 5th Cousin 5th Cousin 3rd to Distant Cousin		
Adrian Nazario Valdez	Nazario Valdez	Male	1997 5th Cousin 5th Cousin 3rd to Distant Cousin		
Zoe Tsamitis	Tsamitis	Female	5th Cousin 5th Cousin 3rd to Distant Cousin		
Alexis Pence	Pence	Female	4th Cousin 4th Cousin 3rd to Distant Cousin		
John Gianoukos	Gianoukos	Male	3rd Cousin 3rd Cousin 3rd to 5th Cousin		
John Gianoukos	Gianoukos	Male	3rd Cousin 3rd Cousin 3rd to 5th Cousin		
Natalie Kaduri	Kaduri	Female	1996 5th Cousin 5th Cousin 3rd to Distant Cousin	Gadgeva, Gadjeva, Gadzheva, Kaduri	
Robert Coates	Coates	Male	1947 5th Cousin 5th Cousin 3rd to Distant Cousin	Coates, Schultz, Teske, Dreger, Ellison, Grafer, Wackernagel, Gruening, Kroneberg, Anderson, Reid, Denure, Greb/Graeb, Robinson	Yorkshire, Northern Ireland, Picardie, Thuringen, Erfurt, Volhynia, Kraft and Muller in Russia-Saratov region
Tom Englezos	Englezos	Male	1943 5th Cousin 5th Cousin 3rd to Distant Cousin		
Danielle Novak	Novak	Female	5th Cousin 5th Cousin 3rd to Distant Cousin		
Joseph Saponaro	Saponaro	Male	1964 5th Cousin 5th Cousin 3rd to Distant Cousin	Saponaro, Sarangelo, Marzano, Rini	
SF		Female	1970 5th Cousin 5th Cousin 3rd to Distant Cousin		
ioanna Katsigiannis	Katsigiannis	Female	4th Cousin 4th Cousin 3rd to Distant Cousin		
Eleni Vogas	Vogas	Female	5th Cousin 5th Cousin 3rd to Distant Cousin		
Joanne (De Pierre) (Wolfe) Babey	(De Pierre) (Wolfe) Babey	Female	1964 4th Cousin 4th Cousin 3rd to Distant Cousin		
Dimitria Costello	Costello	Male	1941 5th Cousin 5th Cousin 3rd to Distant Cousin		
Diane Kapuranis	Kapuranis	Female	5th Cousin 5th Cousin 3rd to Distant Cousin		
Kristina German	German	Female	1989 4th Cousin 4th Cousin 3rd to Distant Cousin	Morris, Manganelli, Monos, German	

Name	Surname	Sex	Year	Rel 1	Rel 2	Rel 3	Surnames	Location
Lirim Turkaj	Turkaj	Male		5th Cousin	5th Cousin	3rd to Distant Cousin	Hasanaj, Kennedy, Chesnutt, Joyner, Turkaj	Albania; Kosovo; Garfield, Emanuel County, Georgia, United States; Vero Beach, Indian River County, Florida, United States; Gainesville, Alachua County, Florida, United States; Assawoman, Accomack County, Virginia, United States; Macon, Bibb County, Georgia, United States; Oklahoma, United States
Louise Ganas	Ganas	Female		5th Cousin	5th Cousin	3rd to Distant Cousin		
Malcolm Dean	Dean	Male		5th Cousin	5th Cousin	3rd to Distant Cousin		
Jade Burruezo	Burruezo	Female		5th Cousin	5th Cousin	3rd to Distant Cousin		
Suzanne Martikas	Martikas	Female		4th Cousin	4th Cousin	3rd to 6th Cousin	Houndros, Huntalas, Martikas	
Marshal Eagle	Eagle	Male	1976	5th Cousin	5th Cousin	3rd to Distant Cousin		
Paraskeve Frances Pantelides	Pantelides	Female		5th Cousin	5th Cousin	3rd to Distant Cousin	Panterlis, Hegoumenakis, Halabalakis, Glinos, Galanaki, Pantelides	Turkey
Esin Saribatir	Saribatir	Female		5th Cousin	5th Cousin	3rd to Distant Cousin		
Matthew Wittig	Wittig	Male		5th Cousin	5th Cousin	3rd to Distant Cousin	Caldararu, Bitu, Wittig	
Jenni Rein	Rein	Female		4th Cousin	4th Cousin	3rd to Distant Cousin		
Claudia Elbert	Elbert	Female	1974	5th Cousin	5th Cousin	3rd to Distant Cousin		
Gabrielle A		Female		5th Cousin	5th Cousin	3rd to Distant Cousin		
Michelle Stephanoff	Stephanoff	Female		5th Cousin	5th Cousin	3rd to Distant Cousin	Stephanoff, Hagotta, Ajovich, Ivan, Nestorova, Kadis, Kadieff, Nedelko, Nickoff	
Julija Zubac	Zubac	Female		5th Cousin	5th Cousin	3rd to Distant Cousin		
Lidia Janeska	Janeska	Female		5th Cousin	5th Cousin	3rd to Distant Cousin		
Ahnna Escobedo	Escobedo	Female		5th Cousin	5th Cousin	3rd to Distant Cousin		
Linda Murray	Murray	Female		5th Cousin	5th Cousin	3rd to Distant Cousin	Demetriades, Tsaffaras, Saffaras, Zounes, Murray	
Margo H		Female	1951	5th Cousin	5th Cousin	3rd to Distant Cousin		
George Hadjigeorgiou	Hadjigeorgiou	Male	1975	4th Cousin	4th Cousin	3rd to 5th Cousin		
Tina Panas	Panas	Female	1928	5th Cousin	5th Cousin	3rd to Distant Cousin		
Elaine Ioanou	Ioanou	Female	1954	2nd Cousin	2nd Cousin			
Peter Wood	Wood	Male		5th Cousin	5th Cousin	3rd to Distant Cousin	Kiritsis, Chekouras, Koletas, Wood	
Eric Jeffers	Jeffers	Male	1988	5th Cousin	5th Cousin	3rd to Distant Cousin	Palm, Jeffers	
Ben Brown	Brown	Male		5th Cousin	5th Cousin	3rd to Distant Cousin		
Lori Sarabian	Sarabian	Female	1963	5th Cousin	5th Cousin	3rd to Distant Cousin		
Hanna Furmanski	Furmanski	Female		5th Cousin	5th Cousin	3rd to Distant Cousin		
Dimitri Glavas	Glavas	Male		5th Cousin	5th Cousin	3rd to Distant Cousin		
Kathy Brandt	Brandt	Female	1958	5th Cousin	5th Cousin	3rd to Distant Cousin		
Joanna Zanopoulo	Zanopoulo	Female		5th Cousin	5th Cousin	3rd to Distant Cousin	Zanopoulo, Michailidis, Iliadis, Chrystodoulou	
Jessica Ebanks	Ebanks	Female		5th Cousin	5th Cousin	3rd to Distant Cousin	Thomas, Olivo, Ebanks	
Andreanna L		Female		5th Cousin	5th Cousin	3rd to Distant Cousin		
Lesley Wylie	Wylie	Female		5th Cousin	5th Cousin	3rd to Distant Cousin	Lawhorn, Leamons, Murray, Wylie	
Triantafillos Katsoudas	Katsoudas	Male		5th Cousin	5th Cousin	3rd to Distant Cousin	Kontoulas, Katsoudas	
Alexandra Williams	Williams	Female		4th Cousin	4th Cousin	3rd to Distant Cousin	Joe Radosta, Anthony Williams, Athena Birbilis, Valerie Apton, Williams	
Lydia Gil	Gil	Female		5th Cousin	5th Cousin	3rd to Distant Cousin		
Preston Plumlee	Plumlee	Male		5th Cousin	5th Cousin	3rd to Distant Cousin		
Avrelia Palivos	Palivos	Female		4th Cousin	4th Cousin	3rd to Distant Cousin		
Justin Kotlarz	Kotlarz	Male		5th Cousin	5th Cousin	3rd to Distant Cousin		
John A Lenic	Lenic	Male		5th Cousin	5th Cousin	3rd to Distant Cousin	Rogish, Lenic	
Jeffrey White	White	Male	1949	5th Cousin	5th Cousin	3rd to Distant Cousin	Elliott, Lewis, Noland, White	
John Kellems	Kellems	Male	1992	3rd Cousin	3rd Cousin	3rd to 4th Cousin	kellems, vlahos, bishop, Kellems	
Teresa Alvanitakis Sunnergren	Alvanitakis Sunnergren	Female		5th Cousin	5th Cousin	3rd to Distant Cousin	Alvanitakis, Mullen, Gurdo, Alvanitakis Sunnergren	

Name	Surname	Gender	Year				Surnames	Locations
Nancy Falb	Falb	Female		4th Cousin	4th Cousin	3rd to 5th Cousin		
Christopher Anagnost	Anagnost	Male		5th Cousin	5th Cousin	3rd to Distant Cousin		
Artemis Gregory	Gregory	Female		5th Cousin	5th Cousin	3rd to Distant Cousin	Asprogiannis, Galatas, Tsipras, Toumaras, Gregory	
Taylor Troehler	Troehler	Female		5th Cousin	5th Cousin	3rd to Distant Cousin		
Justin Adcock	Adcock	Male	1971	5th Cousin	5th Cousin	3rd to Distant Cousin		
Irini Aleksi	Aleksi	Female		5th Cousin	5th Cousin	3rd to Distant Cousin		
Maria Helena Segri	Segri	Female		5th Cousin	5th Cousin	3rd to Distant Cousin		
Lindsey Johnson	Johnson	Female		5th Cousin	5th Cousin	3rd to Distant Cousin		
David Carlin	Carlin	Male	1981	5th Cousin	5th Cousin	3rd to Distant Cousin	Carlin, Santomieri	
Eve Anders	Anders	Female		5th Cousin	5th Cousin	3rd to Distant Cousin		
George Tzimas	Tzimas	Male	1968	5th Cousin	5th Cousin	3rd to Distant Cousin	Basounas, Pappas, Oikonomou, Papathimios, Tzimas	
Richard navis	navis	Male	1966	5th Cousin	5th Cousin	3rd to Distant Cousin	Stoyko, navis	
George Economy	Economy	Male	1958	5th Cousin	5th Cousin	3rd to Distant Cousin		
Demetrios Parliaros	Parliaros	Male	1983	5th Cousin	5th Cousin	3rd to Distant Cousin		
Constantina Petropoulos	Petropoulos	Female	1964	5th Cousin	5th Cousin	3rd to Distant Cousin		
Izzy Fakhreddine	Fakhreddine	Female		5th Cousin	5th Cousin	3rd to Distant Cousin		
Ronnie Nagler	Nagler	Female		5th Cousin	5th Cousin	3rd to Distant Cousin		
Kelsey Wheeler	Wheeler	Male		4th Cousin	4th Cousin	3rd to Distant Cousin	Bruce, Rufie, Wheeler, White, Stipple, Ruffle, King, Rice, Vassall, Loring, Couch, James, Smith, Demichele, De michele, Martinello, Hagerman	Italy; Switzerland; Holyoke, Hampden County, Massachusetts, United States; Cleveland, Cuyahoga County, Ohio, United States; Ontario, Canada; Fitchburg, Worcester County, Massachusetts, United States; Plainfield, Hampshire County, Massachusetts, United States; Westminster, Worcester County, Massachusetts, United States; Lee, Berkshire County, Massachusetts, United States; Amherst, Hampshire County, Massachusetts, United States; Sudbury, Middlesex County, Massachusetts, United States; Cranfield, Central Bedfordshire, England, United Kingdom; Leiden, Leiden, South Holland, Netherlands; Devon, England, United Kingdom; Woodham Mortimer, Essex, England, United Kingdom; Bedford, England, United Kingdom
Neil Stanar	Stanar	Male	1976	5th Cousin	5th Cousin	3rd to Distant Cousin		
Cheryl LaMore	LaMore	Female	1974	5th Cousin	5th Cousin	3rd to Distant Cousin		
Vasileios Gianoukos	Gianoukos	Male		5th Cousin	5th Cousin	3rd to Distant Cousin		
Alexis Harrington	Harrington	Female		5th Cousin	5th Cousin	3rd to Distant Cousin		Arkadia Greece
Ioannis Papadopoulos	Papadopoulos	Male	1974	5th Cousin	5th Cousin	3rd to Distant Cousin	Papadopoulos, Aronis, Bouranis, Georgiou, Vlavianos	
Nick Sakaleros	Sakaleros	Male	1975	5th Cousin	5th Cousin	3rd to Distant Cousin		
Bryan Ortiz	Ortiz	Male		4th Cousin	4th Cousin	3rd to Distant Cousin		
Dianne Chilingerian	Chilingerian	Female		5th Cousin	5th Cousin	3rd to Distant Cousin	Bahadourian, Sarajian, Poonanian, Memleketian, Chilingerian	Diyarbakir, Adana, Gurun, Turkey, Boston, New York, New Jersey, Virginia
Paula Jo Triche	Triche	Female		5th Cousin	5th Cousin	3rd to Distant Cousin		
Nick Pachnos	Pachnos	Male		5th Cousin	5th Cousin	3rd to Distant Cousin	Christopoulos, Leva, Pachnos	
Maria Walsh	Walsh	Female		5th Cousin	5th Cousin	3rd to Distant Cousin		
Dennis Gerbino	Gerbino	Male		5th Cousin	5th Cousin	3rd to Distant Cousin		
Shayne Zroback	Zroback	Male	1975	5th Cousin	5th Cousin	3rd to Distant Cousin		

Name	Short Name	Gender	Relationship	Surnames	Locations
Kristina Lefteri	Lefteri	Female	5th Cousin 5th Cousin 3rd to Distant Cousin		
Jorge Salazar	Salazar	Male	5th Cousin 5th Cousin 3rd to Distant Cousin		
Bert Bradley	Bradley	Male	4th Cousin 4th Cousin 3rd to Distant Cousin		
Venitia Caudill	Caudill	Female	1926 4th Cousin 4th Cousin 3rd to Distant Cousin	Coniaris, Polychronopoulos, Caudill	
Stephanie Rondos	Rondos	Female	5th Cousin 5th Cousin 3rd to Distant Cousin	Rondos, Salem, Sillano	Italy
Gregory Paras	Paras	Male	4th Cousin 4th Cousin 3rd to 6th Cousin	Chaiko, Hussey, Paras, Mennon	
Samantha Leone	Leone	Female	5th Cousin 5th Cousin 3rd to Distant Cousin		
George Tjilos	Tjilos	Male	1964 3rd Cousin 3rd Cousin 3rd to 4th Cousin	Tjilos, Tsilos, Tzilos, Gelos, Gilos, Palazis, Stamboulis, Stovou, Stouyou	Peloponisos, Greece; Peloponesos, Greece; Rhodes, Greece; Rodos, Greece
Spiros Katsanis	Katsanis	Male	4th Cousin 4th Cousin 3rd to 5th Cousin		
C Genis Murray	Genis Murray	Female	4th Cousin 4th Cousin 3rd to 5th Cousin		
Mike T		Male	4th Cousin 4th Cousin 3rd to 5th Cousin		
AP		Male	4th Cousin 4th Cousin 3rd to 6th Cousin		
S Marshall	Marshall	Male	4th Cousin 4th Cousin 3rd to 6th Cousin		
leah bizoumis	bizoumis	Female	1963 4th Cousin 4th Cousin 3rd to 6th Cousin	glynou, kiriazi, dallue, katsiferi, bizoumis	
Dimitrios Zarafopoulos	Zarafopoulos	Male	4th Cousin 4th Cousin 3rd to 6th Cousin		
Peter Ellis	Ellis	Male	4th Cousin 4th Cousin 3rd to 6th Cousin		
PRISCILLA T		Female	4th Cousin 4th Cousin 3rd to 6th Cousin	Andreson, Androutsopoulos, Spelios, Speliopoulos, Couiopoulos, Latchis, Rigopoulos, Patterson, Papandricopoulos, Latsis, Paul	
HB		Male	4th Cousin 4th Cousin 3rd to 6th Cousin		
Ria L	L	Female	4th Cousin 4th Cousin 3rd to 6th Cousin		
Stelyana Baleva	Baleva	Female	4th Cousin 4th Cousin 3rd to 6th Cousin		
JS		Male	4th Cousin 4th Cousin 3rd to 6th Cousin		
Rebecca Mitchell	Mitchell	Female	4th Cousin 4th Cousin 3rd to 6th Cousin		
spero theros	theros	Male	1946 4th Cousin 4th Cousin 3rd to 6th Cousin	Theros, Theoderakolpous, theoderakolpous, theros	
DC		Male	4th Cousin 4th Cousin 3rd to 6th Cousin		
Richard Rizzo	Rizzo	Male	1970 4th Cousin 4th Cousin 3rd to 6th Cousin		
Michel Karkour	Karkour	Male	1990 4th Cousin 4th Cousin 3rd to 6th Cousin		
MT		Female	4th Cousin 4th Cousin 3rd to 6th Cousin		
Stephanie S		Female	4th Cousin 4th Cousin 3rd to Distant Cousin		
Leland McAllister	McAllister	Male	4th Cousin 4th Cousin 3rd to Distant Cousin		
M Beers	Beers	Female	4th Cousin 4th Cousin 3rd to Distant Cousin	Serafini, Stanford, Mason, Leonard, Beers	Quincy, MA; Weymouth, MA; England, Supino, Italy
JG		Male	4th Cousin 4th Cousin 3rd to Distant Cousin	KOTIS, PANOUTSOS, GERANIOS, KLEASON	Greece; Tripoli, Greece
Joan Farmer	Farmer	Female	1945 4th Cousin 4th Cousin 3rd to Distant Cousin	Nash, Koutikas, Marinos, Gummersbach, Farmer	
Aikaterini Dimopoulou	Dimopoulou	Female	4th Cousin 4th Cousin 3rd to Distant Cousin		
Peggie McHugh	McHugh	Female	4th Cousin 4th Cousin 3rd to Distant Cousin		
M Morrell	Morrell	Female	1988 4th Cousin 4th Cousin 3rd to Distant Cousin	Morrell, Vakos	
DP		Female	4th Cousin 4th Cousin 3rd to Distant Cousin		
William Candiloros	Candiloros	Male	4th Cousin 4th Cousin 3rd to Distant Cousin		
RV		Male	1970 4th Cousin 4th Cousin 3rd to Distant Cousin	Bussell	
nicholas B		Male	4th Cousin 4th Cousin 3rd to Distant Cousin	bastounes, elliott, anton	
Veronica Iossifova	Iossifova	Female	4th Cousin 4th Cousin 3rd to Distant Cousin		
G Jenkins	Jenkins	Female	4th Cousin 4th Cousin 3rd to Distant Cousin		
Dharini Shukla	Shukla	Female	4th Cousin 4th Cousin 3rd to Distant Cousin		
P Angelikopoulos	Angelikopoulos	Male	4th Cousin 4th Cousin 3rd to Distant Cousin	kotarinos, angelikopoulos, Angelikopoulos	Egypt
Eric Newcomb	Newcomb	Male	4th Cousin 4th Cousin 3rd to Distant Cousin		
Corin Ross	Ross	Male	4th Cousin 4th Cousin 3rd to Distant Cousin		
PK		Female	4th Cousin 4th Cousin 3rd to Distant Cousin		Turkey; Italy
Jamie L		Female	4th Cousin 4th Cousin 3rd to Distant Cousin		
Anthony Langenstein	Langenstein	Male	4th Cousin 4th Cousin 3rd to Distant Cousin		

Name	Surname	Gender	Year	Relationship	Related Surnames	Places
B Blanks	Blanks	Male		5th Cousin 5th Cousin 3rd to Distant Cousin	Blanks, Nichols, Photopoulos, Rue, Nelson	
N Kenny	Kenny	Male		5th Cousin 5th Cousin 3rd to Distant Cousin		
GW		Female		5th Cousin 5th Cousin 3rd to Distant Cousin		
WK		Female	1972	5th Cousin 5th Cousin 3rd to Distant Cousin		
HA		Female		5th Cousin 5th Cousin 3rd to Distant Cousin		
Tom D		Male		5th Cousin 5th Cousin 3rd to Distant Cousin		
Georgia Apostolopoulou	Apostolopoulou	Female		5th Cousin 5th Cousin 3rd to Distant Cousin	Apostolopoulou, Christodoulou, Lignos, Argyropoulou	Lamia, Athens, Ikaria, Santorini, Salamina
JS		Female		5th Cousin 5th Cousin 3rd to Distant Cousin		
Emilia Knezevic	Knezevic	Female		5th Cousin 5th Cousin 3rd to Distant Cousin		
Nomiki Kastanas	Kastanas	Female		5th Cousin 5th Cousin 3rd to Distant Cousin	Papamichael, Zakas, Avdanas, Kastanas	
LB		Female		5th Cousin 5th Cousin 3rd to Distant Cousin		
Karleen Steinle	Steinle	Female		5th Cousin 5th Cousin 3rd to Distant Cousin		
Melody P		Female		5th Cousin 5th Cousin 3rd to Distant Cousin		Manitoba, Canada; Nova Scotia, Canada; Ontario, Canada; England, United Kingdom; Scotland, United Kingdom; Iceland; Ukraine
CP		Female		5th Cousin 5th Cousin 3rd to Distant Cousin	Bourounis, Karapanagos, Giannakopoulos	Tropaia, Greece; Viziki, Greece
Stephan Schmidt	Schmidt	Male		5th Cousin 5th Cousin 3rd to Distant Cousin		
KO		Female		5th Cousin 5th Cousin 3rd to Distant Cousin		
David Caras	Caras	Male		5th Cousin 5th Cousin 3rd to Distant Cousin		
Kaedyn S		Female		5th Cousin 5th Cousin 3rd to Distant Cousin		
Ramiz Sllava	Sllava	Male		5th Cousin 5th Cousin 3rd to Distant Cousin		
Mathew Crum	Crum	Male		5th Cousin 5th Cousin 3rd to Distant Cousin		
Kalliroe Tasios	Tasios	Female	1976	5th Cousin 5th Cousin 3rd to Distant Cousin	Asprogiannis, Makkas, Galatas, Tsipras, Giannopoulos, Toumaras, Lainis, Tasios	
Terry Geary	Geary	Female		5th Cousin 5th Cousin 3rd to Distant Cousin		
Amanda Cutting	Cutting	Female	1987	5th Cousin 5th Cousin 3rd to Distant Cousin		
NC		Male		5th Cousin 5th Cousin 3rd to Distant Cousin		
DM		Female		5th Cousin 5th Cousin 3rd to Distant Cousin	Mehmetaj, Dautaj	
Tatiana S		Female		5th Cousin 5th Cousin 3rd to Distant Cousin		
Kris M		Female		5th Cousin 5th Cousin 3rd to Distant Cousin		
AL		Female		5th Cousin 5th Cousin 3rd to Distant Cousin	Lazic, Dobricic, Velemir, Milivojevic, Nikitovic	Croatia (Sinj, Tijarica), Serbia (multiple places)
Marie Pantazi	Pantazi	Female		5th Cousin 5th Cousin 3rd to Distant Cousin		
Tyler Heathcote	Heathcote	Male		5th Cousin 5th Cousin 3rd to Distant Cousin		
EH		Female		5th Cousin 5th Cousin 3rd to Distant Cousin		
Ani Apfelbacher	Apfelbacher	Female		5th Cousin 5th Cousin 3rd to Distant Cousin		
TC		Male	1964	5th Cousin 5th Cousin 3rd to Distant Cousin		
Brian Chenes	Chenes	Male		5th Cousin 5th Cousin 3rd to Distant Cousin		
CS		Female		5th Cousin 5th Cousin 3rd to Distant Cousin		
VC		Female		5th Cousin 5th Cousin 3rd to Distant Cousin		
Eric Sullivan	Sullivan	Male		5th Cousin 5th Cousin 3rd to Distant Cousin		
Nicole Terracciano	Terracciano	Female		5th Cousin 5th Cousin 3rd to Distant Cousin		
Paulina Tarr	Tarr	Female		5th Cousin 5th Cousin 3rd to Distant Cousin		
PV		Female	1947	5th Cousin 5th Cousin 3rd to Distant Cousin	Beykos or Beikos, Hall	
Bruce Williams	Williams	Male		5th Cousin 5th Cousin 3rd to Distant Cousin		
Patricia Franzoni	Franzoni	Female	1977	5th Cousin 5th Cousin 3rd to Distant Cousin		
Melissa Livanos	Livanos	Female	1981	5th Cousin 5th Cousin 3rd to Distant Cousin		
Eric Hall	Hall	Male		5th Cousin 5th Cousin 3rd to Distant Cousin		
Scott N		Male		5th Cousin 5th Cousin 3rd to Distant Cousin		
Sophia C		Female		5th Cousin 5th Cousin 3rd to Distant Cousin		
Steve K		Male		5th Cousin 5th Cousin 3rd to Distant Cousin		
Eljon N		Male	1985	5th Cousin 5th Cousin 3rd to Distant Cousin	Celo, Nace, Naco, Natsis	
Sarah Williamson	Williamson	Female		5th Cousin 5th Cousin 3rd to Distant Cousin		
MC		Male		5th Cousin 5th Cousin 3rd to Distant Cousin		Sicily, Italy

Name	Surname	Sex	Year	Relationship	Associated Names	Location
Vesko Georgiev	Georgiev	Male		5th Cousin 5th Cousin 3rd to Distant Cousin		
KZ		Female		5th Cousin 5th Cousin 3rd to Distant Cousin		
MK		Male		5th Cousin 5th Cousin 3rd to Distant Cousin	Gdula, Horvath, Kuzoff	
Alex P		Male	1989	5th Cousin 5th Cousin 3rd to Distant Cousin		
UW		Male		5th Cousin 5th Cousin 3rd to Distant Cousin	Odening, Ulbricht	
Gina H		Female		5th Cousin 5th Cousin 3rd to Distant Cousin		
Elias M		Male		5th Cousin 5th Cousin 3rd to Distant Cousin	Makos, Martinis	Montreal, Quebec, Canada; Epiros, Greece
MR		Female		5th Cousin 5th Cousin 3rd to Distant Cousin		
Vickie Sarelas Egan	Sarelas Egan	Female		5th Cousin 5th Cousin 3rd to Distant Cousin	Sarelas, Panagopoulos, Smyrniotis, Mouzakes, Sarelas Egan	
Lisa Dedvukaj	Dedvukaj	Female		5th Cousin 5th Cousin 3rd to Distant Cousin		
Robert Jovalis	Jovalis	Male		5th Cousin 5th Cousin 3rd to Distant Cousin	Jovalis, Perry, Lutz	
L Vournelis	Vournelis	Male		5th Cousin 5th Cousin 3rd to Distant Cousin		
Melanie Jones Parker	Jones Parker	Female		5th Cousin 5th Cousin 3rd to Distant Cousin	Jones, Manos, Anagnostou, Glidewell, Hodum, Jones Parker	
Nikoleta Koupa	Koupa	Female		5th Cousin 5th Cousin 3rd to Distant Cousin		
John Macias	Macias	Male	2000	5th Cousin 5th Cousin 3rd to Distant Cousin		
LV		Female		5th Cousin 5th Cousin 3rd to Distant Cousin		
Steve L		Male		5th Cousin 5th Cousin 3rd to Distant Cousin	Deluca, Burd	
Mina G		Female		5th Cousin 5th Cousin 3rd to Distant Cousin	Centala, Schad, Drembar, Gorak	
JM		Male		5th Cousin 5th Cousin 3rd to Distant Cousin		
JK		Male		5th Cousin 5th Cousin 3rd to Distant Cousin		
LC		Female		5th Cousin 5th Cousin 3rd to Distant Cousin		
JM		Female		5th Cousin 5th Cousin 3rd to Distant Cousin		
Andrew Ambrosino	Ambrosino	Male	1992	5th Cousin 5th Cousin 3rd to Distant Cousin	Plouffe, Ambrosino	
EC		Female		5th Cousin 5th Cousin 3rd to Distant Cousin		
MP		Female		5th Cousin 5th Cousin 3rd to Distant Cousin		
William Miller	Miller	Male		5th Cousin 5th Cousin 3rd to Distant Cousin		
Marguerite Ruminski	Ruminski	Female		5th Cousin 5th Cousin 3rd to Distant Cousin		
MJ		Female		5th Cousin 5th Cousin 3rd to Distant Cousin		
KD		Female		5th Cousin 5th Cousin 3rd to Distant Cousin		
elana D'Amico	D'Amico	Female		5th Cousin 5th Cousin 3rd to Distant Cousin		
Iskren Chernev	Chernev	Male		5th Cousin 5th Cousin 3rd to Distant Cousin	Chernev, Popovska	Varna, Bulgaria; Shumen, Bulgaria
Christina W		Female		5th Cousin 5th Cousin 3rd to Distant Cousin		
Lisa Gilbert	Gilbert	Female		5th Cousin 5th Cousin 3rd to Distant Cousin		
Antoinette Bonno	Bonno	Female		5th Cousin 5th Cousin 3rd to Distant Cousin	tomasino, Bonno	
Ivy E		Female		5th Cousin 5th Cousin 3rd to Distant Cousin		
Audrey Burger	Burger	Female	1993	5th Cousin 5th Cousin 3rd to Distant Cousin		
Georgia Rhodes	Rhodes	Female	1959	5th Cousin 5th Cousin 3rd to Distant Cousin		
LOUIS B		Male		5th Cousin 5th Cousin 3rd to Distant Cousin		
Therese DeGrace	DeGrace	Female		5th Cousin 5th Cousin 3rd to Distant Cousin	Mario Medaglia, Giosina Medaglia, Giovanni Siciliano, Annuziata Siciliano., Theresa Bouchard, Hector DeGrace, DeGrace	Calabria, Italy
Jerry Hamilton	Hamilton	Male		5th Cousin 5th Cousin 3rd to Distant Cousin		
Zachary Dunn	Dunn	Male		5th Cousin 5th Cousin 3rd to Distant Cousin		
AS		Male		5th Cousin 5th Cousin 3rd to Distant Cousin	Petzetakis, Karydis	
Frannie M		Female		5th Cousin 5th Cousin 3rd to Distant Cousin		
AS		Female		5th Cousin 5th Cousin 3rd to Distant Cousin		
Jennifer E		Female		5th Cousin 5th Cousin 3rd to Distant Cousin	Olivo, Thomas	
Alexandra Papageorge	Papageorge	Female		5th Cousin 5th Cousin 3rd to Distant Cousin		
Sheryl Marchuk	Marchuk	Female		5th Cousin 5th Cousin 3rd to Distant Cousin		
Craig West	West	Male		5th Cousin 5th Cousin 3rd to Distant Cousin		
Megan Shapiro	Shapiro	Female		5th Cousin 5th Cousin 3rd to Distant Cousin		
J Amato	Amato	Male		5th Cousin 5th Cousin 3rd to Distant Cousin	Amato, Anderson	
JW		Male		5th Cousin 5th Cousin 3rd to Distant Cousin		

Name	Surname	Sex	Year	Relationship	Surnames	Places
Nicole V		Female		5th Cousin 5th Cousin 3rd to Distant Cousin		
EN		Female		5th Cousin 5th Cousin 3rd to Distant Cousin		
MA		Female		5th Cousin 5th Cousin 3rd to Distant Cousin		
JG		Male		5th Cousin 5th Cousin 3rd to Distant Cousin		
W Fortier	Fortier	Male		5th Cousin 5th Cousin 3rd to Distant Cousin		
MA		Male		5th Cousin 5th Cousin 3rd to Distant Cousin		
Peter Romas	Romas	Male	1990	5th Cousin 5th Cousin 3rd to Distant Cousin		
costa sakellariou	sakellariou	Male	1959	5th Cousin 5th Cousin 3rd to Distant Cousin	greek on my father's side - his father a sakellariou from ag. petros kynouria, his mother a samiotou from athens/koropi, my mother is anneke van kirk, her father harold van kirk from hudson mi, also harrow, her mother was gertrude weaver, also dom, sakellariou	ag. petros kynouria, athens,; hudson mi, doylestown pa
HD		Female		5th Cousin 5th Cousin 3rd to Distant Cousin		
Susan Wilmoth	Wilmoth	Female	1971	5th Cousin 5th Cousin 3rd to Distant Cousin		
Kevin Maliszewski	Maliszewski	Male	1986	5th Cousin 5th Cousin 3rd to Distant Cousin	Mieszanek, Maliszewski, Tarabek, Mitchell, Matysek	
Benjamin Friedman	Friedman	Male	1995	5th Cousin 5th Cousin 3rd to Distant Cousin		
Esmeralda Kaiteris	Kaiteris	Female		5th Cousin 5th Cousin 3rd to Distant Cousin		Constantinople, athens, lesbos, Mikras asias.
Penelope Tsinaridis	Tsinaridis	Female		5th Cousin 5th Cousin 3rd to Distant Cousin		
Lila Owens	Owens	Female		5th Cousin 5th Cousin 3rd to Distant Cousin		
F Sohaie	Sohaie	Female		5th Cousin 5th Cousin 3rd to Distant Cousin		
Anthony Dracopoulos	Dracopoulos	Male		5th Cousin 5th Cousin 3rd to Distant Cousin	Dracopoulos, Balafoutis, Drakopoulos	Evangelismos, Greece; Shinolaka, Greece; Montreal, Canada;
Jamie Clum	Clum	Female		5th Cousin 5th Cousin 3rd to Distant Cousin		
Flor Veseli	Veseli	Male		5th Cousin 5th Cousin 3rd to Distant Cousin		
Mitchell Sturevski	Sturevski	Male	1997	5th Cousin 5th Cousin 3rd to Distant Cousin		
Ford Jung	Jung	Male		5th Cousin 5th Cousin 3rd to Distant Cousin	Ford, Mumma, Harral, Clark, Cobby, Ahrens, Jung	
Raquel Segri Ferreira	Segri Ferreira	Female		5th Cousin 5th Cousin 3rd to Distant Cousin		
John Christopher	Christopher	Male		5th Cousin 5th Cousin 3rd to Distant Cousin		
Catherine DiVincenzo	DiVincenzo	Female		5th Cousin 5th Cousin 3rd to Distant Cousin		
Jeanette Lynam	Lynam	Female		5th Cousin 5th Cousin 3rd to Distant Cousin		
Cleopatra Milionis	Milionis	Female		5th Cousin 5th Cousin 3rd to Distant Cousin		
Varvara Leventopoulou	Leventopoulou	Female	1962	5th Cousin 5th Cousin 3rd to Distant Cousin	Leventopoulos, Kandilakis, Tsagkaris, Zaharopoulos, Economopoulos, Constantopoulos, Contuzzi, Akrivopoulos, Varvatsoulis, Georgakalos, Thanopoulos, Prapopoulos, Georgopoulos, Leventopoulou	Athens; Corfu; Izmir; Istanbul; Zatouna; Dimitsana; Siatista; Kalavryta; Sifnos; Georgioupolis, Crete
Angeliki Markaki	Markaki	Female		5th Cousin 5th Cousin 3rd to Distant Cousin		
Adela Mirtaj	Mirtaj	Female	1994	5th Cousin 5th Cousin 3rd to Distant Cousin		
Alicia Barlow	Barlow	Female	1969	5th Cousin 5th Cousin 3rd to Distant Cousin	Weinand, Zanglia, Breidenbach, Barlow	
Isis Sartin	Sartin	Female		5th Cousin 5th Cousin 3rd to Distant Cousin		
T Demopolis	Demopolis	Female		5th Cousin 5th Cousin 3rd to Distant Cousin		
Alaina Stacey	Stacey	Female		5th Cousin 5th Cousin 3rd to Distant Cousin		
Jordan Stacey	Stacey	Male		5th Cousin 5th Cousin 3rd to Distant Cousin		
A M		Male		5th Cousin 5th Cousin 3rd to Distant Cousin		
NZ		Male		5th Cousin 5th Cousin 3rd to Distant Cousin		
Paul Jarosz	Jarosz	Male		5th Cousin 5th Cousin 3rd to Distant Cousin	Lancmańska, Jarosz